In addition to his stand-up work, **Ben Elton**'s television credits include *The Young Ones*, *Black Adder* and *The Thin Blue Line*. He has written three hit West End plays – *Gasping*, *Silly Cow* and *Popcorn* – and all of his five previous novels – *Stark*, *Gridlock*, *This Other Eden*, *Popcorn* and *Blast from the Past* – have been major bestsellers. Ben Elton is married and lives in London.

INCONCEIVABLE

Ben Elton

BANTAM PRESS

LONDON · NEW YORK · TORONTO · SYDNEY · AUCKLAND

TRANSWORLD PUBLISHERS LTD
61–63 Uxbridge Road, London W5 5SA

TRANSWORLD PUBLISHERS
c/o Random House Australia Pty Ltd
20 Alfred Street, Milsons Point, NSW 2061, Australia

TRANSWORLD PUBLISHERS
c/o Random House New Zealand
18 Poland Road, Glenfield, Auckland, New Zealand

TRANSWORLD PUBLISHERS
c/o Random House Pty Ltd
Endulini, 5a Jubilee Road, Parktown 2193, South Africa

Published 1999 by Bantam Press
a division of Transworld Publishers Ltd

A catalogue record for this book is available
from the British Library.
ISBN 0593 044797 (hb)
0593 045505 (tpb)

Typeset in 10½/14pt Melior by Falcon Oast Graphic Art

Printed in Great Britain
by Clays Ltd, St Ives plc

For Mum and Dad
and
Bob and Kate

Dear . . .?

Dear.

Dear Book?

Dear Self? Dear Sam.

Good. Got that sorted out. What next?

Lucy is making me write this diary. Except it's not a diary. It's a 'book of thoughts'. 'Letters to myself' is how she put it, hence the 'Dear Sam' business, which of course is me. Lucy says that her friend, whose name escapes me, has a theory that conducting this internal correspondence will help Lucy and me to relax about things. The idea is that if Lucy and I periodically privately assemble our thoughts and feelings then we'll feel less like corks bobbing about on the sea of fate. Personally, I find it extraordinary that Lucy can be persuaded that she'll become less obsessed about something if she spends half an hour every day writing about it, but there you go. Lucy thinks that things might be a whole lot better if I stopped trying to be clever and started trying to be supportive.

It's now five minutes later and I find I have no thoughts and feelings to assemble. Lucy has been right all along. I'm a sad, cold, sensitivity-exclusion zone who would rather read the newspaper than have an emotion. I always thought she was exaggerating.

Dear Penny

I'm writing to you, Penny, because in my childhood you were my imaginary friend and I feel that I'll be more open and honest if I personify the part of myself to which I'm addressing these thoughts. Does that make sense? I do hope so because, quite frankly, if ever I needed an imaginary friend I need one now. The truth is that I want to have a baby. You remember how our favourite game when I was a child was looking after babies? Well, things haven't changed at all, right down to the fact that I still haven't actually got a baby to look after. This thing, so simple to many women, is proving very difficult for me. Sam and I have been trying for five years (I hate that word, we used to make love, or have a good shag, now we 'try'), and so far not a hint. You could set your watch by my periods.

Sometimes I feel quite desperate about it and really have to struggle not to be jealous of women who have babies, which I loath myself for. Occasionally, and I hate to write this, I'm even jealous of women who've had miscarriages. I know that sounds awful and I'm quite certain I wouldn't say it if I'd had one myself, but at least I'd know I could conceive. I don't know anything. My wretched body simply refuses to react at all.

However, and let me say this very firmly, Penny, I'm determined that I am not, I repeat NOT, going to become obsessed about all this. If, God forbid, it turns out that I cannot have children, then so be it. I shall accept my fate. I shall not acquire eight dogs, two cats, a rabbit and a potbellied pig. Nor will I go slightly mad and talk too loudly about topiary at dinner parties. I shall not be mean about people who have children, calling them smug and insular and obsessed by their kids. Nor will I go on about my wonderful job (which it isn't anyway) to harassed mums who've not spoken adult English for two and a half years and have sick all over their shoulders and down their backs.

I will also desist from writing letters to imaginary friends. I hope that doesn't sound hurtful to you, Penny, but I feel I must be firm at this juncture. Whatever the fates decide for me, I intend to remain an emotionally functional woman and I absolutely SWEAR that I will not get all teary when I walk past Mothercare on my way to the off licence like I did last week.

What does she find to write about? I've been sitting watching her for ten minutes and she hasn't paused once. What can she possibly be saying?

The most important thing to remember, Penny, is that there are many ways of being a whole and fulfilled woman and that Motherhood is only one of them. It just happens to be the most beautiful, enriching, instinctive and necessary thing that a woman can do and is entirely the reason that I feel I was put upon this earth. That's all.

However, as I say, despite remaining resolutely unobsessed, I do not intend to give up without a fight. Five years is too long and I have decided that after two more periods I'll seek medical help. Sam doesn't like this idea much. He says that it's a matter of psychology, claiming that whilst at the moment we can still see ourselves as simply unlucky, if we go to a doctor we'll be admitting that we are actually infertile and from that point on we'll be forever sad. Of course the real reason that Sam doesn't want to go to a doctor is because it's the first step on a road that will almost certainly lead to him having to masturbate in National Health Service semen collection rooms. However, we're going to do it, so T-F-B, mate, too flipping bad.

This really is very depressing.

And to think that I had dreams of being a writer. Oh well, at least this sorry exercise serves the purpose of shattering for all time any remaining illusions I might have had about possessing even a modicum of creative talent. If I can't even write a letter to myself, then scintillating screenplays and brilliantly innovative television serials at the very cutting edge of the zeitgeist are likely to be somewhat beyond my grasp.

Oh good, she's finally stopped.

So what I'll do is I'll just carry on writing this sentence I'm writing now for a moment or two longer . . . so that it doesn't look like I stopped just because she did . . . Ho hum, dumdy dum . . . What can I say? Saturday tomorrow, going to see George and Melinda plus offspring.

Brilliant, Sam. Give the boy a Pulitzer Prize. That's it, finito.

Dear Penny

I must admit that going to see Melinda and George with their new baby today was a bit difficult. I hate being envious, but I was. It was so sweet, a little boy and absolutely beautiful. He's got quite a bit of dark hair and is very fat in a tiny sort of way. Couldn't get over his little fingers, I never can with brand new babs. Just gorgeous.

Dear Book

I'm very worried about George and Melinda's new sprog. Ugly as a monkey's arse. Couldn't say so, of course, but I could see that poor old George was dubious. He calls it Prune which I think is fair, although 'old man's scrotum' would probably be closer to the mark; what with that strange black hair and so much skin one could easily imagine him swinging between the legs of some prolaptic octogenarian.

I had hoped that the sight of young Prune (or Cuthbert as he is called) might put Lucy off a bit, make her see that there are enormous risks involved with propagation. Remind her that for every Shirley Temple there's a Cuthbert. The thought of having to face those chasmic, gaping, bawling toothless gums five times a night would, I imagine, make any woman reach for the condoms. Quite the opposite, though. She thinks he's utterly adorable. Amazing. It's like we're looking at different babies. I mean I know he'll probably turn out all right. All babies start off looking like the last tomato in the fridge, but 'cute', 'gorgeous' and 'adorable', which were the adjectives Lucy was throwing about the place with gay abandon, struck me as the ravings of an insane and blind woman.

Quite frankly, I began to see King Herod in a wholly different light.

I got home feeling all clucky and sad but I am determined to resist maudlin 'I'm barren' mawkishness. The truth is, though, I fear that I am barren and if that isn't enough to make me mawkish I don't know what is. I mean, some girls are up the duff straight off. Lucky bitches. Their eggs just seem to be genetically programmed sperm magnets. My friend Roz from college could get pregnant just by phoning her husband at work and if you believe what you read in the papers half the schoolgirls in the country are teenage mums. But some women, I'm afraid, women like me, well forget it. I'm about as fertile as the Lord Chief Eunuch at the Court of the Manchurian Emperor. I couldn't even grow cress at school. All I ended up with was a mouldy flannel.

However, as I say, I am determined to approach this period of my life positively. Hence these letters to you, Penny, the point of which, according to my friend Sheila (who saw an Oprah *on the subject), is that Sam and I become proactively involved in our emotional journeys. We cease to be mere corks bobbing about on the sea of fate and instead become partners with our feelings. Sheila says that according to several American experts whom* Oprah *spoke to, the desire to have children is entirely natural and good and we should embrace it whether it turns out that we are fertile (I* hate *that word, it makes me feel like a failed heifer) or not.*

Sheila does not have children herself but she understands the desire to nurture them very well, being a theatrical agent.

Dear Book

Another evening, another desperate effort to think of something to write about.

God, I'd love a shag. I really really would like a shag. But we can't. We're off sex at the moment and I must say I miss it. Lucy is over there looking saucier than the condiments shelf at

Sainsbury's. The very definition of the word shaggable. Sitting on the bed, wearing nothing but a pyjama top, bare legs raised, tongue pointing out of the side of her mouth, nose wrinkled in concentration. She really is so beautiful sometimes. But I'm not allowed to jump on her. Oh no. Absolutely not. Can't even pop into the lav and give the old fellah a slap to relieve the tension. We're saving up my sperm, you see. It's this month's theory and it's one of my least favourite.

Dear Penny

Sam's rather grumpy at the moment because he's feeling sexually frustrated. I can't deny I miss it myself a bit, in fact to be quite frank, as I know I must be with you, Penny, I wish he could give me a bloody good seeing to right now. But no. No, no, NO! We can't and there's an end to it. I should explain at this point, Pen, that this is an RBM, a Restricted Bonking Month. What's happening is that I'm making him save up all his sperm and when the time's right he's got to bang me as hard as he can, three times within twenty-four hours. It's this month's theory. Wait for the right time and then have one concentrated, day-long, high-density, sperm-rich assault on my ovulating eggs.

But when is the time right? To have it off or not to have it off, that is the question.

When is the optimum ovulatory moment? Some girls say they can feel it when they ovulate, that their bodies send them little messages, but I can't say mine ever does. All my insides ever tell me is 'I'm hungry' and 'How about another gin and tonic?'

The only way I can determine the optimum bonking moment is to apply scientific methods of research, which I've never been very good at, not even being able to programme my mobile phone. In theory it should all be quite simple. Just a question of counting days, studying your pee and taking your temperature all the time. But it really is a horrible and soul-destroying business. I count days, I collect urine, I pee on a little traffic light from Boots, I take my temperature, I fill in my chart, I do some more pee, I put some more little red dots on my calendar until it's completely covered in little red dots and crossed-out little red dots so that I don't know which little red dots are which. It's like trying to have it off in an intensive care unit.

And the biggest problem of all in these meticulous calculations is when do you begin them? When do you start the counting? Are you supposed to start counting at the beginning of your period, or at the end? Joanna (who's good with numbers – she does the accounts at the agency) said she thought it was sort of the end of the beginning, not when you first feel your period coming, but when it properly starts. But Melinda (who has actually had a baby) said you count backwards from the next one, which can't be right, surely? I remember reading in Elle *or some such mag that clues can be gleaned from the colour of your menstrual blood. Well, frankly.*

I preferred last month's theory. That one was a cracker. I loved it. We were experimenting with the 'bonk all the time' theory. Based on the idea that fertilization is an unknowable, unplannable lottery. Which of course it is.

Lucy made a list in an effort to marshal her thoughts. I reproduce this list below. If nothing else it will fill up a bit of space and make it look like I've written more than I have.

Lucy's Shag All The Time Theory List.

1. No one can ever be sure exactly when ovulation occurs.

2. No one really seems to know at what point during ovulation fertility is at its most likely.

3. If you did know these things it would not make any difference at all. Because no one knows how long it takes a lazy and reluctant sperm with attitude to swim what, I seem to recall being told at school, is the equivalent of a piranha fish swimming the length of the Amazon. Hence, even if you did know when ovulation was going to occur you would not know how long before that you should do the business.

The conclusion that Lucy drew from this list was that the only way to be sure of hitting the mark was to shag all the time. When I say 'all the time' I mean once a night which *is* all the time as far as I'm concerned. If she starts insisting on afternoon delight as well I'll have to buy some sort of pill off the Internet.

It was a good month, except when Lucy scalded herself. Nothing to do with me, I hasten to add. The problem was that after we'd done it she insisted on propping her bum up with a pillow for half an hour so that my sperm would be able to swim downhill. This is not an ideal position in which to enjoy a cup of tea and so, one day, over her and the duvet it went.

I must say I thought she deserved it. I resented the assumption that my crappy, lazy, undermotivated sperm would only be able to reach her eggs if given the unfair advantage of being allowed to swim downhill.

The other thing I find a bit sad about Restricted Bonking Month is it means that Sam and I don't really have much physical contact at all at the moment. Sam's not much of a cuddler, he never has been. He really only tends to cuddle as a sort of pre-sex warm-up, which is a shame. Personally I often crave a bit of physical affection that isn't sexual and is, well, just affection. Sheila says that in her experience (which is considerable, she having had it off for the Home Counties in her time), non-sexual physical attention isn't something that men do, and certainly not after about the first year of the relationship. So I might as well forget it or become a lesbian.

Dear Book

First entry for four days. I really must do better or Lucy will think I'm not trying. The whole problem with the theory of writing down your feelings of course is that it takes so long to come up with one. I remember trying to write a diary when I was at school. All I could think of to write was what I'd had for dinner. I'd read somewhere that the cool thing for a guy to record was his sexual conquests, giving them marks out of ten. Well of course I didn't have any sexual conquests at the time and not for many years after, so that was no good. For a while I tried giving marks for my trips to see Mrs Hand and her five lovely daughters but it was pointless, I always got top score.

Lucy is enjoying doing her writing, of course, surprise surprise. She's sitting there now, across the bedroom, scribbling away. She gets the bed, obviously. I have to do mine on the dressing table, which is of course completely covered in bottles of moisturizing stuff. How many types of moisturizing stuff does one woman need? I mean how moisturized can she get, for heaven's sake? Any more and I shall be able to pour her into a glass and drink her.

What the hell is she writing about? I'm not allowed to ask. Apparently, if we read each other's books we'll be writing them for each other, which is not the purpose of the exercise.

I expect Lucy's writing about what an emotionally retarded shit I am. That'll be it. She can never forgive me for being more relaxed than her about whether we have children or not. I know that secretly she thinks this attitude has infected my sperm. She thinks that their refusal to leap like wild salmon straight up the river of her fertility and headbutt great holes in the walls of her eggs is down to a belligerently slack attitude which they've caught off me. She imagines them gently doing backstroke and diving for coins in the idle juices of her uterus saying, 'Well, the boss doesn't care either way about kids, so why should we?'

Dear Penny

Sam hates this. I'm looking at him now, hunched over his laptop, resentment radiating from his every pore. If ever a person's body language said 'This is airy-fairy New Age bollocks,' his does now. I really don't see why he has to be so negative. Perhaps it's because the exercise is making him confront his own shallowness. After all, it must be very difficult to become a partner with your emotions if you have absolutely no interest in what those emotions are. I don't think he even knows whether he wants children. I'm going to ask him. I don't think I've ever really properly confronted him with the question.

Lucy just stopped writing and asked me for the millionth time whether I was sure that I even wanted children because she didn't think I did. God, we keep having these conversations. I think we should just tape one and put it on a loop. It's not that I don't want children. I'm not made of stone, for heaven's sake, but children are not the only thing I want. I happen to believe that when God made me he made me for a purpose beyond that of devoting my entire life to reproducing myself. To which Lucy replied that when God made me he made a million other people the same day and probably doesn't even remember my name, which I thought was bloody hurtful actually. So I suggested to her that if my presence on this planet is so insignificant then there can be no reasonable justification for me aspiring to pro-creation. In fact I should probably just kill myself right now, relieving our overstretched planet of a pointless waste of its resources. She said I was just being pompous and unpleasant and then started to look a bit teary, which is of course a very easy and entirely unfair way of winning an argument. Actually, some-times, I think I'd quite like to die young. That way I could avoid failing to fulfil my potential.

What he dresses up as self-doubt and humility is actually frus-trated arrogance. He only gets depressed about himself because he doesn't write any more. But it's becoming a self-fulfilling prophecy. He says he can't write, so he doesn't write. It's as simple as that. I told him he'd get a lot further as a writer if he spent less time moaning about it and more time doing it. To which he said he'd like to but that I was taking up all his spare time making him write a stupid book of letters to himself. Which is just ridiculous. At least I've made him write some-thing, as opposed to nothing, which is what he usually writes. Actually, I think it might do him good as a writer to get in touch with his feelings occasionally. All he seems to do as a commissioning editor at the BBC is encourage people to write ever ruder jokes. This must surely eventually coarsen his creative soul.

Anyway, he didn't answer that because he knew I was right. He just snorted unpleasantly and now there's an atmosphere.

It's all very well her telling me to write. I can't bloody write. I'm a creativity-free zone. The only thing about me less fertile than my imagination is my bollocks. She *is* wrong about my attitude to kids, though. Of course I want children. Well, I think I do. There's been so much angst surrounding the subject for so long now that I've forgotten what I originally felt. But I'm sure that if I do want children it's because I love Lucy. That's the only way I can think about it. If I try to think of kids in the abstract I very quickly come up against no sleep and vomit in my personal stereo. Having kids seems to me like the end of life as I know it, and I like life as I know it. I like to work, I like to drink, I like to sleep in and have clothes and furniture with no dribble and sick on them. Viewed dispassionately, I'm not keen on the idea of having children at all and I'm not going to lie to Lucy about it no matter what a cold, heartless shit she thinks that makes me.

Kids, however, as a part of Lucy, as an extension and expression of our love, I can relate to, and if it happened I'd be delighted. No, I'd be more than delighted, I'd be in heaven. It would be the greatest thing in the world, but if it doesn't happen it doesn't. That's how I see it. If we have children it will be another part of us, of our love. If we don't, then we'll still have us. Our love will be no less whole. I don't want to get soppy here, but it's how I feel.

I've just said all this to Lucy and she went all teary again, which at first made me think I'd won her over but it turned out that she was crying because she thinks I've already resigned myself to not having kids and that we're going to end up sad, bitter and unfulfilled and destined to a pathetic, lonely old age.

Dearest Pen Pal

I was talking to Drusilla today at work. Sheila (my boss, the one who told me to write to you) had rushed out of the office (she'd heard there was a bloke on Oxford Street selling dodgy fags at a pound a box), so Joanna and I were being slack. In fact we were playing the Spotlight *game, which is great fun. What you do is you get the* Actor's Spotlight *(which is a book full of photographs of actors) and open it at random. Whoever you pick on, you have to sleep with. Not actually, obviously, but just as a thought.*

I'd just been landed with Sir Ian McKellen and was rather thinking that I had my work cut out there when Drusilla popped in. Drusilla is an actress, hence her connection to herbal and fruit teabags is almost mystical. I don't think I've ever seen her when her hand has not been jiggling a little string over a cup of hot water. She's convinced that I only have to get the right combination of herbal teabags and I shall instantly have triplets.

I'm not sure. Fruit-flavoured teabags are a mystery to me because they're not fruit-flavoured at all. They smell of fruit, but quite frankly they taste of bugger-all. The strange thing is, no matter how much I know this to be a fact, I'm always disappointed. You get that terrific whiff of blackcurrant, or orange and ginger and you think 'Surely this time the goods will be delivered.' But no. Yet another mug of hot coloured water to nurse till it goes cold.

Drusilla recently played a mad mystic in an episode of Casualty *and I'm here to tell you that she was typecast. We'd hoped that it might turn into a semi-regular but sadly it was not to be. Shame. I think* Casualty *could do with a witch in it. Anyway, the point is that Drusilla has got very interested in my fears about being barren and is convinced that the answer lies in the runes. She's been reading up on some ancient Druid-like fertility rites or other and came in today waving a crystal about. She says that Western society is the only society which has dispensed with its fertility rites and the only society in which the birth rate is falling. 'Hallo-o,' she said. 'Obvious connection, I think.' Then she suggested an impromptu fertility ceremony.*

Well, I knew she was mad, but this took even me aback. Unbelievably, she wanted me to lie on the floor while she and Joanna squatted over me. I swear I'm not making this up. Then she wanted us all to make some sort of appalling vaginal symbol with our thumbs and forefingers. Whilst doing this we had to chant the words 'womb' and 'flow' in low rich tones so that the sounds reverberated deep within us.

Well, I ask you. The whole idea was absolutely absurd and I said so.

Let me tell you I felt a right fool when Sheila came back with her fags and found us.

If Restricted Bonking Month works and I do finally get pregnant, Drusilla will of course claim victory for her fertility ritual, but I shan't mind. I'm that desperate I'd give credit to the fairies at the bottom of the garden.

Dear Book

Lucy decided that the optimum moment of Restricted Bonking Month had arrived during lunch. My lunch, not hers. She wasn't there, she was at home surrounded by calendars, thermometers, red felt-tip pens and urine. I was lunching at One Nine Oh (so called because it's situated at 190 Ladbroke Park Gate – brilliant, eh)? One Nine Oh is something of a media haunt and I often lunch there in my capacity as one of the BBC's most senior and experienced lunch eaters.

My guests were Dog and Fish, a comic double act who seem to be doing quite well on the circuit at the moment. They are two Oxbridge graduates who are of the opinion that current comedy is 'completely crap and useless' and what we need is a new, post-comedy comedy. Basically, they want to do for the comic sketch what Techno did for the tune. I asked if that meant you had to be out of your head on drugs to enjoy it and they grinned knowingly and said that, 'Yeah, it would help.' I saw their act in Edinburgh and think they're truly and deeply awful in a very real sense. *Time Out*, however, says that they are important and mould-breaking (no mention of funny, but that would be selling out), so the BBC must of course beat a path to their door. If for no other reason than that if we don't Channel Four will get them and yet again look more hip than us.

They told me that they wanted to do a post-modern docusoap

sitcom. The idea being that we supply them with cameras and a crew and that they record their lives. Each week they'll present us with a half-hour of the best bits plus a four-hour version to run through the night 'for the real Dog-geeks and Fish-heads', they said, 'the real post-comedy comedy nutters'. They claim that by this means they'll cut out all that false crap which TV comedy normally gets bogged down in, like scripts and jokes and acting in an amusing manner, and get straight to the raw improvisational bones of their genius.

'Basically, we're talking about existentialism with knob gags,' is how Fish put it.

Sometimes the irony of my job strikes me quite forcefully. I mean, when I was younger all I ever wanted to do with my life was write comic scripts. Now what I do with my life is commission other people to do it. People whom I have to admit I don't normally think much of. That's my tragedy. I mustn't complain, though. I get to eat a lot of excellent lunch.

Anyway. Lucy's call came along with the starters. Finally, it seemed, after days of intense numbercrunching, the ovulation result had come up and we were on. By a curious coincidence I'd ordered Oeufs Benedict to begin my meal. Her eggs were ready at exactly the same time as mine.

I hate mobiles but Lucy had made me buy one for just such a circumstance as this. I'm going to have to work out the volume control, though, because unless I'm being paranoid her voice seemed to be being broadcast through the restaurant PA.

'Sam, I think I'm ovulating. Come home and fuck me now.'

Well, people may have heard and they may not have heard, but either way they could not have helped but hear my reply, which was intended to be in a whisper but emerged as a sort of loud gasp.

'Fuck you? I'm in a meeting.'

Dog and Fish smiled broadly at this and I could tell that in the delicate dance of mutual respect I was losing ground somewhat. Thinking fast, I repeated what I'd said but with a different emphasis.

'Fuck you! I'm in a meeting.'

Dog and Fish laughed out loud at that and Lucy must have heard them because she absolutely made me promise not to tell them what she was phoning about. She thought they'd write a post-modern, après-comedy sketch about it. They wouldn't, of course; the subject did not come within their frame of reference, the single and only thing of interest to Dog and Fish being Dog and Fish.

It was all very well for Lucy to swear me to silence but she was also demanding that I jack in the lunch immediately and hurry home. It's not an easy situation to think up a decent excuse for. I mean cancelling a meeting is easy. Anyone can cancel a meeting. People do it to me all the time. But attending a meeting, a meeting that has been set up for months and then suddenly getting an abrupt phonecall after which you leap up from the table and leave your busy and highly fashionable companions to dine alone, that requires an explanation. What do you say? All I could do was act casual and try to keep it ambiguous.

'Sorry,' I said. 'My wife is ovulating and she wants seeing to.'

Not great, but the best I could do at the time. In fact I think they thought it was a joke.

'Nice one, geezer,' they said and laughed in a grunty, cynical, fag-ashy kind of a way.

I left a credit card number with the Maître d' to cover Dog and Fish's lunch and grabbed a taxi. All the way home I tried to think erotic thoughts, knowing what would be required of me the moment I walked through the door.

Sure enough, when I got home Lucy was already in bed. It's all very well for her. Nobody minds at the agency if she skips a day. Most of her clients only do voiceover work anyway, which is all fixed fee. Personally I think that all Lucy and the other women in that agency do all day is gossip, but I'm not allowed to say that, of course.

'Come on! Come on!' she was shouting. 'The pee traffic light is green! My temperature is optimum and all the little red dots have collided!! My eggs are done *now*! They'll be hard boiled in a minute!'

Oh, the pressure.

Great steaming shitballs, I hate myself sometimes. All month I'd been wanting a shag and now of course I get stagefright. Well, who wouldn't? It isn't easy to get a hard-on when your partner is desperately staring at her watch and bleakly contemplating a lonely and emotionally unfulfilled life of childlessness ahead. An unkind God seemed suddenly to have replaced my dick with a small piece of warm, flesh-coloured plasticine. 'Lifeless' would have been a compliment. Lucy tried her best, of course, but it wasn't much help. I knew that all she was thinking was, 'Come on, get hard, you bastard. My eggs are on the turn.'

We succeeded in the end. I managed to just about sustain a sort of semi-half-master until achieving a lacklustre orgasm. More of a boregasm really. Words cannot describe how annoyed with myself I was. I felt really unmanned and that I'd let Lucy down. She said it was all right, but without a great deal of conviction. I told her that I didn't think I'd produced enough but she said it didn't need much. 'It's quality, not quantity,' she said, which was nice of her.

Dear Penny

It was Bonk Day today, the culmination of Restricted Bonking Month. This sort of thing is definitely not good for the sex life. I mean sex ought to be spontaneous and erotic, not contrived and mechanical, but what could I do? I needed servicing and there's an end to it. I could see that Sam was a bit upset afterwards. I fear that he feels he's being used like some kind of farmyard animal. Nothing more than a breeding stud, brutally milked for his sperm. Not that he was much of a stud today. Frankly, I've seen harder knobs on the door of a bouncy castle. For a minute there I thought he wasn't going to pull it off. I used all my womanly wiles, even 'going down' on him as they say, something I've never been big on. Well, I'm just not very good at it, I never really know what to do. I mean you put it in your mouth, and then what? Chew? You certainly aren't supposed to blow, despite the name of the exercise. Anyway, he did not respond at all well and it was marshmallow in a slot machine time, I'm afraid.

It was all rather disheartening really, Penny. I mean I don't aspire to being a sex bomb but a girl does rather hope to be able to provoke an erection in her husband. It was the pressure, of course. After all my calculations he knew he had to produce the goods. Difficult for him, I'm sure, but as a woman with feelings I do rather wish it hadn't appeared quite such an ordeal.

Anyway, long story short and all that, honour was satisfied. Sam says that all he can say is that if we do score this month the kid will be a strong swimmer because its dad certainly didn't give it much of a start.

When we'd finished he rushed off, of course. I asked him not to because I think it's important to spend a bit of time together after sex or else it's just sex, isn't it? But Sam said he had to go back to work, which, considering he claims his job consists entirely of telling arseholes how clever they are, didn't seem like much of an excuse to me. I told him that at times like these we should make an effort to concentrate on the emotional side of our relationship, otherwise our love life will be nothing more than a mechanical thing, devoid of sensuality and romance. He said, 'Right, yes, romance, absolutely right,' and left.

When I got back to TV Centre there were three messages to ring Aiden Fumet, Dog and Fish's manager. He's also the manager of about sixteen other acts whom *Time Out* and the *Guardian* have sequentially announced as 'quite simply the best in Britain today'. Aiden Fumet is a very aggressive man, which is all right in itself – certain types of agent and manager have always been aggressive. What puts Fumet beyond even the most distant pale is that he is also self-righteous. He seems to see any failure on the part of the BBC to grant a series to any of his acts as evidence of a vicious conspiracy to deny the young people of Britain the comedic nourishment for which their souls are clearly crying out. The idea that the BBC might think some of his acts less than good does not cross his mind.

'What the fuck was that malarkey all about, then, Sam, dumping my boys at One Nine Oh?' Fumet said when I called him back. 'I'd better warn you now, mate, that Dog and Fish are one phonecall away from going to Channel Four. One fucking phonecall and they're with Michael, OK? And the BBC can fuck off.'

Well, I was in no mood for this. Normally I have to admit that I'm a bit of a pushover. To be honest, I just can't be bothered to argue with these people. The worm, however, can turn and show his teeth (if worms have teeth) and a worm who has just been crap in bed with the wife he loves and who is counting on him to fill her up with sperm is likely to turn like a U-bend.

'What is going *on*, Aiden, *mate . . .*' and I commenced to give him the most exquisitely phrased bollocking of his entire life. Unfortunately it was all wasted because after he'd told me to fuck off he'd hung up.

Later, I told Lucy about the whole incident over supper, and that led to a slight misunderstanding. She said that she was sorry about today, and I thought she meant she was sorry about me getting shat on by arrogant, no-talent twatheads. So I told her not to worry. I told her that it was my job. Well, it turned out that she was actually talking about our lunchtime sex session. She's been concerned that I might feel used – 'milked for my sperm like a farmyard animal' was how she put it. So when I said, 'Don't worry, it's my job,' she thought I meant having sex with her was my job and said, 'I hope you don't see it as a job,' in a very tart voice indeed. But I of course still thought she was talking about my work and therefore took her tart retort as a snide reference to the pathetically unfulfilling way I earn a living and said, 'Yes, it's a job, a bloody boring job. There's certainly no satisfaction to be had in it.'

Misunderstandings all round and quite an atmosphere had developed before we got it sorted out, after which I immediately put my foot in it again. Lucy remarked that this confusion perhaps indicated that we should be setting time aside to be tender and close with each other and communicate more. Well, I thought she was just trying to be nice to me, so I told her not to bother on my account as I wasn't bothered either way. It turned out that she was actually appealing for a more tender and sensual attitude on my part, so me saying I wasn't bothered was the worst thing I could have said.

After that we didn't talk any more and she started clearing the plates in a marked manner.

Dear Penny

I got my fucking period today.

I'm writing this with a hotwater bottle clamped to my tummy because of the cramps. Oh, how I love being a woman. I've known it was coming for days.

'What's that dull aching feeling, I wonder?'

'Why, that's a little warning that you're going to be bent double in agony for a couple of days living off painkillers, and by the way it looks like you're barren as well.'

Drusilla says I have to learn to love my periods, that they're part of the sacred cycle of the earth and the moon. Words failed me at that juncture, which was fortunate really because had I thought about it I would have told her to get on her sacred cycle and ride it off a sodding cliff.

It really is so depressing, Penny. The grim, clockwork inevitability of my body failing to perform the functions for which it was designed. A few months ago I broke down on the M6, my car, that is, not me, although quite frankly I nearly did as well. It was awful, just sitting there waiting for the breakdown people to come. Completely useless, sitting in an apparently perfectly serviceable car but not able to get anything to work (it was a blocked fuel line, by the way). Millions of other cars kept whizzing by and they were all working but I was stuck, absolutely stuck, and there was nothing I could do about it. I cannot tell you how frustrating it was. Well, my whole life's like that really. Month after month I'm stuck, my car won't work and I have no idea how to make it go. All there is left for me to do is to try and seek help, to face that long trudge up the hard shoulder in search of a phone that probably won't work in order to call an emergency service that will take for ever to respond and when they do won't be able to find the problem or have the right tool to fix it. Meanwhile, the entire rest of the female sex are whizzing past in Renault people carriers with eight babyseats in the back. Am I dragging out this analogy too far? If so I don't care.

Look, I know I'm whining here, but if I can't whine to my imaginary friend who can I whine to? My periods are absolutely horrible and the crowning nightmare of my apparent infertility is the idea that this abject misery, which I have endured twelve times a year since I was thirteen, might be for nothing. I mean, if it turns out my whole plumbing system is irrevocably buggered and that I might just as well have had a hysterectomy twenty years ago I shall just die.

Dear Book

Failed again. Arse. Lucy says that Sheila says the bloke on *Oprah* said that I'm not supposed to use that word. 'Failed', that is, not 'arse'. Apparently the 'fail' word implies a value judgement. If we say that we've failed then that means in some way it's our fault, which of course it isn't. Lucy has read eight and a half million books on the subject of infertility and while they don't agree on many things they do all seem to feel that a positive outlook is essential.

Well, bollocks to that. We've failed again. Lucy has got her period, Restricted Bonking Month was a complete washout. She's in bed right now, with the light off, groaning. I'm sure the main reason she wants a kid is to have nine months off having periods. They seem to be so awful for her. She says I can never know how bad it feels, but to give me some idea she says it's like being kicked in the balls over and over again for two days. Sounds terrible, although how she would know what being kicked in the balls is like I don't know.

I always feel at such a loss at these times. So impotent. Whoops, wrong word there, but you know what I mean ... I mean I know what I mean ... for heaven's sake, I think I'm going mad. Nobody's going to read this but me and yet I'm beginning to address this pointless exercise to a third person. I must get a grip.

Anyway, as I was remarking, I feel so useless at period time. I watch Lucy groaning away and I really haven't got the faintest idea what's going on with her. All I know is that her gut swells up like a football, which is doubly sad because it makes her look pregnant. I think all small boys should be given lessons about menstruation when they are eleven. I mean, we were never told anything about it when I was at school. I'll bet they still gloss over it, and as you get older you don't like to ask. I mean obviously I know the basics, but the details you have to pick up off the tampon ads on the telly and it's most confusing. They use all this code language and imagery like 'protection' and 'freedom' and 'all-over freshness' and there's wings involved and the blood's blue and frankly you just don't have the faintest idea what's going on at all.

Dear Penny

Felt better today, physically, anyway. Mentally I'm still feeling low. The brutal truth is that it is now sixty-one periods since Sam and I started trying for a baby. That's five years and one month. What's more, when I come to think about it, prior to that we weren't exactly being careful. In fact we had at least a year of relying on withdrawal. I wanted to get preg even then and I remember thinking that if one night he didn't get it out in time I wouldn't mind a bit. I know now that he might as well have left it in until Christmas, it wouldn't have mattered anyway.

Because, basically, I have to face facts. I am Sad. I'm Barren. My womb is a prune.

There, I've said it. I don't care, it's how I feel. What's the point of this book if I can't be honest? Excuse me, Penny, got to get a tissue.

I've been crying, Penny, sorry. I tried reminding myself about the homeless and the starving people in Africa, but it didn't work. Anyway, I'm back now. Don't worry, I'm not about to collapse or have a breakdown or anything, it's just that sometimes I get a bit overwhelmed, that's all.

And, yes, I know that a lot of women wait a lot longer than five years and a month (actually six years and one month in my case, if you count the careless year) and then all of a sudden they start spraying sprogs about the place like a fish spawning. I've heard all the stories. Couples who gave up hope only to have eight kids in a week!

'I know someone who waited decades!' people say.

'My cousin had actually been dead for three years when she had her first. Dead of old age! She was a shrivelled, sundried-tomato-like, cadaverous old corpse and what's more her husband had no testicles, having lost them in the Crimean War. Yet once they'd had one they couldn't stop. Ended up with enough for a football and a netball team plus a crowd of supporters!!'

I've heard them all.

Mum says that she's sure it's all in the mind. Everybody says that. She says I concentrate too much on my career. Everybody says that too. Besides which, career? Ha! Ha ha HA! One thing I do not have is a career. I am not a theatrical agent, I am a theatrical agent's assistant. Negotiating residual repeat fees for cable broadcasts of ancient episodes of Emmerdale Farm *(when it was still called* Emmerdale Farm*) is not what I call a career.*

Melinda says I've got to relax. Everybody says that as well! In fact, that is the thing that everybody says most. They say, 'Relax, the thing to do is put it out of your mind and then it will happen.' It is simply not possible to bloody well relax with your body clock ticking away in your ear at five million decibels, and your eggs getting more dry and ancient by the day.

Melinda and George brought Cuthbert round today, which was nice. No, really it was, I'm not so bloody sad that I can't enjoy my friends and their babies. Sam still refers to Cuthbert as Scrotum, which is ridiculous because he's beautiful. I held him for a while and just wanted to eat him. It's pathetic, I hate myself, but all the time I was saying how lovely he was, all I could think was, 'Wish I had one.'

Dear Sam

Scrotum may have improved slightly, difficult to say. I mean he no longer makes me want to hide behind the sofa like he was a

monster from *Doctor Who*, but then that may just be because I'm
getting used to him. George has overcome his initial qualms,
I'm pleased to say, and given the lad the benefit of the doubt. The
prospects of young Cuthbert ending up wrapped in a blanket outside a police station are receding. I mean it's clear that he's not
going to be a male model, that's for sure, but George thinks he
could probably do something in the City or on the radio. Or a
boxer, perhaps? We certainly wouldn't have to worry about his
looks getting ruined.

I'm probably being unfair here. I suppose all babies look this
way in the very early stages, but I have to be honest and admit
that they do absolutely nothing for me. I try to get clucky but no
go, I don't even want to hold them. I'm an arm's-length man,
thank you very much. That funny pulsating bit on their heads
completely freaks me out. The first time I saw that I confidently
expected the Alien to burst forth from it with Sigourney Weaver
close behind. Of course Lucy went potty over the lad and had to
hold him and I knew that all she could think was that she wished
she had one.

I wish that she did too. I wish that we both did. I would love
to be the father of Lucy's child.

Sometimes, on the rare occasions when I go for my run in the
park, I find myself fantasizing about us being a family. I imagine
Lucy back home with the two cutest little toddlers ever and me
getting back and having my bath with them and then we all have
tea together and then a story.

I'll stop writing now as I'm in danger of turning into a sad fuck.

Dear Penny

Drusilla has suggested aromatherapy. She's given me some
rose and geranium oils, which was nice of her. She says these oils
are oestrogenic. Sam is of course completely dismissive. He says
if women want to bathe in scented oils then that's fine by him but
they should not bloody well pretend there's any further signifi-
cance to it than that. I hate the way he does that. As if there's
some rational and obvious way of doing things and everything

else is just self-indulgent claptrap. I mean it probably is self-indulgent claptrap, of course, but he doesn't have to be so negative all the time. I said to him, 'There are more things in heaven and earth than are dreamt of in your philosophy, you cynical bastard!' which I must say I thought rather a clever riposte.

The thing about Sam is that he protects his feelings by pretending he doesn't have any. I'm sure that's why he suffers from writer's block. I just don't believe you can write anything worthwhile without putting a bit of yourself into it.

Dear Self

The house reeks! Stinks! I do wish Lucy would not talk to Drusilla. I mean I know that Drusilla has considered Lucy her soulmate since Lucy got her the part of a plum in a yogurt advert, but the woman is nuttier than squirrel shit. The aromatherapy business has got out of hand. As I write these very words Lucy, a normally rational person, is boiling up the bark of a hawthorn hedge with the roots of a herbaceous bush in order to make a tincture for her bath. I try not to be dismissive, but Lucy knows how I feel and takes it as evidence of a shallow cynicism on my part. She feels that this is at the root of my inability to write, saying that I live my emotional life at a glib surface level and that I won't write anything worthwhile until I get in touch with my inner feelings. The truth of the matter is, of course, that I don't have any inner feelings and the reason I can't write anything decent is that I am a talent-free zone with the brain of a Brussels sprout.

Dear Penny

Sam is still moaning about my aromatherapy and herbal remedies (I'm currently boiling fennel and ginger, which I admit is a bit whiffy). He's so cold and dismissive of anything remotely spiritual or sensual which is very frustrating for me because I really do feel the need for softness and spirituality in my life sometimes. I mean, what's the point of sharing your life with someone if you can't communicate with them about the things that matter to you? Sam, I'm afraid, thinks that feelings are an inconvenience and never really wants to talk about anything important. He's only interested in his work and trivia like old popmusic. Sometimes I even wonder about whether he still fancies me.

Sheila took on an important new client today. An actor called Carl Phipps. He came into the office. Very arrogant. Good looking, certainly, but what does that signify?

Dear Self

Now she's started using this little candle and dish arrangement in which she warms aromatic oils. The house stinks like a student party. I know I shall have a blocked nose in the morning. On top of which the whole business has made her all upset with me as well. This evening she wanted me to massage nutmeg oil into the crease of her bum (not, I hasten to add, out of any sudden erotic desire but because it's what it said you should do on the bottle). Well, I put down my newspaper and did it, of course, but she could tell that I wasn't overly enthused about the whole thing. She felt I was massaging her bum crease in a perfunctory manner and took this as further evidence of my lack of tactile warmth, similar to the shameful way in which I don't like to cuddle while watching the telly. Lucy thinks I'm uptight and unloving, that massaging her bum crease is something I should relish, that I should be rejoicing in the sensual dialogue betwixt my fingers and her bum. I just think that I wanted to finish my paper.

Look, Book, I'm not saying I don't fancy her. Of course I fancy her, but we've been together for nearly ten years! I just can't get as worked up about her bum as I used to. I know her bum, I'm familiar with it, we've been through a lot together. Caressing it can never again be the same journey of mystery and delight that it was on our first wild nights together. I can't say this to Lucy, of course. She'd be horrified and think me a callous pig. Although

I can tell you one thing: if I strolled up to her while she was watching *EastEnders* and said, 'Stick your fingers up my arse now,' I'd get pretty short shrift.

But it's always the way with women, isn't it? One law for them, one law for us. She's completely irrational. She says that I'd probably be more than happy to massage aromatic oils into Winona Ryder's bum and the truth is that of course I bloody well would! I don't say so, of course, but naturally she takes my silence as an admission of guilt (contrary to all civilized law, I might point out). So she says, 'Well, go on, then, I'm not stopping you,' so I say no, I'm not going to massage oil into Winona Ryder's bum because I love her (Lucy, that is, not Winona) and whatever my unworthy male hormonal response to gorgeous film stars might be, I have chosen to be faithful to Lucy. Also, I have to admit that Winona might not be one hundred per cent keen on the idea and her wishes would of course have to be taken into account.

The extraordinary thing is that Lucy thinks that an attached man finding other women attractive is virtually tantamount to his being unfaithful. Which is bullshit! Only being unfaithful is tantamount to being unfaithful! I have tried to explain that the fact that a man remains faithful despite finding other women attractive (which all men do unless they're dead) is the proof of his love and devotion and should be recognized as such and appreciated, not condemned. To which Lucy says, 'Well, if you're that desperate, go ahead, then. I'm not stopping you,' and I say, 'I don't want to! That's the point! But the reason that I'm not unfaithful is not because I never find other women attractive, but because I love you!' And she says, 'Well, if you're that desperate, go ahead, then. I'm not stopping you.'

And so the long day wears on.

Dear Penny Pal

I feel a bit sad. I know Sam loves me and I suppose he still fancies me, but he doesn't bother to show it very much and he never says it. He says he does, of course. He claims that I have selective ears, that I never hear him when he says nice things but only when he doesn't. I don't think that's true. I think he only really says nice things when I ask him to say them, but I can't be sure. I think that perhaps his mother didn't cuddle him enough as a child or something. Tonight I made him massage some oil into my lower back and although he did do it I could tell that it was a major inconvenience for him, which made the whole thing pointless. I mean, if aromatherapy is going to have any effect at all I imagine it will be a pretty subtle one, dealing as it does with one's most delicate biorhythms. Sam's reluctant vibes will have buggered all that completely. Let's face it, delicate biorhythms are not exactly going to stand a lot of chance against a great big lump of negativity that just wants to read its newspaper.

He used to be much more tactile but now he doesn't even bother with foreplay when we have sex. I mean it's not as if he's In Like Flynn or anything like that. He's not rough or insensitive. In fact I think he's quite a sensitive lover, but he just doesn't try so much any more. He just cuddles up for a bit until he thinks I'm ready and then he's off. I sort of try to talk about it but he gets irritable. You see, he thinks it's inevitable that two people will become less sensuous and erotically aware of each other as the years go by, but I don't. Sometimes I'd rather just stroke a bit and cuddle than have sex, but I don't think Sam would see the point.

Dear Book

I think Lucy is at the end of her tether. She's been a bit quiet these last few days and I know it's because she's thinking about fertility. There's been this documentary running on the Beeb about IVF couples and she seems to have learnt it off by heart. Personally I can't watch it. I just cannot bring myself to be interested in the sad and desperate experiences of complete strangers. Lucy, on the other hand, tapes it. She tapes anything about fertility, even that arrogant pillock Kilroy who's on in the mornings. She cuts articles out of the papers (incredible how many there are) and writes off to all sorts of organizations. It's all a bit heartbreaking, although she's very good about it, determined not to become emotionally dysfunctional, she's quite clear on that one. But I must say I do find it slightly alarming how attractive she seems to find baby clothes. Mind you, this is something I've noticed in many women. They look at a pair of tiny socks and say, 'Ahh, isn't that just so-o-o sweet and just lovely.'

Why is this? I simply cannot fathom it. These are empty socks we're talking about here, socks with no baby in them. How can women go gooey over a pair of socks? I find Winona Ryder attractive (as I think I've said), but I wouldn't go all gooey over her socks . . . Well, possibly . . . I don't know. Anyway, what I'm saying is that the sight of a group of girls picking up a tiny jacket or a little hat and going 'Aaaaah' is a mystery to me.

It's the same with dolls. Lucy likes dolls. She's a woman of thirty-one and she loves them. Of course, because she's a grown-up she has to pretend that there's some kind of pseudo-artistic attraction, it's old dolls she likes, interesting ones. She goes on about the porcelain head with the stamp of the German maker on it. But I know that she just loves dolls and that if she thought she could get away with it without looking sad she'd buy a Barbie.

Better stop. Got to read a script tonight, a comic play which has developed out of a new writing workshop we've been running at the Beeb. The author has already had a one-act piece put on at the Royal Court or some other gruesome up-its-own-arse, over-subsidized London centre of theatrical wankdom. Lucy tells me we actually saw it but I can't remember it for the life of me. The new play is called *Fucking and Fucking*. I told him that we'd have to change the title and he looked at me as if I was some kind of fascist. It's so depressing. It seems only yesterday that I was considered a hip and dangerous young producer because I commissioned sketches about tampons. Now I'm a Nazi for telling young writers they can't use the word 'fuck' in their titles. Of course at the Royal Court they positively insist on having rude words in their titles and anal sex by the end of scene one.

I can't believe how quickly I'm turning into a sad, reactionary old git.

Dear Penny

*I'm not putting it off any longer, Penny. I've made an appoint-
ment to go and talk to my doctor. Five years and a month (soon
no doubt to be five years and two months) is too long for it to be
bad luck. There is obviously something wrong and quite frankly
it will be a relief to know the truth. Anyway, it seems to me that
the best way to get pregnant is to go and start the process of some
sort of fertility treatment. At least it is according to the seventeen
million old-wives' tales and urban myths I've been told over the
last couple of years. You hear constantly of people who know
people who had decided to start IVF only to get pregnant by conventional means on their way to the first appointment! There are
also any number of stories of couples who failed at IVF but then
immediately got pregnant by conventional means or by sitting on
wet grass or something. Add to this the numerous people who
have a cousin who signed up to adopt and then immediately fell
pregnant, plus of course the tales of people who got pregnant in
the five-mile-high club on the way back from trying to get a
Bosnian Baby. All in all I have come to the conclusion that the
only absolutely sure way to get pregnant is to be pronounced
infertile.*

*Carl Phipps, our new star, came in to the office again today to
drop off his current ten-by-eight. He's already had an offer of a
film and he's only been with us a few days! I'm afraid this has
made him rather grand. We call his type Uhoaas which stands for
'Up his own arse actor'.*

Dear etc

Depressed. Very depressed. I met the new BBC1 Controller
today. He's younger than me! This is the first time this has
happened. I mean me being older than one of my bosses. I don't
like it at all. He's a whizzkid from Granada. I think he made
some documentary proving that the Conservative Party is funded
by a gang of Middle Eastern prostitutes, so obviously that
qualifies him to schedule the entertainment of a nation. Looking
at him, I suddenly felt the icy hand of mortality upon my

shoulder. I'm thirty-eight, I'll be forty in two years.

I thought about going for a run. I didn't go, but I thought about it.

I feel very sorry for poor old Lucy at the moment. Not only has she got all this fertility business on her mind, but now it sounds like she's got a real idiot to look after at work. That new actor, Phipps guy, can't remember his first name, Cunt or something, although I doubt that could be it. He sounds like a right pain. She went on about him a bit over dinner, so I could tell he's got right under her skin. As if she didn't have enough to worry about.

Dear Penny

I'm going to see Dr Cooper today. I feel better now that I'm finally acknowledging that there actually probably is a problem and that I'm beginning the process of dealing with it. All the girls plus my mum and Sam's mum continue to assure me that five years and one month (nearly five years and two months) is not that long to be trying. I continue to be bombarded with the same old drivel about various women who tried continually and energetically for seven years and then – bang! – out popped triplets. I do wish people wouldn't all say the SAME BOLLOCKS to me all the time. They might at least vary it slightly. There seem to be more urban myths attached to infertility than there are to famous film stars filling their bottoms with small animals. It will be so good to get an informed opinion rather than all this anecdotal hearsay.

Just got back from Dr Cooper's. He says that five years or so is not actually that long to be trying and that he knows any number of women who tried for seven years and then had twelve apiece. I feel a huge gin and tonic calling.

Dr Cooper has, however, offered to do a blood test to check my hormone levels and a sperm test for Sam. I told Sam about it this afternoon and he took it very well. I thought it might bother him a bit – men are so funny about their manhood and anything remotely associated with their willies – but he was great and said it was simply not a problem and did not bother him in the slightest.

FUCK FUCK FUCK FUCK!!!!
I've got diluted sperm. I know it. My sack is empty! My balls undone! Can't write any more tonight.

Dear Pen Pal

The blood test is all set up for next Tuesday. Apparently this will ascertain if I'm ovulating or not. My God, I shall be so annoyed if I'm not. Ten years of condoms, caps, coils and ab-stinence followed by five years of thermometers, counting days and weeing on traffic lights would all be completely wasted.

Drusilla is horrified at the prospect of me having a blood test. She thinks that modern medicine is totally intrusive (and I suppose wandering about naked at Stonehenge isn't intrusive). She thinks I should employ visualization therapy, which apparently consists of breathing, relaxing (surprise, surprise) and visualizing. She wants me to visualize a baby inside me, in my stomach, in my arms, in my very soul, a complete and perfect part of me. I said, 'Drusilla darling, that's all I ever bloody do,' and she said that was the problem. I'm obsessive, I need to visualize mystically rather than desperately, I need to allow myself the free-dom to dream. Sounds like absolute bollocks to me.

I've booked a class for tomorrow night.

Sheila has suggested that I drink more heavily and take up smoking. This is because the only two times she's ever got pregnant (Joanna and I were amazed, we had no idea she ever had been) were after colossal binges. It happened in her wild youth and resulted in abortions as she had no idea who the fathers were. I told her I've had many a drunken shag in my time and sadly the booze method does not work for me.

Sam seems to be going a bit funny over the prospect of his sperm test.

Dear Self

Heard an interesting fact about sperm today. Not that sperm is on my mind or anything but the subject came up in a taxi, as it will from time to time. Sperm counts, it seems, are generally down in the Western world. Seriously down, in fact, twenty-five per cent since before the war, or maybe fifty, the cab driver couldn't remember the exact figure. It seems that for whatever reason, be it additives in the food, pollution, radiation from our mobile phones, or the gunk at the bottom of Pot Noodles, we modern men are considerably less flush in the sperm department than our grandfathers were. Isn't that strange? I mean modern society's attitude to old people is basically one of contempt. We don't want to look like them and they cost too much to run. Most people think of old-age pensioners as being embarrassing wrinkly sad acts, terminally unhip.

'Poor old Grandad,' we think.

'Look at him, sitting in the corner dribbling and sucking his gums, always wanting to watch a different television channel from the rest of the family.'

Now it turns out the man's got bigger bollocks than all of his patronizing male descendants put together! Spunk is a diminishing commodity. George Formby had more than Tom Jones, who in turn has more than Liam Gallagher. Amazing. Dixie Dean had more capacious testicles than George Best, who had bigger ones than Gazza. Actually, thinking about it, that's probably why old-time footballers used to wear those huge shorts, it was clearly to fit their bollocks in. In fact it's probably why when you watch an old pre-war game on film it always looks so slow and uninspired. It was probably as much as the poor bastards could do to drag their enormous scrotums up and down the pitch.

Recently I've been feeling slightly old, which is ridiculous at thirty-eight. Except is it? I mean of course I can realistically say that I may not even have lived half of my life yet, but come on, my sixties and seventies are hardly comparable to my twenties and thirties, are they? I mean I may have as many years left, but will there be as much life in them? No bloody way. I already get buggered knees if I play too much tennis.

I don't like thinking this way. In fact, I don't really like think-ing at all. I'm not really an introspective sort of person. It's writing these stupid bloody letters that's making me all self-conscious. Perhaps I should cut down on the booze a bit. I'll have a drink and think about it.

Dear Penny

I'm afraid Drusilla's visualization class was a complete and utter washout. Why is it that anything interesting and different always has to be championed by the most unprepossessing people? Honestly, I'm trying to be nice here, but the types at this class made Drusilla (who is madder than the Green Room at the National Theatre) look positively sane.

I arrived at the Community Centre and a large woman with more hair (hennaed) than an old English sheepdog and breasts like Space Hoppers asked me if I wished to purchase some wash-able hessian sanitary napkins! I mean I ask you, Penny! Ugh, or what?! I'm happy to recycle glass, collect newspapers and rinse out tin cans but I do draw the line at recycling sanitary pads. If that is to be the price of saving the world then I fear that the world must die. And hessian? It would itch, I mean, wouldn't it? Surely? These hippy birds must have fannies like tanned leather.

I nearly turned around and ran for it there and then, but I'd made the effort so I decided that I'd better give it a go. There's no point being snobbish about these things, after all. Well, first off there was a 'greeting session'. This involved us all sitting in a big circle and chucking a beanbag at each other and whenever you caught it you had to say your name. A simple enough exercise, one might have thought, but it was astonishing how difficult some of them found keeping the rhythm. I doubt if any of them had ever been on a Girl Guide camp.

Anyway, after that the leading lady (who was American) took us on what is called a 'guided fantasy' which was quite relaxing really when you let yourself go. You have to imagine a cool forest and a path by a stream and things like that, damp mist, a green canopy above, you know the sort of thing. An infinity of calm. I rather enjoyed this bit and nearly nodded off, which was nice because I feel absolutely buggered at the moment. Of course if Sam had been there he would have made some smart Alec comment and ruined it, but if you don't try to be clever some of these alternative things can be quite good.

Anyway, once she'd got us feeling all sort of 'drifty', the American lady told us to try and visualize an imaginary baby being welcomed into our wombs. Well, I'm afraid that was where I lost it. All the relaxation disappeared and was replaced by anger and frustration. My cool forest suddenly turned into London as of now. I tried to get it back but I opened my eyes and looked round the circle at all these other sad, silly women, who were just like me (except I occasionally get my hair done), and I hated them. And I hated myself for being one of them.

Afterwards I told the American lady that I really didn't think that this was the right approach for me. I told her that I spend most of my time trying not to think about babies because when I do I upset myself. She said that she understood but that I have to allow myself to want, to dream and if necessary to grieve over my current lack of baby. She said that I was fighting my body, resenting it, seeing it as the enemy of all my hopes and that this self-created tension might in fact be getting in the way of conception. Actually, it did sort of make sense and I ended up rather liking the woman, but I still shan't go again. I just get too frustrated. I keep screaming inside, why the hell should I have to imagine a baby? Why can't I just have one! Far less nice people than me have lots, and it's just not fair. I know that's a wicked thing to say but I know I'd be a much better mum than half the women I see letting their children put sweets in the trolley at Sainsbury's. And as for these people one sees on the news who seem to have children for the sole reason that they might go on to terrorize entire housing estates and become one-boy crimewaves. Well, the injustice is almost too much to bear. I'd read my child Beatrix Potter and Winnie the Pooh and the only glue it would ever get involved with would be flour and water for making collages.

When I got home I found there'd been a letter in the second

post. It was from Melinda sending me photos of when we were
round at her and George's place with new baby Cuthbert. I'm
holding him and he looks so sweet and it looks like he's mine. I
look like a mother with a child and I'm not. I nearly cried but I
remembered my resolution not to be obsessive so I had half a
bottle of red wine instead.

Sam's sperm test is looming. I had originally thought that he
was taking it well but now he does seem to be dwelling on it
rather.

Dear Self

I had lunch with Trevor and George from work today and was
determined to touch on the subject of sperm. Pick their brains, so
to speak. I mean George ought to know something. He produced
Cuthbert and I wouldn't like to meet the sperm that fathered him.
Trevor's gay so God knows he should have some opinions on the
subject, having encountered the stuff face to face, so to speak. All
in all I had been looking forward to airing my fears re my up-
coming (if that isn't too loaded a phrase) sperm test.

I didn't get the chance, of course. We talked shop. We always
do. It's a funny thing about this biz we call show: whenever
people involved in it get together they can talk about nothing
else. I'm as bad as anyone. I believe that in the army they have a
rule in the officers' mess of no talking shop over dinner. It sounds
like a great idea but it wouldn't work for us, we'd just sink into
an awkward silence. Telling people in showbusiness not to talk
about showbusiness would be like telling the Pope to lay off the
religious stuff.

We were lunching in Soho at a posh place called Quark. All
restaurants in Soho are posh these days. Those nice, rough and
ready little Italian diners are just a distant memory. I'd already
made an arse of myself, of course. I arrived first and the waitress
(wearing a skirt that was little more than a big belt, why do these
girls torment us so?) immediately put this plate of prawny things
down in front of me. I said they must be someone else's because
I hadn't ordered anything yet. Well, she actually laughed at me!

Amazing, she laughed and said they were 'for the table', a complimentary pre-appetizer appetizer. 'Don't worry,' she said, 'you won't be charged for them,' like I was some sad tourist way out of his depth and worrying about his budget. God, I felt every type of turd. My own fault, of course. Silly mistake. Particularly for a professional eater of the sacred meal called lunch like myself. I tried to recoup by cracking a little joke. I asked her for a biro so that I could write 'Prat' on my forehead and, get this, she fucking gave me one.

Amazing! It's this worship of all things American, I fear. They have rude, smart Alec staff in New York so we poor Brits who no longer have personalities of our own must do likewise. The thing is that it works in America. Brittle, wisecracking chutzpah is part of New York culture. It's happening, it's buzzing. When we do it it just comes across as surly. Manners are now seen as totally out of date, a shameful hangover from our class-ridden pre-meritocracy past. There's a terrible modern orthodoxy that has developed which says that to be polite and show respect to other people is in fact to diminish your own status. Therefore people assert themselves by being rude. I think it's sad.

Anyway after the prawny things disaster the half-naked waitress gave me the wine list. Well, I couldn't face a wine list, not after the prawny mauling I'd just taken. I'd probably have ordered a dessert wine to start and been tarred and feathered and thrown out for being uncool. So I said I'd just have a mineral water and she gave me the mineral water list! I mean, for God's sake! An actual leatherbound water list! I've never seen that before. The world is now officially raving tonto.

Anyway, as I was saying, I'd been hoping to draw the others out on sperm, but before I could even bring the subject up (which takes delicate handling in itself) we got into this terrible row about our job descriptions, amazing but true. It all came up because Trevor was talking about some script or other that he wanted to commission and he said . . .

'I don't want to throw my weight around here, but as the BBC Head of Comedy, Television Group South, I feel that . . .'

Well, he didn't get any further because George and I both

protested that we were the BBC Head of Comedy, Television Group South. I knew that George wasn't because I knew for a fact that he was Chief Coordinator, BBC Entertainment Group, Television. I'd seen it on an invitation to a party. I also knew that he was angling for the post of Network Regional Channel Controller because I'd read it in the *Independent* only the previous morning. George insisted that he didn't care what it said on his invites, or what I'd read in the *Independent*, that he was BBC Head of Comedy, Television Group South.

'Well, what are you angling for, then?' Trevor asked, and George said that he was very excited about his current position and had no plans to move, which of course means he's angling for something juicy at Channel Four.

That got us thinking. Because if George did go to Channel Four, and if he is, as he insists, BBC Head of Comedy, Television Group South, then either I or Trevor will be able to take over his job (which we both thought we already had anyway). Now, if one of us takes over George's job it would leave whatever job that person currently held vacant for the other. We could all move on and hence would all be guaranteed that precious mention in the media pages of the *Independent* so vital to the profile of us usually anonymous execs.

Trevor insisted that he knew what my job was because he'd been offered it ahead of me (slightly disheartening). Apparently, I'm BBC Controller, Broken Comedy and Variety, which if true is disappointing because only last year I was BBC Entertainment Chief, Comedy Group, London and South East. Which would mean I've taken a step down without realizing it and am further away from becoming a Network Channel Controller than ever. Anyway, at this point a bike arrived with a package for Trevor addressed to him as Independent Commissioning Editor, BBC Worldwide, which is a post none of us had heard of. Most confusing.

We all agreed that at this year's Christmas drinks we really would pluck up the courage to ask the Deputy Director General what our jobs are.

After that the talk drifted on to other things. Trevor and George had their usual row about booze. Trevor no longer drinks, which George strongly disapproves of, particularly since Trevor has been through 'recovery' (another thing of which George disapproves) and feels the need to mention his 'problem' on a regular basis.

'As an alcoholic in recovery I have no problem with the alcohol on this table,' said Trevor. 'In fact I can enjoy the fact that you're enjoying it.'

'That's nice,' said George. 'Like we give a fuck.'

Trevor protested that he was only saying and George asked him not to.

'Look, Trevor,' he said, 'you don't drink any more, that's great, not that you ever drank that much in the first place, but now you're cured, isn't it time you moved on?'

'But that's the point, George. You can never be cured. I'm an alcoholic. I'll always be an alcoholic. I could have nothing to drink for fifty years and I'd still be an alcoholic.'

This is the bit George hates most.

'Well you might as well have a fucking drink, then!' he said loudly enough for people at other tables to turn their heads.

At this point I thought I could bring up the subject of sperm to smooth things over a bit but George, having dealt with Trevor's obsession, moved on to his own, producing some photos of little Cuthbert. I had thought that producing pictures of one's baby in all-male company was against the law but like everything else that seems to have changed, we're all carers and nurturers now. I blame those posters that were popular in the late eighties showing huge muscular male torsos tenderly holding tiny babies. Soppy, I call it, but then I suppose I'm not in touch with my feelings or something.

As a matter of record, though, I must confess that young Cuthbert is beginning to shape up a bit. He's definitely filling out and losing his scrotal appearance. He looked quite jolly in his togs from Baby Gap. George said that Cuthbert's clothes cost more than his own do, which he thought was obscene. What is the point of giving babies and kids designer clothes? They puke on them, they roll in mud in them, they shit in them. Tonto, absolutely bloody tonto. George says that he's going to give Melinda a serious talking to. Trevor, on the other hand (who is rather an elegant sort of bloke), thought we were both being philistines and killjoys and that he wished his boyfriend had half the dress sense of young Cuthbert. To which George replied that it was all very well for him because being gay he would never have to face the appalling cost of bringing up a baby. Trevor said that George was not to be too sure about that; with a Labour government in who knew what might happen to the adoption laws?

Oh, God. Trevor is going to get kids before I do and he's a homosexual.

Dearest Penny

Sorry I haven't written for a couple of nights. I've been feeling a bit sad.

You know I was telling you that Sam isn't very tactile? Well, I'd been thinking that perhaps it was partly because our sex life has become so clinical. You know, it's got so inextricably wound up in my quest for fertility that I thought perhaps I was turning him off. So I tried to broach the subject. I said to him that I was sorry that things have got a bit dreary for us in the lovemaking department of late and told him that it was only because of the baby thing taking my mind off it. I told him that I still found him desirable and once we got through all this I'd leap on him regularly and purely for the fun of it. Well, I have to say, he didn't seem that bothered either way, which was rather dispiriting. He just pecked me on the nose and said I mustn't worry and that he was fine. Quite frankly, this was not the reaction I was looking for.

I know Sam loves me but he hardly ever holds me any more. I mean he only really holds me, properly (as opposed to perfunctorily), when we're having it off and as I say our having it off is not what it was. I think we need a physical relationship that extends beyond sex. Sometimes I'd just like a bit of a kiss and a cuddle without it leading to anything, but he doesn't understand that. He simply doesn't see the point of snuggling unless it's in preparation for sex.

Except when he's pissed, of course, then it's the other way round, then it's all cuddle and no chance of a seeing to.

'I love you I love you I love you,' he dribbles. 'I really really honestly love you.'

I mean, I ask you. As if any woman desires the sweet nothings of a sad sack of beer and flatulence?

But anyway, I do feel a bit rejected. This evening I tried to snuggle up when we were watching Channel Four News but when Sam watches telly he really watches it, no distractions allowed, even during the adverts. It's amazing. There he is, concentrating on the golden crispiness of a packet of fish fingers or the sheer joy of driving a Fiat Uno and nothing must intrude. If I put my arm round him or my head on his shoulder I can feel him tense up and if I should dare to ask him to massage my feet or some other such pleasantry, well blimey! It's like I've demanded that he sacrifice his entire existence for my comfort. I suppose I must just accept that he is not, nor ever will be, much of a cuddler. I don't think many men are. At least I hope it's not just him.

Yesterday I had one more go at the visualization class. Drusilla made me. She said it was absurd to do it just once and that if I didn't go again then I might as well not have gone at all. So I gave it another chance, but it really isn't for me. We're all supposed to know each other now so the American lady was a bit bolder and she hopped straight in with some cathartic roleplaying. She made us all cry like babies. Ten grown women sitting in a circle, crying and wailing. I think the idea was to physicalize and project our need for children and hence stop us feeling like it was some kind of guilty secret. That may have been it. Anyway, it was bloody embarrassing. After that we had to hug each other and offer comfort, sharing our sadness and recognizing that we are not alone. Well, I tried to be communally supportive but it was pretty gruesome. I ended up clamped to the bosom of a woman who smelt of dogs. I really shan't go again now. I wouldn't have gone at all if I hadn't been feeling so helpless.

One strange thing, though. During the meditation bit of the

class (which happens at the end – we have to sit around and go all dreamy) I found myself thinking about that appalling hoity Carl Phipps, you know, the Uhoaa from work. Can't think why, I don't even like him or find him attractive. Although he does have a nice smile, that is when he deigns to bestow it upon one so lowly as I.

Dear Book

Trevor and I played squash today. God, I am so unfit. I coughed up something that looked like it lived in a pond. I hardly smoke at all any more but I do like a drink. I think I'll try and switch to Spritzers. The beer is beginning to lie rather heavy.

Anyway, I talked to Trev a bit about my impending examination re sperm and we both agreed that it is not a test of my manhood. A poor result, a thin scrotal mix in the pot, does not mean I am any less of a man. Trevor pointed out that I have always prided myself on my liberal outlook and have never had any respect for all that macho bullshit. He was actually very sensitive and nice. He asked me whether I'd think him any less a whole man if it was him who was suspected of having a sad sorry sack full of bugger-all banging betwixt his legs. I said of course I wouldn't.

But I *would*! I know I would. I'd pretend I wouldn't but I would. 'Poor old Trevor,' I'd think, 'not much going on in the bollock department,' I'd think, 'something of a testicular void'.

And that's what he's going to be thinking about me when I fail.

I told Lucy about my fears and, here's a funny thing, she burst into tears, which I wasn't expecting at all. I mean, after all, I'm the man with the suspected empty balls, aren't I?

So I said, 'Hang on. I'm the one with the suspected empty balls, aren't I?'

I thought she was going to hit me. She said that I was already thinking in terms of 'fault', which was pathetic and destructive! She said that the truth was that the problem was far more likely to rest with her than with me because a woman's tubes are a lot more complicated than any stupid horrible little knob and that if my sperm proved acceptable our infertility would henceforward be her 'fault' and I would blame her! This was of course followed by more tears.

'Well,' I said, 'a: I don't care whether we have kids or not and . . .' I didn't get to b, because she called me an insensitive shit, redoubled her wailing and weeping and ran out of the room.

I hate seeing her cry. It really makes me sad. On the other hand I do think it's a bit much that I can't worry about my sperm count without her turning it all back on to herself. I mean, I'm in on this too, aren't I? Or aren't I?

But life goes on. There is after all more to it than my bollocks, although I do tend to forget that fact with a sperm test pending. But turning to other subjects, I've been thinking about the conversation I had with Trevor and George at Quark about our job titles. Perhaps I should be moving on from the Beeb? After all, there's so much independent production going on and what with my Beeb experience, I'd probably be in huge demand. Of course I would. And I must say that I quite fancy a bit of that indie cash that's swilling about the place. Honestly, I see children making five times what I make and all because they've rented three square feet of carpet in Dean Street, a secretary with a nice belly button and commissioned a witty documentary about chalet girls on the piste or something equally blindingly obvious. I mustn't get resentful, but on the other hand I must get off my arse.

Of course what I'd really like to do is write an original script myself but since even coming up with an initial idea seems to be beyond my creative powers I might as well do my present job but for a decent salary, which means the indie sector.

Only eight days to go until the big test and I am definitely feeling quite relaxed about it. In fact, it's actually seven days and thirteen hours, so what's the problem?

Dear Penny

I can't believe it! All Sam thinks about is his sperm test. I mean for God's sake! From what I can gather, as a younger man he practically had a degree in masturbation. His horrid hand was never still! Even now I suspect he occasionally indulges in a sly 'excuse me' when I'm not around.

All in all masturbation is clearly a much-loved hobby to Sam and yet here he is, moping about as if he's been sentenced to be hanged by the scrotum until dead.

What's more, he's desperate *to get a good result! Terrified that he might be found to be lacking in the tadpole department. This is unbelievably selfish of him because basically and in reality what this means is that he's desperate for there to be something wrong with* my *body. I mean, that's what it comes down to, surely? When he prays for a full complement of the damn stuff he's actually praying for me to have shrivelled tubes, or blocked follicles or nodules on my whatsit or something equally ghastly. Because, let's face it, it's either him or me. We can't blame Mrs Thatcher for everything like we used to when we were young.*

And this is the whole *point. There is basically only one thing that can go wrong with a man. N.E.S. Not Enough Sperm. That's it and once you know you know, and you can start to deal with it. I imagine there are creams or possibly vitamin supplements of some kind.*

But with a woman! Well, a woman's plumbing is like . . . well, I don't know what it's like, I'm trying to think of something really complex but also very beautiful. The ceiling of the Sistine Chapel, for instance, or Paul Simon's Graceland *album. There's a hundred things to be checked and every single one of those checks involves a gang of doctors placing something up one's doodah not dissimilar to the equipment they used to build the Channel Tunnel! How could he wish that upon me?*

There was a documentary on this evening about orphans of war.

I wanted them all.

Every single one, disabled, dying. There was one little girl with no mummy, no daddy, no home and no legs. I'd bloody have her any time. Does that make me a patronizing Western imperialist who wants to deprive a child of its culture merely to satisfy my own mawkish maternal needs? Probably, but I don't care. If Sam and I can't have kids (oh God, I'm going teary again) I think I'll try and work for a children's charity. I sent £100 to War Child but didn't tell Sam as we already have a charity covenant and have agreed not to respond to impulse appeals.

Dear Self

I feel much better about the sperm test now.

I've decided that it's actually politically offensive to get all worked up with fear and shame about something which is simply an accident of nature. Would I consider someone who is born with less than fully functioning legs or arms less of a man or woman for that? No, I damn well wouldn't. So enough of this nonsense. I'll take my sperm result like a man and if it's a poor one then so be it. If it turns out that the contents of my balls is all stew and no dumplings then that's fine by me. I'll simply shrug, *c'est la vie* style. In fact I'll take pride in the way God made me.

'I have runny spunk,' I shall announce at dinner parties. 'Does anyone have a problem with that?'

Nonetheless, despite not caring at all, I'm planning to go into a bit of training. Well, you want to do as well as possible, don't you? I might as well give it my best shot, so to speak (quite funny that, must suggest it to one of our ruder comics). I've resolved therefore to cut out the booze for a few days and eat a lot of fruit. Also George told me that he'd heard that zinc was good, so I've bought a tub of five hundred tablets from Boots. I've also got multivitamins, a crate of Energizer sports drink and an American book entitled *The Testicular Workout*. Having said all this, I wish to stress again that I'm not in the slightest bit concerned about my test result.

Turning once more to other matters, I did something a bit devilish at work today. I instigated a bit of tentative job exploration and on BBC time too. I wrote a letter to Simon 'Tosser' Tomkins, with whom I was at college. Old Tosser's done very well of late, having practically cornered the market in supplying the BBC with programmes fronted by posh smart Alecs. He and his partners have had a quite extraordinary run of success, producing quiz shows (fronted by posh smart Alecs), chat shows (fronted by posh smart Alecs) and endless travelogues (fronted by posh smart Alecs). All these shows, I have to say, have been pretty good, not least, I might add, because the BBC itself pioneered most of the formats on radio. Anyway, Tosser recently floated his company on the stock market and it turned out that it's worth seven million quid! Which really is a quite astonishing amount of money. And to think I once saw him shove four radishes up his arse at a May Ball. Blimey. Anyway, I just sent him a friendly note, you know . . .

'Dear Tosser. The Beeb's a bit crap these days or what? Too many shows full of yobs going on about how much they like football. I was thinking of putting myself about a bit. What do you think?'

I signed it 'Sam Bell, Executive Chief Commissioning Editor, BBC Worldwide,' which is actually a post I made up but I didn't want old Tosser thinking I'm not a major player. Of course, being me, as I was putting the note into an envelope I began to worry about it. I suddenly felt all guilty and started to think that I might be burning bridges at the Beeb. Suppose my negative thinking is showing in my attitude? I wouldn't wish to blow the credit I've built up at TV Centre, certainly not before I get a new job. So I also sent a note to the new Channel Controller asking if he'd like to come to dinner. I very much doubt he will, since as I believe I've mentioned he's younger than me and also knows pop stars and people like that, but it's nice to ask him. A bit of smarmy arselick never hurts. I sent the letters through the BBC franking system. Let the licence payers stump up the cash. I've given them the best years of my life.

Dear Pen Pal
I spent yesterday lunchtime at a women's clinic for alternative medicine and therapy. As I've said, all that New Agey stuff is not really for me, but on the other hand it's foolish to dismiss things out of hand. Anyway, while I was there I bumped into Drusilla. She'd just been to an aromatherapy session and she reeked of orange and liquorice oils. It made me think of the school

tuckshop actually. This was unfortunate because of course then I thought of all the girls I knew at school, and then I wondered where they all are now and of course then I thought they've all got babies! Twelve each, no doubt. Which is wonderful, and I'm glad for them, no really I am, but it does also make me feel a bit sad.

Anyway, Drusilla (who seems to be nearly as fascinated by my infertility as I am myself) asked how long we'd lived in Highgate.

'Five years,' I said, to which she positively shrieked and said that this was our problem! I told her not to be ridiculous, of course, but asked her to tell me more (you can't be too careful). Well, apparently it's well known that there's an unfriendly and infertile ley line running right through Hampstead and Highgate. I pointed out that other people conceive in Highgate, but apparently ley lines are very personal and can be a fertility drug for some and an absolute vinegar douche for others. Drusilla is convinced that our problem is geographical. She claims that the most powerfully positive ley line within this, our ancient and magical land of Albany, runs right across Primrose Hill! Well, I half guessed what was coming, but it was still a shock. She wants Sam and me to have it off on top of Primrose Hill!

On bloody top! In the open air. At midnight under a full moon, no less.

It's not on, of course. Absolutely out of the question. Under no circumstances would I dream of doing such a thing. Well, it's ridiculous. She'll have us fellating at Stonehenge next.

Incidentally, I nearly shouted at that arrogant sod Carl Phipps today. I was on my own in the office and he came in to pick up some faxes, from an American producer no less, very grand. I must say he was looking rather nice, wearing a maroon-coloured corduroy suit, so I said, 'Oh you're looking rather nice, Carl,' and he said, 'Well, one tries.' I mean the arrogance! He might just as well have said, 'Yes, I am gorgeous, aren't I?' Which he is not, incidentally. Anyway, then he sat right down on the corner of my desk and said, 'You're looking like something of a sex bitch yourself today, Lucy,' which was simply not true. All I had on was a silly little miniskirt, my kinky boots and that little tight top I quite like. Frankly I looked awful, so it was stupid of him to pretend I didn't.

Carl is terribly popular with the public. He's definitely our biggest client. He gets loads of fan mail from that costume thing he did at the Beeb. I can't think what people see in him.

Dear Book

Good news and bad news. Lucy has vetoed my all-round scrotal fitness plan. She says that the test must not be rigged. If we're to get anywhere with discovering why we're infertile I must present an honest picture of myself and my life. i.e. half pissed most nights and occasionally at lunchtime. Lucy suspects, I fear, that my fondness for booze (which though sociable is by no means excessive) may be the problem. She imagines that the inside of my scrotum resembles the Groucho Club at 1.45 on a Saturday night, i.e. nearly empty but with a thin smattering of pissed-up free-loading liggers who have no real skills or purpose and appear to make no positive contribution to anything whatsoever that might justify their comfortable and socially exalted existence.

Therefore, despite her low opinion of my fertility, Lucy wants it to be presented honestly and for this reason the zinc and the multivitamins have been ditched. Also (rather splendidly) she's told me to keep drinking. Although only at normal levels, what-ever they may be. I find it almost impossible to work out how much I drink. I mean I know it's not that much, but how much is that? If ever I ask myself 'How many did I have last night?' I always answer, 'Oh, only a few.' But when you actually try and work it out, check how much you spent, the state of the whisky bottle still on the kitchen table, the various places you've been, suddenly you're worrying that you're an alcoholic.

Anyway, Lucy's decision not to let me prepare for my test has certainly made life easier. I'm particularly pleased to be able to give up the *Testicular Workout*. It promised firm, full and rounded testicles in a wrinkle-free scrotum inside one month, but it required a kind of tensing of the arse and lower gut muscles which made me frown furiously. I'm glad not to be bothering with that any more. I have enough new lines on my face without deliberately grimacing for ten minutes a day.

Anyway, in four days' time it will all be over. Which means from tomorrow onwards I'm not allowed to ejaculate. Apparently a three-day period of being left alone in quiet contemplation will give my sperm time to consider their characters and pull themselves together a bit. No great hardship, this abstinence. Sex for Lucy and me at the moment is rarer than a decent sitcom on ITV and I'm usually too tired to be bothered with slapping the monkey.

No reply yet from Tosser, or indeed the Channel Controller, but I take this as no slight. They're both very busy men, very busy men indeed, as, of course, am I.

Dear Pen Pal

I gave blood today. This test is to consider my hormone level to see if I ovulate. I did it at an NHS Female Health Clinic in Camden. I didn't do it at my normal GP's because Dr Cooper is on holiday and I don't really like Dr Mason (nothing specific, just don't really like him).

God, Camden's getting gruesome. If you're not out of your brains on drugs the police stop you and ask if you're lost. I walked up the High Street holding my copy of the Big Issue *as a sort of shield. So depressing, all those homeless people. How did it happen? Thatcher, I used to think, but she's been gone for donks and they're still here. You give money to a couple of them but you can't give money to them all and when you've run out of change you want to say to the ones you haven't given anything to that you've already given money to the previous ones, but why would they care?*

The clinic was depressing, as it would be. All these women having their bits and their boobs checked, or barren like me. One tries to maintain a positive outlook but it's not easy.

There was an old TV Times *in the waiting pen (I won't call it a 'room', that would make it sound too cosy; it was just a sort of square of plastic chairs with a couple of broken toys on the floor).*

Anyway, the TV Times *contained quite a good article about Carl Phipps, when he was still in that awful thing* Fusilier! *on ITV. Quite nice pictures, although I must say I prefer him now he's got longer hair. That crew cut was rather brutal. Still, his eyes haven't changed, still soft and limpid. He knows how nice they are, though, like David Essex used to. I'll bet he uses twinkle drops. The text went on and on about how girls are always getting terrible crushes on him. You can see how they might, but God, some women are stupid.*

Dear etc.

Quite astonishing development at work today. I've been to *Downing Street*. I didn't meet the Prime Minister, but it's still amazing. It completely took my mind off my sperm test.

It happened like this. I'd just sat down to another morning of brooding over the lack of direction or passion in my career, leafing through another pile of scripts, wondering why the hell I can't seem to find it in me to write one myself, when Daphne said that the Channel Controller was on the line. Well of course I was thrilled, he could only be phoning personally to accept my dinner invitation! I was mentally leafing through Delia as I grabbed the phone and had already decided on the salmon mousse to start when it turned out that Nigel had called about something even more exciting! He was phoning from Barcelona, where he was (of course) attending an international television festival. Perhaps the single greatest perk of being at the Beeb is the international festival circuit. The BBC don't pay you much, but they do let you lig. Even I get to go to a few. Lucy and I had a fantastic weekend in Cork last April, except that she thought she was ovulating so I wasn't allowed to drink. Controllers, being an altogether superior breed, of course, virtually spend their lives at festivals. You can always find them in some exotic location bemoaning the fact that *Baywatch* is the most popular programme in the world and that cartoons arethe sickness at the heart of children's broadcasting. Anyway, this was why Nigel was calling from Barcelona.

But oh, such news! It turned out that the Prime Minister's office had been on to the BBC about the PM appearing on *Livin' Large*. *Livin' Large* is our current Saturday morning kids' pop and fun show and every week they have a sort of interview spot where the children get to ask questions of a celebrity. Now, unbeknownst to me (surprise, surprise) our PR people had had a brilliant idea. (I must digress here to remark that the fact that our PR people had had a brilliant idea was shocking news in itself and evidence of how much things have changed around the old place. BBC press and public relations used to consist of an office with a large enthusiastic woman in it whom everyone ignored. Now it's a huge and entirely separate company called something like BBC Communications or Beeb COM, whose services I have to *hire*. It's quite extraordinary. In order for me to ensure that BBC shows are plugged in BBC publications I have to pay BBC money to BBC Communications. It seems loopy to me, but George assures me that it's cut away a lot of 'dead wood'.)

Anyway, BBC Communications' idea had been to ask the Prime Minister if he would like to appear on *Livin' Large* and take some questions from 'the kids', thereby cutting through all that cynical adult bullshit and plugging in to the pure unsullied enthusiasm of youth. Astonishingly, it seemed to me, the man was considering it.

The problem for Nigel (the Controller) was that Downing Street (which is a vigorous, 'can do' sort of a place these days) wanted to meet *today*! and no other later date would do because the PM's diary is chockablock with summits and Cabinet crises right through till Christmas. Nigel had of course tried to get a flight back from Barcelona but there was a football match, or the French air-traffic controllers weren't letting anybody out of Europe today or something. Anyway, the upshot of it was that I would have to go to the meeting!

Well, I spent the rest of the morning phoning my mum and Lucy and everybody I knew and trying to get my tie ironed. Of course, one might have thought that in the heart of one of the largest television studio complexes in the world getting one's tie ironed would have been easy. To get someone from wardrobe would, one might imagine, have been the work of a moment. Unfortunately 'wardrobe' no longer exists as such. It's a separate company called Beeb Frox or else something equally awful, and one has to negotiate with it. This Daphne, my wonderful secretary, duly did, and came back with a quote of £45. It seemed a bit steep to iron a tie but apparently Beeb Frox claimed it would scarcely cover their paperwork. I told Daphne that seeing as this was the Prime Minister and all, she'd better get on with it, but it turned out not to be that simple. In order for my office to generate a payment from finance (BeebCash Plc) I needed first to prove that I had secured the most competitive tender for the work. Daphne said that she was required to approach a minimum of two outside costumiers to see if they would iron my tie more cheaply than Beeb Frox. Only when we had three estimates to compare could we commission the work. Meanwhile, it would also be necessary to decide out of what programme budget the ironing of the tie was to come. Clearly this would have to be *Livin' Large*, but if that was the case their Line Producer would have to sign the chit. Also, *Livin' Large* was not made in house but by an independent company called Choose Groove Productions. Incidentally, I must add here that this does not mean that Choose Groove Productions make *Livin' Large* in any practical sense, oh no, the BBC make it, with BBC staff in a BBC studio, paid for by BBC money, the only difference being that some bloke with a ponytail in Soho takes a thirty-grand-an-episode production fee and gets to stick his company logo on the end of the programme. It was to this lucky recipient of the BBC's forced entry into the marketplace that Daphne would have to go to get budgetary authorization for my tie to be ironed.

In the end, Daphne flattened the tie underneath a pile of old copies of *Spotlight* for a stick of my KitKat.

So anyway, to get on with the story, this afternoon there I was, fronting up to the gates of Downing Street and being saluted through by a policeman. It was like a dream. I walked up the street with my briefcase, just like cabinet ministers do on the news, and in through the famous door.

I must say it's bloody dowdy inside, or at least the bits I saw are. Amazing. The entrance hall is like a rundown hotel. Nobody could accuse any of the previous fifteen administrations of wasting money on decoration because I swear that the place hasn't had a lick of paint since Chamberlain was waving his bit of paper about. While I was waiting I noticed an old plastic carrierbag chucked on the threadbare carpet against the skirting board. I remarked to the amiable old doorman that I hoped it wasn't a bomb and he said that he hoped so too but that it probably belonged to somebody.

Anyway, after about ten minutes one of the PM's 'forward planning team' arrived, a young woman called Jo whom I think I recognized from her having been on *Question Time*. She ushered me into a small room with a chair and an old couch and some dirty coffee cups on a table. Here she 'briefed' me on the background to this particular 'outreach initiative'. She told me that the Prime Minister was Britain's newest, youngest, hippest prime minister since Lord Fol d'Rol in 1753 and that her office had the job of reminding people of this fact and generally demonstrating that the PM was neither fuddy nor duddy.

'We want the kids to know that their PM is not just the youngest, most energetic and most charismatic premier in British history but that he's also their mate, a regular bloke who likes popmusic, wearing fashionable trousers, and comedy with proper swearing in it. Which is why we think it's important to place him on *Livin' Large*.'

'God yes, great idea,' I said, pathetically. It's amazing how even the proximity to power seduces a person.

'But in a dignified context,' Jo added firmly. 'No gunk tanks or "gotcha"s. It struck us that some kind of "youth summit" would be appropriate, you know, the boss chats with the future and all that. It could be an extended version of that section where the celebrity guest takes questions from the kids.'

I said it sounded fantastic and that the BBC would be honoured.

'But nice questions, of course, not political. That wouldn't be appropriate. Questions about the issues that matter to kids. Popmusic, fashion, computers, the Internet, that sort of thing.'

My mind reeled. This was *fantastic*. A genuine television

event! Like Mrs Thatcher getting grilled about the *Belgrano* on *Nationwide* or the *Blue Peter* elephant shitting on John Noakes. The Prime Minister himself doing an interview with kids on live TV and I was to exec it! Christ! Like I say, I reeled.

'This means a lot to the PM,' Jo continued. 'Dammit, as far as ordinary people are concerned politics is boring! The kids don't want a lot of old fuddy-duddies telling them what to do. We need to let people know that things have changed. Basically, it's very important to us that the premier gets a chance to point out that he likes popmusic and that he actually plays the guitar. Will that be possible?'

Well, as far as I was concerned he could point out that he liked liver and onions and played the didgeridoo if he wanted, but I said that I thought everybody knew that the PM played the guitar; it seemed to have come up in every interview he'd ever done.

'People have short memories,' said Jo, 'besides which we need to make it clear that it's the electric guitar he plays, not some strummy-crummy, clicky-clacky, Spanish castanets type, classical fuddy-duddy stuff.'

Well, I nodded and agreed and wondered if it would be appropriate to kiss her arse and pretty soon Jo signalled that the meeting was over.

And so there it is. I, Sam Bell, have successfully brokered a historic live TV encounter between the PM and Generation Next. Trevor and I spent the afternoon trying to think of a good hook for the trailers. Trevor kept coming back to 'The Premier meets the Little People' but I'm sure that'd just make everyone think of leprechauns.

I must say this business has changed my attitude to my job entirely. I mean, if I was in the independent sector I certainly wouldn't be meeting the PM. Besides which, it has occurred to me that I could use my newly acquired inside knowledge of Downing Street to write a political thriller. It could be just the inspiration I need.

Good old Beeb, say I. When Tosser offers me a job I'll turn it down.

Dear Penny

Guess what! Sam nearly met the PM today. I could hardly believe it when he told me. Now that's what I call cool. I'm so proud of him. I'm married to a man who deals with the very highest in the land and from what he tells me he handled it incredibly well. The only thing that made me a bit sad is that if we never have kids then I won't be able to tell them that their dad once nearly met the PM. Oh well, I really must stop thinking things like that.

Dear Self

Another bit of good news today. They tell me that I can produce my sperm sample at home! Yes, apparently sperm survives for one hour once outside the body (if kept warm) and as long as you can get the stuff back to the clinic within that time it doesn't matter where you pull one off the wrist. Great news.

Anyway, I went in to see Dr Cooper after work to pick up the sterilized pot (you can't just hand it in in a teacup). You can get the pots at Boots, but I'm not asking some sixteen-year-old girl for a sperm pot. Dr Cooper decided to take the opportunity to offer advice and consultation. He asked me whether I was aware of the manner in which I should produce my sample. I told him that I thought I could just about remember, I might be a bit rusty (it being as much as three or even four days since I last played a solo on the one-stringed bass), but I was sure that it would all come flooding back.

I must say I'm delighted about this 'home-tossing' development, generally much more relaxing I feel. Interesting as well, because this will be the first time in my entire life that I will be able to have a completely legitimate hand shandy. Amazing really, when I think back over all the sly ones I've had over the last twenty-five-odd years, all the lies and stratagems I resorted to, particularly as a child, and here I am positively being encouraged to abuse myself by the National Health Service. Ironic. I thought about ringing my mum, just to rub it in, but I don't think she'd see the joke.

Dearest Penny Pen Pal

I think Sam's quite proud of his pot. He's put it on the mantelpiece in the sitting room like it was a darts trophy. I hope he doesn't imagine that's where he's going to fill it. The bathroom's more appropriate. And I've told him he's got to think about me while he's doing it. Horrible business all round, quite frankly.

I adopted a baby gorilla today. She's called Gertrude. She was advertised in the Big Issue *I bought in Camden. You don't actually get to have Gertrude at home but for £90 they send you a picture of her and a certificate of adoption. There are only 650 of Gertrude's type left on the planet. What are we* doing *to the world? It's so disgusting.*

Sam gave me a rather patronizing look when I told him about the adoption, which infuriated me because I acted out of ecological concern and for no other reason. Although I must say Gertrude does look very sweet, so small and defenceless, absolutely beautiful little thing. £90 well spent.

Dear Idiot

Rather an unfortunate development arose today workwise. And when I say 'rather' what I actually mean is 'unbelievably' and such a bugger coming so soon as it did after my Downing Street triumph.

I was sitting at work trying to read a treatment for a game show that had been sent in by Aiden Fumet on behalf of one of his acts. It was bollocks, of course, and depressing bollocks at that. Something about contestants having to identify their partners by smelling their socks and looking at their bare bottoms pushed through holes in the set. The bit they seemed most proud of was that the game would also feature gay and lesbian couples. This alone, the authors seemed to feel, made the idea important, alternative and at the cutting edge.

Anyway, I was just applying my 'Loved it but seems more Channel Five to me' rubber stamp when the phone rang and Daphne told me it was someone called Tosser. Good, I thought. Tosser has always been a tiny bit patronizing with me and I'd been looking forward to telling him that I was no longer in the market for employment so he'd have to headhunt elsewhere. I relished this chance of informing him that as I'd recently been entrusted by the Channel Controller himself with the duties of executive producer to the Prime Minister, I was now feeling very comfortable at the BBC.

Sadly I was not to have this chance.

'Sam,' said Tosser, 'love to come to dinner, old boy, except I'm going skiing. But as it happens I'm not sure the invite was intended for me anyway. It said "Dear Nigel" on the note.'

Oh my God.

Oh my Goddity God.

I went first hot and then cold and then both hot and cold at once.

Wrong envelopes!

Such a basic farce plot! I would have seen through it in a second in a script and now it had actually bloody happened!

A man did not need to be Stephen Hawking to work out the permutations of the plot. If I'd sent the dinner invitation to Tosser Tomkins, then I'd sent my enquiry about leaving the BBC to . . .

Daphne took another call. I knew even before I had registered her hushed and respectful tone that the sword of Damocles was suspended above me. This would need very careful handling.

'Sam. The Channel Controller on line two.'

I made my excuses to Tosser. 'In shit, Toss, got to go!'

And picked up the phone. Nigel's voice was cold as a penguin's arse.

'Sam, I have a memo here in which you address me as a tosser.'

'It was a mistake.'

'Yes,' said Nigel, 'it certainly was, mate.'

He went on to assure me that he was flattered that I had thought to seek his advice about whether I should leave the BBC and intrigued that I wanted his opinion on whether I should 'put myself about a bit on the job market since after all the independent sector is clearly so much more vibrant'. He thanked me for my consideration and promised to give the matter his fullest and most immediate possible attention.

Click. Dial tone. Bugger.

That was it. No goodbye, no mention of my dealings with Downing Street about which I had copiously emailed him.

Well, I couldn't leave it there, could I? I rushed along the corridor to his office. Television Centre is of course famously circular and I was so flustered that I missed the Controller's office entirely and had to run round the whole building again. I've done that before, of course, many times, but only when pissed and trying to find a Christmas party.

Responding to my urgent pleading (conveyed to him via one of his icy receptionists – he has two, flash bugger), Nigel allowed me into his office.

I can remember (just) that office when it was a friendly place. When the BBC really was a family. A family in which almost every member was a jolly uncle or an aunt. A family of fat boozy old time-servers who earned little and drank much. Men and women who went through their entire lives without once wearing a stylish garment or having a fashionable haircut. Who worked their way up the system, serving the public faithfully (if slightly unsteadily) from Floor Manager to Producer to sad old git in the corner of the bar who was too old and pissed to find his way out of the circle. Well, those faggy, boozy days are long gone and it's probably for the best. None of those jolly old boys would last a second in a climate where there's five hundred channels competing for the audience and the money's all going to cable and satellite. Still, I can't deny that, as I stood there trembling before my Channel Controller (who, I must say again, is *two years fucking younger than me*), I found myself wishing that he was a fifteen-stone, red-nosed old bastard who would just tell me to bugger off and forget about it before commissioning another series of *Terry and June*.

'Look, Nigel,' I said, still dizzy and clutching at a Golden Rose of Montreux for support and nearly cutting myself on its petals. 'This is awful, I wanted to invite you to dinner.'

He answered me with nothing more than a raised eyebrow.

'That note I sent you was meant for someone else. Simon

Tomkins, you know, he was on the panel with you at last year's Edinburgh Television Festival. He was the one who said the BBC was an ageing tart trying to flag down a curb crawler on the information superhighway.'

Well, it put the thing about calling him a tosser to rest but, beyond that, I'm afraid I had dug myself deeper into the hole.

'So what you're telling me, Sam, is that this note dissing the BBC' (he used the word 'dissing' even though he's a thirty-six-year-old white freckly philosophy graduate from Durham University) 'was actually intended as a job application to one of the foremost independent producers in the country?'

'Uhm,' I said.

Not good, but the best I could do at the time.

'Well?' said Nigel.

I was clearly going to have to do better than 'Uhm.'

'Oh, you know, just a punt, Nigel, really more to see what sort of shape the independent sector's in than anything else.'

He did not believe me even slightly.

'Uhm . . . did you see my emails regarding the Prime Minister? Tremendously successful meeting we . . .'

'Yes, I saw them,' said Nigel, and there our meeting ended save for Nigel assuring me that if I was at all unhappy at the BBC I had only to offer my resignation and he would consider it most favourably. He said he was disappointed, that he had always taken me for a company man (which I bloody am actually). He talked about the Beeb being a family, that it was not just a part of one's career but a career in itself, a career that demanded some sense of loyalty.

Yes, Mr Nigel straight from Granada, bloody exactly, until the next time the Chief Exec at Channel Four resigns or Murdoch is looking for a bit of posh to give cred to the management 'team' at one of his tabloid channels. Then the BBC will be a family all right, a modern dysfunctional family in which everybody buggers off at the first chance they get, with Nigel at the front of the queue.

Needless to say, dinner was not discussed.

Dear Penny

Got my picture of Gertrude today and was slightly dis-appointed to discover that it's the same as the one in the Big Issue. *You'd think they'd have taken more than one shot of her. Still, at least it's a better print.*

I do have to admit, Pen, that I'm just a little bit concerned that those less environmentally aware than myself (my mother, for instance) might consider my adoption of Gertrude as reflective of my hopes for a child. This is definitely not *the case. The plight of the mountain gorillas is an international tragedy and my involvement in the issue is entirely political.*

Book

Lucy has put a picture of a baby gorilla into a clipframe and placed it on the mantelpiece. She says we've adopted it. I'm now rather worried that her nurturing instincts are getting the better of her. Interestingly, the baby gorilla (whose name is Gertrude) is, in my opinion, the dead spit of George and Melinda's Cuthbert, although possibly Cuthbert has more hair.

I went for a quickie in the BBC club bar after work today. The club bar always depresses me these days. It's been franchised out and now has a name, Shakers or Groovers or possibly Gropers, I'm not sure, I'm always pissed when I try to read the beer mats. I do know that the Studio One tea bar is now called Strollers. Anyway, I bumped into George and Trevor at the bar and they had clearly been sniggering about something when I approached, but on seeing me they stopped dead. It could only mean one thing. My arse-up with the Channel Controller is now public knowledge and it will only be a matter of time before the whole incident is recounted in *Private Eye*. Not good, I fear.

Still, it's taken my mind off the sperm test.

Dear Penny

Sam's a bit quiet and rather down at the moment. I know he had a row at work with that appalling Channel Controller. (Who else but an arse could spend £7 million of public money adapting Finnegans Wake? FINNEGANS WAKE! *I ask you. A road map of Birmingham is easier to follow. And seven million! That's a million pounds per viewer in my opinion and I said so at last year's Light Entertainment Christmas party. George laughed so loudly something came out of his mouth, but Sam, who can be a fearful toady, told me to keep my voice down.)*

I do feel sorry for Sam. I mean he really does seem a bit depressed, but it's so hard to know how to help. The fact is he doesn't want any help. He'd rather read his newspaper. If it was me I'd want tons of attention, in fact I do want tons of attention. Sam, however, neither craves it nor gives it very much and this leaves me feeling in extreme want of warmth. This evening I knew something was on his mind and I tried to reach out to him but he'd have none of it. He just drank beer and cracked silly jokes about if we do have a kid we'll have to send it out to work at the age of seven because we'll be so poor. Ha ha. So now we're going to be penniless as well as infertile. Hilarious.

Dear Sam

Well, it's done. Conjugal visit to hand completed. Not as easy as I might have hoped, considering my enormous experience in this area, but the required sperm sample is sorted. Funny to think that my sperm is in some laboratory somewhere waiting to be tested, darting this way and that for the benefit of a total stranger. Hope they're looking after it, keeping it warm. I feel very slightly paternal about the stuff.

Producing it was a close-run thing. Originally we had planned for Lucy to attend the masturbation, possibly even lending a hand, so to speak. This was her idea. She doesn't really like the thought of me having sex without her, even if it's only on my own. She's convinced that I'll not give her a single thought throughout the whole proceedings but offer my entire fantastical erotic being to Winona Ryder, and of course she's right. Well, for God's sake! I get to sleep with Lucy every night, I only get to do it with Winona when required to produce a sperm sample. I tried to explain this, saying that psychologists had established that an uninhibited fantasy life was part of a healthy, monogamous sexual relationship. Well, Lucy wasn't having any of it. In fact she acted quite hurt, which I find truly extraordinary.

Women! I simply do not know where to start. They *actually* think that a man can be unfaithful whilst indulging in solitary masturbation! It's positively early Christian in its unforgiving intensity. Thank goodness I didn't tell her I'd also been planning to invite Tiffany from *EastEnders*, The Corrs and Baby Spice to the party.

Anyway, as I said, Lucy seemed to feel it was important that she be involved in the process, so this morning when we woke up I went and got the pot from the sitting-room mantelpiece. I handed it over to Lucy, got back into bed and took up my limp appendage whilst she held the pot out expectantly, clearly anticipating an immediate outpouring.

Well, I'm here to tell anyone who cares to listen that masturbation with an audience (particularly an impatient one which hasn't yet had a cup of tea) is not easy. I mean, of course Lucy and I had done this together before, but only in relaxed mode, in the spontaneous joy of passion, so to speak (and not, I admit, for some time). We had never before attempted masturbation for a solely practical purpose. Book, I am here to tell you that I felt a complete prick, both personally and of course literally. There I was kneeling on the bed, portion in palm with Lucy holding out the pot like some kind of beggar, and nothing was happening. Lucy, bless her, had a rather self-conscious go and disported herself about the bed a bit, you know, cupping breasts in hands and pouting, that sort of thing. I really don't know which of us felt more stupid. After about thirty seconds I could see she was getting bored and beginning to think about breakfast. It was as much as she could do to stop herself looking at her watch. Quite obviously it was never going to work. I love her and I fancy her but a fellow can feel self-conscious even with a woman he's shared a bed with for six years. I just could not get things going and in the end I had to decamp into the spare room and choke the poor old monkey alone.

I could see that Lucy was a bit hurt (though she denied it), but what could I do? You can't masturbate without an erection and you can't get an erection with your wife staring at your dick angrily and saying, 'Come on, it's already eight-fifteen. Don't you fancy me, then?'

Anyway, left to myself I came up with the goods, so to speak. I say 'goods', if that isn't too grand an expression to describe the sad little sample I produced. I couldn't believe it. I've always been under the impression that my ejaculation is as substantial as the next man's. If anything I might have even flattered myself that I was rather a major supplier. Well, let me tell you, you can forget all that once it's dribbling down the inside of a plastic pot. It looks pathetic! I mean pa-the-tic. Like a sparrow sneezed.

Interesting, really, how vulnerable the whole exercise made me feel. I felt genuinely exposed, like my very manhood was being tested. As if the whole exercise was a test of my virility and sexuality. Rather sad, actually. I'd always presumed I'm a pretty relaxed, modern sort of bloke. I didn't think I'd ever bought into any of that macho bullshit about being a big noise in the trouser department. Yet there I was staring at my sample thinking about trying to eke it out with a bit of flour and water.

But one thing you learn as you go through life is that you are what you are and you have to accept it. Besides which, I suddenly realized that I'd spent about two minutes worrying about how little I'd produced and of course I only had an hour to hand it in before the stuff died. I had to get to the clinic or I'd have the whole business to do again.

Now the advice that Dr Cooper had given me was to pop the pot down my pants, because at all costs its contents must be kept warm. In fact he had told me that if possible I was to work it into a warm crevice, which I assume is doctor code for shove it up your bum. It's a very strange feeling waddling along the street try-ing to hail a taxi with a pot of sperm clenched between your buttocks. I was immediately consumed with the irrational con-viction that everybody knew what was going on. Policemen seemed to glare, toddlers tugged at their mothers' skirts and pointed, office girls veered across the pavement apparently to keep well out of my way. I swear I heard an *Evening Standard* vendor mutter 'Dirty pervert' as I passed. Perhaps it was my desperate, hurried air that drew people's eye. Let's face it, a man is hardly going to look his most relaxed and urbane when he is charging along the street, agonizingly aware that his sperm has only minutes left to live.

Every taxi was full, every bus a 'Not in Use. Driver in Training' let-down. The tube station had one of those chalk blackboards outside which regret that two thousand people are stuck in a tunnel below. Eventually I spotted an empty cab but inevitably another bloke spotted it too. We both dashed for it (well he dashed, I waddled) and arriving at the same time we wrestled over the handle together.

'Mine, I think,' I said. Normally I would have given up without a fight but I was desperate by this time, having only twenty-eight minutes left.

'Well, you think wrong,' said the man. 'Bugger off and get your own cab. I'm having this one.'

Honestly, I don't know how some people can be like that, so casually brutal and rude. I couldn't do it if you paid me. It's like when I see people throw litter out of car windows, I just think, are these people from another planet? Are they a different species altogether? *I would never do that.* Oh well, mustn't get depressed about it, it takes all sorts I suppose.

Anyway, on this particular occasion, quaking at the thought of a scene though I was, there was no way I was going to let that cab go.

'Look,' I said, 'I have to have this cab, it's a matter of life and death.'

'Tough,' said the man. 'I've got a very important meeting.'

'Well I've got some warm sperm up my arse and it's dying.'

I'll have to remember that one. The bloke let go of that door handle like it was a live snake.

'I bet you're the sort who drops litter out of car windows as well,' I said as I got in the cab, and I meant it to hurt.

It wasn't an easy journey, unable to sit down as I was. I had to curl up on the back seat in a sort of foetal position and I could see that the driver didn't like it. But we got there in the end, with a few minutes to spare even, and I rushed into the clinic and handed in my sample. Actually that was a pretty gruesome moment too. I was so desperate to get there in time that I just rushed through the front door and went straight up to the reception desk. It was only as I was actually fishing the pot out of the back of my trousers that I realized that it might have been more tactful and polite to have retrieved the thing in private. The nurse stared at it as if to say, 'And you want me to touch that now?' before going off to get some rubber gloves and a bargepole.

My God, I can't believe I've just spent half an hour writing about taking sperm to a clinic! If I could only be half this committed and energetic at work I might not be in the shit I'm in. Things are still very edgy at the office. It seems to me only a matter of time before Nigel finds a way to get rid of me, and if I'm honest I'm really not particularly employable. Lunch-eating is not a skill for which there is much demand these days, it's not the eighties.

Lucy keeps saying I need to start writing again. Touching, really, how she still believes in me.

I sent another note to Tosser (this time I checked the envelope three times) to try asking him again about a job. I didn't bother with any matey-matey, beating-about-the-bush stuff this time. I just basically asked the bastard for a job. Hope I didn't sound desperate. Does 'Give us a job, you bastard,' sound desperate, I wonder? Depends on the tone, I suppose. But how does one imply tone in a letter? You can't write 'Not to be read in desperate manner' because that really would sound desperate.

Looking back over the last few pages I've written, I've come to the surprising conclusion that the American expert Lucy's friend Sheila saw on *Oprah* was right: writing letters to yourself is actually a very good idea. I came home today all fired up with my success at delivering the sample on time and looking forward to telling Lucy the story (particularly the bit about hailing the cab), but she seemed all distant and distracted. She said it had been a difficult day at work and she didn't feel like talking. Fair enough. I almost always feel like that. Still, it's helped to write it down.

Perhaps I should bash it all out into some kind of article and send it to the *Observer* Health section. I bet they'd give me a hundred quid for it, but Lucy would probably not approve. Besides which, I was forgetting, I can't write.

Strange, Lucy not wanting to talk. I hope she isn't working too hard. Actors can be such pains.

Dearest Penny

I have to tell you that something very strange happened at work today, which I hardly like to write about. I was on my own again. Sheila is still bronchial (self-prescribed cure: forty cigarettes a day) and Joanna is in LA with our one other big name, Trudi Hobson. Trudi is playing the icy British bitch in some dreadful action film. It's a sequel called, well, can't remember what it's called actually. Shit Two, I should imagine. Anyway, there I am on my own and who should turn up but, yes! Carl Phipps, all brooding and Byronic looking in a big coat. Well, before I know it he's telling me that fame is a lonely burden and asking me out to lunch! Extraordinary. I can't imagine why he picked on me. I'm sure I haven't given him the slightest indication that I enjoy his company or find him remotely attractive.

Well, as it happened I couldn't go out with him anyway because I was all alone and who would man the phones? (Lots of voiceover work coming in this week, almost every chocolate manufacturer in the country seems to want one of our chaps to say 'When you need a big, satisfying block in your gob . . .'). So I told him that I was too busy, and I said it slightly hoitily. I rather resent the assumption that mine is the sort of job that you can just drift in and out of, even though it is. 'Fair enough,' says Lord Phipps and off he goes in a flurry of brooding, wuthering menace, and I thought that was the end of it.

Well! Ten minutes later he's back with a positive hamper from Fortnum's (perhaps not a hamper, but certainly a large plastic bag), full of fantastic stuff from their food hall. Oysters, olives, foreign nibbles and champagne no less! He said he was celebrating getting a recall for a very big American film. Usual thing,

71

dastardly Brit to play villain. Actually, I must just say that for all that we hate political correctness, it has been a godsend for our posh actors. It seems that the English are the only racial group left on earth whom absolutely nobody minds seeing marmalized. Honestly, ten years ago it was costume drama or nothing for our boys. If nobody was making Robin Hood *or* Ivanhoe, *they didn't work. Now they get to crash helicopters into Bruce Willis!*

Anyway, so there we were in the office, just the two of us, and I asked Heathcliff, if he was celebrating, didn't he have someone special to celebrate with? Do you want to know what he said to that, Penny? He said that that was exactly what he was doing!!!! Arggh!

Oh, my God! I could feel myself going beetroot and that rash on my neck coming back (when I was a teenager, if ever a boy asked me out I invariably instantly looked as though my throat had just been cut). My knees became the knees of a jelly lady and the cheese straw I had been toying with disintegrated and fell into the photocopier (and completely buggered it).

Anyway, of course I told him not to be silly and asked him what he meant by such familiarities. I put on my best snooty, posh 'we are not at home to callers' telephone voice and said that I was a respectable woman. Well, he didn't say anything, he just smiled in a sort of soft way that he knew *brought out his dimples and* took my hand.

Yes!

Smouldering eyes, shy dimples and holding my hand. *Sorry about the breathless style, Penny, but I am much moved.*

Because here, I'm afraid, is the terrible thing (none but you must ever know, Penny). I did not withdraw my hand! Not for a moment, anyway, or perhaps even a bit longer than a moment. A minute or two, possibly, not more than three, I'm sure of that. I left it there and we just sort of, well, looked at each other and his eyes went all melty (just like his close-ups in The Tenant of Wildfell Hall *when he really was very good). He looked like the dispossessed lord of a bleak moorland estate. I swear his after-shave smelt of heather. God knows what I looked like – an electrified rabbit with a rash, no doubt.*

Anyway, time felt as if it had been frozen as I became lost in his eyes. Then, and I don't know if I imagined it, but I think, in fact I'm sure, I felt his finger playing in the palm of my hand which, as far as I know, is silent code for 'I would not be averse to rogering you, ma'am.'

If this is true, I just can't BELIEVE the man's cheek. He knows I'm married. Married to a good, solid, honest, ordinary, boring, far better man than he, if not quite so dishy, bloke.

Anyway, after a bit I did take my hand away, thank God. I don't know what would have happened if I hadn't. I think he would have kissed me. His face certainly seemed to be a lot closer to mine than it had been a moment or two before. And then short of making a scene I don't know what I would have done. He is our biggest client, after all. I probably would have had to kiss him back, which would have been terrible! Anyway, instead I thanked him for the lunch in an extremely cold 'not today, thank you' voice and said that I had to get on with my work. To which he shrugged, smiled a knowing little smile, picked up his fan mail and left.

I must say, I feel most peculiar.

But also very angry.

Yes, all right, he's good looking and famous but that doesn't mean that every girl is going to fall at his feet for a glass of champagne and a cheesy nibble! I love my husband, dull, sexless bore though he may be. What is more, I want to have his children, something which is not proving easy, and I can do without arrogant actors trying to interfere with my already unbalanced hormones.

Dear Sam

No news on sperm.

No reply from Tosser re him giving me an important new job.

No further communications from the Channel Controller.

My life is on tenterhooks, whatever tenterhooks may be.

One good thing is that everyone has been impressed by my visit to Downing Street. Except Nigel the Controller, of course, who still hasn't talked to me about it. Lots of people are trying to get tickets to the show but I'm being ruthless. I say, 'You didn't want tickets when it was just Mr Blob Blob and the two puppet monsters. What's changed?' and they say, 'The fucking Prime Minister's going to be there! That's what's changed,' which I suppose is fair.

I saw Nigel the Controller today and he didn't remind me about my appalling faux pas over the letters, which I think is a good sign. Mind you, he didn't really have an opportunity because it wasn't just him and me, he'd summoned all the commissioning editors in the Entertainment Group (if indeed that is what we are), plus the finance and marketing people, for a big strategy meeting, so there were about ten of us festooned about his office. The subject of the meeting was the BBC's plans to get into movies, so it should have been an exciting discussion, but with the cloud hanging over me I couldn't get worked up. What's more, I was the last to arrive, which is always a dodgy thing to be with a sarky up-himself swine like Nigel.

'Good of you to pop in, Sam.'

I should have told him to stuff it but I didn't, of course, I started to try and explain. What is it Churchill or Thatcher is supposed to have said? 'Never apologize, never explain.' Well, they were right. Nigel didn't let me get any further than, 'Sorry, I was . . .'

'I see,' he said. 'So having wasted our time being late you want to waste more time telling us why. Is that it?'

I couldn't believe it! The bloke is *younger than me*. George and Trevor were both in the meeting but they were no help, they just studied their briefing notes intensely.

'Uhm . . .' I said. Not a brilliant retort, I'm prepared to admit.

'Uhm,' Nigel repeated. 'Well, as answers go it has the virtue of brevity, but I think that completes its list of recommendations.'

Some of the others actually laughed at that! Snivelling syco-phants. Not George or Trevor, of course, but a couple of the accountancy people and a young woman with pink hair who came over from Sky. I'll remember you, I thought, but why bother? She'll probably be my next boss.

Anyway, I slunk into a corner and Nigel got down to some serious pontificating.

'Nobody watches television nowadays,' he said, 'or at least none of my friends do. Television is wallpaper. Television is fast food. Television is arse produce. Movies are the millennial art form. Where do you think I'm going with this? Come on, come on, anyone!'

Honestly, it was like being back at school.

'The BBC should be getting into movies,' said the young woman with the pink hair and Nigel positively beamed at her. 'Hullo,' I thought, but actually I think Nigel could only ever properly fancy himself.

'Exactly, Yaz,' he said and proceeded with great self-importance to rap out the names of recent British movie hits.

'*Four Weddings, Full Monty, Trainspotting, Lock Stock and Two Smoking Barrels, Emmanuelle Goes Beaver Hunting . . .*'

This last one took us all a bit by surprise but we let it go.

'British movies have never been more healthy,' he continued, banging his desk. 'There were at least three last year that the Americans quite liked. We need to be a part of that revolution. We need to reposition our goddamn asses.'

I swear he said it: 'reposition our goddamn asses'.

'We need to be making movies.'

Everyone seemed terribly excited at this idea but I always thought the BBC was a television company and said so.

'Boots is a chemist, Sam. That doesn't stop them selling chicken tikka sandwiches with yogurt and mint dressing.' This got a big laugh from Yaz, who leant forward to pick up her coffee conspicuously pointing her cleavage the Controller's way. Nigel didn't notice, being the sort of man who'd rather harangue his subordinates than look at a nice bosom.

'Jesus Christ, Sam! At least try setting your brain for the twenty-first century! As Britain's premier media provider, the BBC is perfectly placed to connect up with the real cutting-edge talent that is out there making New Britain hip. Writers, producers, directors, women, the cream of Cool Britannia, the tip top of Britpop. We need to interface with these people. We have the resources to make films, we have the budgets to make films, all we need is the ideas.'

Later, discussing the meeting in the BBC bar, George and Trevor were very excited about it. After all, for people like us who spend our time commissioning new ways of humiliating the public for the early Saturday evening schedules, the idea of making proper films is pretty seductive. I tried hard to join in with their enthusiasm but I couldn't summon up much jollity. Jealousy really, I suppose. I don't want to commission films, I want to write one. The idea of going about Soho searching out shaven-headed twelve-year-old film-school fashion junkies with rings through their scrotums made me tired. Unfair of me, I know, but as my mother said, life wasn't supposed to be fair.

George and Trevor saw things differently. They thought it presented a golden opportunity.

'This is your big chance!' they said. 'Commission yourself. Write a script and green light it. The man's crying out for ideas and he's asking us to find them. You'll never get an opportunity like this again! It's gamekeeper turned poacher.'

For a moment I was almost seduced, but then I remembered two things. Firstly my current relationship with the Controller does not lead me to imagine that he'd accept a script with my name on it. And secondly, even if he did, *what* script? I haven't written a thing in years. I've forgotten *how* to write and even if I hadn't I have nothing to write about.

Trevor said he'd always thought that a gay alcoholic in recovery would make a great subject for a movie.

'But that's your story, Trevor,' I said.

'And a monumentally fucking dull one it is too,' George added.

Of course they're both right. Nigel's new initiative is an opportunity I should be seizing with both hands. But I just can't do it. They say comedy is about conflict and pain. Where's my conflict? Where's my pain? I'm a boring bloke in a boringly happy marriage. Apart from my own monumental lack of talent and an impending sperm result there isn't a cloud on my horizon.

Dear Penny

I simply cannot believe it. Sam handed in his sample three days ago and since then he has been jumpy as a kitten. He pounces on the post in the morning even though he knows the result will take five days. He grabs at any envelope that comes through the door, ones containing offers to join bookclubs, others containing enquiries about whether we want to sell our house. He tears them all open in terror that they might also be concealing a failed sperm test certificate. I swear that's what he thinks he's going to get, a certificate, possibly with a ribbon on it or a red wax seal, saying 'sperm test FAILED'. I'm afraid it seems that nothing, absolutely nothing, turns a man into a wanker so much as having to take a sperm test.

Anyway, my blood test result came through with the second post and it seems my body has passed that particular hurdle, insomuch as the indications are that I ovulate. Hooray and whoopidydingdong. There are now only fourteen million things that could be wrong with my sad, dysfunctional tubes. Sometimes it really is hard to be a woman.

I had to send off loads of signed pictures of Carl 'Will you fuck me for a sandwich?' Phipps today. I have very mixed emotions about that whole episode. Obviously I'd never do anything about it, I mean obviously. Nonetheless it's quite flattering. At thirty-four and married it's rather nice to discover that one could still get laid if one wanted to which one doesn't and one certainly wouldn't even if one did.

When I told Sam that my blood test indicated healthy ovulation he acted most unpleasantly. Instead of being pleased that at least one part of my body functions as it should, he immediately took it as proof that he's going to fail his sperm test and that he's some kind of sexless eunuch. It really is most thoughtless of him to be so self-obsessed, and not very attractive. I must confess to having briefly entertained the unworthy thought that Lord Byron Phipps, the brooding, smouldering Tenant of Wildfell Hall, would not be so ungentlemanly or uncaring of a lady's distress.

He would also have more faith in his testicles.

Sam

Still no news on the sperm test.

Also still no word from Tosser about giving me a job.

However, I've also still heard nothing further from the Channel Controller about my sensational faux pas over the mixed-up letters and am beginning to dare to hope that I may have got away with it. After all, Nigel isn't such a bad bloke, is he? He's trying to drag the Beeb into the twenty-first century and all that, isn't he? And he's got a sense of humour, hasn't he? He'd see the funny side, on the quiet. I mean when he was an Arts Editor I remember he did that documentary on Ken Dodd. Marvellous stuff. Really, really marvellous earthy, populist stuff. It compared Dodd to a Shakespearean clown. They did a bit of Dogberry and Verges from *Much Ado* to illustrate the point. Hilarious, particularly when they duelled with loaves of French bread, absolutely hilarious. I must tell Nigel how hilarious I found it. Yanton Nabokobovich did the interview, I recall, and called Doddy a true subversive. 'Isn't every joke really a small revolution?' Yanton enquired. 'An act of rebellion undermining the status quo?' 'If you like, missus! Ha ha!' said Doddy.

Brilliant telly.

Of course Nigel's got a sense of humour and he's a bloody good bloke as well. Old Nige won't let me down.

Had a fascinating debate with the Complaints and Standards people at the weekly programme briefing. George was in the chair and we were debating acceptable names for vaginas. Amazing. There we were, five men earnestly debating whether 'fanny' was an acceptable term to use before nine o'clock. I told Lucy about it and she went back on her old thing about men being intimidated by fannies. She pointed out that there are any number of words for penis that can be used pretty much with ease on the Beeb – knob, willy, percy, portion, member, todger, tackle, dangler, sausage, John Thomas, Dick Dastardly, meat and two veg and Uncle Tom Cobblers and all. However, when it came to female genitalia almost everything was too rude. She's right, of course. 'Vaginas' are ruder than 'penises', even 'fanny' is on the edge. 'Muff' might pass, but again only just. The meeting was quite stumped. In the end we came up with 'fou fou', which is a term somebody's mother used. I can't see our tough young lady comediennes buying 'fou fou'. We'll be lampooned in the media section of the *Independent* before we know it.

Still no news on the sperm test, or did I mention that?

Dear Pen Pen

Drusilla came into the office today and caught me having a cup of coffee. She says caffeine is the enemy of womankind and insisted I drink a cup of squeezed lemon juice to purge myself. Then she asked if I'd given any more thought to the business of the Primrose Hill ley lines, because there's a full moon next Thursday and the long-range weather forecast is good. The woman is out of her mind.

I also had lunch with Melinda and baby Cuthbert. He really is gorgeous and I'm sure that the slightly disconcerting impression of a permanent scowl will disappear as his mouth gets bigger. We ordered our salads (followed by cake) and inevitably Melinda produced her photos. Even though Cuthbert was sitting right in front of me in the flesh (and such a lot of flesh too, great folds of it), Melinda insisted that I look at nearly two hundred pictures of him. Which was nice (because he really is gorgeous, although slightly like a miniaturized Reggie Kray), but a tiny bit tiresome. How I wish we lived in times when the taking of a photograph was a rare and precious thing. When five or ten images sufficed to cover a person's entire childhood. Nowadays people take millions of shots on computerized cameras and then reel them off on their home printers ad nauseam. Besides which, now that video cameras come with little playback screens it's possible for people to show you their ghastly videos as well, sometimes while they're actually recording them. Melinda didn't go that far, but she had had an entire set of prints done for me, which really is too much.

I did think about showing Melinda a picture of Gertrude (just the one from the Big Issue, *not the glossy one) but decided I wouldn't. I thought that she might think it sad. Not that she'd have any reason to.*

After about half an hour Cuthbert started crying and when I say crying what I mean is attempting to reduce London to rubble by the sheer force of sonic vibration. Melinda breastfed him at the table, which I thought was very right and feminist of her, although I do wish she hadn't burped him quite so vigorously afterwards. Most of it hit the floor but I fear a splash or two of milky vomit may have landed in people's food.

Actually, I had thought that you weren't supposed to burp them any more.

I can't deny, though, that it all made me feel broodier than ever. Despite Cuthbert not having a volume-control button and his indiscriminate vomiting and his slightly moth-eaten-looking patch of coarse black hair, looking at him did make me just long for one of my own. Particularly when I saw his little Peter Rabbit jumper. It was just so sweet. All my life I've looked forward to rediscovering Beatrix Potter via my children, so that did hit me rather hard. I must say, though, that I didn't much like the baseball cap Melinda had bought him from OshKosh. It had 'Yeah, I know I'm cute' written on it, which I thought was a bit sickmaking (and sadly not entirely true).

I'd never buy a cap like that for a child because what a parent is really saying with that kind of stuff is 'Look how beautiful my baby is.' Which is not really on, not for the British, anyway. It's not how we go about things. Or is that a wrong thing to say these days?

Also Melinda had just bought one of those 'Baby On Board' stickers for their Fiat. Sam says he's astonished that George allowed it, and that nobody buys those any more. I must say, I can't say I like them overmuch. I mean, what is the parent trying to say to other road users? And what are other road users supposed to make of it? 'Thanks awfully for the tip because I'd been thinking about driving into the back of you, but since you've got a kid in the car I'll cover the brake.' It's absurd. I'm going to have my own sticker made. 'Sadly my husband and I have not yet been blessed with the divine gift of a child but we'd still prefer not to die in a car crash, thank you.'

Anyway, when we'd finally exhausted all the photos and

cleaned the vomit off everything I got round to telling Melinda all about my strangely daunting encounter with Carl Phipps, or Heathcliff as I often think of him. I know I was only going to tell you, Penny, but I just could not keep it to myself. Well, guess what? Melinda thinks I should shag him! Yes! Shag him. *I couldn't believe it! Melinda of all people. She's normally so proper. But she said that this was different, that these were special circumstances on account of the fact that Carl Phipps is acknowledged as one of the most dishy men in the country. Did I think, Melinda enquired, that if Sam got the chance of slipping one to Sharon Stone he would pass it up?*

'Yes, I bloody well do!' I said. Rather too loudly, in fact, because people looked.

I don't think Melinda really meant it. I mean, she's never been at all indulgent of the idea of infidelity. I remember one New Year's Eve George gave me a kiss and she got quite funny about it. I mean it was quite a long kiss, I admit, but it was New Year's Eve and the bonging takes a very long time if you start at one and go on to twelve.

Reading between the lines, my guess is that George is probably not seeing to Melinda's needs properly at the moment. I believe this often happens after a baby. The hubby starts to see the wife as a mother not a lover and feels strange about lusting after the thing that is feeding his child. Also, Melinda hasn't quite got her figure back yet (poor thing). That's understandable, of course, it's only been a couple of months and it's far too early for her to worry about that sort of business. Although I did think that three cakes was a little bit reckless. I only had one and a bit.

Anyway, I told Melinda that I had no intention of betraying Sam because I love him and that sexually he gives me everything I need. Which is basically true, on the whole, I suppose. Certainly it's true about loving him, anyway. Although sexually I must confess to being not particularly satiated at the moment. The problem is that he seems to think of nothing but the result of his sperm test. In fact he's obsessed with it. Which is not, I have to admit, particularly attractive in a man.

Yo, stud!

Yes! Yes! Yes! *Yes*!!! All RIGHT! Result, my son! Here we go, here we *go*! Result! Re-flipping-sult! Sorted. Oh yes! Sorted for sure. Passed! Passed my sperm test.

The letter arrived this morning.

At first I didn't want to open it. It was just like my 'A' levels. I remember I was grapepicking in France and I had to ring home and get my mum to open the envelope. I can remember walking round that French phonebox for half an hour, too nervous to make the call. Of course I couldn't hang around for half an hour this morning because I had to go to work, but I did make Lucy open the envelope and read the letter for me. As she slid a knife along the crease of the paper everything seemed to be in slow motion. I can remember thinking that now at least the waiting was over, whatever fate might bring.

I must say things started pretty grimly. There was no personal element at all, no 'Dear sir,' no 'Brace yourself, mate,' no 'Better get yourself a drink, you sad pathetic excuse for a man, because you have no sperm.' Just a printed form on which they fill in your results with a ballpoint pen. So much for our more caring society. They do not even offer counselling.

Well, Book, I am here to tell you that at first I thought that all was lost. The very opening line (under the deceptively bland heading 'motility') said '30% sluggish'. Honestly, that was the very word they used. *Sluggish*. A horrible, horrible word, reminiscent of slimy snail-like creatures that can't be bothered moving their arses on garden paths in order to avoid being stamped on. Sluggish! It's such a loaded term, not clinical at all. I wanted a doctor's reaction, not a critic's! And if they're going to use unscientific language couldn't they have thought of a more friendly expression? Like 'relaxed', perhaps, or 'unhurried'? If they'd told me I had relaxed sperm I could have handled it. Cool, laid-back sperm, sperm that liked to hang out and chill with the other guys. That would be fine. But 'sluggish'? It's almost as if they were trying to be unpleasant.

Anyway, the next line was worse! Yes, worse! I nearly cried. It said '41% swimming in the wrong direction'! I mean, what a thing to say about the very stuff of a man's loins! My head was spinning. I thought, I've got *stupid* sperm! The stuff's backing away up my dick all these years! Then I thought, 'Hang on, this is ridiculous!' This test is rigged. How are they supposed to know what's the right direction, for heaven's sake? They're in a plastic pot! I had this vision of all my sperm desperately groping about hither and thither, banging their heads against the sides of the container, lashing their tails around like fish in a bucket, thinking, 'We're genetically programmed to find an egg here. Where is it?'

By the end of the letter I was ready to slit my wrists.

In conclusion it said, '90% useless'! Bad swimmers, poor motility. A load of rubbish in general.

So now the full and terrible truth was upon me. I'm not a man. I've failed my sperm test!

I was already asking myself whether they'd let me take it again. If it was like your driving test, I mean I had four goes at that when in actual fact I should have passed on the first time except that my examiners were a bunch of total Nazis. Then of course it dawned on me that the sperm tester must be a Nazi too! A jealous, small-minded petty official dedicated to ruining the lives of better men. A hopeless and inadequate man, embittered because his own sperm were small and sickly and couldn't find their way out of his trousers. A man who took his revenge upon society by becoming a sperm tester and failing anyone who came up with the real goods.

That had to be it. Give a fellow a sperm tester's uniform and suddenly he thinks he's Hitler!

I was on the very point of phoning my MP and demanding a full recount when Lucy pointed out that stamped at the bottom of the form in big letters was the word NORMAL.

Oh, the relief! It turns out that my pathetic percentages are par for the course, that pretty much all sperm is 90 per cent rubbish. Apparently there's only a couple of decent wrigglers in an entire wristful. For all the macho pride and posturing of us men, most sperms just simply aren't up to it. They're sluggish. They're stupid. They're always wandering off in the wrong direction. They don't know where they're going.

Lucy said they sound exactly like a pub full of blokes, which was *quite* funny, I suppose.

Anyway, that was it. Passed. Normal. I was so pleased I danced round the kitchen and spilt my coffee.

'Normal!' I shouted. 'Oh yes! Normal! Ordinary! Run of the mill!' Then I thought, hang on, normal? Ordinary? A bit disappointing, really. I mean, let's face it, 'Superb' would have been a better result. Probably just an off day. Still, whatever, I'm off the hook.

Dear Penny

Well, I must say I did laugh at Sam's letter and not just because it nearly made him cry either. The bit about 41 per cent swimming in the wrong direction! Well, I ask you. I'm surprised it wasn't 100 per cent. What woman doesn't know that sperm swims in the wrong direction? We certainly don't need to invoke the hard-pressed resources of the National Health Service to find that out. Not if you happen to cough half an hour after a bonk and ten million of the little swine headbutt your gusset.

Anyway, armed with both our test results I took an hour off work and went to see Dr Cooper and he said that having established that nothing obvious is wrong with either of us, the problem might be that we are incompatible (I felt like saying that this thought had crossed my mind too, but I didn't). Dr Cooper says that my juices and Sam's sperm may simply not like each other. That my body may be poisoning his tadpoles as they try to 'swim up my Amazon' as Sam calls it. All this sounds completely gruesome but Dr Cooper assures me that it's absolutely fine and normal, normal, that is, in sad infertile old bags like me. Actually he didn't say that last bit but it's how I feel sometimes. I have this vision of my insides as a wrinkled old prune. It's funny. Sometimes it all seems so unreal, like a dream. Me? Possibly infertile? Surely not. There must be some mistake. I want kids, I've always wanted kids, my whole life has been built round the anticipation of bringing up kids, this can't be happening. Why me? Why bloody me! Oh well, I suppose we all think that, don't we? We desperate ones.

Anyway, back to Dr Cooper and his incompatibility test. I must say I was a bit taken aback at the thought. The idea of all Sam's seed drowning in agony in the hell waters of my poisonous vagina made me quite teary. Like a murderess. Well, it seems that in order to discover whether this horrible possibility is in fact the case we must do a postcoital test. Which basically means Sam and me having it off and then a doctor having a look at the aftermath. Quite frankly, one of the most horrible suggestions anyone has ever put to me.

When Doc Cooper first explained it I thought he wanted us to have it off at his surgery which would be not on. I just couldn't do it. However, Dr Cooper said that he would not be doing the test, for which small mercy I should think he is eternally grateful. I imagine that he's absolutely sick of the sight of my nether regions by now, he's been up them that many times over the years. And the thought of encountering them while they are gorged with Sam's sperm is almost too horrible to contemplate.

Anyway, what has to happen is that Sam and I must get up early on the appointed day and get straight down to business. This is not regular morning practice for us, I hasten to add, both of us preferring a cup of tea and a slice of toast first thing. Besides which, the memory of Sam's efforts at morning masturbation are still painfully fresh. Once I've been properly serviced and stonked up, so to speak, I have to go to some ghastly specialist clinic or other (which will no doubt look like something out of Solzhenitsyn's Cancer Ward*) and up me the doctors will go. Surprise, surprise. Who would be a woman? Looking back over the years of smear tests, non-specific infections, fertility bizzo and all, my poor old muff has definitely been a well-trodden path for the medical profession. Sometimes I think I should have a revolving door fitted. Anyway, as I was saying, the specialist, having had a jolly good poke around (with what will no doubt be a piece of frozen metal the size of a grill pan), will then be able to inform me whether or not my insides are filled with dead sperm.*

Ugh!

God, I hate this. Why can't I just get pregnant!?

I rang Drusilla from work and asked her when exactly she'd said that the next full moon was. I'm not going to do it, but I can't afford to discount anything.

Dear Sam

Going to dinner at Trevor and Kit's tonight. Had the usual hoo-hah about what to wear. Not me, of course. I know what to wear. Trousers and a shirt. But Lucy finds these decisions much more perplexing. What's more, she insists on dragging me into her dilemmas and then blaming me for them! She stands there in her underwear and says 'Which do you think, the red or the blue?' Well, I know of course the clever thing would be to refuse to answer, because there's no chance in this world or the next of saying the right thing. Nonetheless, inevitably I have a stab at it.

'Uhm, the red?'

'So you don't like the blue?'

'I didn't say that.'

'I was going to wear the blue.'

'Well wear the blue, then.'

'Well I can't now, can I? Since you obviously think I look horrible in it . . . Now I've got to start thinking all over again . . .'

Madness, absolute madness, particularly since it's only Trevor and Kit, for heaven's sake. George and Melinda were invited too but they couldn't get a babysitter. I pointed out to Lucy that that sort of thing will happen to us if ever we do score. I don't actually think that she's thought the whole social side of having babies through at all. Not being able to go out or get pissed when we want to, all spontaneity wiped from our lives in one single act. I said to her, I said, here we are, two highly educated, fully rounded people and yet we are *desperate* to totally subsume our existence in the abstract concept of a being who will suck us dry physically, emotionally and financially and will not even be able to form a decent sentence for at least five years.

Sam's in the bathroom shaving, having just delivered a little monologue on the downside of having children, and I'm trying very hard not to get upset because I've already done my make-up. How could he be so thoughtless and selfish? He doesn't mean to be cruel, I know, but he just doesn't understand. I was born to have children. There's never been a moment in my life when I didn't want, some day, to be a mother. When he talks like that, as if children are some kind of lifestyle option to be taken or left, I feel a million miles away from him. Children are the reason for being alive.

I just reminded Lucy that kids are, in the end, just another lifestyle option and I think I made her feel better.

On the other hand. Sometimes I must admit that I catch a glimpse of Lucy, or a look at her while she's asleep, and I think how pretty she is, and how much I love her. And I think how much more I would like to love her and how I would like to find new and more complete ways of expressing that love. That's when I think that perhaps having a baby might be the most wonderful thing in the world. Oh well, mustn't dwell.

Dear Penny

Last night's dinner with Trevor and his boyfriend Kit was great fun, despite Sam getting me a bit upset before we left.

Sam and Trevor are of course colleagues in lunch at the Beeb and are terribly funny when they start sneering at the more awful of the artists they have to hand over all our licence fees to. Trevor was telling us about these ghastly Oxbridge-educated yobbos whose job is to make jokes about football on some beery late-night sports chat show. It's called A Game of Two Halves *and it's Trevor's biggest hit. Apparently the rough idea of the show (I haven't seen it) is that clips of various sporting events are played and then the regular panel members compete with each other to see who can mention their penises most often.*

It was nice to have a really good laugh. We always do with Trevor and Kit. Trevor is good at taking the piss out of himself and it seems he's become a victim of his own success with this alternative sports quiz he's developed. Two of the blokes on it have inevitably been picked up for representation by the bull-like Aiden Fumet. Fumet has been to see Trevor and explained that, on the strength of their current 'ballistic' status, his 'turns' must immediately be given their own sitcoms. When Trevor asked if before committing hundreds of thousands of pounds worth of licence payers' money to an untried project it might be possible to see a script, Aiden Fumet immediately turned into the spiritual skinhead he is and called Trevor 'a pointless time-serving cunt'. He also threatened that any suggestion of artistic interference from Trevor or the 'BB-fucking-C' would result in Aiden Fumet's entire 'stable' being no longer available to the Corporation.

Trevor does a very good Aiden Fumet, who has a strange hybrid accent – half bored aristocratic rock star and half East End stallholder. 'What the BBC 'ave gotta under*stand* is that all my boys are *Time Out*-approved geniuses and any more messing abaht and I'll take 'em all to 'ollywood, where they have a proper professional attitude towards the talent and I can get two million dollars a turn, minimum.'

Trevor, George and I all agree that artists are a lot more arrogant with the BBC than they used to be. I suppose it's down to the incredible diversity of employment options that anybody half good (or not even) is presented with these days. I mean, there was a time when there was only one channel and anybody, no matter how talented, who wanted to be on telly did so by the grace of the BBC. That was how we used to get those incredible long runs of things. People did what they were told, and if that meant doing sixty episodes of the same sitcom then that was what they did. These days, with eight million channels available the celebs call the shots, which makes life a lot more difficult for us execs.

Trevor also blames the Montreal Comedy Festival. This takes place in Canada (well it would do) and hence appearing at it is as close to playing in the United States as the vast majority of

88

British comics are ever going to get. Which is why they all go there. Trevor and I go too whenever we can swing it, as it really is the most monumental piss-up, and the restaurants are excellent! The problem is that big Hollywood TV people also go. Well, not actually big Hollywood TV people. In fact, the minions of the minions of big Hollywood TV people. Those so low down the US TV totem pole that they have nothing more pressing to do in LA or New York. In fact, as far as I can make out, the Montreal Comedy Festival is really just an annual holiday for failed Americans because it is the one time of the year where they get to lord it over people even more desperate to make it in the States than they are themselves.

Anyway, these US non-executives swan about the place being bought drinks by British agents and pretending to be important. Then they go up to all the desperate British, Irish, Australian and Kiwi comedians and tell them that they are 'just incredibly interesting and original' and that CBS will probably be very interested in turning them into Eddie Murphy probably or at the very least possibly giving them a sitcom development deal probably.

The sad truth, of course, is that the British comics swear far too much to be of any real interest to the Americans and I have to say that the Ozzies are even fouler. Also, the Montreal Comedy Festival is of only slightly more significance to American Television people than is the Big Knob Comedy Club in Brick Lane. So all that happens is that the British come home (having been drunk for a fortnight and having abused the sacred sexual trust of some poor little nineteen-year-old Canadian publicist), with eye-popping tales of impending and colossal success in the glamorous world of American sitcom. These tales are then circulated by the comedians' managers and dutifully published in the *Independent* and, of course, *Time Out* ('Move over, Robin Williams, here comes Ivor Biggun from Slough!' 'Eric and Ernie couldn't do it, but Dog and Fish just might'). This confirmation of the stories in print then makes the managers, who originally circulated the stories, actually believe them, hence they think that they can push the BBC around.

'Listen, Sam,' Aiden Fumet regularly says to me, 'I've been

faxed by somebody *very* big at *NBC*! So where's the fucking sit-com deal for my boys?!'

It was so funny! Trevor is always good at telling stories about work because you see he doesn't really care about it very much, unlike Sam, who cares desperately and actually thinks that you can 'plan' comedy hits and that festivals and managers and American development deals are terribly important.

Anyway, then Sam (possibly trying to be funnier than Trevor) brought up our impending postcoital business, which I suppose I didn't really mind because Trevor and Kit are very good pals. Although it is slightly disconcerting to discuss one's vaginal juices at the dinner table. We all had another good laugh about it, though, because, of course, it is funny. Trevor and Sam were both being most amusing, saying things about vaginal genocide and Sam's sperm swimming back from the fray carrying little white flags.

We actually laughed until we cried and then I'm afraid to admit I nearly did cry a bit because the truth is, hilarious though it may be, it isn't *very funny wanting kids and not being able to get them.*

Kit was so lovely. He's a set designer for the theatre (mainly fringe; he told me that recently he had to do Burnham Wood moving to Dunsinane for about five quid: 'We use a lot of real twigs, and binliners, of course, can represent just about any-thing'). Anyway, Kit asked what we would do if we failed the test and it turned out that my body really did reject Sam's sperm. Well, before we knew it we were discussing Trevor making a donation! Ha! Apparently, Trevor has already done it for a lesbian couple in Crouch End that he and Kit met on the Internet. He explained that you don't actually have to do it, you know, have sex together ('Not even for you, Lucy love,' said Trevor), you just use a turkey baster! Seems incredible to me, but apparently it's true.

Sam laughed a lot at all this, but I could see he was a bit taken aback at the idea. He really has always been so blusé about kids

that I didn't think he'd mind what I did, but then he went quiet,
so I expect he does mind really.

Life is becoming rather strange. My wife appears to be plotting to conceive with my gay friends using a turkey baster. That'll be an interesting story to tell my mother over the next Christmas dinner.

It has made me think a bit, though. I mean, what if Sam and I aren't compatible? What are the alternatives? Adoption? Artificial insemination? Forgetting about the whole thing? Oh well, I suppose I'll just have to do what I've done many a night of late and try not to think about it.

Dear Sam

A sort of half-exciting thing happened at work today. It started off very exciting, but then got slightly less so. I was just completing a particularly difficult level of *Tomb Raider* on my PC when Daphne looked in and said that the Director General's office had been on and would Lucy and I care to go to dinner at Broadcasting House!

Well, *would I?* All thoughts of Lara Croft's extraordinary bosom fled my mind instantly. I mean the DG's dinners at BH are legendary. He has cabinet ministers, captains of industry, footballers, bishops, *everyone*. But *never*, to the best of my knowledge, has a lowly executive producer of broken comedy and sitcom been invited. I did once go to his Christmas drinks, but it was only the once and, anyway, there were at least two hundred people at that and it was only drinks. This was dinner! Dinner at Broadcasting House, the Ship that sails down Regent Street! What an honour! The DG must have heard of my trip to Downing Street. I doubt he could have missed it: I've talked about it loudly in every single nook and cranny of the Corporation.

Anyway, for whatever reason, we'd been invited. We were 'in'.

I nearly stood to attention when I told Daphne to accept!

'When is it?' I said. 'I'll cancel everything. If my mother dies, she dies alone.'

'Tomorrow night,' she said.

Slightly disheartening. Obviously an invitation at such short notice means we're to be fill-ins for somebody who has jacked. Still, I thought, I'd never have expected to have been asked at all, so even being a replacement is an honour.

Then the phone rang. It was George.

'Guess what?' he said. 'Melinda and I got asked to a DG's dinner for tomorrow night! Incredible, eh, what a coup! Obviously we're a fill-in for somebody who jacked but, still, pretty amazing. The appalling bugger of it is we can't go! Melinda just can't get a sitter she trusts. There's only two sitters in the world it seems who aren't mass murderers and they're both busy. I've threatened divorce but she won't budge . . .'

'When did you get your invitation?' I asked.

'Yesterday, late afternoon,' said George. 'I rang the DG's office first thing this morning to say we couldn't do it. I could scarcely believe I was actually turning down the Director General this morning. I suppose in a way it's pretty cool.'

After George got off the phone I tried not to be miffed. 'Who cares?' I thought. 'So what if I was second choice?' We were still going to dine with the . . .

And then Trevor rang.

'You're not going to believe this,' he said, 'but Kit and I got invited to have dinner at BH with the DG and we can't go! His office rang first thing this morning. It's for tomorrow night so obviously we were to be the replacement for someone who's dropped out, but all the same! Pretty amazing, eh? I had to ring them back half an hour ago to decline. It was like pulling teeth but there's no way Kit can break his rule.'

Kit, sadly, is HIV positive and although he's doing incredibly well and you would never know he carried the virus he does have to be careful about over-exertion. He and Trevor have a strict rule that they have only one social occasion a week.

'And we used it up having *you* to dinner,' Trevor said, and I must say that I didn't much like his tone, the clear implication being that he and Kit had been insane to waste their precious entertaining time on us when there were far more impressive prospects just around the corner. We parted slightly coldly.

So there it is. Lucy and I are to be the replacement for a replacement for a replacement. Nonetheless we are going to dinner with the DG, which is not to be sniffed at. I'll have to make sure that Nigel hears about it. He can hardly sack me if I'm friends with the PM *and* the DG.

I spent all day expecting Keith Harris to phone and say he'd had to turn down an invite from the DG because Orville has a cold.

Tosser also phoned me today. No chance of a job with his company, which was a bit dispiriting, I must admit. I had thought, vainly, that he'd jump at the chance of recruiting me, that I'd be rather a prestige signing for his company. You know, top BBC man and all that, but obviously he doesn't think so. 'The BBC is just another player,' he said to me, which is a bloody ridiculous thing to say considering the BBC is the largest broadcaster in the world and he has a floor and a half in Dean Street. Quite frankly, I suspect him of only giving work to gorgeous young women with pierced bellybuttons and small tattoos of scorpions on their shoulders; there certainly seem to be a lot of them employed at his office, though that might just be coincidence, I suppose.

Dear Pen Pal

I'm writing this having just got back from dinner at Broadcasting House. The Director General was hosting one of his evenings for the great and the good so obviously we'd only been invited to pad out the numbers (Sam did some spying and it turned out that the Editor of the Daily Telegraph *had jacked at the last moment. Sam said other people had been asked to fill in before us, but he was very vague about who they were, very important people he said).*

Anyway, when I say we had dinner with the Director General we barely actually spoke to him, of course, being at the other end of the table, but it was still very nice. BH really is a fantastic building, even though some idiot or other ripped most of the Deco out in the fifties and replaced it with the interior of a Soviet prison. Nonetheless it still feels special to walk in through those same doors that Tony Hancock and Churchill and Sue Lawley have walked through before you.

Of course actually having dinner there (served by very smart staff) is particularly magical, it takes you back to another age, like the twenties or something. You start with drinks in a sort of antechamber and then go through into a marvellous dining room, all wood lined and shimmering crystal. I got sat next to a bishop who was very nice, and a junior member of the shadow cabinet who was not. He immediately made it quite clear that he was not happy at being seated next to a mere 'wife' and, what's more, a mere nobody's wife to boot. I swear that as the swine came through and spotted his place-setting (with me already sitting next to it) his face actually fell! Unbelievable. He couldn't even be bothered to make the pretence of being polite. He *actually* grimaced.

We attempted smalltalk for about a minute.

Me: 'So you're in the shadow cabinet? How fascinating. Although I always imagine that being in opposition must be very frustrating.'

Swine: 'Hmm, yes. So your husband works in television comedy, you say? I really don't think that any of that rubbish is funny any more. There hasn't been anything remotely decent since Yes, Minister.'

After that he completely ignored me until the cheese, by which time he was pissed enough to try a bit of bored flirting in a lazy, patronizing, off-hand sort of way.

Swine: 'I expect with you both being in showbusiness there must be terrible temptations. Do you ever get jealous? Does he?'

I wasn't having any of it. 'What a strange question,' I said, not only hoitily but also fairly toitily and turned back to the bishop, with whom I was getting on like a house on fire. He must have been ninety-three if he was a day and he was telling me about his hobby, which was collecting eighteenth-century Japanese erotic art! Extraordinary! Where does the church get them? What's more, whilst describing a porcelain figurine of a naked ninja (in rather too much detail), he squeezed my leg under the table! The randy old goat. What is it about men? They're pathetic. A couple of drinks and they start sniffing about like dogs. Sam was scarcely being any better than the bishop. He was sitting next to this tart with extraordinary knockers (not entirely her own, I fancy) and I could see him just ogling them. I mean at first he'd at least tried to be discreet, although I knew what he was up to, of course, all that reaching for the salt and passing the bread. Sad, really. And after a few glasses of wine he just gave up any pretence at subtlety and started simply staring at them with his tongue hanging out. I mean it couldn't have been any more obvious if he'd said, 'Phwoar! Look at the jugs on that!' I've no idea who this overly boobed slapper was, she was only about twenty-three or four and clearly a second wife to someone, but I didn't find out whose. I looked for a man with a smug smile on his face but there were too many contenders. It may have been the shadow cabinet minister. On the other hand why would a man with a girl like that be flirting with me? I'm not exactly spectacularly blessed in the knocker department.

All in all, what with Sam drooling and the shadow minister sneering and the bishop's hand beginning to gather a tiny bit too much confidence, it was a great relief when the DG made us all move round for the pudding. I ended up talking to his wife, who seemed very nice. I found myself telling her all about Carl Phipps. Not the hand-holding lunch, obviously, but about being an agent and representing him. I must admit I suddenly heard myself being altogether more enthusiastic about him than I'd intended to be. 'He's so nice,' and 'He's rather dishy,' and 'He's not at all stuck up,' the last of which at least is certainly not true.

I suppose it's just possible that I sounded rather schoolgirly. Oh well, it doesn't matter, I suppose. We shan't be asked again anyway.

On the way home Sam insisted that he wasn't pissed, but he did his usual pissed thing of worrying about whether he'd put his foot in it to anyone. I said he might as well have put his foot into *that woman's cleavage because he'd done everything else but climb into it (which he denied, pathetically). Sam always comes home from parties worrying that he's said something wrong or offended someone. It's incredibly boring and, what's more, it's affected me. I never used to be like that at all. 'Fuck 'em,' I used to say, but he's so bad he's got me doing it as well. Sometimes we come home from going out and spend the whole cab ride asking each other if we were embarrassing and reassuring each other that we weren't. It's sad.*

Anyway, he'd better not have been too pissed. He knows damn well what he's got to do tomorrow morning.

Dear etc.

I *think* it went all right tonight. Bit worried I might have said the wrong thing. I've been over it with Lucy and it *seems* all right. As far as I can recall I only spoke to the Director General twice. I said, 'Good evening,' at the beginning and later on I said, 'Yes, I think things are fairly healthy in the arena of entertainment and comedy at the moment.' I don't think either of those comments could be misconstrued. Surely not? Unless he thought I was being sarky? But why would he think that? No, I'm quite sure I didn't make any faux pas.

Definitely.

What's more, I *certainly* didn't spend the evening staring at that woman's tits, as I've been unfairly accused of. I mean they were *there*, for God's sake! In fact they seemed to be everywhere! I simply couldn't avoid the things. I could hardly sit and look at the ceiling all evening, could I?

Anyway. One thing is for absolutely sure. I am *not pissed*. I was *very* careful about that. Because, as I'm well aware, I have to provide a shag in the morning. What is more I intend to make it a cracker, because I really love Lucy. I really really do. Despite her paranoia about other women's bosoms I absolutely love her. I just told her so and she said I was pissed, but I'm not. I just love her, I really do, I love her, I love her, I love her and tomorrow, before I go to work, I am going to make love to her so passionately and

96

so beautifully that she will remember it always, because I love her.

Dear Penny

This morning I think I had the worst shag I have had in thirteen and a half years of moderately continuous lovemaking. I doubt that I shall ever forget it. Sam reeked of stale booze and fags, plus I was still seething about him spending the whole evening staring down that enormous cleavage, which he continued to deny, of course.

Anyway, we both knew we would have to go through with it. The postcoital examination had been booked for ten and you do not mess with a confirmed appointment on the NHS. I must say that from the moment we woke up it was clear that it was not much of a prospect for me, erotically speaking. Sam staggered back from a rather loud visit to the lavatory announcing that he had a headache but that it couldn't be a hangover as he hadn't been drunk. What's more, we were a bit late already because, although Sam had set the alarm to give us an extra half-hour (it normally only takes us about fifteen minutes), somehow or other he'd managed not to push the button in so it hadn't gone off.

Anyway, I had just decided to ignore the beery, faggy fug that surrounded him and attempt a bit of foreplay when Sam said, 'I'm afraid we're really going to have to be quick, darling, because I've got a meeting.'

Well, I screamed at him! 'Oh, I'm so sorry!' I said. 'Trying to start a family when you've got a meeting! Perhaps if I phoned your secretary we could schedule our sex life into your diary. Just in pencil, of course. Wouldn't want to be inflexible about it or put you under any pressure!' Sarcastic, I know, but I was furious.

Anyway then, of course, the inevitable happened and he couldn't do it. His dick just completely disappeared. I told him to think about Ms 'look at my gargantuanly fulsome funbags' from the previous night but he got all angry and said that he didn't wish to think about other women, but that bonking to order was not as bloody easy as it might appear.

Well, to cut a short story even shorter he just about managed it. He wasn't at all sure that he'd produced enough for the test but Dr Cooper had assured me that it doesn't take much, so I thought that it would be all right. Actually I felt a bit sorry for him. I could see he felt he'd let me down a bit so I said he wasn't to worry because it wasn't his fault that he had a small and unreliable penis.

I really did mean it nicely but it just seemed to put him in an even worse mood.

So, Sam got dressed and went to his meeting, and I went off to the clinic. Obviously worried about all the stuff falling out on the way. Horrible thought. It had been such a gruesome effort mingling our juices in the first place that I didn't want to have to go through the whole ghastly palaver of a pre-postcoital examination bonk again, if that makes sense.

So there I was, hobbling to the car and trying not to cough. Once in the car it was worse. Driving yourself in these circumstances is a mistake unless you have an automatic. It is simply not possible to change gear with your legs crossed, and trying to do the whole journey in third makes things very juddery when you pull away at the lights, which of course shakes things down even more.

Then when I got to the clinic the road was blocked by a car with its hazard lights on.

I hate hazard lights.

They should be bloody well banned. People think that if they have them on then everything is all right. They can do exactly as they please. Park in the middle of the road, reverse up motorways, drive through crowded supermarkets, invade Poland. 'It's all right,' said Hitler's panzer commanders, 'we've got our hazard lights on.' I mean I ask you!!! I'm confident that the day is not far off when the burly and tattooed drivers of getaway cars will claim as a plea in mitigation that as they speeded away from some robbed bank or hijacked security van they had their hazards on!

So of course I had to reverse back up the street (with people reversing behind me, and making V-signs as if it was my fault). By a miracle I managed to park in a space exactly the same size as my car. I don't know how I did it. Extraordinary achievement and it only took seventy-two manoeuvres, which isn't easy when you're trying not to judder your insides. Thank God for power steering!

Anyway, out I got and hobbled back along the street to the clinic, still trying to keep my knees together, past the car with its hazards on. I'm afraid to say that I gave way to anger and snarled at the bloke at the wheel, shouting, 'You're blocking the road, you fool!' which was rather stating the obvious. Then of course I felt all guilty because perhaps he was waiting to pick up a disabled person. On the other hand, there was no yellow sticker, but even so it never helps to be aggressive.

So, feeling all hot and bothered I announced myself at the reception desk. Most embarrassing.

'Hello. I've come to see if my vagina poisons my husband's sperm.'

I didn't actually say that but the receptionist knew anyway. She smiled wearily and told me to take a seat. There were two or three other women waiting as well and I must say it felt very strange and slightly creepy knowing that we'd all been shagged within the previous hour or two and that we were all desperately trying to hang on to the dollop within.

As it happens, the clinic was very good and got through us quite quickly. I only had time to get halfway through a fascinating article in Woman's Own about Prince Andrew's exciting engagement to his new fiancée Sarah Ferguson, who is known to her friends as Fergie. I must say medical waiting rooms are incredibly nostalgic places. They are the only places where you can pretend that the Princess of Wales is still alive. I got quite sad all over again just thinking about that dreadful Sunday when she died.

So anyway, then it was into the torture chamber and all the usual appalling cervical intrusions, legs up in the stirrups, fanny prised apart, invaded and inspected. 'Ah, well,' I thought, 'another day, another duck-billed battering ram shoved up my poked, prodded and provoked privates.' There was a student there as well, having a good old stare.

I hate that!

I absolutely loathe *it. I mean I know they have to learn and all that but I really can do without spotty teenagers wanting to mess around between my legs. It reminded me of being back at school.*

Anyway, what with one thing and another I was in a foul mood as they slapped on the freezing cold lubrication and the doctor shoved up his horrid contraption, cold again, of course, and began scraping out my cervix. And what did he say? Well, of course, he said what they always say.

'Do try to relax.'

Oh well, of course. A perfect stranger is sticking bits of cold, greasy metal up your vagina, staring deep within, tutting in a worried manner and then asking an adolescent boy what he thinks of it, but do try to relax.

I always want to say, 'Sit on a traffic cone, mate, and you try to relax,' which would be brilliant and utterly unanswerable, but of course I never do.

Well, anyway, it turns out that Sam had not disgraced himself. There was enough of the stuff up me for the test and to my surprise I got the result immediately. Normally these things take ages to come through but amazingly the doctor whipped his spatula out of me, slapped the smear under the microscope and gave me the result there and then. Satisfactory, he said. Everything had turned out fine. Except, that is, for the fact that when he extracted the metal duck it made a disgusting loud wet raspberry noise, which was excruciatingly embarrassing. It's all that jelly they use and he used far too much. Every time I braked on the way home I slid off the car seat.

Anyway, as I say, long story short (EastEnders is nearly starting and the new barmaid is considering turning to prostitution to support her child. Juicy, or what?), the news is good. Sam and I are definitely chemically compatible. My juices do not reject his seed (although he's been such a pig lately I would not blame them if they did!). I am of course very pleased about this because despite his being a pig I do love him and I had been dreading having to pop round to our gay friends with a turkey baster and asking them to fill it full of sperm.

So there we are. It seems that compatibility is not the problem. Nor is my ovulation and nor is the motility of his sperm.

And yet we are still not preg! Why? WHY? Bloody why?

It is completely baffling and most distressing. What's more, we're running out of options. I fear a laparoscopy looms. Oh, shit. The very thought of a doctor inserting a television camera into my bellybutton makes my knees wobble! I'm not good with bellybuttons at the best of times; they make me go funny. I won't even let Sam kiss mine (not that he's offered to in years) and now I must face the prospect of a CNN news team clambering through it and sending back live bulletins from my ovaries.

I can scarcely believe I'm going to write this but I'm beginning to seriously think about Drusilla's theory re: ley lines and Primrose Hill. She does seem very certain of her facts. Shagging in Highgate is less conducive to connecting with the ancient forces of rejuvenation and fertility than shagging on Primrose Hill. I know that Drusilla is a witch but she's a good witch, which is a very different thing from the wicked variety.

Dear etc.

Well, this morning was a pressure job all right, our postcoital compatibility test. Doctor's orders. Shag and then straight round to the clinic to check the juices. Not much fun for the woman certainly but let me tell you it's a horrible situation for the bloke who is called upon to provide the wherewithal. I mean it's not ideal, is it? Sex on demand is tricky enough at the best of times, but in the morning, particularly after a big night at the Director General's, it's a very tough call indeed. The truth is we haven't done it on a weekday morning in years, well you don't, do you? We're not bloody students, are we?

Besides which, the whole problem was compounded by the fact that we slept through the alarm, dammit, and I happened to have a particularly early and rather important meeting.

Lucy says, 'When don't you have a meeting?' But actually that's not true. I am, in fact, often there at her beck and call. The point is when I am available to her she's not interested. She's only interested in presuming on my time when she knows I have other things to do.

So, what with the hangover (which I think I managed to disguise from Lucy), the earliness of the hour, and the impending meeting, instant and impressive erections were not massively in evidence.

Lucy tried to be nice about it but quite frankly she didn't try very hard. I don't think women have any idea how difficult it can be. They think that because most men seem to have erections pretty much all the time we can summon them up at will. They do not understand that when it comes to dicks, the captain is not in control of the ship.

Lucy said, 'I cannot believe this! Every morning you have a horn you could hang a bath-towel on. What's the problem now?'

She simply doesn't understand. I admit, of course, that on almost every other morning of my life I have woken up with an erection but that, and this is the point, is because *I didn't need one.*

It really is unfair. Any bloke can get a stiffy when he doesn't need one, and of course he almost always does. On buses; in the checkout queue at Sainsbury's; anywhere, really. But what women do not understand is that these unasked-for horns are normally not bonking horns but useless, sexless, pointless, unlooked-for protrusions.

Anyway the point I'm making is that the dick has a mind of its own, considering itself entirely autonomous and impervious to orders from the bridge. This is something that women need to understand, something that they should be told by their mothers at an early age. The fact is simply this: trying to tell a knob what to do is the very last thing it will appreciate or respond to.

I'm going on a bit, I know, but the injustice of the situation moves me deeply. Anyway, we pulled it off in the end, so to speak, but it was a very, very close-run thing.

I did, however, manage to make my meeting, which I was pleased about because it was a special one, concerning as it did Nigel's major new film-making initiative, an area in which considering my current standing with the Controller I cannot afford to screw up. Actually, I was rather excited about it. After all, film is film and we humble telly people do not normally get to dabble in so exalted a medium.

It was to be a 'breakfast' meeting at a posh hotel, I'm sorry to say. Whichever American it was who invented such a deeply uncivilized idea should have his eggs boiled, his muffins split and his pop-tarts toasted on an open fire. You can't make sense of a meeting over brekkie! How the hell are you supposed to take anything seriously when you're eating Rice Krispies? Or, worse, Coco Pops, which was what I had.

I can never resist the kids' stuff when I eat in hotels. I always want to order sausage, chips and alphabetti spaghetti from 'Sidney the Seal's Jolly Menu for Whizz Kidz'. Well, let's face it, that sort of stuff is normally the only thing that British hotels can actually cook. If you're fool enough to order anything 'steeped' in a sauce or containing the words 'jus', 'julienne' or 'trio' you might as well diary in half an hour in the bog for the afternoon while you're at it.

In fact this was Claridge's, so all the posh nosh was probably superb and I could have ordered porridge or salmon or the full English but I've never been big on breakfast, and the smell of kippers and kedgeree before eleven quite frankly makes me nauseous. Fish for breakfast has always struck me as wrong, like having a croissant for supper or coffee in a pub. Apparently, however, fishie brekkie is the last word in traditional crusty, old English chic ('chic' I believe being the traditional spelling of 'shite'), so Claridge's of course offers it. Not for me, though, nor salmon and scrambled egg on a lightly toasted muffin. Let's face it, how often in my life do I get the chance to have a bowl of Coco Pops?

Anyway, to 'cut to the chase', as people in film say, I was meeting some people from Above The Line Films.

I *do* beg your pardon, I was meeting *with* some people from Above The Line Films. One must of course speak American English when moving in film circles these days (sorry, *motion picture* circles) and since those circles are the ones in which my Controller wishes me to move, American English I must speak when I meet *with* all sorts of motion picture wankers, or, rather, *jerk offs*.

The people from Above The Line are very hip at the moment, the reason being that they recently made a film that some Americans quite liked. It's an interesting thing about the Brit film industry (such as it is) that for all the gung-ho, Cool Britannia jingoism we spout about our cool new British talent, we judge our product exclusively on whether or not people in America go to see it. You could make a British film which every person in Britain went to see twice, plus half the population of the European Community, but unless at least five thousand Americans have also been persuaded to go the style fascists will judge it naff and parochial. On the other hand, if we make a movie which flops everywhere and which *only* five thousand Americans go and see, the director will still be seen as a major burgeoning international talent. This is what the Australians call a cultural cringe. They used to have the same thing about us. In the sixties it was no good being big in Oz, you had to be big in Britain. They've dropped that now and concentrate on America like everyone else. I believe that some New Zealanders still see success in London as important but probably only the ones who supply the lamb to Marks & Spencer.

Anyway, long story short as Lucy would say, there I was, post deeply unsatisfactory shag, sitting at Claridge's 'doing' Coco Pops and kedgeree with three of Britain's brightest motion picture talents. Justin Cocker, an estuary Oxbridge mid-Atlantic drawler who called the toilet the 'bathroom' and asked if they had any bagels and lox. A snarling Scot called Ewan Proclaimer, who took one look at the Claridge's breakfast room and said, 'God, I fuckin' hate the fuckin' English. I mean they are just so fuckin' *English*, aren't they? D'you ken what I'm saying here?'

Also a pencil-thin woman called Petra. On the phone the previous day I had asked Justin Cocker if Petra had a surname and he said that if I needed to ask that question I did not know the British motion picture industry. Which is right, of course, I don't. Which is why I work for sad old telly.

Weird meeting. Like a summit between people from different

planets. The BBC being vaguely located on earth, and Above The Line Films being located somewhere far beyond the galaxy of Barkingtonto. The extraordinary thing is that they think that *they* are the ones who live in the real world. This is because the BBC is publicly funded and is hence some dusty old pampered 1940s welfare state relic which thinks the eighties never happened. Amazing how these days it's hip to assume that the money supplied by vast multinational media conglomerates (writing off their tax losses) is somehow more tough and real and proper than that raised by the public for the purposes of their own entertainment.

Anyway, on this occasion licence fee money appeared to be good enough. (It certainly paid for the breakfast, anyway.) I told them that the BBC was interested in co-producing more films with a view to theatrical release prior to TV screening and that my special area was comedy. It seemed I had come to the right people. They said if I wanted comedy they had comedy. Real comedy. Not crap comedy, they assured me; not all that *fuckin' crap* that the BBC passes off as comedy, not *shite* comedy, but sharp, witty, edgy, in-your-face, on-the-nose and up-your-arse comedy. 'Two words,' they said, 'Zeit' and 'Geist'. In other words, 'Tomorrow's comedy today.'

Well, I can't deny I was excited. This surely was what we wanted. I had only to steer this lot towards Nigel and my standing would again ride high. Ewan Proclaimer produced his script, the eagerly awaited follow-up to his film *Sick Junkie*, which had been 'hugely successful', i.e. some American critics liked it, although it was actually seen by less people than watch the weather on Grampian. *Sick Junkie* had been a career breaker for Ewan, but now he explained that he wanted to move totally away from all that stuff.

His new script is called *Aids and Heroin.*

'It's a comedy about a group of normal, ordinary kids,' said Ewan Proclaimer, 'all heroin addicts, of course. Probably Scottish, perhaps Welsh or Irish . . .'

'Although we'd shoot it in London,' interjected Pencil Petra.

'Well, of course we'd shoot it in London!' Ewan snapped. He

was clearly not a man who liked to be interrupted. 'Morag and I have only just got wee Jamie into a decent school . . . Now these kids survive on the edges of society, right? Dealing drugs, stealing, whoring, ripping off the social. The movie is a week in their ordinary mundane lives. They inject heroin into their eyeballs, they have babies in toilets, they get Aids, they try to raise veins on their private parts in order to inject more heroin, they kill a social worker, they have anal sex in exchange for heroin which turns out to be cut with bleach and kills them, they have abortions, they're raped by gangs of English policemen . . .'

My head was spinning at this apocalyptic vision.

'Excuse me,' I risked an interjection. 'I hope I'm following. This is a comedy we're discussing here?'

'Total comedy,' Ewan assured me, 'but *real* comedy, about what's *actually* happening to kids today, not escapist *English* crap.'

It all sounded very post watershed to me, but you never know these days. Things are moving so fast I confidently expect to see them making bongs out of Squeezy bottles on *Blue Peter*. But anyway, broadcastable or not, I wasn't having any of it. Well really, it makes me so tired. This never-ending diet of sex and drugs and urban horror that well-heeled highly educated young film makers seem to feel duty-bound to serve up as stone-cold naturalism. For heaven's sake, I know that life is tough out there but not exclusively so. There are more adolescents in the Girl Guides and the Sea Scouts than there are teenage junkies, but nobody ever makes a film about them.

I finished my Coco Pops in a marked manner, resisting the temptation to drink the chocolatey milk out of the bowl, and rose to leave.

'Well, thanks for explaining your idea to me, Ewan,' I said. 'Unfortunately the BBC is not in the business of funding cynical tales about drugs and prostitution which purport to reflect everyday Britain merely so that the fashion junkies who make them can swank about at Cannes and then bugger off to work in the States the first chance they get.'

'Look, bollocks to the English bullshit,' Ewan Proclaimer

replied. 'Do you want the picture or not?'

'Ah dinnah,' I said in what I hoped was a Scottish accent, although it almost certainly wasn't. Then I took up the bill and left the room feeling proudly self-assertive. I may not be able to write myself but I can at least protect the public from the self-indulgent witterings of those who can't either.

By the time I got back to Television Centre I had worked myself into a right old self-righteous lather. The first thing I did was to get Daphne to take down a sarky fax telling Above The Line Films where they could shove it. I had no sooner finished doing this and was contemplating a calming game of *Tomb Raider* on my PC when Nigel called and summoned me to his office.

I trudged along the circular corridor convinced that this was it, that the long-awaited shafting was about to be administered. It seemed obvious that Nigel intended to get rid of me before the Prime Minister's imminent visit (set for this Saturday) so that he could take all the credit himself. As I entered the hallowed office, however, it seemed that I was wrong. Nigel was positively beaming at me and actually asked if I wanted a coffee.

'Sam!' he said. 'I just heard you did breakfast with Above The Line and met with Justin, Ewan and Petra.'

I was about to protest that I had only been following orders but he gave me no choice.

'Congratulations, mate! Excellent move. Ewan is a genius and a God-sent antidote to all the crap your department normally commissions.'

Alarm bells began to ring.

'Yes, that's what *he* said,' I replied limply.

'He's just the kind of raw, edgy talent we need for the new film initiative. It would be absolutely sensational if you could bring him and the whole Above The Line ethos into the Beeb. As it happens I'm having dinner with Justin and Petra at Mick and Jerry's tonight so I'll do everything I can to push it along. OK, mate? Well done.'

My coffee had just arrived but I was already rushing out of his office, scarcely bothering even to attempt an excuse. I ran as fast as I could back round the circle, bashing into internal mail trolleys and PAs with trays full of tea as I went. I arrived back in my office just in time to see the fax I had dictated to Daphne emerge from the machine having been transmitted as instructed.

Fate deals me blow after blow.

Dear Penny

I've decided. Since the next medical step for me is a laparoscopy, which is intrusive and not to be entered into lightly (like my bellybutton), it is foolish for me to ignore other possibilities.

Tomorrow is a full moon, my traffic light says I'll be ovulating and Sam will just have to like it or lump it.

Oh my God.

I got home today and Lucy told me that tomorrow night, at midnight, she wants me to take her to the top of Primrose Hill, which is a *public park*, and shag her under the full moon.

I'm still hoping that this is some kind of joke.

Dear Penny

Tonight is the night! Full moon! What's more, the forecast is for a mild night with gentle breezes. Perfect. Perhaps the fates are finally going to be on my side.

Drusilla and I went to a fairy shop in Covent Garden at lunchtime and got some crystals. I don't really believe in that sort of thing but I must say they really are rather beautiful and Drusilla assures me they'll help. We sat together on a bench in Soho Square and energized them. This involved squeezing the crystals in the palms of our hands and, well, energizing them. Drusilla made a sort of low groaning noise but I just con- centrated. I had a tofu pitta bread sarnie from Pret A Manger in the other hand so I imagine that I energized that too, which can't hurt, can it?

I've also bought a nice thick picnic rug from Selfridge's, because you want to be as comfortable as possible on these occasions. Also one of those inflatable pillows that people use in aeroplanes. This is to prop up my bum afterwards because I want to give Sam's sperm as good a downhill launch as I possibly can. I have this vision of millions of them tumbling down some sort of water shoot (like the Summit Plummit at Disneyworld), hurtling off the end and then getting knocked unconscious in a fruitless effort to penetrate my cold unyielding eggs.

I also went to Kookaï and bought an incredible new frock. It's just a sheath, really, and I'm afraid my tum will bulge, but I'll hold it in. The dress cost an entire week's wages but Drusilla insists that this must be a sensual and erotic event, not just a sly bonk in a park. There's to be wine and candles and I must reek of musk and primrose oil and ancient pagan scents. I really didn't know where I was supposed to get ancient pagan scents in London on a Friday afternoon but Drusilla had it all sorted out. Rather conveniently, Boots do a set of soaps that cover the lot and she'd bought me a box as a present.

She also reminded me that I must remember to wear my silkiest pair of split-crotch panties and when I told her that I do not possess any pairs of split-crotch panties, silky or otherwise, she was quite surprised. Drusilla is definitely a dark horse, except I shouldn't be surprised really; in the end being a witch is just about sex, isn't it? Anyway, she insisted that we go immediately to a sex shop and buy some erotic underwear, but when we got in there I just couldn't. It wasn't that I was embarrassed, I was just laughing too much. I mean these places are ridiculous. They have these dildos the size of draught excluders! What on earth you're supposed to do with them I just don't know. Stand them in the hall for people to hang their hats on, perhaps? They also had these sets of Oriental Love Balls, which a girl is supposed to push up and then walk around with them in. I was just saying that I didn't believe any woman ever walked around with Love Balls up her doo-dah when the assistant came over and said, 'How are the Love Balls going, Drusilla?'

'Lovely,' replied Drusilla dreamily, giving her hips a little jiggle and smiling.

Do you know, I swear I heard a clanking sound. I am so parochial.

In the end we agreed that the most sensual thing of all would be to wear no knickers at all. I've always thought naughty underwear was curiously sexless. Except perhaps a sheer silk teddy, or French knickers, but I don't think they'd be right for Primrose Hill and I doubt that you can get grass stains out of silk.

I played Celtic music and clannaed on my Walkman on the tube on the way home to get me into a mood of fertile pagan spirituality. I'm quite excited in a funny sort of way. It's not often I shag alfresco these days. Quite frankly, it never has been a common occurrence with me. Insects and bare bums don't mix.

I hope Sam cheers up about it, though. I regret to have to report that last night, when I told him what was expected of him, he was most unenthusiastic. In fact he got quite hostile. Obviously I can sort of understand his doubting the effectiveness of the plan. It's a long shot, certainly, relying on the faint echoes and rhythms of the ancient world to jolly his sperm along. I'm highly sceptical myself, but I do wish he'd see that we must try everything. We've now been infertile for sixty-two months and all the doctors can think of doing about it is to pump me full of dye and video my uterus. Well, forgive me if I sound feminist, but with that in prospect I feel I have a right to expect Sam to explore every other avenue first.

It's always the way, though, isn't it, Penny? The poor woman gets the short end of the stick. Our bodies are so complicated! *It's like with contraception. The things women have to go through (all pointless in my case, it seems) and yet still men only worry about their own pleasure. I remember when Sam and I first started doing it regularly he wanted me to go on the pill or have a coil fitted because he didn't like condoms. He said they were a barrier between us (well of* course *they are, that surely is the point). He said that they spoiled the sensual pleasure of our lovemaking. Basically what he was saying was that he didn't want to put his dick in a bag. So instead would I mind either filling my body with chemicals or having a small piece of barbed wire inserted into me? In the end, I got a Dutch cap and God was that a palaver! Trying to put one of those in when you've had a bottle and a half of Hirondelle is not easy. The damn thing was always shooting across the bathroom and landing in the basin. Then there was that awful cream you had to put on. The nights that I nearly shoved toothpaste up my fanny and brushed my teeth with spermicidal lubricant! Makes my eyes water just to think about it.*

Anyway, I'm digressing. As I often do when on the subject of the selfishness of men. Well, let's face it, there's just so much scope. But as I was saying re the Primrose Hill bonk, I just have to give everything a try, it's a matter of life and . . . Well, I don't know what, life and no life, I suppose, which is a pretty terrible thought. And anyway who knows what strange and powerful forces there are in the world? I mean the moon does definitely affect people, we know that. You only have to look at dogs. They go potty at full moon. And as Drusilla has pointed out, even vaginal juices have a tidal flow and so, when one comes to think of it, does sperm. I mean it might all just be a case of never having done it when the tide's in. As for ley lines, well I admit that it sounds pretty unlikely. On the other hand certain places do have a special energy. I can remember once feeling very strange during a walk in the Devil's Punchbowl in Surrey, and that's supposed to be a mystic place, I think, isn't it? Sam claims it was the macaroni cheese I'd had for lunch in that pub, but I know it wasn't.

And what's more, apart from any spiritual and mystical considerations, I had hoped that Sam might find the whole idea a bit raunchy. After all, we are lovers, aren't we? Besides being boring old marrieds? Surely we can see all this in the light of a naughty, saucy adventure?

No chance, I'm afraid. Sam didn't get home until half an hour ago (last-minute preparations for the PM tomorrow), and he's insisting that he still has some calls to make. I'm writing this while he whinges and whines about comedy in his study. This was supposed to be our time, a time of erotic and sensual reflection. I've had my bath (by candlelight with rose petals floating on the water) and used all the soaps. I was really beginning to feel quite goddess-like and fertile and Sam is acting like it was just any other bloody night.

I bet Carl Phipps wouldn't be in his study making calls about stupid comedy programmes while his lover lay damp and scented and naked upon their bed below.

No! I must not think that sort of thing. It's wicked.

Sam has agreed to do it and that's the main thing. I can't expect him to suddenly turn into a romantic lead. All I need him to do is shag me at the appointed time and place.

T'will be dark in an hour. The moon is on the wax and the witching hour is nigh. Do you know, Penny? I've got this funny feeling that it might just work.

Dear Self

It's four o'clock in the morning and we've just got back from the police station. They were quite nice about it in the end, once they let me put my trousers back on. I thought I handled the whole matter pretty well, actually.

Dear Penny

Sam was ridiculous tonight, quite bloody ridiculous. I mean you just do not give false names to the police, do you? Particularly 'William Gladstone'. What chance is there of there being a man called William Gladstone having it off on the top of Primrose Hill in the middle of the night? I honestly think that if he hadn't tried to give them a false name they would have let us go. I mean bonking isn't illegal, is it? But of course when he claimed to be a nineteenth-century prime minister they asked for ID and immediately the game was up.

'Oh yes,' said Sam, 'that's it, I remember, my name's Sam Bell just like it says on my credit card. Ha ha. Samuel Bell, William Gladstone; William Gladstone, Sam Bell. Easy mistake to make.'

When they asked him his occupation I said, 'Prat,' which made them laugh and helped a bit, I think.

He looked like one of those men who stand on the end of train platforms. Not much of a turn-on at all. I explained to him as patiently as I could that Drusilla had insisted that a steamy passionate atmosphere was essential. We must both be highly, throbbingly, almost primevally sexually charged. Timeless animals of passion, caught up in the eternal spinning vortex of all creation. After all, I pointed out, if we can't be bothered to put the effort in then we can hardly expect the ancient gods and goddesses of fertility to do so either.

'Hmm,' he said and nodded in a kind of stunned way.

Anyway, I made him go and put on his black tie and dinner suit, which he wears to the BAFTA awards every year. He's always been disappointed when wearing that suit, having never won a single award. They always give them to someone fashionable with smaller ratings. I prayed that the ancient and timeless deities of the firmament would change all that tonight and give him the most important prize of all.

Lucy made me put on black tie, which quite frankly made us look like Gomez and Morticia, particularly since she'd really gone to town with the black eyeliner. I must admit, though, she did look fantastic. Like a beautiful model, I thought. I really did and I said so. 'You look like a beautiful model,' I said and she said, 'Oh yeah sure, I do not.' Odd, that, the way women react to compliments. They'll expend any amount of energy telling you that you never say anything nice to them and that you don't fancy them, but when you do pay them a compliment they say, 'Oh yeah sure, I do not.'

Nonetheless, I think she was pleased.

Sam suddenly started being rather sweet and I must say he looked very nice in his dinner suit. Most men do look good in black tie. Dinner jackets even make a paunch look sort of stately and dignified. Not that Sam has a paunch. Well, maybe a tiny one, but not really. Anyway, I thought he looked lovely, even

113

*though he still insisted on wearing his anorak 'just till we got
down to it'.*

Actually I can scarcely credit it, but it was all beginning to get
rather fun. Lucy had prepared some bits of artichoke on biscuits
(fertile fruit, apparently) and oysters! We had them in front of the
fire with a glass of red wine (just one) before getting in the car.
Lucy had also bought a beautiful black crocheted shawl to keep
her warm and it just looked fantastic with her white skin showing through the black, like a Russian princess or something. As I
say, her make-up was all dark and Gothic around the eyes and
her lipstick was like a gash of shiny crimson. And she'd put on
some long droopy silver earrings I'd never seen before.

All in all, she'd really made an effort, which I loved her for. I
myself had tried to enter into the spirit of things by putting on
the silk boxer shorts I got last Christmas and had so far never
worn.

*I do wish Sam hadn't put on those Donald Duck pants. I know
he was trying to be nice but you don't need Disney characters
when you're trying to be all pagan and ritualistic, even if they are
silk.*

*Anyway, we got there and amazingly found a parking place
almost immediately (were the Gods intervening on our behalf?).
And having got over the usual car palaver (Sam set the alarm
off, I don't know how he manages to do that so often), we stood
there together at the foot of the ancient hill. It was only eleven-
thirty, so we had a good half-hour to climb up it and get down
to it, so to speak. I tried to hold Sam's arm but his hands were
full.*

It probably was silly to take along a stepladder but I thought the
gates would be locked and we'd have to climb over a fence. They
lock Regent's Park up, I know that. Lucy thought it made us look

like burglars and told me to go back and put it on top of the car, which meant five more minutes wrestling with bendy bungies.

It was a very quiet night for London and I must say the hill looked fantastic against the moon. We seemed to have it to ourselves apart from the birds and squirrels and, of course, the spirits of the night. Drusilla had assured me that the spirits would definitely be about. Flitting hither and thither, bringing good fortune for some, a hex for others. I thought I saw one but it turned out to be an unconscious homeless alcoholic slumbering on a bench near the children's playground.

If we succeeded, if the gods really did bring us luck, I was going to bring my children to play on those swings every day.

Funny, as we made our way up the path, to my surprise I really did begin to feel all ancient and beautiful. I tried to close my mind to the fact of dirty, noisy, modern London all around me and allow my body to respond to the timeless rhythms and vibrations of the eternal cycles of life on earth that were swirling about me.

Of course it would have been easier if Sam had not kept telling me to watch out for dogshit, but I suppose he meant well.

I trod in this huge turd the moment we entered the park. Huge. No mortal dog could have passed such a turd. Honestly, I went in almost up to my knee. Any deeper and I would have had to call for a rope. London Zoo is situated at the bottom of Primrose Hill and I was forced to conclude that an elephant must have escaped.

Oh, I do so hate treading in dogshit. I suppose that's what you get for wandering around London's parks in the dark, but why don't people clear up after their dogs? In Australia the council supply plastic bags and special bins. You put your hand in the bag, pick up the turd then fold the bag back over it and drop it in the bin. Superb. And we call them uncivilized. Over here of course the bags would instantly be scattered to the four winds and the bins would be the target of every puerile little prat with a can of spraypaint in the neighbourhood. Graffiti artists? Like hell. God I loathe the way liberal-minded people feel the need to defend this endless depressing scribbling as if it was some kind of vital and vibrant expression of urban culture, rather than just the work of arrogant bored little vandals that it is. I mean, whenever they talk about graffiti on the telly they always show some fabulous mural in the New York style executed over several months and now hanging at the Tate. Of course, people's actual experience of this loathsome vandalism is nothing like that. It's the endless repetition of the same identical scribble, executed purely to flatter the ego of the arrogant dickhead with the spray-can.

Halfway up the hill Sam suddenly started ranting about graffiti, which is a particular hate of his. God knows what made him think of it at that time. I told him to shut up because I was trying to influence my ovulation and I didn't want him spoiling my positive vibe.

At the top of Primrose Hill I was amazed to discover that I was starting to get quite motivated. I mean I had expected to be petrified with embarrassment, but in fact I felt quite sexy. It was such a fine night and Lucy looked so beautiful standing there in the silvery light of the full moon. There's a sort of look-out area at the top of the hill, with benches and a map of the panoramic view of London. We had it all to ourselves and it was suddenly very beautiful, like we were on a flying saucer hovering over London or something. Lucy took off her shawl and put it on a bench, then we stood for a moment, staring at the city all laid out before us. She looked so stunning in just her sexy crimson dress and with a gentle night breeze playing in her hair. I'd been worrying that I might get stage fright under the pressure and be one dick short of an erection, but no way! I was a tiger! I think I fancied her at that moment as much as I've ever fancied her, and that's quite a lot, as it happens.

London looked like a great starry carpet spread all about us. It felt as if we were in Peter Pan *(except that's Kensington Gardens, not Primrose Hill). I thought for a moment about all the thousands of centuries that had gone before, when we could have stood on that very same spot and seen nothing but darkness below us. Suddenly our time on earth and the fact of being human seemed very small indeed. Completely insignificant in the grander scheme of things. Except that what we were hoping to do, what this night was meant to achieve, was in fact as big as the whole universe! New life! A new life was what we had come to this place to make. A brand new beginning. Should we succeed, this very moment would be the dawn of time for that child.*

My baby's entry point into the great circle of eternity.

We chose a place on the grass behind the concrete summit (Sam having first thoroughly checked the area with his torch for dog-do and used hypodermic needles, which was sensible) and laid our blanket on the ground. Then I put out the circle of candles around the blanket (little nightlights in jamjars that would not be spotted from afar) and sprinkled primrose oil about the place.

Then I lay down with the moon on my face and, ahem, raised the hem of my garment. Sam lay down on top of me, and, rather incredibly, we had it off. I must say I was proud of him. I'd been half expecting him to fail to deliver, but apart from complaining a bit about it being painful on his knees and elbows he was quite romantic about it. We kissed a lot (for us) and all that stuff, bit of stroking, etc. I shan't go into detail, but I'm all for that sort of thing, you know, foreplay. It's so easy as the years go by to neglect the preamble and just get straight down to it, so to speak. I regret to say that Sam does tend rather to just roll on top and go for it. He doesn't mean to be insensitive. It's just there always seems to be work in the morning. Anyway, on this occasion we took a bit more time, not much more, but it makes all the difference.

I won't say that I actually had an orgasm, the situation was rather too fraught for that, I'm afraid, but I nearly did and I definitely enjoyed it and when we'd finished I thought we'd done well. After all, it's not every girl that has it off wearing a new satin frock surrounded by candles on the top of Primrose Hill at mid-night under a full moon.

Afterwards we lay there for a little while on the rug (me with pillow under bottom), gathering our thoughts and listening to the breeze in the trees.

Anyway, that was when Sam screamed.

This, I'm afraid, brought an abrupt end to our idyll, as well it might. Unbeknownst to us there had appeared upon the hill a nocturnal dogwalker, a nervous old man who on seeing two pros-trate figures surrounded by candles had thought that a satanic murder was in progress. He had no doubt been suspecting some such occurrence for years and Sam's sudden yelping convinced the old sod that tonight was the night. Off he went to flag down a passing policecar and shortly thereafter we were caught bang to rights (with the emphasis on 'bang') by the officers of the watch.

What had happened was this. As Sam and I had lain there together in the warm and spiritual afterglow of our lovemaking, a squirrel had found its way into Sam's trousers, which Sam had left nearby along with his silk jocks, having stepped out of the whole lot in one. I don't know what had led the squirrel into this dark territory. Perhaps it was after Sam's nuts. What I do know is that the squirrels of Primrose Hill and Regent's Park are in-credibly cheeky on account of the manner in which they are indulged by all and sundry. Anyway, there Sam's trousers lay in a state of sort of concertina'd readiness waiting for Sam to step back into them. As Sam stood bent and hovering above his trousers, one foot in and the waistband firmly gripped, the squirrel popped out its head to see what was what. There was of course a confrontation.

They faced each other in the night, Sam staring down at the squirrel, the squirrel staring up at Sam, or in fact at Sam's bollocks, which it was situated directly underneath.

Amazingly, it was Sam who screamed first.

Lucy says it was a squirrel but if it was a squirrel then someone's been feeding them steroids. This looked more like a ferret or a weasel to me, possibly an urban fox. I'd just risen to my feet, idly thinking of this and that, contentedly contemplating the large and joyful whisky I'd be treating myself to when we got home. I reached down to pull up my trousers and instantly I felt this hot breath upon my bollocks! Looking down between my legs I saw it, eyes blazing, teeth bared, talons poised. Whatever it was, it appeared to me to be getting ready to rip my scrotum off! Of course I screamed. Who wouldn't have screamed with an alien creature hovering beneath his bollocks! Of course I know that Lucy is convinced it was a squirrel and it's true that Primrose Hill is amply supplied with squirrels. It's also true that these appallingly over-indulged tree rats tend to treat all humans as nothing more than sources of free food. Nonetheless I contend that what I saw fossicking around in my trousers tonight on Primrose Hill was like no squirrel I have ever seen. It was big and tough and toothy and wicked-looking and it will haunt my slumbers for many a night to come.

The police were upon us almost before we knew it. We did not hear them coming because Sam was leaping about beating his hands between his legs and shouting, 'Ahh! Ahh! Get a stick! Ahh! It's going for my bollocks!' I think that the squirrel must have seen the coppers first, actually, because by the time they arrived Sam's trousers appeared to be empty (apart from him, of course). They were nonetheless still very much unhitched, which was all rather embarrassing. I was all right because I had only to shake my dress back down, but Sam got into an awful mess trying to pull his trousers up. I think that somehow he managed to get his foot through his belt loop and as the officers breasted the hill Sam was still bent double wrestling to free the whole thing up. He had his back to them and I regret to say that the sight that he must have presented to them in the torchlight could not have been pleasant. I should mention here that Sam's Donald Duck pants were also round his knees so that there was a second full moon shining on Primrose Hill tonight. I think we were very lucky that they didn't do us for indecency.

Anyway, as I say, had Sam not insanely attempted to give the police a false name I think they would have let us off there and then, but instead they took us in. I certainly think that Sam's following up his false name débâcle by warning them that he was an intimate of Downing Street made matters worse. I mean, you do not try and pull rank on the rozzers, particularly if you haven't got your trousers on. I didn't really mind getting run in, it sort of made me feel even more pagan and dangerous, like a witch or an outlaw, as if the forces of order had tried to constrain our tryst but had arrived too late! And anyway, I knew they'd let us off in the end. After all, it isn't a crime to assume a pseudonym, is it? I don't think it is, or what would they do about stage names? In the acting profession if you have the same name as somebody else, Equity actually make you change it, so it can't be illegal, can it?

Well, anyway, we sat about a bit at the police station and after a cup of tea and one or two off-colour innuendos from the young constables they let us go. Sam got quite shirty about the jokes the coppers made, which I thought was stupid since they were no worse than the sort of rubbish he commissions every day. They even dropped us off back at our car, which I thought was nice of them.

Anyway, it's all over now, for better or worse, and here I am, lying in bed. Sam's already snoring, sleeping the sleep of the great and powerful lover, but I'm wide awake, clutching my crystals, humming Celtic hymns and praying to Gaia to deliver new life into my body. Let Mother Nature make me a mother too!

In my heart and my soul I truly believe she will.

Well, it's now the evening following our Primrose Hill tryst and today has not gone well.

In fact, today has gone worse than I could have dreamt possible.

On the plus side Lucy is very happy about our success last night. She seems to have convinced herself that the power of positive thinking has been the missing factor in us getting pregnant. She has therefore decided to believe absolutely and fundamentally that Primrose Hill will work its magic. When I got home this afternoon I found her sitting in front of the fire watching a Saturday afternoon film on Channel Four and looking wistful, sipping camomile tea and gently trying to will her eggs to envelop my sperm. It's a strange thing, but you know she did sort of look pregnant, I can't really say why, but sort of serene and womanly and, well, fertile. I know it's silly to say that, and particularly silly to get our hopes up, but then perhaps it's not. Perhaps Lucy is right. Perhaps positive thinking is what we need. Anyway, if there's any balance of fair play in the world we'll be pregnant; because the rest of my life is double buggered squared.

I have not mentioned my inner torment to Lucy, of course. When she asked me how things had gone today I said, 'Fine.' I did not feel that in her present state of self-induced mystical empowerment she would want to be told that her husband was an utter joke. I did not feel it fair to tell that sweet, trusting, potential nestbuilder that the career of her champion and protector now hangs by less than a single thread. That we are shortly to be paupers. I simply could not bring myself to tell her that the Prime Minister's visit to *Livin' Large* was the most right royal cock-up since Henry the Eighth discovered girls.

Therefore, Book, unable to seek support from my preoccupied wife, I am turning for solace to you. It happened like this.

Despite my late-night run-in with the law on the previous evening, I was up bright and early this morning. *Livin' Large* goes out live at nine a.m. and I had promised to take my niece Kylie along, which meant going to the studio via Hackney to pick her up. Kylie is the daughter of my sister Emily and has apparently, of late, taken an interest in politics. My sister, anxious to encourage this new maturity in a girl who up until now has liked only ponies and Barbie, asked me to take her along. To add to the excitement, Grrrl Gang, a kind of post-post-Spice Girls group, are also appearing on the show and Emily says that Kylie worships the ground they walk on. Or, in fact, more accurately, given their

121

ridiculous shoes, she worships the ground they walk seven inches above.

Kylie was something of a shock. I had last seen her about six months before at a family do and she had been a very sweet and pretty little eleven-year-old who had a picture of a horse in a locket round her neck. I'm afraid to have to report that the butterfly has reverted to a caterpillar and that Kylie or 'K Grrrl', as she now wishes to be known, is a horrid little pre-teen brat. Her nice blonde hair has red streaks inexpertly dyed into it. She has a nose stud (Emily says she got it done on a school trip to Blackpool and that Kylie has threatened to run away if it is removed). She wears enormously baggy army combat trousers into which eight or nine of her could be fitted. Her tummy is bare save for a tattoo of a rat holding a hypodermic needle (mercifully a transfer). Her crop-top T-shirt has the words 'DROP DEAD' printed on it and her once-pretty face is now contorted into a permanent sulky scowl.

I asked her if she was excited about going to the studio. The look of astonished contempt she gave me would have scrambled an egg.

'Oh *yeah*! *Right, as if!* Like I'm *really* going to get excited about going to a crap *kids'* show. Yeah, *right*, that's *really* likely.'

I could not have felt more withered if I had been a sultana. This girl made me feel like a piece of one-hundred-year-old shit. I was grateful that I'd done my duty by Lucy on the previous evening because this child was in danger of un-manning me entirely. I did my best to engage her interest, which was, of course, fatal.

'The Prime Minister will be there.'

'The Prime Minister is a meat-eating fascist.'

'Grrrl Gang will be playing live.'

'Grrrl Gang are crap and sad. They don't even sing on their records because it's all done by a computer, *if* you didn't know.'

'I'll introduce you to Tazz.'

'Tazz is a moronic duh brain who wouldn't have got anywhere if all the sad old men at the BBC didn't fancy her.'

I thought this was extremely unfair. Tazz is an excellent presenter and a lovely girl. Yes, it's true that she's fairly gorgeous and does indeed have the factor that in showbiz is traditionally called 'something for the dads', but there's far more to her than that. Being consistently perky for three hours on a Saturday morning is more difficult than a lot of people think. It takes real talent.

'Don't you like *Livin' Large*, then?'

'Oh *yeah*! *Sure, as if*! *Livin' Large* is crap.'

'Well don't come, then.'

'No, *I'll come, I suppose.*'

And so we went. Kylie, like most young people of my acquaintance, wanted it both ways.

We got in the car and Kylie sorted through my tapes, rejecting every one with pained groans of contempt before turning up the radio full to prevent further conversation. Actually I wished that Lucy had been with us to see her. Kylie has always been such a nice little girl. Lucy tends to see her as an example of the joys we are missing out on by being childless. Up until now I have agreed with her on this point. Kylie's dolls, her love of stories, her obsession with all animals has always been just so cute (a word I hate), but that's what Kylie was. We went on holiday with them the Easter before last and it rained all the time. Kylie spent the week lying on her tummy in front of the fire reading the entire Narnia saga. It was a lovely thing to see and Lucy and I had wished she was ours. Well all I can say is that if ever we do have one she can go to a boarding school for the grumpy pubescent bit, because it is *not* attractive.

Anyway, back to my disaster. Whatever Kylie might have felt, I personally was very much looking forward to the morning and meeting Tazz. She really is gorgeous and quite simply every bloke in the country fancies her. Heterosexual blokes, that is. I realize that these days it is not done to presume that people are necessarily heterosexual. Although, quite frankly, if I was gay I reckon Tazz would turn me around, but then I said that to Trevor and he said, 'Well, does Leonardo di Caprio turn you around?' To which the answer is a very big 'No.' Quite frankly, I think that Leonardo di Caprio looks like Norman Lamont. It's just that Tazz is so *perky*, the most pathologically perky girl on television, perky beyond all reasonable human expectations, a living, breathing perky force. She is also, I'm told, very nice, and a real enthusiast about things like Comic Relief. Besides all this, she wears tiny little crop-tops and microscopic little skirts which for somebody like me who spends his time at TV Centre talking to plump, grumpy, unshaven comedians about whether they can say knob before nine o'clock is a very welcome change.

This morning, rather disappointingly, Tazz was wearing trousers. Probably a directive from Downing Street. I don't think the PM is an ogler, but he's only human, for God's sake. Many a strong man's eyes have twitched downwards to check out the knicker triangle when facing Tazz on the 'Hot Seat' sofas. The word is that even Cliff Richard took a peek. The last thing Downing Street wants is the PM caught having a perv on a twenty-two-year-old's gusset.

Having such a gorgeous girl presenter is an essential part of kids' TV these days. I mean the kids themselves would probably be just as happy to watch an enthusiastic old granny, but the bleary, beery students who haven't gone to bed yet want something sexier, as do the dads who say, 'Let's watch Tazz on the BBC. She's much better than that computer-generated ferret they have on ITV.'

The show started off fine. I got Kylie sat down amongst the other kids whom at first she affected to despise but I soon noticed that she had hooked up with two eleven-year-old sisters whose mother seemed to have dressed them as prostitutes, in so much as their skirts were the merest pelmets and their tops barely covered the fact that there was as yet nothing to barely cover. Having seen Kylie settled in, I went up to the control box. It's rather fun being an executive producer. People bring you coffee and things and I was surprised to discover that I was clearly the most senior figure present. I recall reflecting how generous it was of Nigel to stay away and let me take my rightful place centre stage as the BBC's official Prime Minister host. Ha! And double ha!

Anyway, after the usual half-hour of cartoons ('We hate showing them but it's what the kids want'), Tazz introduced Grrrl Gang. Despite my niece's snooty contempt for them, having

Grrrl Gang on was quite a coup (what's more I spotted Kylie screaming with all the other little grrrls). Grrrl Gang are the newest girl group, tougher and more street than whatever the last one was. None of these groups is ever going to do what the Spice Girls did in '96, but Grrrl Gang are pretty hip at present. They were 'In the Dock', which was another of these sections in which the star guest takes questions from the kids in the audience and on the phones. Which in reality means a series of tremulous voices from Milton Keynes and Dumfriesshire asking, 'How do you get to be a pop star?'

To my surprise the answer to this turned out to be quite simple.

'You just got to be yourself, right? Livin' it large. Kickin' it big. That's all it takes,' the grrrls of Grrrl Gang assured the kids of Britain.

'You gotta kick it, girl! Big yourself up!'

'Yeah, and don't let no one disrespect you, right?'

'Cos it's about babe control, right? Grrrl strength. Like if you tell a teacher you wanna be a pop star, right, or an astronaut? And she says like, *no way, babe*, you've got to work in a factory or go on the dole! You tell her you are going to be a pop star or an astronaut, right? Cos you can be whatever you want, grrrl. A pop star or an astronaut . . . or . . . anything.'

'Yeah, if you want it, grrrl, just grab it. It's a babe revolution.'

That being sorted out to everyone's satisfaction, a tiny voice from Solihull asked if the grrrls had heard that their manager was predicting that they would soon be bigger than the Beatles.

'We're already bigger than the Beatles, aren't we?' said one of Grrrl Gang. 'I mean, there's five of us and there were only four of them.'

The rest of the Grrrls nodded wisely at this.

Then Tazz announced that it was environment week on *Livin' Large* and that the show was committed to biggin' up the environment big time, right. The grrrls from Grrrl Gang all let it be known that they had big respec' for this concept and it was at this point that I got my first intimation that the morning was not necessarily going to go entirely smoothly. Tazz had brought on the *Livin' Large* 'Green Professor', a nice, wacky, bearded git called Simon. The idea was that Simon would discuss green issues with Tazz, Grrrl Gang and the kids.

Sometimes these things can be a little sticky, but one of the grrrls from Grrrl Gang had a question right off.

'Talking about the environment, right,' she said, 'do you know about animals and stuff, then?'

Simon positively glowed. 'Well, a little. I'm Chief Zoologist to the Royal Natural Academy.'

'All right, answer me this, then,' said the grrrl. 'How come birds have rude names, then?'

Simon was clearly not following.

'You know,' the grrrl continued. 'Cock, tit, thrush.'

Up in the control box we all froze.

'Warbler.'

The kids giggled and Simon stuttered.

'Well, I . . .'

In control the phone lines were lighting up already as irate parents all over the country began to call in to complain. The producer screamed into Tazz's earpiece telling her to move on. I could see her wincing on camera six.

'My brother used to have a white mouse called Big Balls,' said a second member of Grrrl Gang.

'Yeah, but that's just a personal name, innit?' replied the first. 'Not a breed.'

At that point Tazz was able to throw to her male partner who was standing next to the Gunk Tank ready to Gunk Dunk the weatherman from *Top of the Morning TV*, a cable channel morning show.

Looking back, I suppose I should have taken it as a warning. The warm complacent glow I had been feeling (Lucy stonked up; me about to be the sole facilitator of a glorious TV moment with the PM) suddenly chilled a bit. This was live telly and things could go wrong. But the panic in the box subsided and I comforted myself that it was probably good luck to get the gremlins out of the way first. A glance at my watch informed me that the PM was due in twenty minutes so I decided to make my way to the front of TV Centre to be ready to receive him.

Oh, how naive I'd been.

To think that I had actually believed that I was to be allowed to glory in this moment alone. Ha! I cringe at my stupidity. When I got to the reception area I discovered that a welcome committee had already assembled. Nigel was there, of course, standing on the red carpet trying to look both relaxed and important in equal measure, but he was way way back, bobbing up and down to see, and you just can't stand on your tiptoes in a dignified and commanding manner. In front of Nigel, all jostling for position, were the Corporation's Chief of Accounting, also the Heads of Marketing, Networking, Global Outreaching and Corporate Affairsing. Besides these, I could see the BBC2 Channel Controller, who was officially junior to Nigel but was ahead on the carpet because he was more fashionable and tipped in the media to shaft Nigel by next Christmas. Also present were the Head of Television and the Head of Radio, also the Head of Television and Radio (Radio and Television Group) and the Chief Programming Coordinator and the Chief Coordinating Programmer and the Deputy Director General, of course the Director General himself, the Chairman of the Board of Governors and the Board of Governors. Basically, the entire senior executive management structure of the Corporation had turned out so that they could say they had met the PM and also no doubt to sneak an ogle at Tazz.

I took my place at the back of the crowd quietly determining to find a moment to proclaim loudly that despite being far and away the most junior senior executive present I was in charge on the ground. It was my gig.

There were five or six Downing Street minders buzzing about the place as well, phones and pagers going off like the martians were about to land. I saw Jo Winston and waved but I'm afraid she either didn't see me or didn't recognize me. A palpable buzz amongst the minders and the cops announced the imminent arrival of the great man. *Livin' Large* was covering the main gate with news cameras and I heard a radio crackle that the PM's car was just coming off the Westway and down into Wood Lane.

Then they were upon us. Outside the main gates heading south towards Shepherd's Bush was the mini cavalcade, two motor-cycle outriders at each end sandwiching three cars of which the PM's Daimler with its darkened rear windows was the middle one. As the procession drew up opposite the main entrance the front motorbikes pulled across the road into the oncoming traffic to block the northbound traffic. Clever idea, I thought. Wish I could do that. A person can sit in the middle of that road for five minutes waiting for a chance to pull across. For the PM's driver it was the work of an instant, however, and, leaving behind the two secret service cars, the Daimler pulled up to the famous IN barrier of BBC Television Centre.

And then came the first of the day's truly momentous disasters.

Book, my hand shakes as I report that the barrier did not rise.

The entire top brass of the BBC (plus me) stood transfixed with horror as the prime ministerial Daimler drew to a reluctant halt whilst a little old man in a peaked cap emerged from the security hut that stands beside the barrier.

'My God,' I heard the Deputy Director General exclaim to the Director General, 'that fellow is asking the Prime Minister if his name's on the Gate List.'

The DDG's voice was the only sound. None of us could speak. We just watched in dumbstruck silence as down at the gate a negotiation began to take place between the BBC guard and the Prime Minister's driver.

I could feel my bowel start to loosen. The BBC gate men are notorious, positively Soviet in their trancelike commitment to the letter of BBC law. Their duty is to defend the gates of Television Centre against all but those who have passes or whose names are on the Gate List, and they discharge this duty with a lack of personal initiative that would have surprised a Stepford wife. In fact only last week a story went round that Tom Jones had been refused entry because his name was not on the Gate List, even though he had got out of his Roller and sung 'It's Not Unusual', 'Delilah' and 'What's New, Pussycat?' on the pavement.

Jo Winston's radio crackled. It was the voice of the Prime

Minister's driver. We could see him talking into his mouthpiece from where we stood.

'They won't lift the barrier, Jo. The guard says there's no name on his Gate List.'

Oh, my fucking giddy bollocks!

'Tell him it's the Prime Minister!' Jo snapped into her radio.

'I have. He says, oh yeah and he's Bruce Forsyth.'

'But it *is* the Prime Minister.'

'I know it's the Prime Minister, miss. I'm his driver, but this man says there's no name on his Gate List.'

Everyone in the reception committee twitched in horror. The Chairman of the Board of Governors turned to the Director General.

'Why has the Prime Minister's name not been forwarded to the gate?' he said.

The Director General turned to the Deputy Director General.

'Why has the Prime Minister's name not been forwarded to the gate?'

The Deputy Director General repeated the question to the Head of Television and Radio who asked it of the Head of Television. He asked Nigel the Channel Controller and Nigel turned to the man who was in charge on the ground, the man whose gig it was.

'Sam!' he hissed.

Before Nigel could ask me why the Prime Minister's name had not been forwarded to the gate, I pushed my way through to the front of the group and grabbed Jo's radio.

'Tell the idiot at the gate that this is Sam Bell, BBC Controller, Broken Comedy and Variety!' I barked, and was rather disconcerted to notice that a number of minders, both BBC and Government, noted down my name. 'The Prime Minister is appearing on *Livin' Large* and he is to be allowed through immediately!'

After a tense moment during which we could all see the driver conveying my message to the guard, the driver radioed back.

'He says he's going to need a programme number for *Livin' Large* to check with the studio. He says nobody told him about any prime minister and he thinks it's a wind-up.'

Of course!

Now I understood the problem in all its horror. Nobody trusts anybody in television any more. That is its curse. There has been such a plethora of shows based on practical jokes and nasty cons on TV over the past few years that everybody in the industry lives in a state of constant paranoia. They check their hotel rooms for hidden cameras, their bathrooms for tiny mikes. Nobody is safe. Impressionists ring up celebrities pretending to be other celebrities, tricking them into making appalling indiscretions which are then broadcast to the nation. Hoax current affairs programme researchers fool naive politicians into commenting on non-existent issues so as to make them look like complete idiots. False charities con publicity-desperate public figures into earnestly espousing ludicrous fictitious causes and campaigns. Candid cameras record people's selfish reactions to prostrate figures in the street and ticking bags on buses. Only last week there was a huge scandal at TV Centre when a left-wing comic from Channel Four managed to blag his way onto *Newsnight* and get himself interviewed as the Secretary of State for Wales. It was only when he said he loved his job because of the ready supply of sheep that they rumbled him.

This hapless gate guard, seeing the *Livin' Large* cameras looming behind him, clearly suspected that he was the subject of what is known in the business as a 'gotcha'. He imagined that if he let the Daimler through, Noel Edmunds or Jeremy Beadle would leap out of the boot and lampoon him.

Nigel had joined me in the little cluster of people around Jo's radio.

'Give the bastard the programme number,' he hissed in my ear.

It was the obvious thing to do and I would have done it, except that I did not have the programme number. Why would I? I am a senior executive. I have people to have that type of thing for me. So does Nigel, of course, and his person is me. He was nearly in tears.

'Sam! You're in charge on the ground!' There was no pretence at hissing now. 'Get the barrier lifted!'

I gave Jo back her radio and set off for the barrier, which was a distance of perhaps fifty metres. For a moment I tried to maintain my dignity but trying to walk at running pace looks even more panicky than running, so I ran. At the barrier I could see that the guard was shaken but determined. For all he knew this could be a test of his guarding abilities. We have all seen films where the guard nods the general through and then the general turns on the guard and bollocks him for not demanding to see a pass. The gate guard did not wish to make that mistake. All in all he had clearly decided that whether it was a hoax or not the safest policy for him was to cling to the rules like a paranoid limpet.

'He hasn't got a pass. His name's not on the list and you haven't got a programme number. The rules are very clear.'

I wondered how the PM was taking all this. It was impossible to say since, as I have said, the rear windows of the Daimler were darkened. To see him I would have had to put my head through the driver's window, which would probably have resulted in my being shot. The shadowy nature of the PM's countenance was of course a contributory factor to the gate guard's doubts. I thought about asking whether the Premier would mind stepping out for a moment and showing himself, but I did not have the nerve.

'Right,' I said, and grabbing the gate I attempted to lift it by brute force. This was pointless, of course. I heaved and I heaved and the guard threatened to call the police, of whom there were four in evidence. I think if I had bent the barrier backwards it might have snapped but supposing it had boinged back and killed someone? A flying splinter might blind the PM!

I had to think straight. Force was not the answer. I let go of the gate and strode back to the guard.

'Ring the switchboard,' I said. 'Ask them to ring *Livin' Large* and get them to give you a programme number.'

There was an agonizing wait for the switchboard to respond. It was a Saturday, after all, and TV Centre is always a bit dead on a Saturday. Eventually the guard got through, but only as far as the switchboard, who refused to put him through to *Livin' Large*.

'They're live on air at the moment,' the guard said, 'and not taking calls in the control box.'

'I know they're live on air, that's the whole . . .'

What could I do? I know these people, people at gates, people on doors, people with lists. They are immovable. They cannot be reasoned with. Over the years they have stopped me going into clubs, pubs, departure lounges, the wrong entrance at cricket grounds and, most days, my own place of work. The mountain would have to go to Mohammed.

I set off to run back to the studio to get the programme number. As I sprinted up the carpark turning circle and back into the studio complex I could feel the eyes of every single superior I had upon me. They burned into my back as I ran past the famous Ariel Fountain and into the Centre. Amazingly, I did not instantly get lost and rush into a drama studio, ruining a take, like I normally do. I pushed my way straight into *Livin' Large*, bursting in on the show while a boy band (called Boy Band) were singing a song about being in love (called 'Bein' In Love'). I grabbed a camera script from a floor manager, noted down the programme number and charged back out towards the gates.

As I emerged from the building clutching the precious number I could see that the Daimler had been allowed through. The police, it seems, had taken charge and threatened the gate guard with immediate arrest if he did not lift his barrier and now the Prime Minister was on the red carpet being profusely apologized to by the Chairman of the Board of Governors and the Director General.

The PM laughed, he smiled, he said that these things happened and that we were not to worry about it at all. Had it not been for the flashing eyes and gritted teeth I might almost have imagined that he meant it.

As they bustled the great man off for make-up I tried to make a face at Nigel as if to say, 'Phew, got away with that, didn't we?' He would not even look at me.

Back in the studio Tazz was telling the cameras that the most mega honour in television history was about to be visited upon the kidz of *Livin' Large*, and that the Prim-o Minister-o, the Main Man UK, was already in the house!

There was cheering, there was shouting, the *Livin' Large* goblin puppets jumped up and down in front of the camera, Tazz beamed, the male presenter (whose name I can never remember) grinned, the floor managers tried to look all serious and then the great moment was upon us, the PM was about to go on. Most of the bigwigs were watching the show in a hospitality suite on the sixth floor, but I was in the control box along with Nigel and the Head of Television.

'Terrible fucking cock-up at the gate, Nigel,' said the Head of Television.

'Heads will roll,' said Nigel.

'Yes, they certainly will, I'll make sure of that,' I said quickly, but I knew that Nigel had meant my head.

Then the bank of TV monitors which faced us over the heads of the vision mixers, PAs, directors, etc, suddenly lit up with the beaming countenance of the Prime Minister. He looked great. The kids cheered. I felt that the worst of the day was behind us.

Tazz, bless her, lobbed him the first ball beautifully.

'Is it true, Prime Minister, that you play the electric guitar?'

'Perfect!' shouted Nigel in the box. 'Well done, Tazz.'

Nigel was clearly attempting to assume credit for the planting of this question, which had actually been my work. I wasn't having it.

'Yes, good girl, that's exactly what I told her to ask,' I said pointedly.

The PM smiled broadly. He raised his eyebrows in a self-deprecating shrug as if to say that he couldn't imagine how Tazz had heard about that.

'Look,' he said. 'You know a lot of kids these days think that politicians are fuddy and they're duddy but it's just not true. Yes, I do play the electric guitar and I love to surf the Internet. I'm just a regular bloke who likes popmusic, comedy with proper rude bits in it and wearing fashionable trousers. Just like you, Jazz.'

We all gulped slightly at this but Tazz quite rightly let it go and threw the floor open to the assembled children. It went wonderfully. The Prime Minister was frank, open and honest. Yes, he had a pet as a child, a hamster called Pawpaw. His favourite meal was egg and chips, but there must be proper ketchup. He loved soccer with a passion and he thought that Britain could again be great at it. He mentioned again how much he liked popmusic and that he played the electric guitar.

We could see that the PM was enjoying himself. Jo Winston had joined us in the box and she was beaming. The incident at the gate seemed to be forgotten. It was beginning to look like we'd got away with it.

Then my niece Kylie asked a question.

'Mr Prime Minister. With more young people than ever living rough on the streets, with your government cutting benefits to young people more than ever before, with class sizes at record levels and with children's hospitals being forced to close, don't you think that it's an act of disgusting cynicism to come on here and pretend that you care at all about what really matters to young people?'

Oh my raving giddily diddily fuck.

The PM was absolutely not ready for it. He was stopped dead. At any other time he could easily have fielded an attack like Kylie's. He would have told her that they were putting in more money than the other lot. That they were tackling a culture of dependency. That they were targeting benefit where it was really needed. I'd heard him do it any number of times in interviews and he always convinced me. But on this occasion he just wasn't ready.

He had thought himself safe. He *should* have been safe.

'Well . . . I . . . uhm . . . I do care . . . but I . . .'

Kylie pressed home her advantage.

'Do you care about the children of single mothers? Because most of them will go hungry tonight . . .'

'Shut that fucking kid up!' the Head of Television screamed. Jo Winston's knuckles were white around the pen she clutched. The control box hotline rang. Nigel picked it up. 'Shut that fucking kid up.' I could hear the voice of the DG himself crackling on the other end.

'Shut that fucking kid up!' Nigel shouted at me and I dutifully relayed the message into the studio link, nearly blowing poor Tazz's ear off.

'No, for heaven's sake, let him answer!' Jo Winston shouted at me, but it was too late.

'Well, we're going to have to leave it there,' Tazz was saying, with a grin frozen on her face. 'So here's the new video from Sir Elton John.'

It could not have looked more terrible. Jo Winston was right. The PM needed to reply but instead Kylie was left with the last word and the Main Man UK looked like a piece of shit.

Jo Winston left the control box without a word. Her look, however, spoke volumes. She thought I'd stitched her up.

'Who supplies us with the fucking kids?!' the Head of Television shouted. I knew which kid he was referring to and I kept my mouth shut.

Even before Elton John had finished his song the Downing Street posse were out of the building, departing in fury, swearing revenge on the BBC and claiming loudly that the PM had been set up. The Director General had tried to tempt the great man to a glass of wine (a grand reception buffet was all waiting). He actually chased after the prime ministerial Daimler round the turning circle with a bottle of claret in his hand. But any hope of post-broadcast jollies, I'm afraid, had been dashed by the as yet unclaimed little girl in the studio.

In the control box an inquiry was underway. The Deputy Director General had arrived and also the Head of Radio and Television. They knew they were in trouble. Relations between the Beeb and Number Ten are always strained and the licence fee always seems to be up for renewal. Everybody was all too aware that publicly embarrassing the Prime Minister on live TV was not the best way to ensure the future of advert-free public service broadcasting in the UK. As my various superiors spoke, contemplating the wrath that they must face from their own superiors, I was painfully aware that below us the studio was emptying. Looking down through the great glass windows onto the floor, I could see that the bulk of the audience had been escorted out and the scene-shifters were beginning to strike the set. Standing alone in the middle of all the activity and looking rather lonely and scared was my niece Kylie. Obviously she had no idea where to go or what to do; I had said that I would collect her after the show. The problem was that I knew that if I went anywhere near her the game would be up.

Then the game was up anyway. Nigel spotted her.

'That appalling little anarchist is still there,' he said. 'I don't believe it! That means she must belong to one of the crew!'

They all stared down. Kylie was looking more isolated than ever. The deconstruction of a TV studio after a programme has been made is a noisy, frenzied business. Large things roll across the floor, even larger things descend from the ceiling. Many men and women bustle about shouting. To be a twelve-year-old child abandoned in the middle of it would be a pretty intimidating experience and I could see that Kylie was starting to think about having a cry. She wasn't the only one.

'If Downing Street get to hear that she belongs to an employee they'll never believe we didn't set them up,' said the Deputy Director General. 'Go and find out who the hell she's with, Bell.'

Hope! A chance! I might just get away with it! All I had to do was rush down, get Kylie out and then blame it on the friend of a friend of a scene-shifter. I would promise a full investigation and then cover the whole thing up. I was about to bound out of the box when I saw Kylie tearfully hailing a passing floor assistant. I watched in horror as the floor assistant put her microphone to her lips. It all seemed to happen in slow motion. My whole life passed before my eyes.

'Hello, Control.' The floor manager's voice floated out of the console loud and clear. 'I've got a little girl here called Kylie, says she's Sam Bell's niece. Is he about at all because she wants to go home.'

Dear Pen Pal

Honestly, trust Sam. Just when I want to be at my absolute most relaxed and non-tense he has gone and made a complete ass of himself at work. He tried not to tell me about it which was nice of him seeing as I'm trying to be as one with my Karma, but he was writing at his book for so long that I had to ask him and it all came out. I feel awful for him, but I'm afraid I've had to tell him that I'm not going to think about it, I just can't. Every fibre of my being is currently dedicated to being in tune with the ageless

rhythm of life and, however you look at it, the politics of tele-
vision are simply not a part of the ageless rhythm of life. Sam
doesn't mind. He never wants to talk about anything anyway.
He's a terrible bottler-upper, like most men, I think. They don't
want to touch, they don't want to talk. They just want to drink,
watch TV, drink and bonk.

Dear Book

The *Livin' Large* story was in all the papers on Sunday (PM
humbled by child) and they're still carrying it today. I've been
named in every single article, of course. Despite me issuing a
very clear statement, nobody believes that I didn't set it all up.
It's just too convenient what with the girl being my niece and all.
The papers tried to go after Kylie as well, but I'd guessed they
would and told Emily that if Kylie said even *one* word to the
press Emily would no longer be my sister. Kylie is now house
grounded with the curtains drawn until it blows over.

I did not go in to work today and took the phone off the hook.
I really am in very deep shit and I don't want to talk to Lucy
about it because she has enough on her mind. Funny how writing this book has actually ended up as a sort of therapy for me,
although it has nothing to do with having kids.

Dear Penny

I feel terribly sorry about Sam's travails but despite that I also
feel curiously centred and at one, almost elated. I know I must
not get my hopes up, but I do definitely feel different. Anyway,
there's nothing wrong with being positive, is there? I don't want
to suppress or fight whatever may or may not be happening in my
body with negative thinking. I'm sure that mental attitude has
enormous power over the physical self. And I do feel differently
this month. I don't know why, but I do. Who knows . . .?

Sam seems to think he's going to lose his job but if only I could
be pregnant I wouldn't mind about us being poor or anything. I'd
live in one room. I wouldn't care, not if I had a baby. Sam always

says, 'Ha!' when I say things like that and of course I know he's right. Nobody wants to be poor and live in just one room, but if all we have would buy me a baby I'd spend it tomorrow.

Dear Book

Lucy keeps going on about not caring about being poor, only about getting pregnant. She says she'd happily see us with nothing as long as we have a child. The problem is that we're probably going to have nothing whether we have a child or not. Penniless and infertile would be a lot to take, I think. On the other hand, Lucy seems very certain that it's going to work this time. She really has started to believe in the power of positive thinking. She's even said that if it's a girl she'll call it Primrose. I hope she's right. She does look glowing.

Actually if it does work I'll get her to do some positive thinking about me keeping my job.

Penny

My period started this morning.

I just want to die.

Why did I let myself hope? How could I have been so pathetic? I don't know why, but I was. What with the crystals and the ley lines and the positive thinking and everything. I just thought for once I'd get some luck. Just for once it would be me who was lucky. But of course it wasn't. Obviously. Shit, shit, shit, shit.

Why me?! Why bloody me?! Some women scarcely even want children and have them.

I want nothing else! All my life I've wanted to have children. Right from the first game I ever played, I've known I wanted to be a mum. It's my life's fucking ambition.

But I can't do it.

Sixty-three periods! Sixty-three fucking months of trying and trying and trying and nothing! I feel wretched, just wretched (quite apart from these God-awful period pains). I keep thinking, why me? I mean, why should I be the one who can't have a little baby to hold? Why? My sister's got two. Melinda's got one. Every bloody woman in Sainsbury's seems to have about twelve. I know I shouldn't resent them but sometimes I do. It just is so unfair! Of course I know that lots of other women are in the same boat as me and all that but I just don't *care about them. That's all. I* don't.

Dear Self

Well, the Primrose Hill Bonk bore no fruit. Bugger.

I'm afraid to say that even I had begun to get my hopes up a bit. Poor Lucy was being so positive that she made me feel positive too. I was even having fantasies about what life would be like if we had one. Just tea-time and story-telling-type fantasies, that sort of thing. Loading up the car to go camping and

I'm going to stop now.

Dear Penny

I was alone at work again today so I spent five hours on the phone trying to get through to Dr Cooper to see if I can get a referral to have a laparoscopy. Most of the 247 'getting pregnant' books that I own suggest that this will probably be the next step and Dr Cooper certainly said it would be. The alternative and homeopathic books of course do not approve of this kind of brutalism but what is one to do? I've tried so many things and honestly if I gave up eating and drinking all the things that some of these books tell you to give up I'd starve to death before I could conceive.

I couldn't even get through to the surgery. There's some sort of flu epidemic on and it's obvious that they're a bit pushed. I'm afraid that we're going to have to consider having it done privately. I don't like to because Sam and I have always felt very strongly about the NHS, but I don't think I have any choice. I mean the waiting lists are so long now that even though you want to do the right thing you can't. Funny, really, because these days I actually feel that because the lists are so long I should go private anyway if I can afford it, just in order to free up a bed. Extraordinary. I remember when Mrs Thatcher had that operation on her hand and said, 'I didn't add to the queue,' we all went potty at dinner parties all over London and now we're saying exactly the same thing.

I am so depressed.

Dear Sam

Lucy wants to have a laparoscopy done privately because she can't get through to Dr Cooper. I said *absolutely not*. I pretended that it was a matter of political principle and expressing our solidarity with the NHS. The truth is it's the money pure and simple. What with my cock-up over Above The Line Films and the fiasco with the Prime Minister it's now pretty much a certainty that Nigel is going to shaft me and until I know what the future holds I can't countenance any additional expense.

I went to Oddbins today and downgraded from single malt to blended.

Dear Penny

I am really quite proud of Sam. He was absolutely immovable on the private operation bit. I had no idea he had retained such a firm grip on his political principles. Good for him.

I've booked the private operation for the end of next month.

I mentioned my political fears to Sheila at work because she's a bit of an old lefty and she said something awful. She said, 'Yes, but the reason that we all worried about Thatcher's hand was because it was about essential surgery, which is what the Health Service is for. Fertility treatment is hardly essential, is it? It's more of a personal indulgence.'

She actually said that, and she was trying to be nice. Well, I suppose it's what a lot of people think. Perhaps I'd think it myself if fate had dealt me different cards.

Dear Sam

Well, I knew that it was only a matter of time before the axe fell and it fell today. I finally lost my job. I think the whole corridor knew before I did. Trevor avoided my eye and Daphne looked distinctly upset. I'm a pretty easygoing sort of boss and I think she's scared they're going to give her to some twenty-eight-year-old Armani clothes hanger who thinks only American sitcoms are funny.

Anyway, there was a warning sign in every face, so by the time I got to Nigel's office to which I'd been summoned I was ready for anything. In a way it wasn't so bad.

'Radio,' said Nigel.

'Radio,' I said.

'Radio,' said the Head of Radio and Television, who was also in attendance. 'I'm extremely keen to up our light entertainment output in sound-only situations. Your massive experience in bringing on the best of the new comedians and writers makes you the perfect person to head up this major new entertainment initiative.'

Which of course means that it would be more trouble and expense to sack me than to shift me to a job where it doesn't really matter what I do. On the other hand I had been expecting immediate redundancy, or, at the very best, the post of Programme Coordinator: Daytime South West, so this was, in a perverse, reverse kind of way, quite good news.

'What's the job title?' I asked.

'Chief Light Entertainment Commissioning Editor, Radio,' said the Head of Radio and Television.

I let it hang in the air a moment, waiting for the words 'deputy' or 'sub' or 'Midlands' to follow. They didn't, but you can't be too careful. I heard a story of a bloke who went to see the DG and thought he'd been offered 'Controller, BBC1' but actually after the DG said the word 'one' he coughed and in that cough managed to add 'Planet Green Initiative, Bristol Environment Unit.' The poor man was on the train pulling out of Paddington before he'd worked out what had happened.

So there I was, the new 'Chief Light Entertainment Commissioning Editor, Radio'.

'What about the money?' I said.

'The same,' Nigel replied, to my delight, 'if you go quietly and *don't* write any bitter whistle-blowing articles in the *Independent* media section or *Broadcast* magazine.'

And so the deal was done, effective immediately. I was to clear my desk that very day. One slightly dispiriting thing. I'd asked Nigel if I could take Daphne with me over to Broadcasting House (where my new office is to be). He said fine but then *she* refused! I could tell that she thought that radio was a definite step down and could see no reason why she should have to share in my reduction of status.

'No, thank you, Sam,' she said. 'It's very kind of you but I'm the personal secretary to the "BBC Controller, Broken Comedy and Variety", which is a *television* post. I am not personal secretary to the "Chief Light Entertainment Commissioning Editor, *Radio*".'

So there you go. Was it Kipling who said they were more deadly than the male? (Women, that is, not personal secretaries.)

I must say it was lucky that Lucy did not require one of her servicings on demand tonight because I don't feel much of a man at the moment. I can still support us in the style to which we are accustomed, but at what cost to my pride? If I thought I had a nothing job before, I don't know what I've got now. A time-serving sideways shunt of a dead-end grace-and-favour pile of shite, that's what. I mean, radio entertainment's fine up at the posh end, the Radio 4 clever quizzes, witty, 'varsity stuff and edgy alternatives, but all that's already spoken for. I've been dumped down at the Radio One yoof end and they don't want comedy. They want attitude and I'm a deal too old to give them that.

Anyway, to my surprise Lucy was quite positive about the situation. She seemed to think that it was a good thing. She pointed out that I'd never liked my job anyway, and now I'd have the time to do what I really want to do, which is write.

Well that of course brought on the same old row.

'Oh yes, that's a good idea,' I said. 'I'll just bash off an award-winning script now, shall I? Except hang on, that's right, I remember, I haven't written a bloody word in years,'

A bit bitter, I know, but it had been a pretty rotten day. Lucy always hates it when I get negative on her.

'And do you know why?' she snapped. 'Because you've given up on your emotions, that's why. If you live your life entirely superficially how do you expect to write anything?'

Well, this sort of thing carried on back and forth until we went to bed, both pretty depressed. Lucy was out like a light, emotionally exhausted, poor thing, what with all that infertility about the place and having a completely useless husband. I, on the other hand, couldn't sleep. What Lucy had said kept ringing in my ears. Maybe I do avoid my writing so that I don't have to explore my emotions? Or is it the other way round? Do I ignore my feelings so that I'll be sure that I'll have nothing to write about? Either way it's a pretty sad effort. Then I began to wonder what my emotions would be if I had any. What was happening inside me? Did I care much about losing my job? No, I didn't really care much about my job because I was no good at it. In fact I didn't deserve it in the first place. I was no good as a commissioning editor because I was too bloody jealous of the people I was commissioning, which was pathetic. So what did I feel? When I wasn't avoiding my feelings? That I want to write? Who cares? That I love Lucy? Well that's not a bad subject. Love always goes down well. That I want Lucy and me to have children? I certainly feel that. I may never say it, but I want more than anything else in the world for Lucy and me to have children.

And then it struck me! It was such a shock that I went cold. It was so obvious! How could I have missed it! That's what I would write about! I sat bolt upright in bed. The whole thing seemed to leap into my mind fully formed. It made me dizzy there was so much of it coming to me at once.

'I've got it, Lucy!' I shouted and she nearly fell out of bed in shock.

'Got what?'

I could hardly form a coherent sentence I had so much to say. The words tumbled out in a stream.

'My theme. The inspiration I need! It's so obvious, darling, I can't think how I've missed it. I'll write about an infertile couple!

It's a real modern drama, about life and the absence of life . . . There's jokes, too. But proper jokes. Sad jokes, which are the best kind. Sperm tests, postcoital examinations, guided fantasy sessions . . . Imagine it! The disintegration of this couple's sex life, the woman beginning to think about nothing but fertility, going all tearful over baby clothes . . . Adopting a gorilla . . .'

Writing it down now I admit it looks a little insensitive but I swear I didn't mean it to be. After all, I was talking about writing a *story*, a fiction, about two fictitious people, not *us* at all. Perhaps I could have put it better, but I was so excited. This was the first decent idea I'd had in years.

'The thing will write itself,' I said and the ideas just kept tumbling into my head and straight out of my mouth . . .

'How about a scene where the woman can't decide which herbal teabag would be most aromatherapeutically conducive to her biorhythms? Or some sort of open-air ritual . . . It'll be bloody hilarious . . .'

I would have gone further. I could have gone on for hours. I was really on a roll, as they say, but at that moment Lucy stopped me. Well, when I say stopped me, she threw half a cup of cold herbal tea in my face.

'How about a scene where the woman throws her herbal tea all over the callous bastard who wants to rape her soul for a few cheap laughs,' she said.

It took me a moment to cut through the bitter irony to realize the point she was making. I was astonished. I'm not astonished now, of course, having had time to reflect on what she was getting at, but at the time I couldn't work out her attitude at all.

'What!' I exclaimed. 'But you said! You said! You told me to look within!'

'I didn't tell you to try to turn our private misery into a public joke!' I've hardly ever seen her so angry. 'Maybe it's a good thing if we are infertile. If we did have kids you'd probably expect them to pay their way by becoming child prostitutes!'

This was pretty strong stuff. I mean, I understood that she was upset and everything, but child prostitutes? Come on.

'You don't understand anything!' she said. 'I'm thirty-four. I've been trying for a child for over five years! I may well be barren, Sam!'

Well now I admit that I lost it a bit too. I mean it seems to me that Lucy has developed a habit of seeing the fertility thing as being pretty much exclusively her problem, just because I deal with it in a different way to her. I mean I'm in this marriage too, aren't I? I have feelings and I had thought that I was under orders to get in touch with them. I mean, maybe we are infertile. I don't know, perhaps we can't have children. But if we can't, what does she want me to do about it? Go into mourning? Weep and wail over the absence of a life that never even existed in the first place?

I'm afraid I put this point to Lucy and she took it as confirmation of her long-nurtured suspicion that I don't care whether we have a baby or not. In fact I probably don't even want one. After this I probably said too much. It's just that I don't think she was even trying to see it from my point of view.

'And what if I don't?' I said. 'Does that make me a criminal? Have I betrayed our love because I happen to place some value on my own existence? On my career and my work? Because I have not committed my entire emotional wellbeing to the possibility of some abstract, non-existent life which we may or may not be able to produce?'

Lucy was near to tears but like the bastard that I am I pressed my advantage.

'I mean isn't this near deification of the next generation all a bit bloody primitive? A baby is born. Its parents devote their lives to it, sacrificing everything they might have hoped to have done themselves. Then, when that baby is finally in a position to fulfil its own destiny and also the dreams its parents had for it, that baby has its own baby and the whole thing starts again. It's positively primeval.'

Lucy got up and went and made herself a cup of herbal, which I hoped she wasn't planning to throw at me. When she came back she said, 'It's life, Sam! It's what we're here for, not . . . not to make bloody films.'

But that's the point, isn't it? As far as I'm concerned I am here to make films! Or at least to fulfil and express myself in one way or another. I mean I only have one life, don't I? And it's the one I'm living, not the one I may have a hand in creating. I know that sounds selfish but is it actually any more selfish than seeking to replace yourself on the planet? I don't know. Anyway, I tried to calm things down a bit, so that we could get some sleep if nothing else.

'Look, Lucy, I'm sorry . . . I don't want to upset you. Of course I want us to have a baby, it's just . . . it's just . . .'

Lucy was not in the mood to be calmed.

'It's just you want to write a comedy about it,' Lucy said. 'Well, if you *ever* even so much as *mention* the idea of exploiting our personal misery for your profit again I'll leave you. I will, Sam. I mean that, I'll leave you.'

With that she turned her back on me and we lay there together in grim, wakeful silence.

Dear Penny

I had a pretty rotten night last night. Sam and I had a row. He thinks I'm a mawkish self-indulgent obsessive and I think he's an arrogant self-obsessed emotional retard. However, I'll write no more of that at the moment because there was dreadful news this morning which certainly puts my little worries into perspective.

Melinda rang at about nine to say that Cuthbert had been taken into hospital with suspected meningitis. He's at the Royal Free in Hampstead and Melinda is in with him. We won't know the full picture for a day or two, but it might be very serious indeed. Poor Melinda must be going mad. If it is meningitis then even if Cuthbert survives it's going to mean brain damage and all sorts of complications. Of course it might not be. All we can do is wait. I can hardly bear to think about it. Sam, of course, seems completely unmoved by the news. I know that he isn't, but that's how he seems.

Dear Book

I don't know what Lucy wants from me. We heard horrible, horrible news from George and Melinda today. Cuthbert has suspected meningitis. Lucy's got herself very upset about it indeed, which I think is unhelpful. There's no point presuming the worst, after all, and so far it's only suspected. Of course I understand that Lucy is feeling particularly emotionally raw at the moment where babies are concerned, but I don't see what she thinks I can do about it. When we heard I said, 'Oh dear, that's absolutely terrible. Poor George and Melinda.' I could see immediately that she did not feel that this was a sufficiently emotionally charged reaction, so I said, 'Oh dear' again, but it just sounded worse. It's frustrating. Of course I'm worried about it and terribly sorry for George and Melinda but I don't know what else I can say. I rang George and asked if there was anything I could do but of course there isn't. I felt an idiot even asking. What possible thing would I be able to do?

Dear Penny

No news on Cuthbert. Tests still being carried out.

I went for my interview with the private doctor today. Dr James. He seems quite nice but he won't actually be doing the operation. All he'll do is refer me to some clinic in Essex or somewhere else miles away. One ten-minute appointment, one letter, one hundred pounds, that will do nicely, thank you.

I was nearly late for the appointment, in fact, because the address was in Harley Street. 298AA Harley Street. Well I couldn't believe it, this poxy little flat must have been half a mile from Harley Street! All the way along Weymouth Street. It's absolutely ridiculous that these doctors can attach a snob value to an entirely false address. I mean, honestly, we might as well all say we live in Harley Street. Anyway, Dr James saw me promptly, which was a new experience for me, and they also offered coffee and biscuits which I did not have as I imagine that in the private sector the going rate for a custard cream is about ten quid. I told Dr James how far I'd got with investigating infertility and as expected he booked me in for a bellybutton broadcast. It makes me feel quite ill even to think about it.

Afterwards I went up to the Royal Free in Hampstead to see Melinda and Cuthbert. It was heartbreaking. All these tiny babies and little toddlers so sick and scared. It just isn't fair. Melinda is bearing up but has had very little sleep and looks pretty grim. Cuthbert was in an isolation ward and I didn't see him, but Melinda says he looks so vulnerable and fragile that she could hardly bear it. She says every fibre of her being wants to do something to protect him but there's nothing she can do. So she just sits and waits, consumed with weird feelings of guilt plus fear and also terrible visions of Cuthbert in pain or dying or becoming damaged. Then she started crying and I cried too, which was absolutely ridiculous as I was supposed to be comforting her. So I told her about Sam and me shagging on top of Primrose Hill which made her laugh, but of course the story doesn't have a funny ending because it didn't work. Then she asked me about Lord Byron Phipps and I told her not to be silly and that that was all forgotten about. Little did I know.

Anyway, when I left the hospital I had to go and sit on a bench on the Heath for a while because I was too upset and emotional about poor little Cuthbert. I mean obviously he's not mine but I know him pretty well and quite frankly any baby in torment has always broken my heart. I suppose it would do anyone. I rang Sam on his mobile just for a chat, but he's in the process of tying up the loose ends of his old job and I could tell he was busy. 'So no news, then?' he said, which really meant, 'Why the hell are you calling me?' Sam is very practical in that respect.

Anyway, I wasn't feeling much better when I got back to work, which I'm afraid was not necessarily a very good thing. You see, when I got to the office, in, as I must point out again, a highly vulnerable and emotional state, the place was empty save for Carl Phipps! He was standing over my desk reading a contract.

There is no point denying that he looked handsome. Very handsome. He'd hung up his big coat and was standing there in a baggy white shirt open to the chest. What with his tight black Levi 501s and his Cuban-heeled boots all he needed was a rapier and he could have fought a duel.

'Sheila and Joanna are down at the Apollo press call,' he began to explain, but then he said, 'You've been crying.'

'No, I haven't,' I lied pathetically.

'Tell me what's wrong, Lucy. I hate to see you cry.'

Well, that was it. Suddenly I was in floods and before I knew it he had his arm around me and was comforting me. I honestly do not think that at this point he was making a move on me. At least if he was it was a very subtle one. No, I genuinely think that he was just trying to be nice. Although I'm not sure if men are ever entirely non-sexual in their actions. Anyway, first I told him all about little Cuthbert and how worried I was for George and Melinda. He was quite wonderful about that actually, genuinely concerned and in fact he knew rather a surprising amount about the symptoms.

'The majority of suspected cases turn out to be just that, suspected.'

'How do you know?' I asked into his chest.

'I'm an actor,' he replied. 'It's my job to know.'

Well, even in my highly charged state this was a bit close to luvviedom for me and I think Carl felt the same because he quickly went on to explain.

'I played a junior doctor in three episodes of Angels a few years back. Tiny part but that's never an excuse for not doing the research.'

He was stroking my hair now, just in a comforting way.

'The symptoms in these cases are quite generalized and sometimes the real cause of the problem is never known, the baby just gets over it. Babies are very tough, you know, and very brave, even though they don't look it.'

I must say, he made me feel a lot better about things, although I still scarcely dared hope, but it was just so nice talking to him, such a change from Sam, which I know is a horrible thing to say but it's how I felt. Anyway, I ended up telling him all about myself, even all my infertility fears. He was a really good listener, which is quite rare in an actor and really seemed concerned. Of course he came up with all the same old stories that everyone

149

comes up with about friends and cousins who tried for years and then had ten, but somehow coming from him they seemed genuinely comforting.

All right. Here we go.

Long story short. I can't put off writing it any longer. I admit it. I kissed him. Yes, I kissed him and it was fantastic. We were talking and talking and talking and then he brushed a tear from my eyelash and then he took my hand and suddenly we were kissing. And proper kissing, too, a genuinely fully charged tongue-twanging passionate clinch.

Oh my God, I go weak to think of it.

I suppose it went on for a minute or two (maybe three, no more). Just big kissing. He didn't try to push his luck, which was damn lucky really. He did slowly clasp me more closely to him but not in a gropey way, although my (ahem) breast did end up pressing rather hard against his. I was braless today and in a soft cashmere poloneck and what with him just being in a cotton shirt I could really feel myself against him and him against me. Christ, my heart was pounding. He must have felt it like a bloody sledge-hammer.

Anyway, in the end I pulled away. Well, it really was either that or progress further, which would have been terrible! My God, what am I even thinking of? He was ever so good and nice about me wanting to stop (not that I did want to!). He just got up, kissed my forehead gently and said, 'If ever you need someone to talk to, I'm one call away. One call.' Then he was gone.

Well, work was out of the question after that, so I just staggered home and here I am, reflecting on it all. I haven't been kissed like that in a long time. Of course I feel guilty but also I can't deny I feel very exhilarated. But then I think of Cuthbert and my own infertility and feel completely wretched about being excited by a kiss. I do wish life was easier.

It's a little bit later now and I feel worse. I got to thinking about Sam, you see, and obviously started feeling guilty. Not just about the kiss but also about last night. He suggested writing a screenplay about an infertile couple and I absolutely exploded, which I'm not sure was quite fair. I mean I still hate the idea and if he ever did it I'd kill him, but I think I should have been more sympathetic to his point of view. After all, it's been me that's been pressing him to explore his emotions further and use his feelings in his work. I mean obviously I did not mean quite such specific emotions. Him exploiting our most private agonies for easy laughs and cheap emotional stings is out of the question, but I still think I should have been a bit more gentle in rejecting the idea.

By the time he came home I was feeling very loyal to him, in need of his love and in need of showing him mine. I had resolved to demonstrate to him how much I care and to be much closer than I have been of late. Well, it didn't work, of course. I tried to hold him and to hug him and to bond in both a physical and emotional sense but, surprise, surprise, he just gave me a peck on the cheek and went to his bloody study to brood about his career. If he wants to drive me into the arms of Heathcliff-style Byronic actors then he's doing a good job.

He didn't even ask if I'd heard how Cuthbert was.

Dear Sam

I got home and found Lucy all clingy and wanting to talk about the strengths in our relationship. Well I'm sorry but I just can't do that stuff at the moment. I don't think she realizes how much my life has been screwed up recently, or if she does realize she doesn't care. As far as she's concerned I'm there to offer either affection or sperm as and when she feels she needs it. *My* worries, my complete humiliation at work, the ignoble end to a career I've worked on since leaving university, she sees these things as selfish and unworthy obsessions. Stuff I ought immediately to thrust aside as unimportant when real stuff like our relationship or not having a child comes up.

I mean, for God's sake! The world doesn't need any more babies! Millions and millions starve every year, millions more live in a misery of deprivation and abuse. Why don't a few people start *not* having babies? Why don't a few people start living their own lives, fulfilling their own destinies? That's what

I say. Being childless Lucy and I have a unique opportunity. We're young(ish); we're fit; we have a dual income (for now); we could be doing anything! Learn to fly a plane, walk to the source of the Andes, save the rainforests, get completely arseholed in the pub every night, *anything*. Yet all we do, *all* Lucy cares about is trying to have a baby.

I suppose the truth is that I'm lying to myself because I want us to have one too. It may not be all I care about, but it's what I care about most.

Poor Lucy. She only wanted me to show her that I love her and my God I do love her. I love her and fancy her so much. That night on Primrose Hill was just magical, even though it didn't work.

It's just that I'm not very expressive, I suppose.

Bugger everything.

Dear Penny

Melinda rang at seven o'clock this morning. It's not meningitis. They don't know what it is but it's definitely not meningitis. I'm so happy for her because it would have been almost unbearable. Cuthbert's going to have to stay in for a while under observation but he's really rallied and Melinda sounds like the entire universe has been removed from her shoulders.

I told Sam and he said, 'Oh great, that's absolutely brilliant, I mean really wonderful news, fantastic,' but after a minute he went back to looking at the media appointments section of the Guardian.

Anyway, when I got to the office today Sheila said, 'What's happened to Sam? Have you been injecting him with monkey glands or something?'

I had no idea what she was talking about but I soon found out. On my desk there were a dozen red roses and the card attached said, 'You're beautiful and I must have you.'

That is honestly what it said. 'You're beautiful and I must have you.'

I mean, it was there for all to see. No wonder Sheila presumed it must be Sam. I mean, for someone to leave a message like that, open, for all to see, he's got to be pretty confident of his ground, hasn't he? I must have gone a red so deep it would have been visible in Australia. Sheila spotted my confusion, of course.

'Unless it isn't from Sam,' she said wickedly.

'Oh no!' I said, far too loudly. 'They're from Sam. We've had a row. I expect he's trying to make up. How embarrassing.'

I'm so angry I could . . . Well, I don't know what I could do, but honestly! I mean all right, yes, I kissed Carl Phipps. In fact it could even possibly be suggested that I snogged him, which was very very wrong of me, but that does not give him the right to start making public requests for intercourse, does it? Surely not? I mean I'm a married woman! What's more, it's the appalling arrogance. I mean the swine is so damn sure of himself. He's so used to the amorous fantasies of stupid little fans that he just presumes he can get his leg over whoever he likes. It's horrible.

I mean yes, I admit it, I fancy him, he's gorgeous. But this is too much. The moment Sheila went out for her cigarettes (she had four with her first cup of coffee, four, it's quite incredible), I phoned him at home.

'Yo,' said his answerphone (yes, 'Yo', gruesome), 'the Phipps man here. I'm either out, busy or too shagged out to pick up the phone. If it's about work then you can call my people' (my people! That's us!), 'on 0171, etc . . . Or if it's about stuff in LA you could talk to Annie on 213, etc . . . If it's about New York you could call William Morris on 212, etc . . . Otherwise, hey, do that message stuff after the beep thing.'

Well, having sat through that, I'd had plenty of time to prepare myself.

'Carl, it's Lucy from the office. Just who the hell do you think you are? I think you're horrible! Do you imagine I'm a slut? Do you think I'm some old slapper who you can just . . . just . . . knock off when you choose? Well, let me tell you that just because you're quite good looking doesn't mean I'm going to sleep with you, all right? I'm a married woman so you can just bloody well forget it! Oh, by the way we need an answer on that soap powder ad script we sent you. Goodbye!'

I felt a lot better after that.
Great news about Cuthbert.

Dear Self

Now I really am hurt. I felt so mean this morning about every-thing that I sent some roses to Lucy at her office. I sent rather a saucy message too. I said she was beautiful and that I must have her. I thought she'd be pleased. I thought when I got home tonight she'd leap on me. But no, nothing. She didn't mention it! She just carried on writing her book and when she'd finished that all she did was go on and on about how much she hates their new actor, Carl Phipps.

I think she fancies him.

Anyway, then I thought perhaps the flowers didn't arrive, so I asked her if she'd had any surprises on her desk that morning.

I swear she went white.

'What?' she said. 'What do you know about it? Who told you? Have you been talking to Sheila?'

'I haven't been talking to anyone,' I said. 'I just wanted to know if you got my red roses this morning.'

Did I say that she went white before? Well, it must have only been pale because *now* she went white, she actually shook and clutched about herself for support. It's this bloody baby business, she needs a rest.

'The roses . . . you sent me?' she said.

'Yes, with the saucy note. Did you get them?'

'Oh, yes,' and her voice sounded like that of a dying hamster, a hamster dying of a sore throat. 'I got them.'

Then she became almost hysterical.

'Why?!' she shouted. 'Why did you send them?! My God, and that note! It was stupid! Stupid, stupid, stupid.'

Well, that was it. I walked out. I'm actually writing this in the pub. I mean, all the times she's gone on about me not showing her any affection ('Show me some affection,' that's all she ever seems to say, particularly when I'm trying to watch the telly) and

154

now, now I try to do something sexy and romantic and she screams at me.

I'm sorry. I know I'm not supposed to say this. I know I'm not supposed even to *think* it, but *bloody* women!

Dear Penny
I want to DIE. I JUST want to DIE.

Dear Sam

My first day in the new job today, which meant a ridiculously early 5 a.m. start. Lucy brought me a cup of tea which was very nice of her although frankly I'm not sure she'd been to sleep. She kissed me and thanked me properly for the flowers. She said she was sorry about last night and it was just the tension of everything what with the looming laparoscopy and all. I told her not to worry and I think that we put the atmosphere behind us, although I can't say that things feel particularly close at the moment.

My new office is located at Broadcasting House, which I like. It's so old and truly BBC. It's also in town rather than miles out west and very easy for me on the tube.

My new job is awful. My principal responsibility seems to be the Radio 1 breakfast show. This is because what used to be primarily a pop show is now much more a light entertainment programme with a bit of music thrown in. They have a sensational new signing at the moment, a bloke called Charlie Stone, who is supposed to be the absolute last word in post-modern youth broadcasting, which means he cracks knob gags in places where knob gags were previously considered taboo, i.e. at seven-thirty in the morning on the nation's number one radio show. He's actually very good in a completely indefinable way, which is what star quality is, I suppose. He's both hip and mainstream at the same time, which is a very tough trick to pull off. Of course he gets an enormous amount of complaints. Which I believe the Channel Controller finds very encouraging.

The Controller's name is Matt Crowley and I had been emailed to meet him at the studio to 'check out' Charlie's show live.

'He's at the very cutting edge of post-modern zoo radio,' my new controller assured me. 'Satirical, confrontational, anti-establishment and subversive.'

Which of course as always means knob gags.

When I arrived Crowley was already there (bad start) and we stood together behind the glass wall watching Charlie and his posse entertain the waking nation. I joined him at the end of a song called 'Sex My Sex' from a singer called Brenda, who is incredibly pretty and is always appearing in her bra on the cover of *Loaded*.

'All right,' said Charlie, 'that was another very sexy waxing from the very sexy Brenda. It made me want to reach for the knob . . . To turn up the volume, I mean! Tch, what are you lot like? And what a very sexy lady Brenda is, what a very very sexy and of course talented lady. She makes my tackle taut. How could she not? She makes my luggage leap, my stonker stand, my hand pump hard and she bucks up my old boy. Sorry if that sounds sexist, but I'm sworn to speak only the truth.'

I was pretty astonished actually. It's so long since I listened to Radio 1 I hadn't realized how blokey it had got.

'And speaking of sex,' Charlie went on, 'tell me, lovely listeners, when did you first feel sexy? I want to hear about your first bonk. Yes, I do, and we know you're dying to tell. Did the earth move? Who ended up on the wet patch? Did you smoke afterwards or just gently steam? Think about it and give us a bell.'

Matt turned to me with a pleased proprietorial look.

'Brilliant, right?'

'Oh, right,' I assured him.

'So, here's how it is, mate,' Crowley continued. 'I may be your controller, but he's your boss, OK? *The Breakfast Show* is the station flagship. It's his show and you work for him. He's a radio genius and your job, your number-one occupation, is to stop him getting poached by Virgin or Capital.'

Later on, alone in my new office, I made a decision.

A big and terrible decision, a decision I never imagined myself making, a decision I hate myself for even thinking about. But I've done it now and deep down even though I know I'm wrong, I know I'm right.

Dear Penny

I've taken the week off work. After the way I've shamed myself with Carl Phipps I may never leave the house again. I mean, what must he think of me? How must he feel? He kisses a girl, she kisses him back and the next thing he knows he's being foully abused on his answerphone and told that the girl will not give him one when he hasn't even asked her to in the first place! My God! Every time I think about it I want to kill myself.

What am I to do? I'm bound to see him sooner or later. Perhaps I'll give up my job. After all, now that Sam has been transferred to radio (Sam keeps saying 'the shame of it' but I don't see what's so wrong with radio), the threat of our immediate financial ruin seems to have lifted somewhat. If I left the office I'd never have to see Carl again. I must say it's tempting.

Cuthbert is out of danger and home, by the way. Melinda brought him round and he projectile vomited all over me and an antique cushion cover. Melinda said that the doctors had warned that this might happen and I wasn't to worry because Cuthbert was fine. A slightly insensitive thing to say, I thought, as I mopped up the bile. I mean us non-mothers do have lives too and we do care about our cushion covers. Still, I mustn't be mean. Any mum who's been through what Melinda has recently been through with Cuthbert is entitled to place him at the centre of the universe and exclude the needs and feelings of all other beings.

Dear Traitor

Well, I've done it. If Lucy ever finds out, which in the end she must, I cannot bear to think what her reaction will be. But whatever the harvest, I've done it. I've pitched my idea about an infertility film to George and Trevor at the BBC. I know it's terrible and madness and I'm putting at risk everything I hold dear but I am a writer. Writers write about themselves, all artists draw upon their own experiences and emotions. It's part of the job.

Reading this back, it all looks a bit like special pleading, but I think it's fair. Lucy has no right to ban me from the source of my inspiration. It may be her story but it's my story too. Anyway, I'll change the names, for God's sake.

I spent all last night writing a synopsis. Lucy thought I was doing this book, which I felt pretty guilty about . . . except in a way I think I'm sort of doing what we originally intended, just in a different form. Anyway, I did it and I must say I thought it looked fantastic. If I was a commissioning editor I'd commission it. The maddening thing of course is that until a few days ago I *was* a commissioning editor.

I managed to get my treatment down to just under a thousand words which in my experience is about right. You don't want to offer too much at first, just a few crisp ideas succinctly put. That's what I used to long for when I was reading people's treatments. God, the depression when something the size of a telephone directory lands on your desk and you're supposed to respond to it overnight. Besides, Trevor and George had agreed to meet me right away, being such good mates, and I didn't want them to have an excuse for not having read it. I biked it over to the BBC first thing this morning and we all met up at noon at Quark, meeting for the first time as suppliant and God-like commissioners, rather than as honoured partners in lunch. I can't deny I was nervous.

When I arrived Trevor was alone. I didn't bother with any of the smalltalk that's normally the rule on these occasions. Dammit, I've known Trevor for years.

'What do you think?' I asked.

The news was good. He loved it. I cannot describe the relief.

'I think it's a fantastic idea, Sam,' he said with real enthusiasm. 'Dark, dramatic. Even the Controller's excited.'

I was amazed. 'You've shown it to Nigel?'

'We didn't tell him it came from you, of course.'

This was extraordinary news. Bringing in a network Controller at such an early stage was scarcely common. In fact it was unheard of.

'It's the Zeitgeist, Sam, the issue du jour,' Trevor explained to me, as if I didn't know. 'For Christ's sake, everybody knows somebody who's doing it. The whole country's obsessed. That IVF documentary we ran got eight million viewers even on the repeats and there wasn't a laugh in it.'

Just then George came up. He was late because he'd been up at the Royal Free taking Cuthbert for a check-up. Cuthbert appears to be getting back to his old self, insomuch as George was still trying to get sick out of his breast pocket.

The gorgeous waitress who had so humiliated me on my previous visit to Quark was hovering about waiting to take our order. I longed for George to say something loud and forceful about my treatment, which would let her know that I was not a sad git at all but a hot new screenwriter with a project hurtling towards a green light. He didn't, though. George doesn't let anything get in the way of his ordering food. He made up for it, though, once we'd ordered and even without a sexy young audience it was still pretty heady stuff.

'Now look here, Sam,' he said. 'We've all had a gander at your idea and everyone thinks it's marvellous . . .'

'Yes, I've been telling him,' said Trevor.

And suddenly they were both talking at once.

'The scene in the restaurant where she rings up and demands her Restricted Bonking Month bonk.'

'And then the bloke can't get an erection.'

'Brilliant. Did that really happen?'

I admitted that it did.

'I love it when she spills the tea because she's propped herself up on the pillows,' said George. 'How's Lucy taking it, by the way? I mean, it's pretty intimate.'

This was, of course, a pretty tricky point. After all, Trevor and George are both friends of Lucy's and here I was, hoping to convince them to enable me to betray her.

Just then the waitress arrived with our starters and of course everything had to stop while George went into his 'Modern restaurants are crap' routine. He has a particular hatred of what in the 1980s was called nouvelle cuisine i.e. small portions pretentiously presented.

'Hate these poncy joints,' he said, loudly, so that the waitress would hear. 'Plates the size of dustbin lids, portions so small you think you've got dirty crockery and it turns out to be your main course.'

If the gorgeous, icy young waitress cared what George thought about the food or its presentation she certainly did not let it show on her sullen, impossibly perfect countenance. She simply smiled her 'You're not so special, I meet two thousand wankers like you a day' smile, turned and left, leaving George and me to gape at her wonderful bottom as she returned to the kitchen. George observed that she could probably crack walnuts between those splendidly athletic-looking buttocks, which he knew would annoy Trevor, who asked him to keep his witless, sexist, juvenile heterosexual banter to himself.

After this we returned to the difficult subject of what Lucy would say about my treatment.

'I'm amazed she's letting you do it,' said Trevor. 'I really am. I mean, I know it's a story and not about her but all the same, you've had to get your research from somewhere.'

It was time to come clean and admit that I hadn't actually told her about my plans yet. After all, I reasoned, there was no sense in getting her all excited if it came to nothing. Movies are a notoriously dodgy business.

'Even if you do give me a commission, I'm going to keep my new job in radio and work incognito.'

I could see that George and Trevor were not entirely convinced that I was embarking on a sensible course of action, but it is not really their problem and one thing I'm sure about is that they love the treatment, as, it seems, does Nigel. Astonishingly, for the first time in as long as I can remember, I seem to be getting somewhere.

Dear Penny

I went back to work today and there was a note in an envelope on my desk. It was from Carl. I knew it was from him because the envelope was made out of pressed rag paper and it was sealed with wax! I simply do not know anyone else rich enough or theatrical enough to deliver a note in such a manner. This is what it said.

'You are obviously hurting in some way. Perhaps I have hurt you. I know that I never meant to. The truth is, Lucy, that I have felt drawn to you from the very first day we met. It is not just that I find you beautiful, although I do, but there is also a kind of sadness about you, a longing from within that fascinates me and makes me want to know you more. Of course I have no right to feel this way. You are a married woman and the thoughts that I have about you are entirely wrong and inappropriate. Therefore I shall not come into the office again if I can help it and I promise that I will do my best to keep out of your way from now on. Always know, though, that I am your friend and am there for you if you need me. Yours respectfully, Carl Phipps.'

Well, I mean to say!

That has to be the loveliest note that anyone has ever sent me. How does he know so much about me? A longing within? I mean it's absolutely spot on, isn't it? I don't think I've ever met such an intuitive man in my entire life! I mean I've never told him about my wanting a baby . . . Well, I suppose I might have mentioned it, but only in passing, so it's still amazingly sensitive of him. And so generous not to be furious about my answerphone message. I mean, for heaven's sake! I called him up and told him to forget about sleeping with me when he hadn't even asked to (well, not in words anyway).

Oh well, it's all over now, isn't it? All over before it even began, which is the best way, and I'm really pleased. Of course in a different world, on another planet, it might have been nice to . . . No! I mustn't think that way, it's pointless and shameful. Carl has shown me the way with his dignified restraint.

But how amazing. I do believe he's actually got a crush on me.

Dear Sam

Lucy had her laparoscopy today. Superb material. I feel awful writing this because obviously it wasn't much fun for her but really, this script is going to write itself. I've never felt so motivated. I do wish I could share this sense of purpose with Lucy because it's just what she's always been wanting for me, but for obvious reasons I must keep my own counsel.

We got up at five-thirty. Lucy was not allowed to even have a cup of tea because of the operation. The drive was a nightmare, of course. Rush-hour starts at about three in the morning these days. I'll definitely be voting Green next time. The frustrating thing is that transport is the only area where we all collectively agree to ignore the evidence of our eyes and believe instead in the myth. I'm worse than anyone. I mean, let's face it, the propaganda that the car industry puts out would give Goebbels and Stalin a run for their money in terms of pure Utopian disinformation. They always advertise cars by showing some smug smoothie driving at speed along a gorgeous empty road, with not another car in sight. When in the real world did anyone ever drive along an empty road? I don't think that I've once been in that position in twenty years of driving. They always tell you what the make of the car is. I don't give a toss what the car is. Why don't they tell me where the *road* is? Just once in my life I'd like to drive on a road like that.

It really was a near-surreal experience, sitting there in fifteen thousand pounds' worth of machinery, machinery that was supposed to liberate mankind, crawling along at a walking pace, hating every other car owner on earth. That's what we were all doing. Every single person for miles and miles and miles sitting in a steaming metal box hating every single other person. Every morning in every town in Britain virtually every adult gets into his or her tin box and starts hating. Then, having taken all day to calm down, we get back into our boxes and start hating all over again. Yet when asked the question 'Why not get on a bus?' I'm the first person to say, 'No way, they're horrible.'

Dear Penny

I'm writing this while sitting alone in a depressing, plain little hospital room waiting to be done over like a kipper.

Sam drove me to the clinic this morning, which was nice except for the fact that he insisted on doing his 'This traffic is insane,' rant as if somehow we weren't as guilty as everyone else. Not easy to stomach without so much as a cup of tea inside me. On the other hand he was solicitous about my forthcoming ordeal, asking lots of questions which I thought was good of him since I know he hates the whole ghastly business. As indeed do I, but as I say, I appreciate him showing an interest.

I took the opportunity of the traffic jams to get some background detail out of Lucy regarding the laparoscopy. I must say it sounds absolutely dreadful, but not without its comic possibilities.

I know what happens backwards from the eight million books about fertility I've read in the last year or two. Sam was fascinated; he even jotted one or two things down when the car was stopped in traffic. First they feed a tube into your tummy and pump you full of gas so that they can see your insides better, then they make another hole just above your pubic triangle, or map of Tasmania as Sir Les Patterson would say (I can't believe I'm writing this), and they shove a probe in to move things about a bit so that they can take their pictures. They also pump in a lot of dye which apparently will bring out the finer features. Sam actually laughed at this, but I think it was just because he was nervous.

It's amazing what women have to go through, so weird. I wonder if it would be funny to have a scene where the doctor (possibly gay) offers the woman a choice of colour dyes to see which one would go nicest with the shade of her intestines. Maybe a bit over the top. I'll have to think quite carefully about the tone of this script. I mean, is it mainly funny with a bit of emotion, or mainly emotion with a bit of funny? Somewhere in between, I think.

Anyway, once they've got everything pumped up and dyed and prodded into position they make a hole just under your belly-button and put a long fibre optic telescope through with a camera on the end. God, what a thought. As I was telling Sam, I was actually beginning to feel sicker and sicker. It was lucky that I didn't have anything in my stomach to throw up as we've just had the car valeted. One strange thing was that as I was telling Sam the gory details I suddenly remembered that I'd meant to have my bikini line done and I was really annoyed that I hadn't. I mean why would I worry about that? It's absurd. I never worry about a bit of escaper normally, not for smear tests and all that, sometimes don't even bother for the beach. But for some reason today I just felt like looking my best. I can't imagine why. Perhaps this whole business makes me feel less like a woman and I wanted to reassert my softness and my femininity.

One brilliant thing Lucy told me was that she had wanted to have her bikini line waxed! Superb stuff! I improvised a line there and then ... I said, 'Blimey, Lucy, it's a laparoscopy, not lap dancing,' which I think cheered her up and I'll certainly keep it for the script.

Sam just made stupid jokes, which was a bit irritating, although I know he meant well. The thing is that I don't think he really understands how demeaning and dehumanizing the whole process is. You're not a woman any more, you're just a thing under a microscope, like in biology at school. I shan't write any more now because I can hear a trolley clanking in the corridor and I fear my hour has come.

Lucy was pretty zonked out when I picked her up this afternoon, so I couldn't get much out of her on the journey home. The doctor said it had all gone fine, anyway, and that they would give us the results in a few days, 'When we've got the photos back from the chemist,' he said. I hate doctors who crack glib little jokes like that. I mean, that's my wife's internal organs he's talking about! I think I'll use him in the movie, though. Stephen Fry would play him brilliantly.

The trip home was even worse than in the morning. What are we *doing* to the world? Actually, more to the point, what are we doing to ourselves? At one stage I spent twenty-five minutes in a virtually stationary battle to prevent a bloke getting in front of me from out of a side street. Every inch of road that became available I filled, in order to prevent him from edging in, never once allowing myself to catch his eye. Why? Why did I do that? It's something about cars. They shrink our souls. If I met the same man on foot I'd say, 'Oh, excuse me,' and make way. Instead I spent twenty minutes of my life, when I could have been relaxing, obsessed with stopping a bloke getting two feet in front of me in a stationary queue. I really am pathetic.

When we got home Lucy went straight to bed. I'd intended to spend the evening doing some more work on my script but somehow I don't feel like it. What with Lucy in a drugged sleep upstairs, I'm feeling a bit cheap. Guilty conscience, I'm afraid. I do hope I'm not weakening. I must see this through. It's the first thing I've felt genuinely excited about in years.

Dear Penny

Well, yesterday I had the laparoscopy and today I've got a very sore throat. Sam was particularly interested in that, wondering how you could end up with a sore throat when the business was so very much down the other end. He seemed quite excited for a minute as if there might be some extraordinarily exotic reason for this phenomenon. When I explained it was just where the anaesthetist had stuck a breathing tube down my throat he actually seemed quite disappointed. Very strange.

I think this new job at Radio is getting him down. I must say, it doesn't sound very stimulating.

Dear Book

There really is no job for me at Broadcasting House. They just made one up to avoid a run-in with the union. Ostensibly my responsibility is to commission youth-orientated comedy, but I have absolutely no money whatsoever to do this with. The entire youth entertainment budget, and I mean all of it, has been spent on Charlie Stone's wages. I couldn't believe it when I found out. The breakfast show is considered such a flagship for the station that every resource has been sacrificed to its success, which basically is Charlie. I dropped in on his show again this morning to have another look at what we're paying for, and because, frankly, I had absolutely nothing else to do. It was rather traumatic for me actually, as he was interviewing a couple of the grrrls from Grrrl Gang. I'm afraid it brought back very painful memories of my *Livin' Large* disaster.

'All right,' said Charlie, and those words alone cost the licence payer about five pounds. 'Coming up now we've got Strawberry and Muffy from the all-conquering Grrrl Gang, and my trousers are swollen to bursting point. No doubt about it, these girls give me a third leg! You should see them! Grrrl Gang? More like Phwoar Blimey Gang from where I'm sitting! Anyway, grrrls, I know that it's very important to you that you write a lot of your own lyrics. Tell us a bit about where the band is coming from.'

'It's about everything, right!' replied Strawberry or Muffy, I don't know which. 'It's a whole philosophy! It's whatever you want it to be. It's about having a totally positive attitude and kickin' it big for your babe mates and all your sistas! So get on the case! Get a grip! Get with the plot! You gotta go out and grab whatever you want! Like a degree in physics or a cute bloke's buns! Just grab it, grrrl!'

I don't think I've ever heard anything quite so fatuous in all my life. Certainly not since I last attended a BBC targeting and strategy meeting (entitled 'Meeting the Future: Policing the Gateway').

I was glad I popped in, though, because it strengthened my resolve about my film. I mean I can't spend the rest of my career pretending to laugh at Charlie Stone's knob gags, I just can't. My script development is my way out. Lucy would understand, I know she would.

Not that I'm going to tell her.

Dear Penny

Sam and I went to see Dr James, my consultant, today. Actually I think he's called Mr James. I've always found that confusing about consultants. It seems that the higher a person rises in the medical profession the less grand the title they get. Probably quite healthy really. Stop them getting too pompous.

Anyway, the good news is that they've found nothing wrong with my innards. I do not have endometriosis, which is an enormous relief. Also there are no adhesions on the abdominal cavity and I have recently ovulated.

'Tremendous news, that,' said Mr James, who is a brutally cheerful type. 'Can't make an omelette without eggs, and by omelette, of course, I mean baby.'

There are no fibroids on the outside of the uterus and to the best of Mr James's knowledge no congenital problems in the womb ('can never be one hundred per cent sure, though'). There are also no cysts, thank God, as the very thought makes me feel sick, and no apparent abdominal diseases. It was quite shocking really to hear the catalogue of things that could have spelled disaster.

We were also shown some photographs of my insides, which Mr James described as 'beautiful' but which Sam and I agreed were absolutely obscene. All yellow and red and purple. They were like stills from a horror movie. Strange to be looking at one's own innards. Stranger still to have someone admiring them.

'Lovely,' said Mr James. 'Absolutely lovely. You've got tip-top guts. Good big healthy bowel, too. That's the orange splodge. Beautiful bowel, facilitates a superb movement, I imagine. Well

done. Don't worry about it being orange. It isn't orange, it just comes out orange on the slide for some reason.'

After we had all admired my digestive system, Mr James got back to the subject at hand.

'So, as I say, most encouraging, most encouraging indeed. We didn't find a thing wrong.'

So that's all right, then. Lovely. Couldn't be better. Except for one tiny little thing, of course. I am still not fucking preg! *To this I'm afraid Mr James had no answer. Sam and I remain cursed with what is described medically as 'non-specific infertility', or, to give it its full scientific description, 'We do not have a fucking clue.'*

'Very common condition,' said Mr James. 'Very common indeed . . . amongst people who can't have babies, that is.'

So what now?

Well, what else? IVF, of course. Mr James said we could easily wait, we're relatively young, we might *just have been unlucky. It might* work out conventionally. *Mr James says that actually quite a few previously infertile women do conceive after having a laparoscopy. Something to do with it flushing out the tubes, but nonetheless he felt it was probably time to begin some form of treatment.*

Bugger. I never thought it would come to this. It would actually have been easier if he'd said, Look, the photos are the worst I've ever seen. No eggs. No tubes. No chance. Forget it for ever. Except that would have been unbearable. I just don't know what I would have done if he'd said that, I really don't.

Dear Sam

Today we went to see our consultant and got Lucy's lapa results. Good news and bad news. They found nothing wrong, which is good; on the other hand, they found nothing that they could 'cure', so to speak, so that's bad. Poor Lucy now faces the prospect of IVF treatment and she is pretty down about it. Well, I can't say I like the idea much myself. Of course it does mean that I'll get first-hand knowledge of the whole horrible process for my film, which will be extremely useful, but that is absolutely and completely beside the point. In fact I want to make this quite clear, right now, lest in future years, when I'm a big Hollywood player, I ever look back and doubt the motives and feelings I had at this juncture. I'm aware that I'm secretly exploiting Lucy's misery (and my own) for our future gain, but I'd happily give it away right now. Film or no film, if there was anything on earth I could do to make Lucy pregnant, I'd do it. Anything. I mean that. But it just doesn't seem that there is anything I can do, beyond shagging her when required and playing my part in the IVF business if it comes to that.

Honestly. It's important that I set this down on record. The film means nothing. If tomorrow Lucy fell pregnant naturally I'd be the happiest man in the world.

I can research IVF stuff without her anyway.

Dear Penny

Despite the fact that we are now definitely on the road to IVF, I've decided to make love to Sam every day this month in the hope that the laparoscopy 'tube clearing' theory will bear fruit. We started last night and I have a dreadful confession to make. About halfway through I found myself thinking about Carl Phipps. I forced him from my mind, of course, but I'm afraid to say that my subconscious was being more honest than my conscience because I often find myself thinking about him.

I love Sam, of course, absolutely. But it's different.

Dear Sam

Lucy has decided to begin a cycle of IVF after her next period (presuming we don't score in the meantime with her newly flushed-out tubes). Dr Cooper, our GP, is writing to the people at Spannerfield Hospital, which is one of the top places for fertility treatment, to get us an appointment to see them.

I had a big meeting at Broadcasting House today. Infuriating, really, because I'm getting along splendidly with the script and the last thing I want to be bothered with is my actual job. The Beeb have now officially commissioned my film, by the way, which is absolutely wonderful. For the first time since I used to write sketches for radio when I was young and wild, I am a professional writer. It's not a bad deal at all for a first film. Forty thousand, but in stages. Final payment to be made on completion of principal photography, so I'm only actually guaranteed ten thousand at the moment for the first draft. I've asked Aiden Fumet to look after my business. I must say, now he's on my side I like him much better. I didn't go in with him myself when the deal was made. George and Trevor didn't feel that Nigel was quite ready yet for the news that the brilliant new writer they'd found is, in fact, the despised and sacked Sam Bell. Nigel probably imagines me as some spiky-haired punk, since Aiden Fumet normally only represents fashionable people.

Anyway, as I say, I'm now a professional writer with a script fully in development at the BBC, which is an absolutely thrilling thing to be. The only fly in my professional ointment is that I still have my job at Radio which I must keep up in order to avoid making Lucy suspicious, and of course for the cash. We can't survive for the next six months on ten grand plus the minute sum Lucy makes at the agency.

So, bright and early this morning, after Lucy and I had had a three-minute quickie ('Don't worry about me, just get on with it,' were her bleary, sleepy words), I left her lying in bed trying to eat toast with three pillows under her bum and her legs propped up against the wall and rushed off for my meeting. They like to start early in Radio because it's very much a daytime medium, unlike TV, of course.

The meeting was fascinating in its banality. It was a seminar pertaining to the Director General's Regional Diversity Directive (the DGRDD), which is called 'The Glory of the Quilt'. I don't know why it's called 'The Glory of the Quilt'. Somebody in the lift said they thought it related to Britain being a patchwork, but for all I know QUILT may be an acronym for Quasi Utilitarianism Initiative Long Term. Or something else altogether. Nobody ever knows these things. I don't think we're supposed to.

The seminar was being chaired by the Head of Youth, BBC Radio, whose name is Tom. Tom and I had already met. He called me in to impress upon me that he did not mind jokes about drugs or even anal sex. In fact he positively encouraged 'cutting edge' material, as long as it was on after nine in the evening and was in no way exploitative or offensive to minority groups.

Anyway, Tom kicked off in pretty general terms.

'Hi, yo. Welcome to this session of the ongoing series of seminars under the Director General's Regional Diversity Directive. The Glory of the Quilt. As you all know, today's on-going subtopic is Regional Diversity and Youth.'

I hadn't known, actually, but I let it go. Up until now all the seminars of the Director General's Regional Diversity Directive had been bogged down in debating why all the regional diversity debates were taking place in London, but they had obviously bitten the bullet on this one and moved on.

'So, BBC youth radio and the regions,' said Tom. 'As you all know, the Director General is one hundred per cent committed to the BBC diversifying into the regions and I fully support him in his view . . . Bill, I asked you to formulate a comprehensive de-centralization strategy.'

I have not yet discovered what Bill's post is. Nobody I asked knew either (including Tom). My theory is that Bill wandered in-to BH one day, possibly to be interviewed on Radio 4 about bird-watching or to deliver an envelope of money to the playlist compilers at Radio 1 and he never found his way out again. Broadcasting House really is something of a warren.

'The key to regional diversification,' said Bill, 'is accents. We need more accents about the place. Northern accents, Scottish accents, at least one Welsh accent.'

Tom leapt on this like a thirsty man hearing the bell at closing time.

'I agree,' he said. 'Accents are the key and I think we need to stress right from the word go that wherever possible those accents should be genuine.'

Everybody nodded wisely at this, although Tom himself could see problems.

'The BBC is, however,' he continued, 'an affirmative action employer. We have quotas and we're not ashamed of it.'

The problem was that a vast percentage of BBC senior staff are of course from either Oxford or Cambridge, people unlikely to possess overly strong regional accents. The choice, the meeting felt, was pretty stark. Either BBC executives stop giving jobs to their old university friends, or some of those friends will have to pretend that they come from Llandudno.

'I'm not entirely unhappy with that,' said Tom. 'If we're going to teach the kids to speak badly let's at least have people doing it who know the rules that are being broken.'

Dear Penny

I got my period today. One more infertile month to add to the long long line of them that stretch back into my distant past. Sam and I will go and see the people at Spannerfield tomorrow. He's dreading it, I know, although strangely he seems to have suddenly become a lot more interested in the process. During the last day or two he's asked me really quite a lot of questions about ovulation and LH surges and things like that. It's good that he asks, but I'm sure he's only trying to be nice. Still, that's better than nothing, I suppose.

Dear Sam

We're going to Spannerfield tomorrow. I'm pretty nervous and a bit depressed about it. I've been using some of these feelings in my script (just as Lucy always wanted me to, I might add), and it's working out rather well. Interestingly, the film is going to be less of an absolutely full-on comedy than I originally thought. Not that it won't be funny. You couldn't avoid it with that many knob gags at your disposal, but it's also going to have its serious side.

I tried a bit out on Trevor and George today. I was really nervous because I've never attempted anything but jokes with them before but I wanted to give Colin (that's the name of my lead bloke) something of what I'm feeling. I'm going to paste the speech straight across from my Film Document because I think it's relevant to this book too.

COLIN (*Reflective. Depressed*): So it seems that we've reached the end of the fertility road and we're going to have to try IVF. I know it's a positive thing and all that, but it just feels so sad and ... well ... grown up ... Funny how the penny finally drops that you're not young any more. That moment when all the clichés that affected your parents and their friends start happening to people you know. All those dreadful, embarrassing, failure-type things that were for older people. Alcoholism [Trevor nodded wisely at this], divorce, loneliness, money-troubles ... or childlessness like Rachel [that's the girl's name] and me, childless and trying for a test-tube baby ...'

I must say when I read it out to them I thought it sounded far too mawkish and indulgent, but George and Trevor were very supportive. They think that a bit of emotion will really add depth to the piece and that it will play well against the comedy, which I agree with absolutely.

They still love the comedy. George nearly fell off his chair when he read the bit about me taking in my sperm sample and having to dig it out from down the back of my trousers in front of the nurse. He thinks I made it up and simply will not accept that it really happened.

Dear Penny

Well, we've had our meeting at Spannerfield. Our new consultant's name is Mr Agnew and he seems very nice. He explained that there are two more tests he'd like to carry out before we commit to an IVF cycle. A hysterosalpingogram (HSG) for me and another sperm test for Sam. His old test is no good because apparently the Spannerfield IVF people always test the sperm themselves. The hysterosalpingogram is an X-ray of the uterus and Fallopian tubes. This involves injecting dye into my cervix (again), which I am so looking forward to. Sam's test involves him having another wank. But, yet again, he is the one who's kicking up a fuss! I can't believe we're back to all that again. I said to him, I said, 'My God, Sam, it's not the end of the world! I'm asking you to have a quick one off the wrist, not fuck a hedgehog!' He laughed a lot at that and jotted it down on a piece of paper. I don't know why he did that but somehow I thought it was quite touching.

Dear Sam

Lucy says it's just a quick one off the wrist like the last time. Oh yes, just like the last time, except this time they won't let me do it at home! I have to go and masturbate at the hospital! Christ, I can't imagine a more horrible prospect. Unfortunately I made the mistake of saying this to Lucy and she said that she could imagine a more horrible prospect as a matter of fact . . . having long telescopes pushed through your bellybutton, having dye injected into you, having your gut pumped full of air and photographed internally, and above all having every doctor in Britain staring up your fanny on a day-to-day basis.

Well, if she's going to play the woman's card then there's nothing I can say, is there?

She said a great line about a hedgehog which I'll definitely use.

Dear Penny

Carl came into work today. He had to sign some contracts. We hardly spoke. He smiled a nice smile but then went straight into Sheila's office. It's what he said he'd do in his note and absolutely the right and proper thing, but I can't deny it gave me a jolt. A very large part of me desperately wished he'd stopped and had a chat, you know, just about inconsequential things. Of course, I must never forget that the last time we saw each other we kissed, long and hard, in fact. And Carl is right: that's a fire which must definitely not be fed. All the same, I did wish he'd felt able to say more than a perfunctory 'hello'. Except he is right, I know that. I mean basically I've already been a bit unfaithful to Sam. I mean not really, of course, but a bit, and that's terrible.

Let's face it, if I discovered that he'd been pashing on with some-
one at work, even if it was only once, and totally out of character,
I'd still be pretty bloody angry, to say the least. I don't know
what I'd do but I do know I'd be terribly upset.

Dear Book

Well, I must say that this morning has to rank as one of the more gruesome mornings of my life.

Communal masturbation in West London.

Actually that makes it sound better than it was. It makes it sound friendly and inclusive, like a dance or a musical. Dale Winton and Bonnie Langford in *Communal Masturbation in West London.*

It wasn't friendly or inclusive at all.

My God, it was grim. They say they'll see you any time between nine and twelve but Trevor told me to get there at least fifteen minutes before the place opened, as a queue develops. Trevor is an old hand at the sperm test game (ha ha ha), because when he donated to those lesbians they insisted that he have his sperm checked out first. Actually Trevor felt slightly offended about that and accused them of social engineering and trying to create a lesbian master race. The lesbians said that before they wasted a perfectly good turkey baster they wanted to check that his sperm weren't all immotile, two-headed or dead. Charming, I must say, but I believe people can be very frank in the lesbian community. It comes from years of having to be politically and socially assertive.

Anyway, there must be a lot more wankers around than in Trevor's day, because although I slunk in at eight-forty there were already four blokes ahead of me. All sitting about in this depressing waiting room with posters about the dangers of smoking all over the place. I can't imagine why they have such an obsession with smoking in a masturbating facility. Perhaps some blokes have been having a cigarette after they ejaculated?

Anyway, as I say, I slunk in and sat down as far away from any of the others as I could and almost immediately another man arrived. Luckily for me he must have done it before because the first thing he did was go to the empty desk and sign something before sitting down. Instantly I was on the alert! Was there some queueing system of which I was unaware? Did one clock in for a toss? On sneaking over and inspecting the desk I realized that there was indeed a system. 'Please sign list on arrival and wait for your name to come up,' it said on the form. On the form, that is, not on a big poster on the wall, but on a poxy little form on a clipboard on a desk. Couldn't they have put 'Smoking may harm your unborn child' on the little form and 'Sign up!' on a great big poster?

So now, instead of being fifth man in, I was sixth. I thought for a moment about appealing to the man who came in after me, explaining that I had in fact been there before him but did not know about signing the form. I didn't, of course. Let me tell you now that one thing I learned today is that *nobody* talks to anybody in the wanking queue. The hospital could be burning down and we'd all rather burn to death than shout 'Fire!' You sit, and you wait.

Anyway, the long minutes ticked by and at nine o'clock a couple of nurses emerged from various corridors and began to take an interest in things. By this time three more men had turned up and we were being forced to sit right next to each other on the little square of chairs, which nobody liked at all. One of the nurses went to the desk and called out the first name. Up gets the bloke, goes to the desk, gets his pot and is directed down the corridor to the wanking room.

So now we all know the score. One room. One fucking room. We're going in one at a time in a slow, agonizing tosser chain. Each of us realizes that the amount of time that we're going to have to spend in that hellhole is entirely dependent on those in front of us in the queue. The chain moves at the speed of the slowest wanker.

After about ten minutes the door at the end of the corridor opened and the first man hurried out. He dropped his pot off at a little hatch in the wall, handed some kind of plastic-coated form back to the nurse and he was out, lucky swine. After what I considered an unnecessary minute or two of faffing about, the nurse called out the next name and up got another man, picked up his pot and the plastic-coated form and trundled down the corridor to the masturbation chamber. I must say I found this plastic-coated form a bit disconcerting. What was it? Wanking instructions? Surely most men were up to speed on that one? And *plastic-coated*. That was a bit of a gross touch, I must say.

It's always struck me as a strange thing about instructions in general, the way people feel the need to give them out whatever the circumstances. Perhaps it makes us feel more in control, like the way we still give all the details on an outgoing answerphone message: 'If you'd like to leave a message please speak clearly after the tone.' I mean, we all know that, don't we? Perhaps we should add, 'Oh, and don't forget to put the receiver back afterwards or your phone will be rendered useless.' Lucy and I had a frozen pie last night and on the box it said 'Remove cardboard box before putting in the oven.' I mean I suppose some people might make a mistake with that, but surely it's better to let them learn by experience or else one day they'll be near a fire with some cardboard and no instructions and hurt themselves.

The ballpoint pens they give us at work have a warning embossed on the plastic tops advising us not to put them in our mouths as choking might ensue. That is a fact. I'm not making it up. Surely the same thing could be said for eggcups or toilet roll tubes or carpets? The world is definitely going mad.

Anyway, back to the tosser queue. The next bloke in took nearly fifteen minutes. *Fifteen minutes* to have a wank! I mean I've pulled them off in fifteen seconds in my time! I could see I was not the only one who thought this. Everybody was shuffling their feet a bit and looking at their watches. Eventually, of course, he emerged, and nearly ran past us to get out of the place, and so the long day wore on. There was a coffee machine available. I say coffee but what I mean is hot water with little brown islands floating in it. Worse than useless, really. Strange, I mean we all knew the machine served liquid shit but because it *said* it served coffee we drank the stuff. If it had said 'Liquid Shit' machine I suppose we would have left it alone. Instructions, you see, we're all caught in the headlights.

Finally at gone quarter to ten, my number came up. 'Mr Bell,' the lady said. It had to be a woman, of course. Like when you're a kid buying condoms at Boots, you could wait for hours for a lad to take over the till but he never did and you had to buy them off a teenage girl your own age. Anyway, the nurse gave me my pot and the plastic-coated instructions, and when I say plastic-coated, I don't mean neatly laminated, no, I mean a twenty-year-old form in an old plastic bag. That form has seen some sights, I bet.

'Last room on the left,' said the nurse. 'When you've finished leave your pot at the lab hatch and return the form to me.'

Well, I must say I've masturbated in more pleasant environments. Don't misunderstand me: I don't think that the NHS should be consuming its precious resources providing sensually lit boudoirs draped in red velvet and reeking of sultry scents for sad acts like me to wank in. I'm just saying it was all a bit depressing.

There was a chair, a magazine rack, a handbasin and a waste-paper basket in the room. That was it. Apart from that it was completely bare. The plastic-coated instructions informed me that I should carefully wash my hands and knob before getting down to the business of the morning. Already in the wastebasket were the crumpled paper handtowels of the previous tossers on which they had no doubt dried not only their hands but also their knobs. Strange to think that only moments before I had entered the room another man had been . . . I decided not to think about it.

So I scrubbed up and viewed the chair. It was a municipal easy-chair consisting of an upright and a horizontal cushion. The sort of chair you would have found in the teachers' common room of a secondary modern school in about 1970. I regret to have to report that it was stained, not in a truly horrid way, but just with age. There was a dark triangle on the front of the seat, left where a million men's legs had worn the material around it. In the magazine rack were some old dirty mags. It's a long time since I've seen the inside of a dirty mag and for a moment I thought, 'Hello, bonus,' but really, you just couldn't get into them at all, they were so *old*. I don't mean interestingly old, like 1960 or something. Just old; about three years or so. On the wall there was a sign saying, and I kid you not, that any donations of spare 'reading material' would be welcomed. Reading! We live in a world where five-year-olds can dial up snuff movies on the Internet and yet a hospital calls wank mags 'reading material'.

I don't know why they don't just write to *Penthouse*. I'm sure the publishers would be delighted to make a donation to assist all those men in making their donations.

Then suddenly I became aware of the time!

Oh my God, I must have been in that room for two or three minutes already! Instantly I had a vision of all the men outside, shuffling their feet, looking at their watches, thinking to themselves, 'How long does it take to toss yourself off, for fuck's sake!' Just as I had been cruelly thinking myself only moments before. Suddenly I was convinced that they were all out there gnashing their teeth and muttering, 'He's reading the articles in the magazines, I'm sure of it.'

Must get down to it! Must get down to it! Don't want to hold up the queue. But how *do* you get down to it under that kind of pressure? It's impossible. I sat on the chair, I stood up, I glanced at a magazine. Panic rose within me and panic was the *only* thing that was rising!

In the end, by a supreme effort I managed to calm myself down a little. I did it by telling myself that the door was locked, that I would never have to see any of those men outside again and that I would take as long as I damn well liked.

So I sat down on the horrible, worn-out old chair and resolutely concentrated on the job. With, I might add, the added pressure of knowing that I *must get the first bit in*! They make this clear in all the literature, and the plastic-coated instructions were also very very firm on the subject. The first bit is the best bit, of that there seems to be no doubt. All the rest is rubbish, full of sound and fury, signifying nothing.

Well, I did it. Sort of. I think there was enough. I hope so, anyway. Only time will tell. Looking at my watch I realized that I had been in there for over twenty minutes. I could feel the wave of resentment greet me as I emerged and walked past them all to hand in my pot. I was so embarrassed and flustered that I tried to walk out of the building still holding the plastic-coated form and had to be called back, which was humiliating.

Like I say, I've had better mornings.

Personally, I think it's possible that I'd rather have dye inserted into my cervix, but I'm not going to say that to Lucy, of course.

Dear Penny

Hysterosalpingogram today. It's not supposed to hurt much, but they say you should take along someone to drive you home just in case you're upset or in discomfort. Sam, of course, had a very important meeting, which he did offer to cancel but I said, 'No, don't bother, I'm fine.' Drusilla came along, which was nice of her, except she seems to view all hospitals, especially the women's-only parts, as places of unnatural torture and intrusion where nature is excluded and man insults the gods. This is slightly embarrassing when she talks about it loudly in the waiting room.

'You know half the problems they deal with here can be treated herbally,' she said so that everyone could hear. 'There's very little in life that a rose and lilac enema won't go some way towards curing.'

The hysterosalpingogram itself was all right. Legs up as per. Quick prod about, as per. Bunch of spotty students staring up me in an intense manner, as per. Then in goes the dye, they tilt it back so that the dye can flow through the tubes. Actually, it was very interesting, because you can watch the progress of the dye on a little television screen. I thought I'd be too squeamish to look, but it was fine, as it turned out. Then they took a few X-rays and that was that. The doctor was in and out in ten minutes and I was in and out in twenty. It was all right, although I did feel a bit sick and faint afterwards. Apparently some women find it more painful. Perhaps my insides are getting desensitized.

Drusilla and I went for a coffee afterwards and I told her about Carl. Amazingly she's of the same opinion as Melinda was when I talked to her about it. She thinks I should 'put the poor boy out of his misery and shag him'! I had no idea all my friends were so cavalier about the concept of fidelity. I think with Drusilla it's actually because she's sex obsessed and believes that anything and everything should be shagged whenever the opportunity arises. Preferably in groups and at Stonehenge.

I said to Drusilla, Hang on, perhaps we're jumping the gun here, perhaps poor old Carl doesn't particularly want to shag me anyway. I mean I know we kissed, but I was upset and he was comforting me. Perhaps he really is just a very nice guy who just wants to be my friend.

'Ha!' said Drusilla and she said it so loudly that other ladies spilt their coffee. Drusilla never minds about being noticed. I do.

I must say that whatever Carl's intentions may or may not be towards me, I'm a bit sad about the way all my pals seem to view Sam. I mean obviously as far as they're concerned I'm married to a sort of sexless, emotion-free geek whom one can betray with impunity. I put this to Drusilla and she replied, 'Well, you said it, babes,' which I thought was bloody mean.

Dear Sam

Lucy had her pingowhatsit today. She wanted me to go with her but for heaven's sake I have a job. The BBC pays me to sit twiddling my fingers at Broadcasting House, not at Spannerfield Hospital. Besides which, today I actually had something to do, believe it or not.

The Prince's Trust are putting on a big concert in Manchester. Radio 1 is going to broadcast it live and the whole concert has been designated a Light Entertainment Brief, i.e. my responsibility. There are two reasons for this. Firstly there will be comedians on the bill (comedy of course being the new rock 'n' roll. Like hell). Secondly, the bill will mainly be made up of ageing old rockers, and nobody at Radio 1 who's into music wants to touch it with a bargepole. They all think that because some of the artists who are to perform have committed the cardinal sin of being over forty (and doing music that has tunes) the whole thing is terminally uncool and should be on Radio 2 anyway.

So there we are. It turns out that it is to be me who's heading up the BBC Radio side of the operation, which is why today I found myself back in Quark in Soho having lunch with Joe London. Yes, *the* Joe London, as in lead singer of The Muvvers, a man who bestrode the late sixties and early seventies rock scene like a colossus. They might sneer, back at the office, all those shaven-headed boys wearing yellow sunglasses indoors and girls with little tattoos of dragons on their midriffs, but I was bloody excited to meet Joe London. This was my history. Joe was big when I was at school. I can remember him when he didn't have a courgette to put in his trousers. Bloody hell, that man couldn't half rock in the old days.

'We're all absolutely delighted at Radio 1 that you can do this show for us, Joe,' I said.

'Oh yeah, tasty, nice one, as it 'appens, no problem, geezer.'

'And of course the Prince's Trust are very grateful too.'

'Diamond geezer, the Prince of fahkin' Wales. Lahvly bloke, know what I fahkin' mean? Likes 'is rock does Charlie, big Supremes fan, and so good with the boys.'

Joe quaffed an alcohol-free lager.

'What's it in aid of, ven, vis concert?' he said.

'Well, Joe, principally helping young kids with drug abuse.'

Suddenly Joe's amiable manner changed.

'Well, I fink vat is fahkin' disgahstin', vat is,' he sneered. 'Lazy little sods! When we was young we 'ad to go aht and get our fahkin' drugs ourselves.'

I was just clearing up this misunderstanding and explaining that the point of the show was to help underprivileged youth when we were joined by Joe's manager, a huge, spherical man with a cropped head and a cropped beard and no neck. His head just seemed to develop out of his shoulders like the top of an egg. He wore a black silk Nehru suit and silver slippers and he was bedecked in what must have been two or three kilos' worth of gold jewellery. His name was Woody Monk and he greeted me with a nod before turning to whistle with approval at our waitress whose skirt was even shorter than on the last occasion I'd seen it. I imagine it had shrunk before the gaze of a thousand middle-aged media leerers who stare at it each lunchtime.

'I remember this place in the sixties when it was a knocking shop,' said Woody Monk. 'The birds working 'ere didn't look much different actcherly.'

I really was dining with the old school. Joe and Woody were rock 'n' roll as it used to be, and it made me feel like a kid again. These days most pop managers look like Tintin with sunglasses.

I asked Woody Monk if it might be too much to hope that Joe would do some interviews to promote the show.

'He'll do as many as you like, we need the profile,' Monk replied, and then, as if to quell any protests that Joe might have, he showed Joe a copy of the *Sun* featuring an article about the current Rolling Stones tour.

'Look at that, Joe!' Monk said. 'Just look at it. I mean, it's obscene, disgusting. That is just a totally ridiculous figure, out of all proportion.'

Joe took off his sunglasses and had a look. 'I don't know, Woody, I like a bit of silicone myself.'

Monk tried to be patient. 'I am not talking about the bird, you divvy! I'm talking about this new Stones tour, one hundred million, they reckon! And the Eagles got the same. It's the arenas and the stadiums,' Monk explained to me, 'megabucks, these places gross in humungous proportions. In the old days when people talked about gross on tour they meant waking up with a mouthful of sick and a strange rash on your naughties. But nobody tours for the shagging any more. They do it for the gelt. Every gig is worth millions of dollars. Can't stop for a bit of the other, accountant won't let you.'

Basically, Monk's point was that Joe needed to tour again in the near future. His latest greatest hits album would be out for Christmas and it needed supporting.

'Are we releasing another greatest 'its album, then?' said Joe.

'Yeah, but a prestige one. Nice classy cover, all in gold, the Gold Collection . . .'

'We done the Gold Collection.'

'Orlright. The Ultimate Collection.'

'Done vat too, and the Definitive Collection and the Classic, and the Unforgettable . . .'

'Look, Joe!' Monk snapped. I could see that he was a volatile chap. 'We'll call it The Same Old Crap in a Different Cover Collection if you like, it don't matter. What we have got here is the Prince of Wales flogging your comeback.'

There, it was out, and Woody Monk did not care who knew it. As far as he was concerned this concert was a marketing exercise for Joe London and that was it. I didn't mind. It meant Joe would promote it for us which was more than any of the modern stars would do these days ('I'm not doing any fooking press, all right?!'). Joe, however, seemed a little embarrassed, though not, as it turned out, about the charity angle.

'Vis ain't a fahkin' comeback! To 'ave a comeback you 'ave to 'ave bin away and I 'ave not bin. So vis is not a fahkin' comeback.'

'Orlright,' said Monk. 'It's a fahkin "still here" tour, then.'

'Vat's right.'

'You can go on stage and everyone can shout . . . Fahk me! Are you still here, then?'

I honestly cannot remember when I have had a funnier lunch, and to think I wasted all those years lunching with comedians.

'Anyway, I gotta go,' said Monk, turning to me. 'We're all sorted, aren't we?'

I said that as far as I knew we were extremely sorted.

'Good, 'cos we don't want no fahk-ups. Vis gig is very important.'

'That's right,' said Joe. 'What with the underprivileged kiddies and all vat.'

'Bollocks to the underprivileged kids,' said Monk, hauling his massive bulk to his feet. 'They should get a bloody job, bleeding scroungers. Fahk 'em.'

So that was that.

Anyway, enough of my day job, time to get down to my script. Lucy is sitting opposite on the bed, looking lovely as she always does. She's very pleased with me at the moment because I seem to be doing so much writing. She thinks it's all for my book. I'll have to tell her soon because things are really progressing with the film. I've called it *Inconceivable* and I've been in to see Nigel to admit that the writer is none other than my despised self. He was a bit taken aback at first but then he laughed and was actually very nice about it. He congratulated me and said that sacking me was the best thing he ever did and that when I picked up my Oscar I was to remember to thank him. It's interesting. Ever since he commissioned my movie script I've been warming to Nigel and now consider him to be a thoroughly good bloke. Is that desperately shallow of me or evidence of my generous and forgiving nature?

Anyway, the very exciting news is that the BBC really want to get on with it. Nigel feels that the idea is very current and that everybody will be doing it soon. Besides which, the film will be extremely cheap to make, which means that the Beeb can pay for it all by themselves. The reason films usually take years to get together is because that's how long it takes to raise the money, but we're already past that hurdle and Nigel is impatient to become a film producer.

'Movies work in a yearly cycle,' he explained. 'The festival circuit is essential for a small picture. Venice, Sundance, Cannes. You need critical heat under you before the Golden Globes in February.'

He actually said 'critical heat under you'. Strange. Whereas before I would have thought he sounded like a pretentious wanker, now I think he sounds knowledgeable and cool.

The reason Nigel is in such a hurry is that the whole thing about being a Controller at the BBC is that you have to make your mark. When you start looking for a fat job in the independent sector you have to be able to say, 'It was in my time that we did *The Generation Game*,' or, 'Oh yes, I commissioned *Edge of Darkness* and *Noel's House Party*.' These days the scramble to be seen to be successful is becoming ever more urgent. People move on so quickly that you have to make your mark quickly too and it seems that, thank you, God, I am to be the beneficiary of Nigel's haste.

Dear Penny

We went in to see Mr Agnew today at Spannerfield. He gave us our test results and everything remains clear. Sam's sperm is fine (about ninety million of them, which is enough, surely?) and a sufficient number of them heading in the right direction to pass muster. Also my pingy thingy seems to have come up normal. Mr Agnew assured me that my tubes aren't scarred, also there are no adhesions, fibroids, adenomyosis, or polyps in the womb, and that the area where the tubes join the uterus is similarly polyp-free. These polyps, it seems, are things to be avoided. I don't really know what a polyp is. I suppose I think of them as sort of small cysts. Actually, I try very hard not to think about them at all. Quite frankly, just hearing about the eight million things that can go wrong inside a woman's reproductive system is enough to make me ill. All Sam has to worry about is whether his sperm can swim.

Anyway, Mr Agnew was very nice and agreed with me that since we have uncovered nothing operable or treatable and yet we remain stubbornly infertile, the time may now be right to commence a course of IVF. Mr Agnew said that not only would this give us a chance of becoming pregnant (obviously) but it might also prove useful in a diagnostic sense, i.e. we might discover what, if anything, beyond the most incredible bad luck, is the problem.

'Fine,' I said. 'When can we start?'

Seven months, said Mr Agnew.

'Bollocks to that,' I replied (in so many words), and Mr Agnew explained that if we go private we can start next month, so that is what we'll do and I don't care what Sam says. If I'm going to have to do this I'll do it as soon as I possibly can and start the long horrible process of getting it over with. Quite apart from anything else, as far as I can see, the NHS is under such a strain that if we can afford to pay we ought to do so and not take the place of someone who can't. Sam says that that attitude simply reinforces the two-tier system. Well, what if it does? I have a home while other people are homeless, isn't that a two-tier system? Should I go and sit in a doorway to avoid reinforcing it? I eat

ready-prepared meals from Marks & Spencer while people in the Third World struggle to grow a few grains of wheat. How many tiers are there in that system, I wonder.

Anyway, it's not posh at all. We all get lumped in together and all the profits that Spannerfield makes out of the private patients go straight back into the unit to fund the research programme. Personally I thought that us making a contribution to funding research sounded like a pretty good thing but Sam says that NHS hospitals using private patients to fund their activities is the thin end of the privatization wedge. He says that the people who manage the NHS budget will say to the hospitals, 'Well, if you're partially self-funding already, we'll cut back on your allocation of public money and force you further into the marketplace.' Hence the financial necessity of having a private system will become entrenched within the funding bureaucracy.

At that point I couldn't be bothered to argue any further and told him to give all his food and clothes to Oxfam if he felt that strongly about it, which he doesn't.

Sam has just asked me whether Hysterosalpingogram begins with 'HY' or 'HI'. He seems to have suddenly got very enthusiastic about doing his book and getting all the details right. I know I should be glad, and I am in a way. After all, it was me that made him start it in the first place. It's just that I wish he'd share some of those thoughts and feelings with me. The way we talk to each other and react to each other has become just a little bit mechanical and predictable. Is that what happens in a marriage? Is it inevitable? I'd love to talk to Sam about that sort of thing but I know he'd just try and change the subject.

Oh well, at least now he's writing down his feelings, which I'm sure is the first step towards him being able to share them.

I'm trying not to think too much about wanting a baby at the moment. I find it drains me. I wake up feeling all fine and then I remember that according to my life plan I ought to have a couple of five-year-olds rushing in to jump into bed with me. That's when a great wave of depression sort of descends, which I then have to fight my way out of by reminding myself how incredibly lucky I am in so many ways. Sometimes it works.

Dear Self

Long meeting with George and Trevor at Television Centre today. Nigel was there for the first hour but then he had to rush off to Heathrow (two-day seminar in Toronto: 'Children's TV: Did Bugs Bunny Win? Cartoons and our children's mental health'). *Inconceivable* is moving at a hell of a speed now. They're already talking about casting and a director, which is quite unprecedented. They do have some problems with the script, though. Nothing major, but it's something I'm going to have to think about very hard. It came up after we'd all been laughing at the 'communal masturbation in West London' scene. We'd been improvising some gags about Colin sneaking a funnel in because those pots are far too small and of course ejaculation is scarcely an exact science. Then George brought up what was worrying them.

'It's too blokey, mate. Colin's stuff is really good, hilarious, in fact . . .'

'And touching in a strange sort of way,' Trevor added.

'But Rachel is a worry,' George went on. 'Frankly she's a bit two-dimensional.'

I couldn't deny that I'd been worrying about her myself and was pleased to have the chance to discuss it. We all agreed that she has some good lines, but George and Trevor (and the ninety other BBC bods who seem to have read the thing) felt that she was clearly being drawn from a male point of view.

'There's no real heart there,' said Trevor, 'and let's face it, essentially this has to be a woman's story. You can't base a movie about infertility simply on a load of knob and wank gags.'

'Excellent though they may be,' George added.

'You have to get inside the character of the female lead. Maybe you should take on a woman co-writer.'

I can't even bear to write down the terrible thought that leapt immediately into my mind when Trevor said that.

This will need careful consideration.

Dear Penny

The die is cast. I'm booked in to start after my next period, presuming, that is (and I must at all times remain positive), a miracle hasn't happened naturally.

Oh God, I do so want a child. Sometimes I think about praying. Not like going-to-church praying, but just at home in the quiet. In fact, if I'm honest I do occasionally offer up a silent one, just in my head when no one's about. But then I think that that's wrong and presumptuous of me because I don't believe in God in any conventional sense so I have no right to pray to him (her? it?), do I? On the other hand, if he doesn't exist I've lost nothing and if he does exist then I imagine he'd prefer even a sceptical prayer to no prayer at all so I can't really lose, can I?

I'm certainly not an atheist anyway because there must be something bigger than us. There are so many questions that scientists can't answer. Who are we? Who made us? Is there a reason? The easy answer to all that of course is God. The universe is a mystery and we shall call the author of that mystery God. That's how I see it, anyway. I suppose I'm an agnostic, which I know is the easy way out. And also very self-indulgent because basically it means not believing in something except when it suits you.

Actually I think it's amazing how arrogant we've become about God. He used to be a figure of fear and majesty, the ultimate authority before whom humanity was supposed to prostrate itself in humble repentance for our sins. Now you hear people talk about God as if he was some kind of rather eager stress coun-sellor or therapist. I was watching a bit of daytime American chat show the other day and someone said, 'I hadn't talked to God in a long time but when I needed him he was there for me.' The presenter nodded wisely and added, 'You have to make time to let God into your life.' This unbelievable banality actually got a round of applause! I couldn't believe the arrogance of it! Like this person and God were equals, pals! It's amazing, this ready appro-priation of the supreme being as some sort of spineless yes man who is on ready call to tell you that you're beautiful and that everything is fine whenever you feel a bit low. I can just imagine God sitting in his heaven amongst his mighty host thinking to himself, 'Oh no, some self-indulgent, self-obsessed sad sack of de-caf and doughnuts hasn't called ... If only these people would make room in their lives to let me in.'

I really don't know what I feel about religion but I do know that if I'm going to have a God I want a great and terrible God, a God of splendour, mystery and majesty, not one that spends his time chatting to whingers about how stressed they are.

Perhaps I'm just being mean. If people find comfort that way why should it worry me? I wish I could find comfort, just a little, because I do want a baby so very much and sometimes the feelings are so strong I don't know what to do with them.

Dear Sam

Lucy got her period today. We've drained the dregs at the last-chance saloon and now it's time to put our trust in the medical profession. Lucy asked me if I'd thought about praying and I said I hadn't but I was happy to give it a go if she wanted me to. We must leave no avenue of opportunity unexplored. Who knows, it might work. It seems to me that the idea of an old man with a white beard sitting on a cloud dispensing goodwill doesn't sound any more absurd than the bollocks most physicists talk. I mean really, every single bloke I know bought *A Brief History of Time* and not one of them, including me, understood a single word of it.

Why do we have such faith in scientists? When I was at school they told us that in days gone by simple folk believed the world was balanced on the back of a tortoise. How we laughed! 'What a bunch of prats,' we said. Ho ho ho! Because we know better, don't we? Apparently, according to Stephen Hawking and his pals there was this tiny lump of infinitely dense stuff the size of a cricketball, contained within which was the entire universe. Where this cricketball was and where it had come from are questions which apparently only stupid people ask. Anyway, one day the rock exploded and all the energy and stuff blasted out from the epicentre and formed into stars and galaxies which are still hurtling outwards to this very day.

Now why is that any more convincing than the tortoise?

They keep saying that if we spend another trillion or two on a new telescope they'll be able to tell us exactly how the universe began. They keep telling us how close they are, saying things like, 'When the universe was three seconds old, protons began to form . . .' Well maybe, but I think that a hundred years from now they'll discover that the universe got farted out of the arse of a giant space elephant and school kids will all be laughing to think that anybody ever believed in the big bang theory.

Sometimes the self-righteousness of the scientific profession really gets on my nerves. They always seem to assume that science is sort of outside society, that what scientists do is pure and that it is other people who corrupt it. I saw a documentary about Einstein and Oppenheimer on the Discovery Channel the other day and it was going on about what simple, peaceful men they were and that during the war they sent a letter to President Truman pleading with him not to drop the bomb. They said that it was too big, too terrible and man had no right to unleash such a force. All I could think was what a couple of hypocrites! For years they'd struggled. For years they'd devoted their colossal brains to developing a bomb which the rest of us would have to spend our lives living in the shadow of, and then they reckon they can get out of their responsibilities by saying, 'Please don't drop it,' and go down in history as sad-eyed, white-haired old peacemakers.

I went in to see Nigel today. He'd rung me twice from Toronto sounding me out about directors and co-producers. He feels we need to bring some experienced film-making talent into the mix. He's right, I think. I mean George and Trevor are great but what do they or I know about doing a distribution deal with a chain of movie houses in France? Besides which, Nigel feels that the budget will need to expand somewhat and put it outside the reach of the BBC alone. The reason for this is not because the film has got any more expensive but because Nigel feels it has such potential that we need to take it to a name director, someone with a proven track record. That of course means paying the going rate, which can run into a great deal of cash. It's a fact that with most movies, particularly the Hollywood variety, a very large chunk of the vast budgets that are quoted so gloatingly in the press is actually spent on the wages of just a few individuals.

Anyway, as I say, Nigel wants to make this movie in partnership with another production company.

'We need someone with experience,' he said to me over the phone with the voices of Canadian TV execs crackling in the background, 'but hip. We must remember at all times that we are positioning ourselves at the cutting edge.'

I knew what was coming and I wasn't wrong. Today I had my second meeting with Justin, Petra and Ewan Proclaimer from Above The Line Productions.

I must say it was a very different affair this time. Petra actually smiled at me and Justin gripped my shoulder saying, 'On the money, pal. Kickin' ass.' Even Ewan stopped snarling and treated me with a degree of civility. It seems that he's even hotter than he was when I met him at Claridge's. He's landed a three-picture deal to direct in Hollywood. I doubt any of these films will be the *Aids and Heroin* project he showed me. In fact he mentioned something about a sci-fi thing with Gary Oldham and Bruce Willis. Anyway, it seems he has a six-month 'window' before he begins pre-production 'across the big pond', and he loves my script.

'I love romantic comedy,' he explained. 'I've always liked romantic comedy but not *shite* romantic comedy. I like romantic comedy with edge, with bite, with *bollocks*! To me *Macbeth* is a romantic comedy, so's *Oedipus*. I mean what could be more romantic than a man loving his ma so much he wants to shag her? And what could be more comical?'

Slightly worrying, but I let it go. After all, Ewan's name attached to the project certainly ups the ante all round. And of course his timetable makes the whole thing even more urgent, which is fine by me. Every film I've ever heard of seems to have spent years in the planning and here I was taking shortcut after shortcut.

That brought us on to the script, with which there are still two problems – one little and one big. The little problem is that I haven't given the story an end yet. I say this is a little problem because I've actually worked out two endings that would work dramatically, one happy and one sad. I haven't been able to choose which one I want to go with yet. I suppose because Lucy and I are just starting IVF ourselves I don't want to tempt fate.

The bigger problem remains the woman's voice in the film. Everyone agrees that I haven't got it right yet and that it's crucial. It's not a big thing, the story's fine as are the jokes, it's just a matter of tone and emotional emphasis. I have to try and find a way to make the female perspective more convincing. I'm trying. I've been trying for days but the more I try the more Rachel turns into a bloke.

Time's running out. Petra and Justin are setting up auditions. Ewan is scouting for locations. I must find the woman's voice.

Dear Penny

Picked up my first sackload of drugs from Spannerfield this morning. Me and a bunch of other women, all feeling a bit self-conscious. I have to sniff the first lot, which I'll begin tonight. You sort of shove a pump up your nose and give it a blast. It doesn't sound too difficult so far. Incidentally, although we'll be paying Spannerfield for the process, Dr Cooper says that he'll pay for the drugs. Apparently some local health authorities will fund fertility treatment and some won't. Ours will, which is very lucky because the drugs cost literally hundreds of pounds! Life is such a lottery, it really is.

Sam's going to Manchester for a night the day after tomorrow. It's this huge charity concert for the Prince's Trust he's involved with. The BBC are broadcasting it and for some reason it's fallen to Sam to represent them. I could go, of course, and normally I'd love to, but I've told Sam that I'm still feeling a little under the weather after the pingogram and I could really use a quiet week.

This is a lie!

My God, I can scarcely believe what I'm writing, but I've decided to see Carl. He rang me at work and asked me out to dinner and I said yes! Of course there's no reason for me to feel guilty or anything, I'm just going to have a bite to eat with a friend. *I'm not going to do anything with him, obviously! But nonetheless, I can't say that my conscience isn't troubling me a bit. Because let's face it, I'm not going to tell Sam about it. Well, how can I? I can't say to him, 'Oh, by the way, while you're away I'm going to have dinner with the dishiest man in England whom incidentally I have already snogged,' can I? Of course, I could say, 'Oh, I'm having dinner with a friend,' but then he'd say, 'What friend?' and I'd say, 'Oh, you don't know him,' and he'd say, 'Him?' and I'd say, 'Oh, for God's sake, Sam, it's not like that,' and he'd say, 'Like what?' and . . . Oh well, before we knew it the Green-Eyed Monster which doth mock the meat it feeds on would be knocking at the door, suitcase in hand and planning a long stay.*

Dear Self

I'm writing this in my room at the Britannia Hotel opposite Piccadilly bus station in Manchester, which is, I imagine, what Kremlin Palace must have looked like at the end of October 1917. Magnificent gilt, glittering crystal, carved marble and hundreds of pissed-up yobbos wandering about looking for the bar and a shag. I love it. It's real rock 'n' roll.

Most of the BBC posse are staying at the Midland Plaza (which is a Holiday Inn but posher than most). However, Joe London and Woody Monk *always* stay at the Britannia.

'Vey understand a drinking man here,' said Joe. 'Not vat I bovver wiv all vat now, but I like ta rememba, you know wot I mean?'

'And the disco's always full of lahvly fahkin' birds,' Monk added.

On inspection Monk was proved right about this. The disco was full of lahvly fahkin' birds, but very, very tough-looking. Northern girls never cease to amaze me by how tough they look. I think it's the temperature. They seem to be impervious to cold. They never wear tights! It's amazing. In the middle of winter in Newcastle or Leeds you'll see them, making their way from bus station to club, groups of determined-looking girls in tiny minidresses, naked but for a square inch or two of Lycra, bare arms folded against the howling wind, translucent white legs clicking along the sodden pavement in their impossibly precarious shoes. Never mind Scott of the Antarctic, these girls would have done it in half the time and got back before the chip shop closed.

I must say I'm glad I'm married and past all that trying to pull birds business. I'd be far too terrified to talk to girls these days (actually I always was). Still, you can have a bit of a sad old look, can't you? And Monk, Joe and I have just celebrated the end of a great night by having a last drink in the Britannia Hotel disco.

And it has been a great night, I must say. A genuine rock extravaganza. Everything went brilliantly, not like on *Livin' Large*. Believe it or not my bloody sister rang and actually asked if I could take Kylie! I'm afraid the language I used was not very fraternal. I haven't sworn at her like that since we were teenagers. Kylie's such a little anarchist these days, she'd probably try to assassinate the Prince.

The show was at the Manchester Evening News Arena, which is just vast. There must have been fifteen thousand fans in there. Amazing. I had a doddle of a job myself, which was to . . . well . . . quite frankly, I don't really know what my job was. Hanging around, I suppose, while the engineers did all the work. That's what executives do, isn't it? And eat lunch, of course, but it was far too late to eat lunch.

We had an incredible bill. Representing the wrinklies was Joe London, Rod (obviously) and Bowie. We were to have had Phil Collins but there was fog at JFK. Besides this, we actually had a pretty impressive turn-out of current acts. Maybe the Prince is getting hip again. I certainly noticed that when the final bill was announced some of my fashion junkie colleagues at BH looked quite miffed not to be involved. The biggest booking of the night was Mirage. They're colossal at the moment and being from Salford were almost local. The lead singer's name is Manky (I think) and he hates absolutely everything, particularly, it seems, his own band. I went along to the sound check in the afternoon and he was on stage having a fight with the principal songwriter in the band, an ugly-looking bastard called Bushy. What a show! All the mikes were on and this vast concrete arena was echoing to the sound of these two lads yelling abuse at each other and pushing each other around.

'Ya fookin' cont! Ya can't fookin' sing!'

'Ya fookin' cont! Ya can't fookin' write songs.'

My heart sank because Mirage were the top of the bill (although Joe and Rod were pretending they were) and it didn't look as if Manky and Bushy would survive until the evening. These boys may have been hooligans but they were professional hooligans. One of the other members of the band started strumming his guitar. 'Look, are you fookin' conts just fookin' fookin' about? Or are we fookin' sound fookin' checkin', ya conts?'

'Fook it,' said Manky, turning to the mike while Bushy picked out the familiar opening notes of 'Get Real', Mirage's current smash. I must say, Manky can certainly sing. He has a wonderful sneer in his voice which really does sound like he doesn't give a fooking fook.

> *Strawberry Lane and Penny Fields.*
> *Norwegian Walrus yeah yeah yeah.*
> *Who's bigger than Christ now?*
> *I don't care.*
> *D'ya get my meaning with your psychedelic dreaming.*
> *I'm a Somewhere Man and we'd all love to see the plan.*
> *Hey Maisonette Bill.*
> *She's just a fool on the pill.*
> *Cos getting on an E*
> *is like having a cup of tea.*
> *Or is it?*
> *Get real.*

Some people detect a Beatles influence.

When the song was over, Manky snorted with contempt and burped hugely into the microphone. It was amazing. This colossal belch rang around the vast aircraft hangar, bouncing off the walls and the concrete floor. I thought it would bring the ceiling down.

'Ya disgosting cont,' said Bushy, 'I'll 'it ya with me knob, ya sweaty twat.'

After that the whole band had a fight.

As they left the stage I could see two familiar figures approaching across the vast acreage of the venue. It was my old lunch buddies, Dog and Fish, who were to compere the night and provide the 'comedy' element. From experience I knew that basically this would involve them coming on between each act and pretending that they did not really want to be there. The strangest aspect of modern compering (or perhaps I should say post-modern compering) is that the host of the evening invariably seems to feel the necessity to disassociate himself from the proceedings, as if it was all some sad joke they're indulging in for a laugh. You see it at award ceremonies all the time. Some young blade comes on and basically says, 'Look, we all know this is a pile of self-indulgent shit and it's probably fixed, but welcome anyway.' I think it's a shame. Bring back Michael Aspel, I say, but you see my problem is that I like things to be nice.

'Hullo, Sam,' said Dog. 'Shag the Mrs that day, did you?'

For a moment I was at a loss but then I recalled the circumstances of my hasty retreat from One Nine Oh. I didn't know what to say, so I laughed a bit and left it at that.

'Yeah, sorry you got shafted out of telly,' added Fish. 'You were a straight geezer. Best thing that could have happened to you, though. Radio's the only truly post-modern no-bullshit medium. It's the new TV.'

'So my successor didn't give you a series, then?' I asked.

'No. Bastard,' Fish said morosely. 'I couldn't believe it, even after we stormed it in Montreal and all the Yanks were queueing up.'

Oh well, it wasn't my problem any more. I had this evening to worry about.

'Now, you do know you can't swear, don't you?' I said.

'No fucking problem, Sam,' said Dog and laughed as if this was a brilliant joke and they headed for the stage.

I could see why. Brenda was starting her sound check. Brenda is a singer but her real claim to fame is that she is heart-stoppingly gorgeous. A regular star of the cover of *Loaded* magazine and a new-lad icon. She usually performs in tiny see-through nighties and sings like she's having an orgasm. The number she was rehearsing is called 'Sex Me Again Sexy Baby'. It's the follow-up to her big hit 'Sex Me Sex Me Sex Me'. Unfortunately 'Sex Me Again Sexy Baby' seems to have flopped. And our sound engineer told me he'd read that she was going to have to do another *Loaded* magazine photo spread to revive her career but that the editor has insisted that this time there was to be none of this coy stuff and it would have to be nipples out. In our sad modern world female pop stars have to be very success-ful indeed before it's allowable for them to perform with their clothes on.

Brenda was not doing a proper sound check because she was performing to a tape, but obviously a rehearsal was required so that the director of the concert video could ensure that Brenda's body would be well covered by the cameras if by nothing else.

Brenda's voice thundered out of the sound system as she strutted and pouted, miming the words.

> *Sexuality, feel my physicality.*
> *Baby, you and me. Let's get it on.*
> *Sex sex sex sex sex.*
> *My body is for you, do what you want to do.*
> *Use me and abuse me,*
> *Caress me and undress me,*
> *Sex me sexy baby.*
> *Deep inside. Oooh, oooh.*

It was all a bit too much for me. More of that and I'd have had to have a lie-down. I wandered off to have a mooch around the hospitality section. I can't be standing about in vast empty arenas ogling young girls like that. It's not good for me. Besides, what would Lucy have thought? I always feel very close to her when I'm away, absence making the heart grow fonder and all that. It made me a bit sad to think of her sitting at home, probably having a solitary bowl of soup or something in front of *EastEnders*. I called her, but she sounded a bit distracted. She said she was tired and was going to put the answerphone on and go to bed really early.

Dear Penny

We met at Quark. I've never been there before but I know Sam goes quite often on his numerous important lunches. It's very posh and they give you little plates of nibbles the moment you arrive. I got there first (of course!) and sat there feeling like an absolute slut! *I mean of course I hadn't actually done anything wrong but it just seemed to me that everybody knew I was there for a clandestine dinner with a man who was* not *my husband.*

I knew the rash on my neck was coming up. No red wine, I told myself, in fact no wine at all. My God, if I got pissed there was no telling what would happen.

The next thing I knew was that this dashing maître d' was opening a bottle of champagne in front of me.

'Meester Pheeepps 'e 'as call to sigh 'e will be a leetle light. 'E sigh to geeeve the liedy shompine.' Well, long story short, as they say, I'd had two and a half glasses by the time Carl turned up. I didn't want to but when one is just sitting there like a lemon, one does.

Carl looked incredible. Everybody turned to stare. He's grown his hair and sideburns again (for a part, Dick Turpin, American cable movie, silly script but fun) and what with his dark curls and big coat he looked as if he'd just come back from writing epic poetry and fighting duels in Tuscany. Anyway, he strode straight across to me and without so much as saying 'hello' or anything he kissed me on the mouth! I mean he didn't try to slip me the tongue or anything but it was quite lippy and totally took me by surprise. Then he stood back, stared at me with his smouldering coal-black eyes and said that I looked absolutely ravishing, which I did not, *although I must admit that I was wearing a new silk blouse with no bra (silk does rather flatter the smaller bosom like mine).*

Anyway, he was full of apologies about being late, rehearsals or something and terribly important meetings. He said he already felt cheated because he knew that my husband was only away for the evening and that he'd already wasted forty precious minutes of it.

Well, that made me think, I must say.

'How did you know Sam was going to be away?' I asked.

Carl looked me in the eye. 'I'm ashamed to say that he wrote to me on behalf of His Royal Highness asking me to read a poem at the Prince's Trust Concert and instead of agreeing, as naturally I normally would have done, I . . . Well, it seemed like fate.'

I was amazed. He had waited until he knew my husband was out of town and had then brazenly asked me out to dinner!

'This is a planned seduction!' I exclaimed and he continued to stare me in the eye and replied that he certainly hoped so.

God, I must have been the colour of a shy beetroot.

'Carl, I'm married! I . . . I love my husband. You can't possibly be serious! I shouldn't even be here.'

'Then why did you come?' he asked, and I'm afraid to say he had me there. I mean I could have protested that I had accepted his invitation entirely innocently, but after what had gone on between us before? Hardly. And me sitting there with my hair done and a breast-flattering new silk top on? The truth of the matter was that there was no way that this meeting could be innocent. I was just avoiding the truth because I was scared of it.

Carl answered his own question. 'You're here because you're lonely, Lucy. Because you need tenderness and passion and you're not getting it. I can see the longing in your eyes.'

I tried to protest that it wasn't true, but I'd lost the power of forming a coherent sentence, what with the champagne and the fact that in some ways . . . Oh God, he was right.

'I've tried to do the honourable thing and keep away as I said I would,' Carl said, 'but when this chance came along I couldn't fight it any longer. I've wanted you from the first day we met, Lucy. You fascinate me. I don't know any other women like you.'

This couldn't be true, surely? I mean Carl Phipps is a star, a heart-throb. He could have the pick of the bunch. I put this to him but he insisted that I was different, that he really did want me above all others. Before I knew it, there we were holding hands again. I really don't know if I encouraged this but I do know that I had left my hand lying prone between us upon the table and when he elegantly rested his hand upon it, I did not withdraw.

Therefore, I suppose I'm as guilty for what ensued as he.

The hospitality backstage was really buzzing. Charlie Stone was doing some interviews to be cut into the broadcast whenever any of the old rockers got into a particularly long guitar solo. I hung around with him and his recordist for a while, partly to let people know that I did have some status and also, let's face it, because he was interviewing absolutely gorgeous girls, including Brenda.

'So, Brenda,' said Charlie. 'What do you say to people who call you a sexist stereotype?'

Brenda drew herself up to her full height, which was about five feet nothing, and answered the charge.

'Well, I think they're the sexists because they don't understand that me being proud of my body and getting my kit off is actually all about being strong, and female empowerment and the me I want me to be.'

'Well, it certainly gives me the horn,' Charlie said, getting to the point, so to speak. Brenda smiled a gorgeous smile as if her point had been proved and honour satisfied.

Next I found myself in Joe London's dressing room. Woody Monk was there, of course, and Wally, the drug-addled lead guitarist of The Muvvers and Joe's sidekick for nearly thirty years. Wally looked quite extraordinary, like a mummified corpse. He reminded me of that Stone Age hunter they found after he'd been frozen for twenty thousand years in the Alps, except Wally had a feathered haircut with a spiky top which had only been preserved for about thirty years. They were rehearsing one of The Muvvers' early hits and Joe and Wally seemed to be having a little trouble remembering exactly how the song went.

Joe said, 'Nah, man, you go fahkin' da da da dum after the second line when I sing, "Youngest gun, dream won't stop" awight?'

This threw Wally completely. 'Is that the lyric?' he mumbled with apparent surprise.

'Of course it's the fahkin' lyric. I mean we've only done it eight trillion fahkin' times, geezer!'

'Well, that's amazing, man,' said Wally. 'I always thought you were singing "Currant bun, cream on top". In't that amazing?'

Then Joe saw me. It took a moment for him to focus, but he recognized me, which was nice and he seemed genuinely pleased to see me. I told him how proud and happy the BBC were that he and the band had graced us with their presence and he couldn't have been sweeter about it.

'I larve a big gig, me. A nice big charity gig. 'Ere, Wally, you remember that one we done for RockAid with Mark Knopfler and the Straits?'

'Nah,' said Wally. Silly question really because it was quite obvious that Wally did not really remember anything at all.

'Mark done this guitar solo,' Joe continued, 'you know, the one in the middle of "Sultans of Swing" . . . dabadaba dabadab dabadaba daaaa daaa, he would not stop, daaaa dabadaba dabadab dabadaba daaaa, people was nodding off, going out for fags, getting married, 'aving kids, dying. Mark's still giving it dabadaba dabadab dabadaba daaaa. "Pack it in, you ponce!" we was all shouting, but old Mark was off in Dabadabaland. In the end we just left 'im to it. I think it's still going on somewhere as it 'appens.'

Just then Rod Stewart puts his head around the door to say hello. I must admit it was all pretty exciting.

'Rod! 'Ow's it going, you old bastard? Orlright?' Joe said. 'Nice one. 'Ow's Britt? Sorry Alana. 'Ow's Alana?'

This was of course something of a faux pas.

'Not Alana, you pillock,' said Monk. 'He moved on.'

'Oh, yeah, sorry. 'Ow's Rachel?' Joe corrected himself.

'I don't fink it's 'er any more eiver,' said Monk.

'Well, whatever, ven, the new one, 'ow is she?' Joe seemed impervious to social embarrassment. 'I saw that calendar she done. Lovely girl, beautiful.'

'Very tasteful,' Monk added.

'Yeah, that's right, it was tasty, very tasty, that one with the sand stuck to her bum that was well flipping artistic, that was . . . Yeah, see ya, Rod, keep rocking, mate.'

Rod having gone on his way, Joe turned back to me.

'Lovely bloke, top geezer. Diamond. 'Asn't changed at all. Still loves his soccer. That's what I like abaht gigs like this. They bring out the best in all of us. We're here to support starvation abroad and drug abuse at home. Just a bunch of top geezers and stunning birds coming together to help uvver people. No ego. No attitude. Just cats wot care.'

At this point, Toni, Joe's supermodel wife, entered. All seven and a half feet of her. She had to stoop to get through the door. I recognized her from the pages of *Hello!* She seemed angry.

'Here, Joe,' she said. 'I've just been having a natter with Iman Bowie . . .'

'Lovely girl,' Joe interjected, 'stunning bird. She 'as been so good for David.'

'Yeah well, they've got champagne in their dressing room and what have we got, bleeding Australian Chardonnay, what if Iman or Yasmin or any of the girls come in and I offer them that? I'll be shamed . . .'

Seeing as how it was the BBC who were in effect hosting the event and hence responsible for the catering, I made my excuses and left. The show was about to start anyway. I really wanted to ring Lucy to tell her about meeting Joe and Rod and Mirage and Brenda and about the whole fantastic show, but I knew she wanted a quiet night and was probably already in bed.

Three bottles of wine between us, a quick 'Perhaps we should have coffee somewhere quieter,' and suddenly I'm in a taxi heading for his place. Yes, we were snogging and, yes, now there were definitely tongues involved and, yes, he was using his hands, upstairs and outside only but when all you're wearing is a silk blouse, quite frankly it might as well have been inside.

Before I knew it we were in his flat. I know it sounds ridiculous to say 'Before I knew it' but it really was. I mean I have never done anything like this before and it felt as if I wasn't really there, as if some other more wicked self had escaped for the night. Carl was being wonderfully provocative. I mean he didn't just leap or anything. He was, well, 'sensitive' is the best way of putting it. After the initial pash in the taxi he really held back and I didn't feel at all pressurized. So how did I end up on the couch with him? With George Michael's Older on the CD and six-year-old brandy being ignored on the coffee table while we writhed together? Because I wanted to, that's why. The booze had knocked out my inhibitions and I wanted to be there, with Carl breathing sensual nothings into my ear and expertly removing my shoes as if he'd been doing it all his life.

And then suddenly I'm floating through the air as he swept me up into his arms with hardly a jolt or a shudder and carried me through to his bedroom, beautifully neat with a vast king-sized bed covered in crisp fresh white linen. This is a man who has a woman who does, no doubt about that. He laid me on the bed and we kissed a little more and then he began to unbutton my blouse.

That was when I stopped it. I don't know how I did because I don't think I've ever felt so turned on, but I stopped it. His other hand was beginning to work its way up under my skirt, beautifully and gently but under my skirt nonetheless. It was the absolute final point of no return. Somehow I managed to find a voice and against every desire and hormone in my body I asked him to stop.

He did so, immediately. I mean he was still half on top of me but he suspended his exploratory hand actions, even going to the effort of doing up the button he had just undone. On the other hand, he did not remove his lips from my ear into which he whispered, 'Lucy, please. I want to make love to you all night, tenderly and gently and completely. I want to massage your body and touch every inch of your beautiful skin. I want to be a part of you, as one, until the morning.'

Oh God, I wanted it. How many years is it since Sam wanted to touch every inch of my skin? And massage! Christ, it takes me all evening to get Sam to give me even the most perfunctory shoulder rub and here was this gorgeous man . . . Except all that has nothing to do with anything. I'm married and I love my husband.

'And in the morning? What happens then?' I asked. After all, a night of passion is a lovely thought, but I had a lot more to lose than he did.

'Then we'll make love again, and again in the afternoon and then I'll ask you to stay another night, and another and always. I love you, Lucy. I think I want you in my life.'

It's what he said. He's a man of strong and volatile passion, that's for sure. He really has got a thing for me. I swear he meant it too. He wants me to go and live in his flat with him. He thinks life should be lived on the impulse. Did I mention that he'd taken his shirt off? He did that after he'd laid me on the bed. He looked absolutely superb, more muscular than I'd expected but not too much. I think saying no was the hardest thing I've ever done.

'Carl. I can't. You're wonderful, beautiful, and I could fall in love with you in an instant, perhaps I already have. But I'm married. I love my husband, it's not exciting like this, but then nothing is exciting for ever, is it?'

'Isn't it? That's a rather bleak view to have of life, Lucy.'

And of course he was right. Oh God, he was right. What an appalling thing to have to say. I want it, I crave it, I need it, but I'm going to deny myself because I believe that life is better lived sensibly and unexcitingly. Nonetheless that is what I believe. You can't just go doing exactly what you like the whole time. Not if you want to look after the things that really matter to you.

'Please, I have to go now,' I said. 'I can't be strong for much longer. Will you call for a cab? Please?'

And to his great credit he did not try to persuade me further. He just said, 'Of course,' and rang for a taxi. I could see that he was as upset as I was. For some strange reason he really has convinced himself that he's fond of me. Christ, I hated leaving that big beautiful bed.

'This time I really won't call you again, Lucy,' Carl said as he kissed me goodbye (on the cheek). 'It wouldn't be fair on either of us.'

The gig was pretty dreadful. I don't think I've ever heard anything so loud in my life. The engineers assured me that it sounded better on the radio, but it was rough going for the audience. I think all arena shows should be banned. They're utterly soulless. I don't care how good the act is, it could be Elvis come back from the dead but if you have to watch it at two hundred metres in what is basically a concrete aircraft hangar it's going to be pretty dull. Anyway, the kids seemed to enjoy themselves or at least they acted as though they did. Then again, if you've paid twenty quid you're going to make the effort, aren't you?

Afterwards there was a line-up to meet the Prince, but I was excluded because the Head of BBC Manchester had muscled his way in and nicked my place. I didn't really mind. I imagine you'd feel a bit of an idiot in one of those royal line-ups. I'm sure the royals do.

Anyway, as I say, me and Joe and Woody Monk ended up in the bar at the Britannia. I managed not to drink too much, although I did have more than I meant to. Joe kept getting the rounds in. I've noticed that about people who've given up the booze. They're always very anxious to buy other people drinks. Vicarious pleasure, perhaps, or else they just don't want you to think that they disapprove. Anyway, after Joe had got me my fifth bottle of Pils I had to explain that I was taking it easy as I was likely to be called upon to provide sperm samples in the near future.

'Oh, blimey,' he said. 'Paternity suit, eh? I get one of vose a veek. Fahking DNA, ruined the art of the casual shag.'

Well I'm home now, drunk and feeling very strange. Angry with myself for so nearly doing something very stupid, and angry with myself for not doing it. I know I'll feel terrible in the morning, even without the appalling hangover that I'm definitely due. But the main thing is that in the end I resisted temptation. Whatever I may have thought or desired, I did not actually do *anything. Well, almost nothing anyway, and that's what matters. I know I let him feel my breasts, but I've decided to pretend even to myself that this hardly happened. Ditto tongue-sandwich style kissing.*

Yes, I freely admit that I wanted him to shag my brains out for hours and hours, but we didn't and I'm glad.

One thing I do feel is that I'm very much in love with Sam. I hope that's not the booze and the guilt talking because I do feel it, perhaps not often, and not in the way Carl excited me tonight, but I do still fancy him. I mean it. It's not just because I'm drunk. He does still turn me on, and that's because I love him. And love is something to be cherished and protected. You can't go through life hopping from bed to bed. You can't just keep redoing the first few nights of a relationship, can you? Of course not! If you want the love and the security that a proper relationship brings then you have to go for the long haul. Even if you do really really really want to shag another bloke.

Anyway, what I really want to say is that I feel very close to Sam now. I rang him at his hotel and told him so. I hope I didn't sound too drunk because I have specifically asked him to cut down on the booze because of our IVF business, which I did not give a thought to tonight like the disgusting slapper that I am. Also I hope I didn't make him suspicious. I mean I do sometimes ring up to tell him I love him. Well, it's not the first time. I'm far more effusive than he is. Oh well.

Actually I think I'm going to be sick.

I just spoke to Lucy, which I'm really glad about. I'd just been thinking how much I missed her when she phoned. It was so nice. I haven't heard her as affectionate in ages. I suppose she was feeling the same way I was. It's not often we're apart.

I really am a lucky man. A lucky, lucky man. I just don't deserve a girl like Lucy, she's beautiful and funny and interesting and I'm just a git. In fact I'm worse than a git. I'm a bastard, a deceiving bastard, because I've already betrayed her trust over my movie script, and now I'm planning a second and even greater betrayal that I can hardly bear to think about, let alone write.

I hope I didn't sound like I'd had a drink.

Dear Penny

Well, it's been a week since the night I choose not to mention and I feel a bit better about it all. The weird thing of feeling guilty and frustrated isn't easy to deal with because there's no doubt that I do like Carl and in another world I could easily see myself with him but I've been really trying to push these thoughts from my mind because I'm absolutely committed to my love for Sam and there's an end to it. In fact we're really getting on at the moment. I don't know why. Perhaps it's doing this IVF thing or perhaps I'm making more of an effort because of 'you know what', but we do seem to be happy together.

I think it's partly Sam, actually. He seems very positive about things and about himself, which is quite a change from the way he's been, well, for years really. It's very nice.

I've been sniffing my drugs every night. This way of pumping them up your nose is all right, but it does mean that you go to bed making the most appalling honking snorts. I can't believe Sam can still fancy me, although he assures me he does. It doesn't matter anyway at the moment because sex is now out for us. I think theoretically we're still allowed to do it but I don't feel like it. These weird hormonal drugs are taking effect, I expect. That and concentrating everything on the big day.

Dear Self

Lucy is snorting and honking like a pig in bed, poor thing. It's these drugs she's taking up her nose. I've had to come through into the spare room, which is where I'm writing this. To be honest I don't think I'll get much sleep anyway. You see, I've finally made my big decision.

I'm going to read Lucy's book.

I have to if I want this script to be as good as it can be. If I want to have any chance at all of it having genuine heart and soul then the heroine's voice must be authentic. I'm sure I could get it right in the end on my own, if I had time. I could talk to Lucy, coax it out of her. I've already used lots of her lines. There was one about telling a doctor to sit on a traffic cone and see if he could relax that I put in only today. But you see I don't have time. This script is hot now. It's coming together now and I have to finish it.

I mean Lucy would want me to get the woman right, wouldn't she? Of course she would.

I tried taking a look tonight while she was in the bath. I felt like a thief, which of course is what I am. The damn thing was locked, of course. She's got one of those leatherbound journals from W. H. Smith. It'd be easy enough to pick but I might break it and then the game would be up. What I must do is go and buy another one. I'm certain that all the keys are the same. They only cost about a fiver.

I feel terrible about this, but what can I do? If I don't blow it, within six months or so I could have my own movie. The ultimate dream of every single wannabe writer on the planet. Courage, Sam. You have no choice.

Dear Penny

I went into Spannerfield today for a check-up. It seems the sniffing business is not moving fast enough, so they're going to switch me over to injections. Just shallow ones in the leg, which I can do myself, but I can't say I'm looking forward to it.

There was a lady waiting there who's on her sixth cycle! I felt so sorry for her. She's from the Middle East and it's terribly important to her to have a child. I think the pressure on women is greater in some cultures. At least I don't have to put up with that! Christ, some men can be bastards, as if a woman doesn't have to deal with enough sadness when she can't conceive without a load of pressure and guilt from her husband.

In so many ways I'm lucky with Sam, apart from loving him, that is, which goes without saying. He really is very gentle and supportive in his own way and he certainly never puts me under any pressure. I've asked him to give up the booze completely, by the way, in order to get his sperm into tip-top condition. I thought he'd sulk but he's been very nice about it. He said it didn't bother him at all.

Dear etc.

Damn, blast and bollocks. I hate being off the booze. Somebody had a leaving do today and I had to drink Coke. It's surprisingly difficult to kick the sauce. You say to yourself, 'It can't be so hard, I'll just take a month off,' but then suddenly Trevor's having a dinner party and you *have* to drink for that. Then there's the pub dominos team reunion coming up and you *have* to drink for that. And of course you're having beans on toast in front of the telly tonight, and you *can't* not have a drink with that.

Ah well. I'm going to stick with it. I love Lucy and I'm not going to let her down, particularly now that I'm actively planning to deceive her. My local Smith's was out of Lucy's type of journal today and I didn't have time to go further afield, but I'll do it tomorrow. My resolve is hardening. Lucy is being ever so nice to me at the moment as well, which doesn't make betraying her any easier. We seem to have entered a new stage of affection. Perhaps it's the treatment. Apparently it plays havoc with a woman's hormones. Well, that is, after all, the point. Also I imagine Lucy is feeling quite emotional because there is now the actual, real possibility that the treatment will work and in a couple of months' time we'll be on our way to becoming parents. My God, imagine that. We've got so used to just presuming upon the inevitability of Lucy's periods that this is a thought that takes some adjusting to. I always stress how small the chances are when I'm talking to Lucy because I don't want her to be too disappointed, but I suppose it *could* happen! And what then?!

I got a taste of it today actually. George and Melinda brought Cuthbert round for tea. He's crawling now, that is when he can find a moment in his busy shrieking, shitting and vomiting schedule. My God, that lad can puke. There seems to be a constant flow of milky vom emanating from his mouth. I mean he doesn't *hurl* it, not often anyway. It's not as if he's coating the furniture or anything, it's just always *there*, sort of falling from his toothless gums. Which of course means that eventually he *does* coat the furniture because everywhere he goes, and he can get about a bit these days, he pushes his face against things, leaving a stomach-turning slimy, milky, gobby patch behind him. I've seen it on George's shoulder many a time. It's as if a large and angry seagull hovers permanently above him, waiting for him to put on a decent suit.

Cuthbert also broke a model of a Lancaster bomber I made when I was ill last year and had painted with meticulous care. The model (which I admit was a kit, but a *bloody* difficult kit) was perfect in every detail. I even sent to Germany for the authentic eggshell blue paint for the underside. Ironic, isn't it? That you have to send to Germany to get the right paint for a Lancaster bomber. They're a big modelling nation, of course, and let's face it, in the end they did win the war. Anyway, I'd thought that I'd put the model way out of reach. 'Everything precious three feet off the ground,' Lucy had warned me, but Cuthbert seems to have an extension section in the middle, like a dining room table. Out of the blue he can suddenly reach twice his physical length. You don't see it happen. You don't know anything about it until there's an unholy screaming. Then you turn to see him surrounded by glass or china or in this case plastic (he'd sort of rolled himself on it, crushing it totally), at which point you have to comfort *him*! It's unbelievable. I mean, *he* didn't spend a week making it, did he?

Penny

I'll probably be writing to you a bit less from now on. The original intention of the letters was, as you know, in order to become a partner with my emotions and to avoid feeling like a cork bobbing about on the sea of fate. Well I no longer feel like a cork because by beginning this cycle of IVF, gruesome though it is, I really feel a lot better and that I've taken control of my destiny. I don't like to admit it, but I feel very slightly confident. I mean, although the chances are reckoned at about a fifth, I'm top of the list in terms of the perfect patient. I'm still relatively young, very young for IVF, I have nothing apparently wrong with me. My husband appears to be packing a full scrotum. All the signs are good. I don't even feel strange about trying to get a baby this way, which I thought I might. In fact just the reverse. I'm quite combative on the subject.

   I was talking to Joanna at work about it and she said something I hear quite a lot. She sort of shook her head in disbelief and said, 'Wow, isn't it amazing? I mean we really are playing God these days, aren't we?' Now she wasn't trying to be mean, quite the opposite. She's very supportive, but nonetheless I bridled. People do still seem to see IVF as a deeply unnatural process and so it is, but no more unnatural than taking antibiotics or flying in an aeroplane. Left to themselves people's teeth would fall out in their twenties and they'd die of pneumonia. Everything we do is unnatural but nobody ever shakes their head in disbelief about eating apples out of season or talking on the phone to people in Australia or being able to get from Highgate to Spannerfield Hospital, which is in West London, in under an hour (depending on the traffic). It's just babies that people get funny about. But I won't have it. All IVF is, when you get right down to it, is the process of getting the sperm and the egg to meet outside the body. That's it. It's my egg. It's Sam's sperm. If it works it'll develop inside me. All they do is create more ideal conditions for the moment of conception than the inside of my plumbing. As far as I'm concerned, it's like a Caesarean but in reverse. Millions of women have their babies removed by the hand of man. I'm just going to have mine inserted, that's all. I said all this to Joanna and she said she hadn't meant to offend and I said that she hadn't, but I suppose in a way she had. I don't feel remotely different or weird because I have to go through this, and I can do without people shaking their heads in gentle disbelief at my situation and talking about playing God.

   I just took a moment out to inject my leg. Sam hates this and turns away (as if I enjoy it!). Just wait till he starts having to give me my bum injections, that'll give him something to think about. Actually, he probably turned away because my legs look so horrible. These injections leave awful bruises (maybe I'm not doing it very well). I look as though I've been beaten up by a midget.

Dear Sam

Nigel and Justin have been asking again about the ending. They want to know when they can expect to see it. I've told them that I'll do it soon, but I'm not sure when. Lucy's and my IVF cycle will last a few weeks and I can't decide whether to commit myself to saying how my story ends before I know our result or after. After, I think, so I've told them that it'll be a month and a half. They don't like it because we've planned to begin shooting by then, but I'm being firm. Surprisingly, Ewan is being tremendously good about it. He says it's only one out of a hundred scenes and since the whole story is one of doubt, hope and unanswered questions he rather likes the idea of leaving the ending ambiguous for as long as possible. He says it'll be very healthy for the actors to discover their parts in the same ignorance and confusion that the characters are in themselves. I find myself warming to Ewan.

I've now bought four diaries from W.H. Smith identical to the one Lucy uses for her journal. One of them is bound to have a key that fits hers. Tomorrow, when she's gone off to work, I intend to return to the house and read her story.

Dear Penny

I wasn't going to write to you tonight but then I thought I would because Sam's been acting very strangely this evening. From the moment I got back from work it's all seemed rather odd. He's been alternately offhand and angry-looking and then suddenly very huggy and affectionate. Normally he doesn't express much emotion either way but tonight he seems to be aglow with it. Perhaps it's his hormones. I've heard that when women are pregnant their partners sometimes react in sympathy with them, experiencing the same symptoms. Who knows, maybe it's the same with IVF?

I must say I'm feeling pretty strange myself, in fact. I've started having hot flushes, so the injections must be working. Their purpose is to sort of shut down my reproductive system so that the hospital can take over. Amazing, really, and pretty scary.

Basically they induce a sort of premature menopause. That's nice, isn't it?

Dear Sam

Well, I'm devastated. I just don't know what I think any more. They do say that eavesdroppers never hear good of themselves. Well, nor do diary readers.

Lucy very nearly had an affair.

I'm stunned. Absolutely amazed. It is the absolute last thing I would have expected of her.

What's more, I have to seethe in silence. I can't say anything about it, of course, because the way I found out is absolutely unforgivable. And what would I say, anyway? I don't really know what I think about it at all. Of course part of me is riven with jealousy. The thought of that *fucking shit* Carl Phipps sneaking about trying to screw my wife and actually managing to get his hands on her, albeit briefly, makes my blood boil. I'm furious. I'm livid. I want to punch him and give her the biggest piece of my mind in history.

On the other hand, she was pissed, and she didn't do it, did she? There she was, drunk, with a top star, a star whom she has always fancied, a star who was putting the hardest of hard words on her (That bastard. I'd like to kill him) and she didn't do it. She pulled back because she loved me. Would I have done the same? Me, who is capable of sneaking about and invading the private diary of the woman I love? I mean if I honestly ask myself, if I was drunk, on Winona Ryder's bed, and she'd taken her top off and offered to kiss me all over and shag me all night, would I have held back the way Lucy did?

That's why I feel so confused. Part of me is angry and hurt and jealous and part of me is thrilled. Thrilled that after all these years, and with me being such a grump most of the time (plenty about that in her book), Lucy still loves me the way she does, loves me enough to walk away from a fantasy when the crunch came.

When I read about it I was furious. I literally felt I was burning up with anger, but now I've calmed down a bit, in a way I think it makes me love her more. I'm still seething, though, and very angry with her and I still hate Carl Phipps's fucking guts.

Of course one positive thing is that now I know she nearly betrayed me it makes me feel slightly better about betraying her. Well, I think that's fair, surely.

Dear Penny

I feel pretty awful, I must say. Now I know how Mum felt a couple of years ago. Looking back, I don't wonder that she was moody, and I'm not even allowed to slap HRT patches on my bum.

Sam's not himself either. He seems emotionally confused. He kisses me a lot, but then I catch him glaring at me. I think in a strange sort of way he's jealous, control of my body now being in the hands of the hospital and him reduced to the role of a near bystander in this dreadfully and intimately intrusive process.

Dear Sam

I've read the rest of Lucy's book now and it's wonderful. Just what I'd hoped for and exactly what I need. It's stuffed with really funny thoughts and poignant bits. Quite difficult for me to read, of course, since I'm the butt of most of her barbs, but in the end I don't feel that I come off too badly. I felt very guilty reading it and not just because it's so wrong to be doing so but also because it's clear that I haven't always been as attentive to Lucy as I should have been. I'll definitely try to be more sensitive to her needs from now on. Perhaps the appalling revelation of her near infidelity is what the Americans term 'a wake-up call' and the pain I'm feeling will serve a purpose. I'm not one for fatalism but perhaps I was meant to find out about what so nearly happened so that I can work harder on my marriage before it's too late.

Anyway, I've copied out loads of good stuff from Lucy's book and really feel that I can get down to finishing the script.

Obviously I'll give Lucy some kind of co-writing credit, depending on how much of her stuff I use. That'll of course mean telling her, which clearly I shall have to do anyway in the end. Oh Christ, how am I going to do that?

Dear Penny

Sam came with me to the hospital today to pick up all the needles and drugs for the next series of injections.

The last couple of days have been uncomfortable for me, but not everything has been negative. Since the other night when he went all moody Sam has been very loving towards me. He's really making an effort, for which I'm very grateful as IVF does make me feel low. The fact that it seems to be bringing out the best in Sam is a great help. He's also got very enthusiastic about his work, which is a huge relief for me as his negativity had got very wearing. I must say I can't quite see what the enthusiasm is based on. We listened to a bit of Charlie Stone's show this morning on our way to Spannerfield and it struck me as being about the most puerile thing I've ever heard. I said so and Sam agreed with me, so I asked him how he'd managed to get so absorbed in it. He said that he had things in the pipeline. I definitely get the impression that there's something Sam isn't telling me, but I don't mind. He's allowed his secrets. After all, I have mine. Looking back I can scarcely believe that episode with Carl ever happened. How could I have been so stupid? To so nearly throw away everything I have. I feel particularly strongly about that now that we're really moving on with the IVF. Could it work? Will we be parents soon? I try not to let myself hope too much, but I can't help it.

Sam

I'm filling in the final details on the IVF part of the script now. Well not the *final* detail – I still can't decide about the ending – but I'm very pleased with the way I've dramatized the process. Ewan is delighted, too, as are the rest of the team. We had an excellent meeting at his house this evening. His wife Morag made us a fabulous dinner and was very interesting about the script. She's one of those uniquely Scottish beauties, almost eerily white with green eyes, a hint of pale freckles and a great mane of strawberry-blonde hair. Quite gorgeous. Not a patch on Lucy, though. Well, let's face it, no woman is. It's probably an awful thing to admit, but I think the terrible shock about Phipps has sort of *reminded* me of how beautiful Lucy is. I mean of course I knew anyway, but maybe I'd begun to take it for granted. I think being brought up sharp against the fact that other men fancy her has rocked my complacency a bit and shown me how lucky I am.

I really really do love Lucy. More than ever, I think. And that's not because of how much she's improved my script, although let's face it she has.

Ewan laughed and laughed at the new stuff. Particularly the business about the injections. The surprising thing was how excited he was at the thought of being able to put a needle on the screen that wasn't full of heroin. He seems to think that this in itself is an incredibly original idea.

'So liberating,' he said. 'Hasn't been done in years. Although it did cross my mind that we might be missing out on some comedy here. What if somehow the IVF drugs got mixed up with Colin's drugs stash and Rachel injected that instead? Could be big laughs.'

Instantly I sensed some confusion. A fundamental misunderstanding, in fact. I said that the idea would be great apart from the tiny fact that my character Colin doesn't take drugs.

Ewan was genuinely surprised at this. 'He doesn't?'

At first he thought I was joking, but I managed to persuade him that I wasn't.

'That is *fascinating*,' he said. 'And that business about the arse injections, about you practising on an orange, that's actually true, is it?'

I assured him that it was. In fact Lucy and I were doing it only yesterday. Ewan turned to George and Trevor, who were attending the meeting, and commented on the extraordinary idea of grown men and women having to actually be *taught* how to use a hypodermic needle. George and Trevor assumed suitably sympathetic expressions of surprise that there could be such naivety. What a couple of idiots! Trevor knows about needles because of Kit's various health crises, but both of them would run a mile from hard drugs. Trevor may have had an E at some point and he and Kit certainly smoke grass, but that's it. George is strictly a Scotch and beer man. What suburban souls we must be.

Dear Penny

Well, Sam administered his first injection into my bum this evening. He had his last practice try on an orange and then prepared to go for the real thing. All I could say was what I had been saying ever since we first saw the bloody things at the hospital, which was, 'That fucking needle is four inches long.' I mean honestly the damn things are not needles at all, not in any normal sense. More like spears or lances. They belong in a museum of military history. The doctor explained that they have to be like that because the purpose is to administer an inter-muscular injection. I said, 'That fucking needle is four inches long.'

Ewan is anxious to know all the details about the process, which I think is healthy. I explained to him that the inter-muscular injection introduces a hormonal drug, which provokes the female subject into a sort of hyper-ovulation, producing far more eggs than is natural. It is, of course, physically intrusive and rather upsetting. Quite aside from having a four-inch-long needle stuck into your arse.

Ewan was sympathetic about this and Morag, who was sitting in on the meeting, nodded vigorously.

'Exactly,' said Ewan. 'This is a crucial scene, a crucial image. Actually, I think we should call the picture *My Arse Is an Orange*.'

To my dismay there was a lot of enthusiastic nodding at this from Nigel, Justin and Petra. Even Morag (whom I had thought seemed sensible) murmured that it was a 'brilliant idea'. I felt rather alone but nonetheless tried to fight my corner.

'Yes, brilliant idea, except that the film is called *Inconceivable*.'

'Oh, aye, at the moment,' said Ewan casually.

I turned to George and Trevor for support, but they just stared at the bowl of Kettle Chips.

Anyway, the deed had to be done. Sam looked as nervous as I was as he filled up the ghastly weapon with the ampoules of hormone solution, tapping the damn thing to make sure all the air was out. If you don't get rid of the air, apparently it can kill you. How nice.

'Are you ready?' he said.

'That fucking needle is four inches long.'

'And it's not going to get any shorter,' Sam said. 'Drop 'em.'

And so that was it. Up went the skirt, down came the knickers and there I was bent over the bed like a condemned woman with Sam hovering at my arse end with a spear in his hand. Most un-dignified. I could feel Sam drawing an imaginary cross on my right buttock with his sterilizing swab. Upper outside quarter is the rule. That way there is less chance of skewering a major nerve centre and rendering the patient paralysed. Very comforting, I must say. One, two, three, and in he plunged. You have to do it all in one easy movement, holding the needle like a pen or a dart. I must say he did it very well, I hardly felt a thing until he depressed the plunger and pumped in the hormone solution, which wasn't very nice, but bearable.

I must say Sam looked quite pale when I came up for air. He said he felt he'd earned a drink, but that of course he wouldn't have one. He said it nicely, as a joke. I really think this whole business is bringing us closer together.

Later on, after we'd all left the Proclaimers' house, I turned on Trevor and George for not helping me defend my title.

'Oh, come on, Sam,' said George. 'It's a pun, for Christ's sake. *Inconceivable* is just a rather poor pun. Surely after all the years we've spent at TV Centre deleting crap puns you don't expect me to defend one now.'

George can be a hurtful bastard when he wants to be.

'You liked it before,' I said.

'Oh yes, before,' he said airily. Yes, before a fashionable young director with a three-picture deal in Los Angeles said he didn't like it. God, I never thought George could be so spineless. We're all caught in the headlights of fashion and fame.

I'm going to sleep now. Sam's still at the dressing table doing his book. It's amazing the way he's come round to the whole thing. I wonder if he'll ever let me read it. I'd never ask because that wouldn't be fair, but I'd love to have a look. Maybe one day when we're both feeling very secure in our love. Of course I could never let Sam read mine, not unless I removed the Carl Phipps entries. Like Stalin rewriting history.

I must be sure to lock my journal very carefully. I found it open in the drawer today, so I must have forgotten to lock it last night, although I can't think how, I always check. Perhaps I didn't turn the key the whole way. Oh well, lucky Sam didn't find it open. He might not have been able to resist a read. Actually I think that's unfair. I think he'd do the right thing. I'm not sure if I would.

After the disagreement over the title, which I think I won, we got back to discussing the hypodermic scene. Nigel was not sure about the 'You might feel a bit of a prick' line, which I was appalled at because it's one of my favourite lines. I also think that objections on the grounds of taste are pretty rich coming from a man who virtually ordered me to make sure there were more sheep-shagging gags on our Saturday variety shows.

Of course I admit it's pretty broad humour, but the whole scene is meant to be a bit over the top. It's a big comedy moment. Colin is bending over Rachel with the needle (which should be funny in itself if they get a decent actor) and he says that the nurse had told him that as long as he does it quickly and confidently it won't hurt, so he jabs it in, she screams and he faints. Brilliant stuff, I think, and Ewan loved it.

Anyway, when Colin comes round Rachel says, 'The nurse said it was me who was meant to feel a bit of a prick,' which I think is a very strong line. I mean it's good to give the girl some rude, earthy lines. Quite feminist, I think.

Nigel just said he didn't think it was funny and George, damn him, said it was a very old joke and a pun to boot.

Anyway, I was just getting all heated and defensive as we writers do when Ewan really alarmed me by saying, 'It doesn't matter, anyway, we won't be hearing the dialogue. I always play thrash metal music over my injection scenes. It's a personal motif. I'm known for it. Have you ever heard of a Boston grunge band called One-Eyed Trouser Snake? They'd be perfect.'

A bit worrying, that, but there's nothing I can do about it. Everyone knows that in movies the writer is lower than the make-up girl's cat.

Anyway, then Nigel asked Ewan if he'd given any thought to casting.

'Well, the girl's what? Twenty-two? Twenty-three?' Ewan replied.

I quickly interjected that in fact I'd been thinking early thirties and unbelievably Ewan just laughed! He could see he'd shocked me, so he tried to explain himself.

'Look, Sam. I think we'll need to be pretty non-specific about the girl's age. I mean obviously we're not looking at teenage waifs but she's got to be vaguely shaggable, for Christ's sake. I'll tell you what I'll do. I'll accept anything from an old-looking twenty-one-year-old to a young-looking twenty-eight.'

I couldn't reply. His pragmatism (I might almost say cynicism) had temporarily rendered me speechless. There was worse to come.

'What about the man?' Nigel asked.

'I was thinking in terms of Carl Phipps,' Ewan replied.

I can't write any more tonight. All I can say is that it'll be over my dead body.

Dear Penny

I saw Carl Phipps again today for the first time since what I think we must describe as 'that night'. It was a bit of a shock. I knew it would happen soon but I still didn't find it easy. I mean it's not as if I've suddenly stopped fancying him or liking him just because I've decided I must not do anything about it. Anyway, I don't know if he was as flustered as I was because we avoided each other's eye. He'd come in to talk to Sheila about a movie script that's come through. It's small-budget, mainly BBC money, but Sheila thinks it's interesting.

'It's a pretty funny script,' she said, 'although it hasn't got an end yet for some reason. I've never heard of the author, but Ewan Proclaimer's slated to direct and you can't get any hotter than him.'

Carl enquired what the theme was and you could have knocked me down with a feather when Sheila said infertility.

'It's absolutely the theme of the moment,' she said. 'Lucy, you're our expert on the subject. Would you like to cast an eye over this script for us? Tell Carl what you think.'

I wonder if there's a scientific name for the depth of the colour of red I must have gone.

'No thanks,' I replied with as much dignity as I could. 'I can get all that at home.'

Dear Sam

We held auditions today for Rachel, which was very exciting and also most disconcerting since the casting director has definitely erred on the lower end of Ewan's age range. The venue was a church hall near Goodge Street on the Tottenham Court Road. Ewan sat behind a long trestle table with Petra, also a PA with blue hair and an earnest-looking young man with a ponytail who is to be the second assistant director. George and I slunk around at the back trying not to ogle the actresses too much. Trevor had come down but had left again; he said he found me and George too sickening. George as usual could not resist doing battle.

'Look, Trevor, when I fancy a girl I just look at her. I don't try and shag her behind a tree on Hampstead Heath.'

'We don't *all* do that,' Trevor replied. He really will have to learn not to rise to it.

Ewan was getting the girls to read one of Rachel's speeches, which I had basically lifted straight out of Lucy's book. It's from the bit where she tried a guided fantasy. Wonderful stuff. There were a couple of actresses who made it sound absolutely marvellous.

' "I mean, why the hell should I have to *imagine* a baby? Why can't I just *have* one! Far less nice people than me have lots. I know that's a wicked thing to say but I *know* I'd be a better mum than half the women I see letting their children put sweets in the trolley at Sainsbury's . . . *I'd* read my child Beatrix Potter and *Winnie the Pooh* and the only glue it would ever get involved with would be flour and water for making collages." '

Listening to it was both exhilarating and excruciating. I mean it works so well and yet of course it's Lucy's voice, Lucy's feelings. I really have done a terrible thing. Standing there watching all these gorgeous young women, all ten years younger than Lucy, mouthing her thoughts, made me feel very awkward about myself indeed. But what's done is done. It'll be worth it for us both in the end. And I can't go back now. George was thrilled.

'Very nice speech, Sam,' he said. 'The woman's voice is so much more clearly defined. You've obviously really unlocked something.'

That made me feel both better and worse.

Perhaps I should just tell Lucy, make a clean breast of it. But I can't. Not while she's all hormonally messed up with IVF. Besides, supposing she stopped me? This is my big break, my chance, and the BBC would probably sue me for the money they've already spent. Anyway, Lucy said to me that if I did this thing that I have done she'd leave me, so I can't tell her, can I? Not yet.

There was one girl who I thought read particularly well. Her name was Tilda, I think. How is it that all these actresses have such ridiculous names? Darcy and Tilly and Saskia and the rest.

They're their real names, too. I don't think they assume them. It's as if their mothers know at birth that they're going to be actresses and christen them accordingly. Or else possibly it's the other way round and that any girl who has to go to school with a name like Darcy has to get so mouthy there's nothing else for her but to become an actress.

Anyway, Ewan clearly thought that Tilda had talent, as did I, although like all the girls attending the audition she was ridiculously young for the part.

'Now then, Tilda,' Ewan said.

He was studying the script as he said it and did not even look up from it as he spoke. He did that to all the girls, just to show them how important he was. Power definitely does corrupt and absolute power corrupts absolutely. Well you don't get power more absolute than that of a movie director. In their own little world, they are absolute monarchs and it can lead to some pretty off-hand posturing, I can tell you. Especially where nervous quaking little twenty-one-year-old cuties are concerned.

'Now then, Tilda,' Ewan repeated. 'Bearing in mind the nature of this story, I'm anxious to underline the fact that despite Rachel's fears for her fertility she remains a sensual and a sexual being. Would you have any problem with that?'

Tilda was confused. So, actually, was I.

'Uhm, no, I don't think so,' she said. 'In what way exactly?'

'Well,' said Ewan. 'I think it's thematically absolutely essential that we see Rachel's breasts.'

I must say I was nearly as taken aback as Tilda was. She went bright red, which was of course highly attractive, gulped a bit and replied, 'Well . . . I don't suppose I'd have a problem with that, probably, if the part really required it.'

'Good,' said Ewan perfunctorily and for a minute I thought he was going to ask her to get them out there and then. I could feel George craning forward in eager anticipation. Thank God he didn't. I mean I bow to no one in my appreciation of the youthful female form, particularly the bosom, but there are limits.

'Thanks. We'll be in touch,' said the PA and Tilda retreated as fast as she could. I suppose in some ways Ewan's question was perfectly fair. It does seem to be something of a rule these days that, whatever the movie, at some point the girl will have to get her tits out. I'm sure that if they were making *The Wizard of Oz* today poor little Judy would have been caught in the shower when the hurricane struck or at the very least it would have blown her dress off. Some more right-on directors try to make up for it by including an equal and opposite shot of the leading man's bum, but it's not the same. I don't think you'll find many women sat on their own in front of their videos late at night trying to freeze-frame the bum shots.

Reading back over the last few pages I note how much I seem to be mentioning attractive women. I think that this is possibly a symptom of the fact that Lucy's and my sex life is currently non-existent. I must say, I'm seriously beginning to miss it, but there you go. Yet another irony in the life of couples like us, infertile couples, IVF couples, is that when we try for a baby, we stop having sex.

Dear Penny

Drusilla has come up with another plan. I blush even to report it. She rushed into the office at lunch today with a map of Dorset and the train times from Paddington. She says that Sam and I have to go to the West Country, walk to the village of Cerne Abbas, go out onto the hillside and prostrate ourselves naked upon the penis of the great chalk man that is set upon the slope. Then, well, you guessed it, we have to have it off! It seems that this is an even more fertile and spiritual place than Primrose Hill, far far more so, in fact. Drusilla says that hundreds of couples use it and the conception rates are considerably higher than with IVF. On summer nights apparently there's a queue and the local druid has to bless one of the big toes as a sort of back-up bonking area. Drusilla says that in reflexology the feet are connected to the genitalia so doing it on the foot is nearly as good.

I must say the idea of standing in a queue of hippies waiting to have it off on an ancient penis which would no doubt be still warm from the last lot did not appeal to me much, but Drusilla claims that there's actually a colossal sense of community. She says people who meet there often become lifelong pals, going off to India together in their camper vans and swapping partners. The very least they do is exchange cards at the winter solstice. Anyway, she demanded, what's preferable? Standing in a queue with some horny hippies or having my body taken over by a gang of mad scientists from outer space (she means the doctors at Spannerfield).

Well, I told her that I was now committed to the IVF cycle and that I certainly did not intend to interrupt it now. After all, if the ancient spirits have waited since the dawn of time for Sam and me to shag on top of a huge chalk knob then they can wait a bit longer. I told her I'd think about it for future reference. I've kept the train timetable, just in case. Not that it'll be of any remote use in a month or two. These new railway companies keep changing them and they don't even mean much in the first place.

I will say this, though. If this cycle doesn't work (which statistically I know it won't, although I can't help feeling sort of hopeful), I might give Dorset a go. Sam and I could use a bit of a holiday and I do love him particularly at the moment. We had such a good time on Primrose Hill (until the arrival of the squirrel) that I think it would be fun to do a little tour of the fertile spots of Britain and shag on all of them.

Dear Sam

Rather an unpleasant day on the movie. We were back in the church hall near Goodge Street looking at men, and of course that complete fucking bastard Carl Phipps was reading for the part of Colin! I have to tell you that it was excruciating sitting there being quiet while the smug, philandering, wife-snogging rat was saying *my lines*. Honestly, it felt like he had Lucy's tits in his hands all over again, but no I mustn't dwell on that, it makes me bloody livid and I know that I've no right to get on my high horse. All the same, I wanted to punch him.

We were seeing the men one at a time instead of bringing in a crowd like we did for the women. This is because Ewan wants a 'name' for the bloke and so they have to be handled a bit more carefully. Actually, I've begun to notice that there's quite a lot of casual sexism in the film industry, which is surprising considering that they're all supposed to be so right-on. It's the old rules of the market. There are far fewer decent roles for women than there are for men and so even the talented women are more desperate, hence they can be paid less and treated worse.

Ewan was using the scene where Colin gets his sperm test results to hear the actors read, and I must say it was quite exciting to see the scene come to life. The little blue-haired PA was reading in the part of Rachel. She was wearing a pair of hipsters that hung so low you could almost see her bum, most distracting, particularly since she had a tattoo of a naked Chinese devil at the base of her spine. Girls these days, eh? Amazing.

'"Forty-one per cent swimming in the wrong direction,"' she read out in that peculiarly depressed delivery that only people who 'read in' can achieve.

Carl Phipps brushed her aside and addressed Ewan directly.

'I've got stupid sperm!' he shouted, far too loudly in my opinion. Anyone can shout. 'The stuff's been backing away up my dick all these years. What is it with sperm! It's lazy, it's sluggish, it's got no idea where it's going. It sounds like a pub full of blokes!'

Ewan laughed heartily, which was fair enough because it's actually a bloody good line, but I thought the delivery was abysmal. Crap, absolute crap. A performance hewn from solid mahogany. Personally I thought that what with the disappearance of the rainforests it was ecologically unsound of him to produce such a wooden performance and I whispered as much to George.

'Actually, I thought it was pretty good,' said George. 'The line's a bit obvious, though. You don't need to spoonfeed us the gags, you know. Trust the audience.'

I hadn't really noticed before quite what a pompous arse George can be when he wants.

'Superb, Carl, absolutely superb,' Ewan was saying.

'Yes, and so good of you to agree to come in and read for us,' Justin added.

This was a reference to the fact that Carl is a star and hence should not really have to do such a mundane thing as actually audition for a part because we should all be aware of how brilliant he is anyway. As if the fact that he turned in a passable Tenant of Wildfell Hall should instantly alert the world to the fact that he'd be brilliant at playing a frustrated and infertile executive at the BBC.

'No actor is too big to read for a part, Ewan,' Carl crawled.

What a pretentious twat.

After the low snake had slithered off (no doubt pausing on his way out to try and shag the cleaning woman) we all gathered round to discuss his paltry efforts. I had expected an instant and resounding raspberry, and was bitterly disappointed when Ewan announced happily that he felt we'd found our Colin and everybody readily agreed. I was horrified and protested loudly. Normally I wouldn't have had the guts, but this was personal.

'Oh no, hang on,' I said. 'I mean, hang on! I completely disagree. He's wrong for it. Totally wrong. I mean, everything he did was wrong for Colin.'

'How's that, then?' Ewan enquired.

'Well, he was anal, uptight, repressed and terminally stiff.'

'Exactly,' said Ewan happily. 'A completely convincing Englishman.'

Dear Penny

I'm writing this entry in my book with an extremely sore arse. Well not with my arse obviously, but you know what I mean. Sam, who has been very good up until now, made a bit of a mess of tonight's injection and it really hurt. He didn't mean to, I know, and he was really apologetic. I was telling him about the script we had in at the office about infertility and IVF. It's called Inconceivable *and is to be a co-production between the BBC and Above The Line Films. I've been feeling a bit bad about it ever since I heard, having stopped Sam from developing exactly the same idea. He told me not to worry about it, but I do worry. I mean I've always been on at Sam to search within himself for his writing and the one time he did, I banned it. What's more, I actually think that it's quite a good idea that they're doing the film. Sam seemed surprised at this – eager, almost. I wonder whether he still harbours dreams of persuading me to change my mind. Not much point, I'd have thought, now that someone else has had the idea. Anyway, I'm not going to change my mind, I'm afraid.*

Nonetheless, I do think it's a good thing that the BBC are covering the subject. It's important for people like us who are actually going through these things that the issues are brought out into the open and discussed. They need to be normalized so that infertile people don't feel so marginalized. I do think that comedy can help with that. I know it's not very fair to be saying all this, particularly to Sam, but then again it's not really so strange. I like to see sex in a movie but I wouldn't want my own sex life exposed on screen (not that it would make much of a movie, I'm afraid).

I explained to Sam that whereas I shall definitely go and see Inconceivable *when it comes out I just couldn't have borne for it to be based on our story directly. I mean it would all go just too deep. The pain and all.*

Dear Sam

I got a bit of a shock tonight. I'd just been getting ready to give Lucy her nightly injection when she started talking about *Inconceivable*. I should have expected it, of course. I knew that the Phipps fucker was on Sheila's books or how could he have stalked Lucy in the way he did. Nonetheless, it was still a shock. For a little while I was thrilled, actually, because Lucy was being very positive about the whole idea. She seems to think that bringing the subject of infertility into the realms of normality via the medium of comedy is a very empowering thing. I could not agree more, of course, especially if I win a BAFTA.

I was soon to be disappointed, though. She still hasn't relented about her own privacy and I can see that it'll be a little while before I can even think about telling her.

Anyway, I was just getting the needle ready for the plunge,

having prepared my target on the outer, upper quarter of her bum as I have done every night for a week, when she brought up the subject of casting. She said that there'd been an offer put in on Carl Phipps to play the husband. I gritted my teeth and resolved to change the subject when she started to eulogize about the bastard. Saying that she thought he would be superb, being such a nice man and a truly sensitive actor and of course so good looking. I swear I did not mean to jab the needle in so clumsily, well obviously I didn't, I'm not a thug. I just jerked involuntarily, hearing her being so nice about the snake. It brought back all the memories of what I'd read and shouldn't have read and reminded me that although Lucy had maintained her honour she had done so reluctantly and that she still fancies him.

Anyway, I feel terrible now for being such a clod with the needle and have just brought her Horlicks and some toast in bed. God, she looks gorgeous, sitting there under the duvet cupping her mug in both hands. I resolve this night to look after her for ever and never let her be hurt. After, that is, I've broken her heart by revealing my black treachery. But she'll understand, won't she? I mean surely.

Dear Penny

I did something today that I swore I wouldn't do. I went to Mothercare. Only for a few minutes at lunchtime, but it was probably not a good idea. Everything looks so lovely. The clothes, the toys, all these amazing new buggies with their great big fat wheels. I love all that stuff. I don't know why. I bought some things too. Well, why the hell shouldn't I? Just a couple of baby-gros and a fluffy ball with a bell inside it. I don't see how it can do any harm to have a positive attitude and if the IVF does fail then my cousin's just had one and I can send it all to her.

Dear Sam

Things are moving at an incredible pace on the film. One of the good things about it being produced by a television company is that they're not afraid of tight schedules. And with Ewan set to begin pre-production on his first US feature in only five months, the schedule could not be tighter. It's all cast now; Carl Phipps as Colin (my God, fate has a sick sense of humour) and Nimnh Tubbs as Rachel. Nimnh is not as big a star as Carl but she's very highly regarded, having played most of the younger Shakespeare totty at the RSC and recently a '*Hedda Gabler for the Millennium generation*' (*Daily Telegraph*) at the National. I have not yet discovered how to pronounce Nimnh but I must make sure I do before rehearsals begin which, believe it or not, is at the beginning of next week. Normally you don't rehearse much with film, but apparently Ewan always does a week with the principals 'Just to create a sense of community,' he says.

Dear Penny

I went to the Disney store in Regent Street in my lunch break today. I really must stop this. Except actually I've always wanted to own the video of Snow White, *which is a genuine movie classic. As for the other toys and videos and the little Pocahontas outfit I bought, well, they'll be useful to have around when friends come over with their children, even if I don't have one of my own. I've been thinking a lot about where we'll put the nursery if we succeed (which I know is statistically unlikely). The spare bedroom is the obvious place. We only ever use it occasionally when Sam gets drunk and snores so loudly I make him go away. It's got a lovely tree outside it so it'll be possible to watch the seasons change and with a bit of encouragement I'm sure we could get birds to nest in it. One of those hanging bags of nuts from a pet shop, I should imagine. I'll buy a book.*

Look, Penny, I know what you're thinking, or what you would be thinking if you existed, in fact I know what I'm thinking and you're wrong. I mean I'm wrong. There's nothing sad or unhealthy about me occasionally buying toys. Why shouldn't I dream? Why shouldn't I indulge in a few delicious fantasies? And just supposing they're not fantasies. Supposing they come true, eh? Oh dear, it would be so wonderful I can hardly bear to think about it.

Dear Sam

Whatever I may think about Ewan casting Carl Phipps, I can't fault him with Nimnh Tubbs. She's wonderful. Beautiful and heart-breaking. She was going through some of the stuff I pinched from Lucy's book today and you could have heard a pin drop. She manages to make it funny and sad at the same time. When she read out that stuff about praying and feeling guilty for only believing in God when she wants something, people clapped, as indeed did I.

And I suppose if I'm absolutely honest, Carl Phipps isn't bad either. He does seem to have a kind of natural intensity which doesn't look forced or anything. When he does the lines it's possible for me to almost forget it's me talking. They were looking at the part where Colin tries to explain to Rachel about what she thinks is his indifference towards the idea of kids and he admits that in the abstract sense he doesn't want children . . .

'"But as a part of you, as an extension and expression of our love, that I do want and if it happened, I'd be delighted. No, I'd be more than delighted. I'd be in Heaven."' Phipps sort of paused here and looked into Nimnh's eyes. I swear they'd both gone a bit teary, both the actors, that is, not both Nimnh's eyes, although that as well, obviously. I'd heard that actors achieve the watery-eyed look by pulling at the hairs in their noses but if they did that they did it bloody slyly because I didn't notice. Anyway, then Carl took Nimnh's hand and said, 'But if it doesn't happen, it doesn't. That's how I see it. If we have children it'll be another part of us, our love. If we don't then we'll still have us and our love will be no less whole.'

Well, it's *exactly* how I feel about Lucy. Not surprising, really, seeing as how I wrote it, but still, it was very moving. Even George, who's a tough, thick-skinned bastard, seemed quite emotional. He told me that it was good stuff and I told him that I'd meant every word of it.

After that Ewan called a short break and went off to sit in magnificent, moody isolation while cute girls with spiky hair and yellow-tinted glasses brought him coffee. All the actors and crew made a beeline for the tea and biscuit table as actors and crew always do. I decided to introduce myself to Nimnh who, being an actress, was holding a cup of hot water into which she was jiggling some noxious herbal teabag or other.

'Hi, I'm the writer. I'm so glad you've decided to do this, Nimnn . . . Nhimmn . . . Nmnhm . . .'

Of course it was only then that I realized I'd forgotten to check up on how to pronounce the woman's name and that I had absolutely no idea. I think she was used to it. Well she would be, wouldn't she?

'It's pronounced Nahvé. It's ancient Celtic,' she said and there was a delightful hint of Irish in her voice which I could tell she was rather proud of. 'I feel my Celtic roots very deeply. My family hail from the bleak and beautiful Western Isles of the Isle of Ireland. My blood is deep, deep green.'

Well there's no answer to that, as they say. As it happens, I didn't need one because just then Carl came up, all blokey and matey.

'I'm Carl. You're Sam, aren't you? I know your wife slightly. She works at my agency.'

Yes, you know her slightly, mate, I thought, and slightly is as much as you're ever going to know her, you lying sneaking bastard.

'Tremendous script, mate,' Carl continued. 'Really tremendous.'

I thanked him and then when his back was turned managed to surreptitiously put ketchup in his tea. A small but important victory. Then the PA called the company back to rehearse. As Nimnh passed me she pointed to the script and the speech Ewan wanted to look at.

'I cried when I first read it,' she said.

The terrible thing is, so did I.

I'd only just put it into the script that morning. I couldn't put it in earlier because Lucy hadn't written it. She takes her book to Spannerfield and if the queue's long, which it normally is, she sometimes jots down her thoughts.

Nimnh sat on a chair in the middle of the rehearsal room, with a pen and a book in her hand (I've even used that device in the film. It acts as a sort of narration), and read the speech.

'"I don't know. As we get closer to the day that will either see me reborn or on which I'll just die a bit more, the longing inside me seems to become almost physical, as if I've swallowed something big and heavy and very slightly poisonous. A sort of morning sickness for the barren and unfulfilled. Do I dare to hope that perhaps soon the longing will end?"'

I could hardly bear it. Nimnh was reading the speech (and reading it very well), but all I could hear was Lucy. All I could see was Lucy, sitting in a crowded waiting room all alone. Scribbling down her thoughts, thoughts I was now making public.

'". . . every mother and child I see begs that question, a simultaneous moment of exultation and despair. Every pregnancy is a beacon of hope and also a cruel reminder that for the present at least there is nothing inside me except the longing. And perhaps there never will be. I don't know why it is that women feel such a deep need to create life from within themselves, to yearn for a time in which their own flesh will bring them comfort, but I know that they do. That's the one experience that women who have children easily miss out on in life . . . The intensely female grief which accompanies the fear that those children might never exist."'

Everyone was very positive about the speech. Ewan loves the way I'm 'building the script in layers', as he calls it. George said that he really felt I'd cracked the female protagonist.

'Nothing to do with me, mate,' I told him. 'Didn't I tell you? I took on a woman co-writer.'

Dear Penny

I've just re-read some of the stuff I've been writing recently and quite frankly I'm a bit embarrassed. Mawkish, self-pitying drivel. I'm sorry I bored you with it. All that stuff about the 'longing within' and 'morning sickness for the barren'. Great Christ, three-quarters of the world is starving! How can I be so self-indulgent? All I can say is thank GOD no one will ever, ever read it. Still, it does help to get it all out, even if I do sound like an absolute whinger.

I went for another blood test today as per. That's about it. Nothing else to tell.

Not long now. My ovaries feel like sacks of potatoes having got about fifty eggs on them apiece.

Dear Sam

I've now officially handed in my notice at BBC Radio. It'll mean going into debt because the advance they've given me for my film is nothing like enough to keep us, but it has to be done. I've taken so many days off in the last couple of months that they'd even begun to notice at Broadcasting House. Normally, if you don't push your luck they'll let you bumble on until you retire but even they have limits so I thought I'd better go before I was pushed.

I dropped in on Charlie Stone's studio on my last morning, to say goodbye.

'Right, OK, nice one,' he said. 'Who are you?'

Which is, I think, a fitting epitaph for my career in youth broadcasting.

I haven't told Lucy about me chucking my job. How can I? She hasn't got the faintest idea what I'm up to. Oh well, one lie more or less won't hurt.

There was a big script conference today prior to commencement of principal photography. It was held at Above The Line in Soho because Ewan didn't want to schlep all the way out to White City. Therefore George and Trevor and even Nigel had to schlep into town. Interesting, that. It strikes me that Nigel's not as tough as he'd like to think he is. The BBC are putting up most of the money but Nigel lets the Corporation get treated like junior partners to three haircuts with half a rented floor in Soho.

And why?

Film, that's why. The whole world is bewitched by film, the inimitable glamour of the silver screen. Or at least the whole of the London media world, which is the whole world as far as we who live in it are concerned. All other narrative art forms have come to be seen as drab and joyless compared to film. Novels, theatre, TV? All right in their way, but in the final analysis boring. Boring and old-fashioned, to be seen as a stepping stone, no more than that, a stepping stone into the only real place to be, the glorious world of film! If a novelist writes a novel the first question his first interviewer will ask is, 'Will it be made into a movie?' If an actor gets a part in a ten-million-pound TV mini series they'll say to their friends, 'Of course it's only telly.' The directors of subsidized art theatres sweat out their time commissioning plays which are as much like movies as four actors and a chair will allow them to be, waiting for that longed-for day when they'll have amassed enough credibility to get out of theatre and into film. It's Hollywood, you see. After ninety years we're all still mesmerized. We still want to get there. Nobody working at the BBC is going to get to Hollywood but somebody from Above The Line might and in Ewan's case will. Which is why we come to him.

Fortunately for me it was a very positive meeting indeed. Everybody agreed that the current draft of the script is good. Superb, actually, was the word being bandied about. Ewan made it clear that he was very happy.

Taking her cue from Ewan, Petra produced sheaves of faxes and declared that LA and New York are also very happy, that everyone in fact is very happy.

It was an absolute love fest.

Then of course came the inevitable caveat. This is a thing that always happens to writers in script discussions, no matter how enthusiastic those discussions might be. Somebody says 'except for'. I've done it to hundreds myself; 'Everybody is absolutely delighted, except for . . .'

'The ending,' Nigel said, and they all nodded.

It was a fair call, I had to admit.

'Vis-à-vis the absence thereof,' said Petra putting the unspoken doubt into words.

I knew I would have to stick to my guns. With Lucy and me so close to a conclusion for better or for worse, I just don't feel that I have it in me yet to decide how my story ends. It turns out that Lucy was right all along. You do need to write from the heart. It does have to come from within, and at the moment I don't have the heart to decide on the fate of my characters. I don't know how I'll feel when the news comes through, so I don't know how they'll feel. That doesn't mean I'm going to make Colin and Rachel's result the same as Lucy's and mine. I might but I just don't know yet.

'It's only the last page,' I said. 'The last few lines, in fact. I'll hand it in when I said, in a few days.'

'But Sam,' Nigel protested. 'Ewan starts filming next week.'

'Well, he doesn't need to start with the end, does he?' I said, looking at Ewan, who stared into his Aqua Libra in a suitable 'I shall pronounce my conclusions in my own time' manner.

'With respect,' Petra said – in fact very nearly snapped – 'it's a bit difficult keeping the American distributors *and* their money in place when we don't know how the story comes out.'

'Well, I don't know how the story comes out,' I protested. 'I'm sorry but I don't.'

Ewan hauled himself from the depths of his futon and reached for an olive.

'Look, it's my movie, you ken?' he said, which is directors all over for you. I'd written it. Various people were paying for it. Hundreds of people were going to be involved in making it. But it would, of course, be 'his' movie, a 'Ewan Proclaimer Film'. On another occasion I might have said something (although I doubt it), but it turned out that Ewan was on my side so I let it go.

'As I've made clear before,' he continued, 'if Sam wants to hold back on the ending then that's fine. It's good motivation for the actors and it keeps us all on our toes. They're playing two people over whom hangs a life or no-life situation. I'm very happy to help them to maintain that ambiguity. Improvisation is the life blood of creative endeavour.'

Well, that shut them up, let me tell you.

There's a church in Hammersmith next to the flyover which I call 'the lonely church'. I call it that because it's been almost completely cut off by roads from the community it was built to serve. Millions of people see it every year but only at fifty miles an hour. Its spire pokes up beside the flyover as the M4 starts to turn back into the A4. It's a beautiful church, although you wouldn't know it until you were about ten feet away from it. I found myself there today. I'd just sort of wandered off after my appointment at the hospital and I must have walked two or three miles because suddenly there I was standing outside the lonely church of Saint Paul's as I now know it to be called. I'd never seen the bottom two thirds of it before but I knew it by the vast elevated roads that roar and fume around it. I didn't go in, but I sat in the grounds trying to find the faith to pray. I don't know whether I managed it. I don't know what it would feel like to really believe in a prayer, I don't suppose many people do. I mean, you'd have to be pretty majorly religious. I do know that I concentrated very hard and tried to think why I deserved a child and came up with the answer that I deserved one because it was the thing that I wanted more than anything else on earth. I suppose in a way that was a prayer, whatever that means. A prayer to fate, at any rate.

Not long now. A couple of weeks at most and then we'll know.

George and Trevor took me out to lunch today. We begin shooting tomorrow and they absolutely insisted that I join them for a final conference. I was delighted to. Now that I'm no longer a BBC exec and on a budget to boot I don't get to dine at Quark quite as regularly as I used to and I thought it would be almost like old times.

They were both already seated when I arrived and looking very serious. George didn't even bother to stare at the waitress's backside, which must have been a first for him, and Trevor refrained from commenting on the fact that though he did not require wine himself he had no hesitation whatsoever in encouraging us to imbibe.

All in all, it was not like old times one bit. They got straight to the point.

'Sam,' said George, but I could see that he spoke for both of them. 'You're going to have to tell Lucy about this.'

It took me completely aback. Silly, really. George and Trevor are both good friends of Lucy and it should have occurred to me that they would be worrying about the obvious autobiographical details that I was exploiting even if they were ignorant about the depths of my betrayal.

'I can't,' I said. 'Not now. We're just about to complete a cycle of IVF.'

'Yes, do tell us how it turns out,' said Trevor, slightly acidly. 'Or perhaps we should wait to read it in the script.'

They were both genuinely concerned. It was as obvious to them as it was to me that a pseudonym would not disguise me for ever.

'People are very excited about this project,' George insisted. 'What are you going to do if it's a hit? You won't be able to hide from the media, you know. My God! Imagine if they found out before she did and she read it in the papers, or, worse, got doorstepped by a hack?'

'Even if it's a flop you can't possibly keep the fact that you've written a movie a secret,' Trevor insisted. 'She's your wife, for heaven's sake.'

They're right, of course, and I certainly didn't need a fifty-quid lunch (courtesy of the licence payer) for anybody to tell me. They meant well, of course, but in the long run it's my business, mine and Lucy's.

I told them that I'd tell her when I know how the story ends.

Dear Penny

Sam gave me the last injection tonight before egg collection, which we go in for at seven a.m. the day after tomorrow. Rather dramatically, the injection had to be done at midnight. It's now twelve fifteen but I know I shall have trouble sleeping. Sam's been very good about the injections. Apart from that one time, they haven't hurt at all. Talking to some of the women at the hospital, it seems that some husbands (partners, I should say) can't bring themselves to do it at all, so the poor women have to go in at seven every morning for weeks. Imagine that. It's boring enough just going in to keep them topped up with the endless amounts of blood they seem to require. Sam told me that he was scared at first but he'd got used to it. I know that I wouldn't like to have had to inject him with huge needles. I think he's been quite brave. In fact I think he's been very good about the whole vile business which I know he would never have got into at all without my insistence. He's given me a lot of strength. Taking such an interest and always being around when I need him. Some husbands hate it all so much that they try to pretend it isn't happening. Sam hasn't been like that at all. Quite the opposite. He's been fascinated, which has made things much easier for me. I tried to thank him a bit tonight because I know he's never really, really wanted children. I mean not really.

She's wrong about me not really wanting children and I told her so. I told her I really do want us to have children, that I want it with all my heart, and I do. I told her I wanted it because I love her and that our children would be an extension and expression of that love. Another part of us. But if it doesn't happen then we'll still have us, that our love will be no less whole . . . and then I realized that I was quoting the bloody script! And I couldn't remember whether I'd said it before, or written it in my book, or made it up for the film, or nicked it from Lucy's book! I suddenly realized that I no longer knew whose emotions were whose. I thought I've got to tell her, right now. And I did try. I started to, but I couldn't. Not now. She's having her eggs collected tomorrow.

Sam was a bit distracted, actually. Probably the fact that he's got to have another hospital wank tomorrow. He hates that so much. Oh well, maybe it'll be for the last time. Who knows? If we could only score. Anyway, he didn't say much. I think he wanted to but he didn't and I didn't press him. We just held each other. In fact it got quite heated for a minute, but I reminded him that if we made love tonight we could end up with twelve. So we stopped.

I feel incredibly close to Sam tonight. I told him that I love him and that it gives me strength to know that whatever happens I'm safe in that love.

I thought he was going to cry. Then I thought he was going to tell me something. Then he didn't say anything.

Dear Sam

This morning Lucy and I went to Spannerfield for the big day of egg and sperm collection. We got there at 6.50 a.m. for 7 as instructed, to find a lengthy queue of cold, sheepish-looking people already there. Most of them were women in for injections because they don't have husbands like me who have the sheer iron guts to do it themselves. Some of us, however, about ten couples, were in for the full business and we were duly led off to a ward with a row of curtained-off beds in it.

There was a rather nice nurse called Charles. Lucy knew him already but it was all new for us husbands (or partners).

'All right, Lucy,' said Charles. 'We'll just pop this on and hop into bo-bos and, Sam, we'll be wanting a little deposit from you for the sperm bank, so I'll just leave a paying-in pot here and I'll call you when there's a service till free.'

Another wanking pot. Great. When I was a kid blithely spanking the plank at any opportunity that arose I never would have even dreamt that I was in fact rehearsing for what would one day be perhaps the most important day of my life.

Lucy had to put on a sort of nightie-smock that was entirely open at the back. She made a comment about it that nearly made me drop the tossing instructions that I was idly perusing, as if I didn't know them by heart by now.

'Dignified little number,' she said. 'Think I'll wear it to a première.'

For a moment I was completely thrown.

'Première!' I said with what could only have been incriminating alarm. 'Première of what?'

'Nothing, just any old première,' she replied, looking at me rather strangely. 'I was joking.'

Just then Charles returned and summoned me to do my duty. He did this by poking his head round the curtain and beckoning me with an ominous-looking finger.

'Your chamber awaits,' he said. And with grim resignation I took up my pot and went.

There are at least two rooms at the actual unit so the pressure of the queue was somewhat alleviated. In fact Charles told me that I had as much time as I liked because we were all in for the whole day anyway.

Well, that was some small comfort, but having said it you've said everything, because this was the most pressurized visit to Mrs Hand of them all. This, as they say, was shit or bust time and as I sat there alone, in the little room, trousers round my ankles (having duly washed my knob as instructed) I contemplated the awesome nature of my responsibilities. My wife, whom I love very very much, has just gone through six weeks of the most appallingly intrusive therapy. Drugs have been pumped into her at every hour of the day, forcing her body to shut down in a premature menopause prior to it being taken over and coerced into a grotesque fertility, over-producing eggs until her ovaries have become heavy, bloated and painful. Every other day for weeks she has traipsed across London to sit in queues with other desperate women, waiting to have various body fluids taken from her and to have her most intimate womanly self probed and manipulated. The reason for all this is of course her desperate, heart-rending longing for a child, a longing which this day may possibly heal.

Now if at this point I fail to ejaculate successfully into a pot, making absolutely sure that I catch the first spurt, this whole dreadful business will have been a total waste of time. So there I sat with all that pressure, alone in a room, attempting to coax my penis into a firm enough condition for me to masturbate successfully and fulfil the trust and the dreams of the woman I love.

Sam looked quite pale when he returned from doing his duty. He said he thought he'd got enough. I said I damn well hoped so. They only need one.

The egg extraction was a rather weird experience. Being there with Lucy while the doctors take over makes you feel like an awkward guest at your own party. When our time came they wheeled Lucy into the theatre, while I padded along behind feeling a complete prat in my green gown, raincap and plastic galoshes.

I sat up at the non-business end and Lucy was soon snoring rather fitfully, having been put out for the count. They had her legs up in stirrups and a doctor lost no time in getting down to business. There was a little television screen on which he could see what he was doing through some ultrasound technique or other and he talked me through it.

'So the white dot on the screen is the needle. Can you see it moving? I'm lining it up with the follicle, which I pierce. Can you see it deflating?'

I didn't answer because it was clearly more of a statement than a question. Besides, I felt too intimidated to speak. I didn't wish to distract anybody by word or deed. Nonetheless, I could see what he was describing – shadowy translucent bubbles being popped by the little white dot and then collapsing as he sucked them out.

'Now we're removing the fluid from inside the follicle, within which should be the eggs.'

Sure enough, they were siphoning out test tube after test tube of pale red liquid and then handing them through a little kitchen hatch into what I presumed was the lab.

It was extraordinary. The lady through the hatch kept shouting, 'One egg . . . two more eggs . . . another egg,' like a dinner lady. It reminded me of that scene in *101 Dalmatians* where the nurse keeps rushing out excitedly saying 'More puppies!' Anyway, in the end the doctor had got the lot and so he backed up the Pickford's removal van between Lucy's legs and started to dismantle the scaffolding rig he'd put up her.

On the way home in the car Sam told me all about it. I was feeling pretty woozy anyway and I can't say that stories of doctors sucking eggs out of my vagina made me feel much better. Still, at least it's over. Sam says they told him they got twelve eggs, which was about what they wanted. He said he hoped he'd managed to provide twelve sperm, but I think he was joking.

It was so strange to think that at that very moment, as we drove home, back in the hospital his sperm were being whirled round in a centrifuge prior to being shaken up in a tube with my eggs.

We both agreed that the whole experience was one that we were not anxious to repeat. I said that perhaps we wouldn't have to. After all, twins are quite common with IVF, even triplets (my God!). Sam told me not to jinx us, but I don't know. I just have this funny feeling that it's going to work.

'I feel good inside,' I told him, and then I was sick into the glove compartment, but it's all right, the doctors said that might happen. All right for me, that is, not Sam, who had to clear it out.

Dear Sam

We began principal photography today. God, it was exciting. We're filming in an old warehouse in Docklands, which they've done out as the hospital. I took the light railway which is not a bad service. They offered to send a car for me but I said no. Lucy might have wondered why commissioning editors of Radio were suddenly being treated so grandly. When I left she was still in bed. I took her a cup of herbal and longed to tell her where I was going. It would have been so wonderful.

'Bye, darling, I'm just off to a film location where about a hundred people are working on MY FILM.'

It's the thing I've dreamt of all my life. What's more, Lucy has shared so many of those dreams, and now they've come true I can't even share it with her. How cruel is that? Fate can be an absolute bugger.

I'll tell her soon, I swear it. The moment we're through this IVF cycle. George says it's pointless to put it off and that there'll never be a good time, but I can't possibly tell her now, she's too fragile. She's taken the week off work (although they say you don't have to) and seems to be in a world of her own. Sort of serene, but very delicate. She says she's trying to be entirely relaxed and meditative. Aspiring, apparently, to an absolute calmness within. Well, I don't think she'd be very calm within if I said to her, 'Oh, by the way, darling, I've turned our mutual agony into a movie and what's more you've unwittingly written half of it.'

How did I get into this? I can't believe it's such a mess. I'm sure I had no choice. Didn't I? I definitely seem to remember having no choice, but it's all gone a bit hazy.

I must say, though, that the day was wonderful. Incredibly exciting. Just seeing all the cameras and cables and trucks and catering and actors and crew, and all because of me. It felt fantastic. People kept coming up to me and asking if I was OK for coffee and saying, 'It's a wonderful script. When I read it I cried.'

Ewan was starting with Rachel's laparoscopy and at first I thought he must have sacked Nimnh because an entirely different actress was on set in the operation smock. I was just getting up the courage to protest to Ewan because I think Nimnh is wonderful when I noticed Nimnh sitting in a folding chair smoking a cigarette. On further investigation it turned out that the new actress was a bottom double! Imagine it! Grand, or what?

It seems there'd been a row earlier that morning when despite Nimnh's protests Ewan had been adamant about filming Rachel from behind getting into bed with the open-backed smock on.

'For Christ's sake, it's not about perving on her arse! It's about her vulnerability! Can't you see that?' he exclaimed. 'This woman is a piece of meat, stripped of dignity. Her arse is *quite literally* on the line and we need to see it!'

Well, Nimnh had simply folded her arms and refused point blank. She said she did not do two Desdemonas and a Rosalind at the RSC in order to have her bum used to sell videos. I thought she was absolutely right, actually, although like every man on the set I would have loved to see the bum under discussion.

Thinking about it, that's probably another good reason why

she shouldn't have to show it. Frankly, I find balancing my sexual politics with my sexual desires is a constant struggle.

Dear Penny

It's three days now since the egg extraction and today was the day to have it all put back in. That is if there's anything to put back, which was the first anxiety. All the way in in the car we were quiet, both of us wondering if our eggs and sperm had even managed to conceive at all, which they might very well not have done.

Well it turned out all right, in that we had managed to create seven embryos, which they said was good. A doctor took us aside into a little room and it all got very serious as she explained that some of the embryos are good and some are not so good, and one was useless because although the egg had been fertilized the embryo had already gone wrong, etc., etc.

Anyway, the long and the short of it was that we had two very good and two pretty good. The doctor said that they were prepared to insert three if we insisted, but she strongly recommended that we do only two, which I was very happy to go along with. I mean the possibility of triplets is pretty daunting. I had been hoping that they would freeze the other two good ones but they don't seem to encourage that at Spannerfield. I don't know why. Anyway, although the consultation was presented as a series of choices for us, in the long run, let's face it, you do what you're told, don't you? I mean I don't know one end of a two-celled embryo from another (if indeed they have ends). That's why you have doctors. Anyway, that was it. We agreed that two embryos be reinserted and the rest would be donated to the hospital for research, which is apparently their usual procedure if the donors have no objections, which we didn't.

The reinsertion was very quick indeed. No anaesthetic or anything. They just wheel you in, spread your legs, and squirt them up. It's incredibly low tech really when you consider the dazzling medical science that has led up to it. First they show you the fertilized embryos on a little telly screen, then a big tube appears on the screen (actually it's about a hair's breadth) and sucks them up. Then a nurse brings the tube through to the doctor (it's like a very long thin syringe). The doctor puts it up your fanny and, guided by an ultrasound picture, she injects the embryos into your womb. It takes about a minute unless the embryos get stuck in the tube, which they didn't with us.

It's a hell of a lot easier than the egg extraction. The only real discomfort is that they make you do it with a full bladder because for some reason this makes for a clearer picture. Afterwards they won't let you wee for about three quarters of an hour, which is absolutely excruciating and you keep feeling that the terrible pressure must be crushing the life out of your poor embryos.

Then they let you go home. As we were getting ready to leave, Charles, the nurse, came in with a printout of the computer image of our two embryos, both of which were already dividing into further cells.

'This is them,' he said. 'Good luck.'

When we got home Sam made some tea and I just sat in the sitting room staring at the photo, thinking that this could be the first photo in an album of our children's lives. It's not many kids who get to see themselves when they were only two or three cells big.

Sam reminded me that the chances are that these ones won't either and I know that, of course, but I'm sure that mental attitude has an effect on the physical self. I know I can't will it to happen, but the least I can do is give Dick and Debbie the most positive start in life that I can.

Yes, all right, I've given them names! And I'm not embarrassed about it either. They're mine, aren't they? They exist, don't they? At least they did when the picture was taken. And now? Who knows? I could see that Sam was not at all sure about personalizing things in this way. But why not? They're fertilized embryos! That's a huge step for us. Something we might easily not have been able to do. We have to be positive, we're so far down the road.

Sam reminded me yet again that it's only a one in five chance. Well, I know! I know. Of course the odds are long, but they're not impossible. Twenty per cent isn't a bad shot. When my photo was taken they were alive.

'Think about that, Sam,' I said. 'Two living entities created from you and me. All they have to do now is hang on inside for a few days. They just have to hang on.'

It's funny, but Lucy's enthusiasm, the strength of her will, is infectious. Because the more I looked at that photo, the more real those two little translucent splodges became. They are, after all, already embryos. They've already passed the beginning of life. And I couldn't deny that in a way they looked pretty tough, I mean for three-celled organisms, that is, obviously.

'Of course they're tough,' said Lucy. 'Think what they've been through already! Sucked out of me by vacuum cleaner, pumped out of you into a cold plastic pot. Whirled around in a centrifuge, shaken up until they bash into each other, smeared on a microscope slide then sucked up again and squirted through a syringe. It's a positive assault course. Dick and Debbie are SAS material!'

She's right, of course. If they do make it back out of her they're going to be either commandos or circus performers. And they might make it. They could make it. I mean, why the hell shouldn't they? If they can just hang on for a few more days while they grow a few more cells.

Then Lucy whispered at her stomach.

'Come on, Dick and Debbie,' she said. It was sort of as a joke, but I could see that she meant it, so I said it too but louder.

'Come on, Dick and Debbie!'

Then we started shouting it.

Funny, really, the two of us sitting there, laughing and shouting at Lucy's stomach.

Whatever happens now, that was a good thing to do.

Dear Penny

I wonder if this will be the last sad letter that I ever write you? The long wait is coming to an end. One more vaginal suppository is all I have to take (there's heen nine, plus three more spikes in the bum). I hope Dick and Debbie realize what I'm going through

248

for them. Sam says that if they're as tough as we hope they are, in eight and a half months I'll be able to tell them. I hope we're not hoping too much. It's only a one in five chance, after all.

Sam said that any child of mine would be one in a million.

Then we kissed for ages.

I can't deny that I feel good. I'm not even slightly periodic and normally I can feel my period coming for a week. Sam agrees that that has to be a very good sign.

Oh well, the day after tomorrow we'll have the blood test and then we'll know. I've made Sam promise that he'll take the day off. He's been working so hard recently (God knows what on – Charlie Stone just seems to say the first thing that comes into his head, which is usually 'knob'). Anyway, I definitely don't want to get the news alone.

After we had kissed, Sam got very serious and said that when it's all over, for better or . . . well, hopefully for better, he wants to talk. I said fine and he said, 'No, really talk, about the last few months, and all that we've been feeling and going through together.' This is a very encouraging sign for me because as I've said before, Sam is not always the most communicative of people. He says he wants to talk about where he wants to go as a writer and what sacrifices we would both have to make for it and, well, lots of other things.

He says he wants to go away this weekend. Whatever the news is and . . . well, talk.

I said that I thought it was a great idea. We can take Dick and Debbie on their first trip.

We thought about that for a while and then we kissed again and then he said he loved me and I said I love him and there was more kissing and Sam put his head on my tummy, where it is now. One thing is for sure: whatever happens, whether Dick and Debbie make it or not, IVF has been good for Sam and me. It's really brought us closer together.

It's twelve-thirty at night. Lucy and I have had a lovely evening together and we've agreed to go away together next weekend. I'll tell her everything then.

She's been asleep for an hour now. But I couldn't sleep because as I lay there thinking about Dick and Debbie I decided on the way my film is going to end. I've just written it up and faxed it to Ewan, who, as far as I know, never goes to bed.

INT. DAY. COLIN AND RACHEL'S HOUSE.

The news comes in the afternoon. Colin and Rachel are sitting, anxiously awaiting a phonecall. They take strength from each other's presence. They hold hands. The phone rings. Colin tries to answer it but Rachel is holding his hands too tightly. There's a moment of comedy and emotion as Colin has to remove a hand from Rachel's traumatized grip in order to pick up the receiver. He listens for a moment. In Rachel's eyes we see the hope and the fear of her entire life. Colin smiles, a smile so big, so broad it seems to fill the screen. He says, 'Thank you,' and puts the phone down. He looks at Rachel, she looks at him, he says, 'They made it.' The End.

That's it. Whatever happens to Lucy and me, that's the end of my movie. It's the ending I felt tonight, the ending I want.

Ewan just phoned. I hope he didn't wake Lucy.

'It's mawkish, over-sentimental, middle-class English shite,' he said. 'I love it.'

Everybody seems to have been up late tonight. Petra called as well and George, who never sleeps at all any more because of Cuthbert.

Petra was hugely relieved. 'The right decision, Sam,' she said. 'I might as well tell you now. If I'd gone to LA with anything other than a developing foetus, they'd have withdrawn their funding.'

I'd unplugged the phone in our bedroom and was having a last whisky (which I've been allowed since making my last deposit) when George phoned.

'Well done, mate,' he said.

I told him it was what I felt like writing.

Somehow I think that now everything will be all right.

Dear Penny

Today I got my period.

It started at about eleven this morning. It came without warning but it's a heavy one and it means that all my dreams are dead.

I'm not pregnant. I've never been pregnant. The two embryos I called Dick and Debbie died a week ago.

I sat on the lavatory for about an hour, crying. I don't believe I've ever cried as much in my whole life as I did today. My eyes are swollen and sore. They feel like they have daggers in them.

I wasn't just crying for the loss of the babies that never existed. That was only the beginning of my trouble, the beginning of the nightmare that was today. I've been crying for the loss of my whole life, a life I thought I knew but it turns out I didn't know at all.

I'm writing this alone in bed. I'll be on my own from now on. Sam isn't here and he won't be coming back. I don't know where he is and I don't care. I've left him.

I'm going to write down what happened so that I never forget.

After I'd cried so much that I thought I would dehydrate I knew that I should tell Sam. We'd been through it all together and I felt that he'd want to be with me at the end of it. Besides, I needed him. Having gone about for a week half believing that I had a child inside me, or even two, I suddenly felt more desperately alone than I could have imagined possible.

But when I spoke to his office at Broadcasting House I was amazed to discover that Sam no longer worked there. The woman I was speaking to said that he'd left weeks ago. She didn't want to tell me where he was, either, as she said it was very private. I told her that I was his wife and I was ill and that she had to tell me where he was. She gave in in the end but she didn't want to. I could tell that she was wondering why Sam's wife didn't know where he was, or that he'd changed his job. I was wondering that too.

When I was riding in the taxi I think I believed he was having an affair. That's what I expected to find at the address the woman had given me. Sam in the arms of another woman. I wish that that's what I had found.

The address was a film location. A big warehouse in Docklands with the usual trucks and trailers and generators outside and inside, a vast darkened hangar where a number of sets had been constructed. There were people everywhere. I passed a group dressed as nurses and as I walked in I could see immediately that one of the sets was a hospital operating room for women, with stirrups and that sort of thing. I stood there for a while, hidden in the shadows, not knowing what to think, not really thinking at all. Everything was so confused, and I felt scared. Scared of what I was about to discover. Slowly it all began to swim into focus. I could see that all the lights and the attention were concentrated on what was a bedroom set, a bedroom very like my own, in fact. There were two actors on the set, one of them, to my astonishment, Carl Phipps. The other was a woman I recognized as Nimnh Tubbs from the RSC. Someone called for quiet and the two of them began to play out a scene. It was a rehearsal. I knew that because I could see that the camera was not being operated. Carl sat at a desk and pretended to type into a laptop.

'What the hell do you find to write about?' he said. 'What an emotionally retarded shit I am, I suppose. I know you secretly think I'm holding my sperm back. You think their refusal to leap like wild salmon up the river of your fertility and headbutt great holes in your eggs is down to a belligerently slack attitude which they've caught off me.'

I could feel myself going cold. Surely that was exactly the sort of thing that Sam always used to say to me? What was going on? Why was Nimnh Tubbs sitting on the bed holding a journal just like I do every night? Just like I'm doing now, in fact.

Then a young Scottish man who was clearly the director stepped into the scene.

'Obviously we'll pick up a reaction from you there, Nimnh,' he said. 'Semi-distraught, emotionally dysfunctional, pathetic little woman stuff, OK?'

Nimnh nodded wisely. She knew that type.

Perhaps I'm stupid. Maybe the last few months have made me stupid, but at this point I still didn't know what was going on. I just stood there, convinced that I was in some horrible dream. They started rehearsing again, more words I knew.

'I just happen to believe that when God made me he made me for a purpose beyond that of devoting my entire life to reproducing myself.'

And she replied, 'When God made you he made a million other people on the same day. He probably doesn't even remember your name.'

Then I knew. Those were my words! My actual verbatim words! Just then I saw Sam. I don't know whether I'd realized what was going on before or after he appeared, but either way I was no longer confused. I knew what had been done to me.

The director had called Sam over. Nimnh was having trouble with the motivation behind the scene and the director wanted her to hear it from the writer.

The writer. I was the bloody writer.

'You see, to me, Nimnh,' said the man who had been my husband, 'this scene represents the beginnings of her descent into a sort of sad madness, a kind of vain obsession. To me the line about not crying outside Mothercare on the way to the off licence is crucial . . .'

Then I realized the full extent of his betrayal. I'd never told Sam about Mothercare and the off licence. I'd only told you, Penny. He'd read my book.

Sam wittered on, posing importantly, loving himself.

'Don't forget that this woman is beginning a journey that will see her lose all dignity and sense of previous self,' he said. 'Before she knows it she'll be making a fool of herself at hippy visualization classes, adopting a baby gorilla and claiming it's got nothing to do with her infertility. She'll have reduced her sex life to a series of joyless, soulless, cynically calculated servicings, treating her poor, hapless hubby as some kind of farmyard animal, brutally milked for its sperm . . .'

They laughed at this. They laughed at it all. Why wouldn't they? It's funny, I suppose.

It was then that I walked forward on to the set. I still can't decide whether it was a good idea, but I was in a daze. Some young woman with blue hair and a walkie-talkie tried to stop me, but I was not to be stopped. They all heard the young woman's protests and turned and saw me. I don't know what Sam thought.

But I knew what I thought. One word.

'Bastard,' I said. It was all I could say. 'Bastard.'

Carl was nearly as surprised as Sam was, but I had no time for him. My whole being was taken up absorbing this new Sam, this Sam whom I'd never known.

'You bastard, Sam, you utter, fucking bastard.'

I hated him and I still hate him. He tried to speak, but I wouldn't let him.

'I got my period if you're interested,' I said. 'We failed. Dick and Debbie didn't make it.'

I didn't care that the director and Carl and Nimnh and the woman with blue hair could hear me. I didn't care about anything. They all began to turn away with embarrassment, but I told them to stay. I told them that they might as well listen now because they'd hear it all soon anyway, that Nimnh would be saying it all tomorrow.

George ran up. My God, George! They were all in on it. I remember wondering if Melinda knew as well.

Carl seized the moment to ask me what I was doing, what was going on.

'Ask him!' I said, and all eyes turned from me to Sam. 'He's told you everything else about me . . . My God, Sam, you've been stealing my book. Stealing my thoughts and feelings, like a thief!'

I don't know whether I actually said all that or whether I just stuttered at him. I do know that I was crying, which astonishes me, looking back on it. I'm certainly not a person who makes scenes in front of strangers lightly. I think that failing IVF had already pretty much destroyed what emotional defences I had. And then all this.

Then both Sam and Carl tried to take my arm to lead me away. Sam was stuttering apologies. Carl was trying to get me to calm down and explain. Then Sam rounded on Carl.

'You keep out of this!' he said, and he looked like he was going to cry too. 'I know all about you!'

254

Carl was astonished. It was the last thing he expected.

'Now look here . . .' he started to say, but I didn't let him get the chance, I just went for Sam.

'Yes, that's right, Sam!' I shouted. Everyone really was backing away now, even the Scottish director, who did not look like a man who would embarrass easily. 'You know all about Carl! That he took me out and that I kissed him. You know everything about me, don't you? Because you've stolen my bloody thoughts! Well, here's another little piece of me and you can have it for nothing. You won't have to sneak about picking locks on people's diaries for this! I hate you! I hate you more than I ever believed I could hate anyone, and I never want to see or speak to you again . . .'

That's what I told him, in that or so many other words, and I meant it. I still do.

Then I ran out of the building with both Carl and Sam running after me. If it wasn't the worst thing that has ever happened to me it would be funny.

We stood there, the three of us, on a pavement in the Docklands, Sam desperately protesting that he'd never meant it to be like this, Carl hanging back wondering whether to intervene or not.

'I meant it, Sam, what I said,' I told him. I was calmer by this time, calm enough to look him in the eye. 'I told you once that if you did this thing I'd leave you and that's what I'm going to do.'

He tried to say that I wasn't myself, that I was over-reacting because we'd failed IVF. Over-reacting. That's a phrase I won't forget in a hurry.

'You've read my book, Sam,' I told him. 'You know that having a child with you was the thing I wanted most in the world. Well, it isn't any more, it's the thing I want least. I'm glad Dick and Debbie are dead! Do you hear! I'm glad they never fucking lived!'

He looked at me for a moment. He was numb, I could see that. Then he started to cry.

He knew he'd lost me.

Tonight is the first time I've opened this 'book' document on my computer since that night when I finished my script and Lucy and I held each other for the last time and I was happy for the last time.

That was three months ago and not one minute has gone by since then, waking or sleeping, when I haven't missed Lucy with all my soul.

I don't know why I've decided to write something in this book now, I just thought I would. I suppose the truth is that I've bored my friends enough with how unhappy I am and the only person left whom I can safely bore without risk of further increasing my solitude and isolation is myself.

I made the biggest mistake of my life when I did what I did to Lucy. Every day I've asked myself how I could have been so stupid and I still don't have an answer. I suppose that I just never thought Lucy really meant it when she said that she'd leave me. I keep going over it all in my mind and I still think that if she hadn't found out about it in such a terrible, brutal way she might not have reacted quite as she did. I don't know, maybe she would. Either way it's academic now, and one thing's for sure: it's all my fault.

We haven't started divorce proceedings yet, but I imagine that it won't be long. We've scarcely even spoken, although there have been numerous exchanges of notes, just practical stuff, not nasty but very cold. I imagine that the final separation when it does come will happen in that tired inevitable modern way. No court case, no drama, no dreadful scenes or confrontations, just the required passage of the allotted amount of time. Lucy won't have to stand up in court and cite my pathetic career and ambition as a co-respondent. The fact that I betrayed and deserted her is of no concern to the law. It's enough that Lucy no longer wishes to be my wife. These days marriages just fade away.

The film is finished, or at least what's known as principal photography is finished, and the editing process has begun. I take no interest in it, of course. In fact I've had nothing at all to do with the project since the day I ran out of the studio chasing vainly after Lucy in an effort to persuade her to forgive the unforgivable. George and Trevor keep me informed. They say that everybody remains very excited. Funny, this is the fulfilment of a lifetime's ambition and I don't care. In fact I actually tried to stop the whole thing. How many writers have done that? After the full extent of my appalling behaviour was so ruthlessly exposed I felt that the only honourable action I could take was to put an end to the film immediately. It turned out that I couldn't. It was no longer mine to stop. The BBC own it in partnership with Above The Line and having already spent over two million pounds on it they were reluctant to cancel. Saving my marriage was not number one on their list of priorities.

I told Lucy what I'd tried to do and she wrote me a pretty caustic note about it saying that she didn't care whether the film progressed or not, that what I had stolen from her she didn't want back anyway. Perversely, I think that the fact that our story no longer belongs to either of us but is instead the sole property of a large corporation has made it a little easier for her. Further evidence of the fact that we as a couple had ceased to exist.

I've given her all the money I got from the film. It's not a vast amount, although I'm told that if it's successful I'll get more from what's known as 'the back end' (George said 'Ha!' to that). Half of it's Lucy's anyway and the rest is to go towards me buying her out of her half of the house. She doesn't want to live in it any more. She couldn't even bear to enter it. She got her sister and her mother to organize her things. That nearly broke my heart. In fact it did break my heart.

She's bought her own place now but it appears that she doesn't live there very much. The final level of my torment is that she and Carl Phipps have become an item. Lucy hasn't told me this herself, of course, because as I say we don't speak, but she knows I know because she tells Melinda and Melinda tells George. It's not a very satisfactory line of communication but it's all I have. I torture myself trying to find out more, begging George for every gruelling snippet. It makes us both feel pretty uncomfortable, but what can I do? I'm desperate. I think about Lucy all the time. Apparently the relationship between her and Phipps is all very perky and positive and keen at the moment, which of course I'm very happy about and which of course I loathe and despise.

I do hope Lucy's happy, though. I really do and I hope Carl Phipps realizes how lucky he is. Not that I've any right to say that. I didn't.

I've started writing another script. I'm doing what Lucy told me to do, drawing it from within. It's about a stupid, lonely, pathetic, weak, useless bastard who deserves everything he gets. It's a comedy.

Another six weeks gone by.

Six miserable weeks.

I've discovered something interesting during the long grey days since I destroyed my life. I've discovered that despite what they say, time is not a great healer. Every morning I wake up hoping that the simple fact that a few more restless empty hours have elapsed will in itself provide me with some relief from the pain of my self-inflicted wounds, and every morning I'm disappointed. Time has healed nothing. I still have the sickness in my stomach and the hopelessness in my head. I still loathe myself and I still love Lucy, who is at this very moment in bed with Carl Phipps (it's two in the morning). Trevor says that four and a half months is not long enough and that if you want time to have any real chance of healing then you have to be thinking in terms of years, possibly decades. This, not surprisingly, is little comfort.

I'm afraid to say that I'm in danger of turning into a very sad act indeed.

I get pissed every night and I haven't washed my sheets in a month.

I'm writing this entry in my book, by the way, because I got a letter from Lucy today and I don't know what else to do with myself. Actually it's not a letter, it's an email. This amazed me, incidentally. When we lived together Lucy couldn't even work the timer on the cooker. I suppose the bastard has taught her. I shouldn't think someone as cool as him would want a girlfriend who did anything as terminally unhip as post a letter.

I'd written to her asking if she wanted a divorce and also if she knew where the key to the garden shed was, because the lawn is now about a foot high.

I'll download Lucy's reply into this file. I want to keep it and this book seems as good a place as any.

Dear Sam

The key to the garden shed is under the second fuchsia pot on the right of the door. If this is the first time your thoughts have turned to the garden then I imagine that all the plants will be dead. If they are not, please give them TLC immediately. There is plant food in the shed. If greenfly or similar is in evidence fill the hand spray with soapy water and administer a gentle soaking. Do NOT use chemicals as the garden is entirely organic. Actually I should imagine that it's entirely cat shit by now because you have to go round and trowel it up once a week or it mounts up.

I suppose that I want a divorce in that we're clearly not married any more and perhaps it's time to formalize that. However, I don't think it's fair that it's me who has to say to you that I want a divorce. After all, I clearly don't want a divorce in that I never wanted our marriage to come to an end. The only reason I want a divorce is because of what you did and I wouldn't want a divorce if you hadn't done it, therefore in a real sense it's you that wants a divorce. Having said that, I suppose I do want a divorce. But not right now. I just don't think I could face it at the moment.

I can't believe it's come to this, Sam. How could you have been so stupid?

Yours, etc., etc. Lucy.

She actually wrote 'etc., etc.'. I don't think I'll open this document again.

Dear Sam

Four more months have passed and once again I find that I feel the need to collect my thoughts.

Next week is the première of *Inconceivable*. Everyone is very excited about the film and the opening is to be rather a grand affair. We're promised television cameras and the presence of celebrities. The film is already being spoken of as *the* new British movie. I must say, there seems to be a *the* new British movie about once a week these days. I don't want to be cynical about my own film, but the phoenix of British cinema has risen from the ashes so often it must be getting quite dizzy.

Lucy is going to attend the première.

I didn't think that she would, but the publicist has just confirmed that she's coming, and will of course be on the arm of Carl Phipps. The publicist assures me that she expects them to be very much the golden couple of the night and to attract a lot of press. Along with Nimnh and Ewan Proclaimer, that is. Ewan has left his wife Morag for Nimnh. This sort of thing is of course very common in the world of films. He really is the most appalling bastard. One gorgeous, sensitive woman isn't enough for him. He has to have a whole succession of them. Well, I've discovered that one gorgeous, sensitive woman was certainly enough for me and I lost her and now I'm not remotely interested in any other and don't think I ever will be.

The première is of course a real emotional issue for me. At first I thought I'd stay away, not knowing if I could face seeing Lucy with Phipps. George and Trevor, however, say that I have to come. They point out that the film is very good and that this should be celebrated. Actually I've seen a tape and I think that it's good too. Ewan Proclaimer may be an arrogant, heartless bastard, but he certainly deserves his reputation as a hot director. Perhaps the two go hand in hand. George and Trevor also point out that the story is mine (and Lucy's) and that if anyone should be present at the moment of triumph it should be me. After all, George argued with his customary brutal honesty, I've fucked up my entire life and sacrificed the only thing I had that was worth having in order to write this movie. I might as well go to the party.

Dear Penny

I never expected to open this book again. It ended so sadly I imagined I'd want nothing more to do with it. Now, however, I have something to say that should be recorded here because it's the end of the story and also the beginning. Besides this, I have no one else to talk to, Penny. I don't want to talk to Carl because it might be nothing and if it is nothing I'd prefer never to have to think of it again, and if it isn't nothing then I don't want to speak until I know for sure. This is why you, Penny, must be my only confidante.

You see, I think I might be pregnant. I'm three weeks late and the tester from Boots has proved positive. I've made an appointment to see Dr Cooper tomorrow.

I can hardly allow myself to believe that it might finally have happened.

PENNY!

Dr Cooper has confirmed it. This is the single happiest moment of my life. I am numb with joy.

I must stay calm, however. These are very early days; it could all still go wrong.

I've been concentrating very hard on my breathing.

A baby, Penny! Imagine it. It's all I've ever wanted from life.

It's now a little later. I've been making some camomile tea and attempting to centre myself. My heart has been pounding so mightily since I got back from the surgery that I'm scared I'm going to shake everything right out of me. I must struggle to control my joy.

Perhaps it'll help if I confess to you, Penny, that this joy is also tinged with one tiny element of sadness. You know what it is, of course. I've written to you so often about my love for Sam that you will not have expected the passing of that love to leave no mark on me at all. It is of course very sad that Sam, whom I loved so much and for so long and with whom I shared so many disappointments, can be no part of this wonderful moment.

It's not that I wish that the baby was his, not at all. I loved Sam with all my heart but love when it is not reciprocated is a pretty useless thing and I walked away. I thought that Sam loved me and I'm quite sure that he thought he did too, but he didn't. What he did to me proved that. If you love someone you do not use them and abuse them, you do not betray them utterly. Love has to include respect and consideration and trust. It's a partnership in which one partner protects the other. Sam didn't protect me and he didn't love me. He didn't love anyone, certainly not himself. Poor Sam.

It wasn't easy getting over him or coming to terms with what happened to me, but thank goodness I had Carl. Carl has been a true and loving friend and has seen me through the most difficult time of my life. I don't think I could have got through without him.

He wrote to me the day after the awful scene on the film set and asked if he could see me. I admit I flew to him, I was so upset and confused about everything that I was happy to get comfort and affection wherever I could find it. I'm very glad I did.

We didn't sleep together that first night, or the next, but I admit that it was not long afterwards.

My God, Penny, it was wonderful!

Perhaps it was the rawness of my emotions and also the rather defunct nature of my sex life in the preceding months that made me so receptive, but credit must also go to Carl. Some men just have a knack, that's all. I know that now. He made love to me as if it was the only thing that he wanted to do on earth at that moment. And do you know? I think it was.

It went on for weeks, Penny, that first glorious fling. I just took a complete holiday from everything and pretty much lived to make love to Carl. Sheila issued all sorts of dire warnings about being caught on the rebound and displacement of unhappiness and things like that but Drusilla said that passion is its own reward and she was right!

Carl is the first man I have ever been with (there have not been exactly many) who really seems to relish massaging a woman. I don't mean feeling her up prior to leaping aboard, I mean massaging, properly applying himself to the job of soothing and relaxing her with no other thought in mind than that. It's a wonderful thing. He still does it (although perhaps not quite as often). We lie together naked on his bed and he's happy to work at my neck and shoulders for an hour or more. One thing I did notice is that he likes to watch himself while he does it. He has a large mirror at the end of his bed and I often catch him drinking in the rippling muscles of his image as he massages me. Fair enough, I suppose. No reason why he should be watching me. I can assure you he has a lot better muscle definition than I have.

We don't actually live together, but we spend a lot of time in each other's place. I love the weekends. Carl is very big on Sunday mornings, lots of croissants and real coffee, big dressing gowns and the papers, just like being in a hotel, which is lovely. Those are some of my favourite times. That and occasional trips to a little cottage he has in the Cotswolds, all logfires and stone walls, very Wuthering Heights. We do have a lot of fun together, we really do. I can't say it's been perfect, of course. I've had my low moments, as, no doubt, has he. The truth is I was in love with Sam for six years and you don't get over something like that in a couple of minutes, particularly if you had no idea that the thing was going to end. Carl also carries baggage with him. It's not another girl, it's more . . . well, Carl loves himself rather a lot, not in a horrid way, don't get me wrong, in fact it's quite charming. It's just I sometimes feel that simply being Carl Phipps is often enough for Carl. He doesn't need anyone else.

That's why I must be very careful about this business of our baby. Carl often says he loves me and how much he regrets the fact that I seem to be unable to have kids, but I don't know how he'll feel when confronted with the fact that I'm having one. I shan't force him. Of course I want more than anything for him to be as pleased as I am and for us to be a family, but if he's not ready for it then I'll simply have to think again.

I do love Carl, I know I do. It is not the same as my love for Sam was, of course. I don't think that any two loves can ever be the same. If they were they'd be interchangeable and what would be the point of that? In one way my love for Carl is more exciting (I think you can guess in which way, Penny) and I suppose in other ways it's less so. I must say it's very strange living with a man who likes to talk so much. By rights I should love it. Sam, of course, was famously the man hidden behind the newspaper and I hated that. It's just that Carl's preferred topic of conversation is himself. It's great fun and very charming and terribly interesting at times and it's also rather impressive. I'm constantly astonished at the skill with which he seems able to bring the most unlikely topics back to the subject of Carl Phipps. Mention metaphysics and Carl will tell you that he has for a number of years been working on a verse play about John Donne; mention Schleswig Holstein and Carl has made a toothpaste commercial in Flensburg. It's his work, really. It possesses him. Basically Carl is and always will be a very very dedicated actor. His art means everything to him, and that is as it should be. It's just that occasionally I do want to say to him that there might be tougher and more emotionally draining jobs than acting – fireman, for example, or paramedic. In fact I did say that to him quite recently and he told me that in fact it has been scientifically proven that the amount of adrenalin released into the body when an actor tackles a lead Shakespearean role is equivalent to that experienced by the victim of a car crash.

Perhaps I just attract men who are obsessed with their work. At least Carl is enthusiastic about his, unlike gloomy old Sam. At least Carl believes in himself.

I'm writing this at Carl's flat. I have a key and of course I want to tell him the wonderful news as soon as I possibly can. I tried his mobile but he's on set and mobiles are banned. Not the Inconceivable set. That was finished months ago. He's guesting on an ITV detective thing, playing a charming killer. I'm sure he's wonderful in it (he says he isn't but I can see he knows he is). Inconceivable is about to be released and there seems to be rather a lot of excitement about it. In fact, I've agreed to go to the première, which is the day after tomorrow. At first I was adamant that I wouldn't, but in the end I was persuaded. The whole thing is still sort of unfinished business, and I think that seeing the film might finally draw a line beneath it all.

Also I do want to see Sam again and perhaps at his moment of *triumph (our moment of triumph; I'm a credited and paid-up writer, ha!) will be a good time.*

I can hear Carl letting himself in. Time to tell him the news.

I've told Carl and he's absolutely thrilled. He went all misty-eyed and talked a lot about fatherhood and his own father and the circle of time and the scheme of things and replacing himself on earth. Then he put on his big coat and went for a very long walk, returning looking windswept and very serious. I suggested that we should go out and celebrate but he didn't want to. He says that creating a life is a huge responsibility and he wants to spend some time in meditation. Each to their own, of course, but nonetheless it would have been nice to chink glasses for a moment even if I can only drink water.

Perhaps he'll be more fun at the première. I know there's to be quite a party.

Dear Sam

I'm writing this on the evening of the première of *Inconceivable*. I should be tying my bow tie because it's all going to be rather a posh do, but I can't find it. I can't find my trousers either. I can never find anything in the house any more. This is because everything is on the floor, which also happens to be where I keep my pizza boxes and my empty bottles and cans. Therefore there's much confusion. George is in the other room waiting for me. He's kindly agreed to be my date for the night but only if I wash my hair and trim my beard. This I've done. I'm also wearing the brand new underwear that Melinda kindly sent round. I must presume that I was beginning to smell.

I'll see Lucy tonight at the première. I think that's why I'm writing this now, just to sort of focus myself.

I don't know how I'll be able to bear it when I see her, particularly when she arrives with another man. I love her so much, you see. Every day I'm amazed at how much I love her. I certainly didn't know that I felt this strongly when I had her. When I think of all the evenings when I turned down the chance to hold her and to touch her because I wanted to work or read the paper. My God, if I had my time again.

Actually, I've finally finished my next script and it's about just that. It's called *Don't It Always Seem to Go* and it's about a bloke fucking up his life and then realizing what he's lost. Amazingly, I've got it commissioned. George and Trevor think it's even better than *Inconceivable*. Lucy was right. All I needed to do was draw from within.

Dear Penny

Tonight has been very strange. I hardly know what to think.

This evening I attended the première of Inconceivable, *which, first of all, I must say I thought was wonderful. Sam really did do a marvellous job. I always knew what a good writer he is. I won't say that it was easy seeing all that pain played out again on screen (and revisiting my own thoughts), but it was done very sensitively and also extremely amusingly. I do think that it's good to be able to laugh about the subject. It's sort of empowering. Perhaps it's my current happiness that made it possible for me to enjoy the film, but I don't think so. I really believe that I would have appreciated it anyway, although it would of course have been much more difficult to watch.*

The whole evening was much more glamorous than I expected and also more exciting. Well, I suppose it's a pretty exciting thing, going to the première of a movie you didn't even know you'd half written. I went with Carl and it was a very strange experience to be at the centre of all that attention. Cameras flashed, microphones appeared from nowhere, and people with autograph books shouted 'Carl! Carl!' and also occasionally 'Gilbert!' which I know he didn't like because he made The Tenant of Wildfell Hall *nearly three years ago. He looked lovely, I must say, like James Bond's intellectual brother. I had on a new dress from Liberty's, which I was quite pleased with, very posh and rather daring at the front. The Wonderbra has of course done wonders for the smaller bosom, and now I'm pregnant perhaps I'll grow my own.*

Of course a great deal of the excitement that surrounded Carl and me was that it was our first time out at a big event as 'an item'. Lots of journalists wanted to know about our future plans but we just smiled gaily and said how thrilled we were about the film.

Tonight has been the most extraordinary and may just possibly turn out to be the happiest of my life.

And not because the film was a great success, although it was, which was wonderful. They cheered at the end and I don't think they were just being nice. We had a real star-studded première with lots of celebs. Quite a few that I used to know had rallied round which I was touched by. There was a real crush in the foyer with TV and radio people grabbing interviews from anyone they recognized. I was trying to fight my way through to the booze and I heard Dog and Fish being very nice about the film.

'Brilliant,' said Dog. 'If you like your comedy with big laughs, this is it.'

'Personally we prefer our comedy with a small side salad,' Fish added. I think they're improving.

Charlie Stone turned up, which was very nice of him because he really is hip at the moment, and the press went mad. Particularly because he had the gorgeous Brenda on his arm as well, which guaranteed pictures.

'Gagmongous!' I heard him saying to a *Morning TV* crew. 'Megatastic! And what about that Nimnh totty, eh? Did she give me the horn or what!'

'Yeah, she's a real strong babe,' Brenda added.

Even Joe London was there with his wife Toni, and also Wally the guitarist. Joe was positive about the movie if a little faint in his praise.

'Not bad,' he said. 'Fort it was a bit of a bird's film myself. What jew fink, Toni?'

'I loved it,' Toni bubbled, ''cos it was funny and sad. In't that weird? I mean, you wouldn't think it could be both, would you?'

The interviewer asked Wally what he thought of the film.

'What film?' he said.

Anyway, all this is beside the point. I've only written it down because it was exciting and I don't want to forget it. The main event of the evening was about to happen, and it was not the film at all. It was Lucy.

Well, now comes the crunch, Penny. There are no future plans. Carl and I are not an item. I've left him and I think that he was mightily relieved.

Well, let's face it. From the first moment I told Carl about me being pregnant I knew in my heart that he doesn't want to have a baby. He said he was delighted, but he was lying. Although in fairness I will say that I think he was lying as much to himself as he was to me.

I finally tackled him about it in the limo on the way to the première. As good a time as any, I thought. I asked if he really was genuinely happy that I was pregnant.

'Happy? Of course I'm happy, darling, I'm delirious.'

Oh dear, Penny. He's a better actor on screen than he is off. There was a long and uncomfortable pause before he added, 'I'm happy because you're happy. That's what matters.'

Which is as much as to say, I'm devastated, my beautiful little life is about to be completely ruined by your bloody baby.

'But you have to be happy too, Carl,' I said, 'or it won't work.'

He sat quietly for another minute, trying to find the courage to start to wriggle out of it. He looked magnificently tortured in his beautiful dinner jacket.

'It's a shock, that's all,' he said finally. 'I mean, you said you couldn't have kids, that's why I didn't use protection.'

'Well, I thought I couldn't, but now it seems I can.'

'And that's great,' said Carl, not looking at me at all. 'Really great.'

And that's when I realized, finally realized, what I'd known all along, but was afraid to admit to myself.

He doesn't want a child, Penny, why the hell would he? He's happy. He has everything he wants, except to be big in the States, and a mewling, puking infant won't get him that. The truth is, Carl doesn't want to be tied down at all. He wants a girlfriend, not a wife, and he certainly doesn't want a mother.

We suddenly found ourselves facing each other in the crush at the bar.

Oh my God, she looked lovely. So glamorous, so sexy, so beautiful. I was crushed by her presence, I just wanted to stand there and worship her. I did stand there and worship her.

I think it was the saddest moment yet. Here I was on the greatest night of my life, standing before the woman of my dreams (and I mean that literally) who looked more gorgeous even than I remembered her. We'd written a hit movie together, and yet I knew I'd lost her, that she hated me.

We made smalltalk for a moment and then she told me her news. It came absolutely out of the blue. Lucy's pregnant.

I really was happy for her, honestly I was, although I also just wanted to die. I told her that I was thrilled and delighted and that Carl is the luckiest man on earth. I meant it too, I really did. Jealous as Othello though I may have been, I knew that I wished Lucy all the happiness she desired.

Then the evening began to take an unexpected turn.

'I've left Carl,' Lucy said, and my heart lurched. 'This evening, in fact, just before the film started, during that speech when the Chairman of BritMovie was telling us that the phoenix of British film had risen from the ashes.'

I just stood there, open mouthed.

'He doesn't want a child, so I'm going to go it alone. No more men for me. It's the modern way, you know, and at least I'll have a bit of money, thanks to you and our film.'

Well, I was aghast. Was this my chance? After all, he'd caught her on the rebound, why shouldn't I? The second bounce, the double whammy. The possibilities of the situation were only just beginning to sink in when a publicist came over to get Lucy for an interview. She was in far more demand than I was this evening, by the way, even though I was the top-billed writer.

Hardly surprising, really. She was gorgeous and in a sexy frock and I was Mr Beardy in an unironed dinner jacket. I know who I would have wanted to interview.

Suddenly she was leaving.

'Well . . . goodbye, Sam,' she said.

I made my decision. Well, it was more of an impulse than a decision. Let's face it, I was desperate. I had one chance.

'Lucy,' I said. 'Come back to me! Please, please come back. I'll do anything. I made the stupidest mistake of my life, but I didn't mean it. Tell me how I can make it up! Please, I love you . . .'

'Sam,' she said. 'Don't be absurd. We can't go back. I'm pregnant with another man's baby.'

Then inspiration struck. Maybe I could get her back after all.

'I'll look after it!' I blurted. 'I'll help bring it up. I'll be its father.'

And I meant it too. I'd love to bring up Lucy's child. I don't care who else's it would be. Lucy's child would be part of her and there's nothing about Lucy that I would not love.

It was a stunning thing to say. I felt winded, suddenly everything seemed to be in slow motion, like I wasn't actually there but was sort of hovering above it all, watching. The publicist kept tugging at my arm. She can't have heard what Sam said, or if she had she didn't care. Publicists at premières have to be very single-minded. After all, you only get one shot at a thirty-second grab on Greater London Radio.

'Sam,' I said. 'You didn't even want children of your own, let alone somebody else's.'

Perhaps it was just the noise of the crowd but my voice sounded very strange to me. Sam looked absolutely desperate, wild even, like Rasputin, although I think that was mainly the beard. The crowd around us were getting louder, everybody calling for drinks and congratulating each other.

'Can't a man make a mistake, for fuck's sake?!' Sam shouted, inevitably choosing the very moment when the room went quiet.

It was fate's favourite practical joke. Kill the volume just when the idiot with long hair and a beard is shouting obscenities. Everybody turned to look. Lucy went red. God, I wanted to ravish her there and then.

For a second I thought she was going to hit me. Instead she just stared at me for a moment and then left with the publicist scuttling after her.

Dear Penny

This morning when I woke (I hadn't thought I'd been asleep at all but I must have been, I suppose) there was a huge bunch of flowers on my doorstep.

This is what the card said:

If I have to serve a life sentence for what I did, can't I at least serve it with you?

Which is not a bad line, I must say, and I swear if he ever uses it in a script I'll kill him.

I am of course very confused. So much is happening at once. I do love Sam, of course I love Sam, but I can't just pick things up as if nothing has happened.

Can I?

Except of course something has happened. Something really extraordinary. Sam has offered to help me bring up my child. He loves me, there can be no better proof of that. I do believe that my joy is complete.

I've just received an email from Lucy. She will have me back. We are to be a family. I have never in my entire life been so happy as I am now.

Dear Penny

Today has been a very upsetting day, although now that it's over I feel curiously strong.

I'm not pregnant. Dr Cooper says that I was pregnant, at least he thinks I was, but I'm not any more. He says that I've suffered a very early miscarriage, which is very common, if indeed I was pregnant at all. Whatever the problem is with me and fertility, it's not yet solved. Sam came with me to the doctor and afterwards we sat in the car and cried a little together. After that we went and got pissed.

Dear Sam

Lucy and I have been back together for six months. The happiest six months of my life, despite the fact that we've just been through our second IVF cycle and failed it. The doctors said that there were some signs of it having begun to work (they know this from the blood tests) but that ultimately Debbie and Dick Two could not hang on. Lucy was very upset, of course, we both were, but we're OK. We had a wonderful holiday in India afterwards, no replacement, of course, but still absolutely fantastic and something we've always wanted to do.

I'm writing this sitting on the bed in a lovely little room in a country hotel in Dorset. Lucy is wearing nothing but a silk slip and is making my heart ache with love and desire. She's packing up a knapsack with champagne, chocolates and a big rug. It's a beautiful warm summer evening. In an hour or so we'll creep out into the night and make our way up the hill to the great and ancient chalk giant's penis. It might work, it might not. Either way, I can't wait.